LOCK UP

The Secrets of Mylin - Book III

Joe Klingler

Cartosi LLC

PRAISE FOR AUTHOR

Praise for RATS
International Rubery Book Award - Fiction Short List

"Klingler's debut is an intelligent, non-stop page turner."—Manhattan Book Review (5-Stars)

"A deep logistical jungle sure to entertain buffs and newcomers to the techno-thriller genre."—Kirkus Reviews (Featured Selection. Recommended List)

Praise for Missing Mona
London Book Festival Winner

"Reads like a good old private investigator novel from years ago."—San Francisco Book Review (5-Stars)

"Klingler's Chicago...was exciting and gritty."—Manhattan Book Review

Praise for Mash Up
Winner National Indie Excellence Award - Thriller

"Effortlessly clever prose...a thoughtful, well-constructed tale."—Kirkus Reviews

"Makes the perfect detective read...a classic addition to the noir genre." —San Francisco Book Review (5-Stars)

Praise for Tune Up

Winner Pacific Book Awards—Thriller of the Year

"A spiderweb of secrets, sex, blackmail, and murder."—Kirkus Reviews

"Recalls the work of James Ellroy. Suspenseful mastery in its best form. Not to be missed."—Seattle Book Review (5-Stars)

Praise for Burn Up

Winner New York City Big Book Award—Best Multi-cultural Fiction

"Surprise after surprise...players come alive on the page."—The Pacific Book Review Starred Review

"Crisp and edgy writing...enhanced by cliffhanging chapter endings." —Clarion Reviews

ALSO BY JOE KLINGLER

Qigiq and Dreeson Thrillers
Mash Up
Tune Up
Burn Up

A Tommy Cuda Mystery
Missing Mona

A Daemon Thriller
RATS

For the latest news, please sign-up for
The Klingler_Report
at
www.joeklingler.com

For Gary Woodcock

"Bad weather always looks worse through a window."

—TOM LEHRER

CHAPTER 1

FOUR MONTHS AND SEVENTEEN DAYS before my twenty-first birthday, my life ended. I sat cross-legged on concrete in the one place that sunlight touched the gray room holding me. I pulled the zipper of the orange jumpsuit down to my navel. They had given it to me after stealing my shimmering outfit from our final concert. The rough materiel grazed my shoulder as I pushed it to my elbow. The yellow glow of the sunbeam warmed my bare breast. My right hand held a single chopstick I had secreted up a sleeve and stolen from the cafeteria. It was my bow. My left held plastic tubes for inserting tampons: three assembled end to end to create a makeshift fingerboard.

If they found the chopstick, they would punish me.

I lifted the tubes to my chin where I had been placing a viola for fifteen of my years and glided the chopstick gently across them. Back and forth and back and forth over the smooth plastic surface, as my inner ear heard the music and the fingers of my left hand danced up, down, over; finding what would have been the deep, rich opening notes of *The Viola Concerto* by Jennifer Higdon.

If I possessed an instrument.

Her composition had won a Grammy. I had never performed it. I longed to.

My viola had died in the inferno that destroyed the orchestra. Without it, I felt my skin being pulled away from my body, like an astronaut without her suit, exposed to the vacuum of space.

Forty of my friends died because of a madman—my horrible brother.

My horrible *dead* brother. By *my* bullets.

I stopped the chopstick. My thigh ached inside where Qigiq's knife had tried to stop me. Before he died, Father watched the news. Then he ranted about the rampant racism in the United States of America. What were forty dead Asian girls to three hundred million Americans? Foreigners in a country that had more mass shootings than days in a year. Fifty dead in Las Vegas—sniper. Dozens of kids killed in schools—automatic weapons. I blinked back tears. Hundreds of people dead in a shopping mall or a subway—humans with dynamite strapped to their bodies. Trucks ramming into pedestrians on busy sidewalks.

My world had been razed; the buzz-buzzing mind of the Internet wouldn't even notice.

I closed my eyes and moved the chopstick.

The resonant sound of a viola filled my ears the way people hear voices when they read. I dreamed of sheet music. Of learning new pieces to fill my days with beauty and keep the bad thoughts away. Ever haunting thoughts—awake or asleep.

A key rattled against metal.

I hid the chopstick in a crack where the concrete floor met the wall. I had shot my brother; they would assume I meant to stab someone. I tossed the tubes on the bed. They didn't fear tampons.

They do not understand. My brother was special.

I pulled the cloth of the jumpsuit up to my throat.

A burly guard who needed a shave and better cologne arrived.

"You have visitors."

I had seen him only once before; the guards changed often. This one had said it was 'to avoid friendships' with the prisoners. The leer in his eyes as he said 'friendships' had frightened me.

He remained on the other side of the barred door he had yet

to open, his face serious.

But I wasn't allowed visitors. I wasn't allowed to be near other prisoners except at an occasional meal. I wasn't even supposed to speak to the guards. I had killed my brother in cold blood. With a pistol my Uncle Gan had given me as a gift, so the courts ruled it premeditated. My brother hadn't been armed. The gun a meter from his body didn't seem to count, because he wasn't holding it at the moment I ended his life.

I hesitated. "Visitors?"

He grinned. But didn't tell me to be quiet.

"Not the kind you're thinking." He wagged his head. "Let's go."

I turn around. He handcuffed my wrists, opened the door, and led me down a long hallway constructed so I couldn't peek into other cells, and the occupants couldn't see who was being moved. My internal metronome measured four minutes of walking before he deposited me in a room the same size as my cell. It held a table and four brown metal chairs, two per side facing each other in regimented rows. No windows except for a tiny one in the door. One silent light above the table, no buzzing of a fluorescent tube. The room smelled of fear.

He released my wrists and pointed.

I slipped into a chair facing the door. It wouldn't move. I leaned forty-five degrees to place my elbows on the table and glanced down. Bolts held the chair legs to the floor.

The guard looked at me with the 'friendships' stare and pulled the door closed as he retreated.

I smiled. New surroundings. And soon, someone to talk with.

Someone not my lawyer.

A short bald man named Mr. Rillado had been assigned to me. He came to visit every other day wearing the same brown suit with a smudge on the collar. He looked me in the eye and asked the same questions over and over. But my answers never changed. Yes, I was trying to kill my brother Shen when I shot him. Yes, he had raped me, beaten me, pimped me. Yes, I knew he didn't have the gun; it was visible in the grass. No, I didn't know if he had another weapon. No, I did not wish to plead guilty to a lesser charge—I had done what I did on purpose.

The dragon gods would take care of the rest.

I waited on the hard, immovable chair. I grew cold. Without motion, time became fluid, distant, as if it were on a long journey and had become too tired to keep on ticking. Eventually the door swung inward and two men wearing American business suits with white shirts and subdued blue ties entered. Thin gray stripes crisscrossed the ties.

No man in such a suit had ever been nice to me for long.

The big athletic black man sat to my right. He had a black satin handkerchief folded carefully in his breast pocket. The slender white guy with a red spot on the side of his neck took the chair to my left. His hands twitched like he had lingered at a Starbucks too long. Americans were so silly with their stimulant drugs. But I loved the sound of that name: *Starbucks!* Though I had no idea what it meant.

"Are you Mylin Wu?" the black man asked.

My eyes flicked between their faces. They knew who I was or they wouldn't be in this Nevada prison asking questions.

I said, "Am I allowed to speak?"

His eyebrows raised. "Yes, of course."

"I was told I must remain silent. No speaking on the row."

They looked at each other. The thin one said, "It's okay in here. You can talk to us."

I would bet many American dollars they would like me to talk to them. But what did they want me to say? Who did they want me to lie about? What facts did I possess that I didn't even know were secrets? I looked from dark eyes to pale blue ones, from one unsmiling face to the other.

"Yes, I am Mylin Wu."

The black man said, "I'm Agent Carr, David Carr, and this is Agent Bain. We're with the FBI." He paused as if reluctant to say more. "Your father was an informant for our agency."

My chest stopped moving. Not like there was weight on it

—more like the motor that made it go up and down had run its battery low. I blinked at him.

"You apparently didn't know," Bain said. "Not many people did."

I coughed; the motor restarted. "My father hated the police."

Carr smiled slightly, his mouth wide, lips closed. "Yes, I know. I met with him on many occasions. He made it clear he believed cops fell to the bottom of the criminal food chain. Pawns of corrupt governments, etcetera. Regardless, he helped us." He studied me, no doubt perceiving disbelief in my eyes. "And we helped him."

Astonishing.

Father never accepted assistance from the police. He preached: *The only good cop is one who can't find you.* That sounded like an incompetent cop to me, but Father would have punished me for saying such a thing to his face. The two men appeared to be waiting for a response, yet they hadn't asked a question. I delayed, enjoying being out of my cell and in the presence of these new men, though I didn't have much use for men.

"Why would my father help you?"

Bain said, "We had something he wanted." He paused and looked to his partner, who nodded. I wondered what cops could have that would interest my father. Money? Connections? "We made sure the local authorities looked the other way while he ran his little prostitution band."

"We weren't a *band*, we were a string orchestra."

Bain shrugged. "Simple deal. We didn't shut down his prostitution business. He gave us information."

"My father wouldn't do that. He would lie."

Bain shook his head. "Everything he told us checked out. Purchase girls from rural villages in China, Cambodia, Vietnam. Train them for years to be able to play." He coughed. "The musical instruments, I mean. But also training them in the ways of the Geisha."

"Geisha are Japanese entertainers. We learn the ancient *Ways of the Plain Girl*. They are much more effective."

Carr laughed. Bain waited for him to stop before continuing. "And the trick for smuggling sex workers into the United States using sports fishermen."

"Very happy fishermen," I said, remembering what I had done for a pudgy gray-haired white man with a round face and bright red cheeks. With his white knuckles squeezing the wheel for hours, he had piloted us safely over whale-size waves for forty-two miles across a lake named Erie. I thought the howling black wind that night had been sent by angry dragon gods to kill us all.

Bain said, "Picked up in Port Clinton or Toledo. Then they disappear."

I had learned to read the skin around eyes and the tightness of cheeks while men gazed upon my body. The black man called Carr was hiding anger. The thin guy enjoyed hearing himself talk.

"Are you asking me if this is true?" I said.

"No," Carr said. "We know it's true. We're telling you now so you'll believe that your father was keeping us informed." He paused. "He told us a good deal more."

How many secrets had Father revealed? How many lies had he told?

I nodded, agreeing to nothing.

"But that's not important," Carr continued. He rubbed his palm in one spot on the table as if polishing it. "Well, parts might be significant." He reached inside his jacket and removed a sheet of paper. He unfolded it, placed it down flat, then pushed it across the table until it touched my arm.

It was covered in that language the kindly professor Pemberly had invented—at my request. Well, at Uncle Gan's request. In the early days, using a handmade dictionary, I wrote love letters to the professor. But Uncle made me stop. I looked down and scanned the paper. Two symbols jumped out: *air* and *death*.

"My father gave you this?"

"No," Carr said. "It came to us through other means. Do you recognize it?"

How could I answer to help myself? I had no reason to trust this man. But what was I protecting? Only two girls remained from the orchestra. I sat up straighter with the realization that maybe they were gone too. My eyes wandered, seeking comfort, finding it in a speaker on the wall. A speaker could play music. How I would love to hear music.

"Well?" Bain said.

I faced him and blinked. "I don't know."

He jerked back as if I had slapped him. "You don't know if you recognize it?"

The authorities wanted to put me in an electric chair because this place where I shot my brother had something called capital punishment. Why did anything else matter?

"I don't know if I want to tell you."

Carr laughed for a second time. "I appreciate your honesty."

Bain frowned. The spot on his neck appeared to get redder.

Carr said, "Let's leap forward. I suspect you know exactly what that paper says and where those scribbles came from. On that assumption, let's discuss why we're here."

Bain said to Carr, "This is classified information."

Carr faced him. The smaller man appeared to shrink. "What are we going to do, not tell her?"

Bain shrugged, moved his eyes to my face, and said nothing.

Carr continued, "Mylin, your trial is coming up. Reliable witnesses saw you shoot an unarmed man to death, possibly with premeditation. You were carrying an unregistered weapon. You're a known prostitute. A motivated prosecutor will seek the death penalty for an illegal immigrant who comes to America and scoffs at our laws."

I knew this. Shortly after arresting me cops tried to scare me. Yet somehow, now that my father and brothers were dead, I was calm. In prison, no one made me turn tricks, or tortured me, or raped me. In many ways, it was better than working in the orchestra—except there was no music.

I stared at Carr and waited. Again, he hadn't asked a question.

Bain cleared his throat, but didn't speak.

Carr said, "What I mean to say is, your future doesn't look so bright."

"My future was never bright."

The room was quiet. The men looked at each other, then back to me.

"Let's change that," Carr said.

I removed my arms from the table and sat up straight in the chair, like I was preparing for the first notes of a symphony. "How can you do that?"

"That's why we're here," Bain said.

Carr held up a finger to silence him. Waited. Then he said, "We would like your assistance in a matter of national security."

I tried to stop my lips, but failed. These men would assume my smile meant I would be pleased to help with their mission. But I was smiling because in flashing back over all the men who had ever asked for my assistance in satisfying their carnal desires, I thought I had heard every excuse a male could possibly fabricate. But not once had a man ever thought to claim that it was a *matter of national security.*

I said, "What nation?"

"The United States, of course," Bain responded.

This man seemed to grow both smaller and more aggressive, reminding me of Silkworm, Aunt Win's toy terrier. It had once leapt from a nearby chair and bitten my bottom while I stood practicing a Bach Prelude.

"Of course," I said. "None of the other hundreds of nations in the world could possibly matter."

Carr laughed yet again, showing the most perfect white teeth I had ever seen. This black man seemed to not care about trivial things, perhaps because something more profound troubled him. I began to like him, which made me cautious.

Carr leaned forward and stared into my eyes. "That scribbling was invented for you, Mylin. We have other samples. We want to know how many more there are." He paused without taking his eyes from my face. "And exactly where they went."

The professor had invented this writing. Uncle Gan insisted, but never told me why. I said, "And you think I can help you?" I pressed my lips together, afraid to hope. "For this you will give me a better future?"

Carr's handsome head nodded. "Yes, Mylin. Fortunately, the man you shot had led the police on a high-speed chase, was an illegal alien, and had a firearm nearby." His eyes penetrated mine. "We studied the surveillance tapes of the concert. You and I both know your brother murdered your orchestra. As we say in my line of work, he needed killing. Times the way they are, Americans won't much care about one more dead illegal, so we can—" He paused, glanced at Bain, "Make adjustments. You'll never see the inside of a courtroom."

This was truly unusual news. What would Uncle Gan advise me to do? First, do not trust them.

"What must I do…for this future you promise?"

"We are in possession of a dozen paintings done by a talented amateur." He pointed to the paper in front of me. "Most have that hidden beneath the paint. We've decoded the messages."

"I don't know anything about messages. Or paintings."

"We think you do," Bain said.

I faced him, and studied his red spot. It was not so much different in color from the mark on my neck made by my viola. "Opinions are like noses. Everyone has one. I will tell you mine if you wish."

Carr chuckled.

"Sure," Bain said.

I said, "You fear something."

Carr watched his partner for a second, then said, "Nail on the head, eh Thomas?"

Bain grunted and pulled a notebook from a case on the floor

I hadn't noticed. He removed a photograph from the back and pushed it across the table. I tried not to show emotion, but feared my face betrayed me. My grandmother had this picture in her apartment.

"People you know?" Bain asked, more gently than he had spoken since arriving.

I nodded slowly, unsure of what was safe to say, but feeling a warm ember starting to glow inside of me. I had felt this sensation before; in the darkest moments, I must remember to do my best…and hope.

"Let's make this easy," Carr said. "Three of the four people in that picture are dead."

"They are?" I said, trying to sound surprised.

Carr smiled. "It's a decade old. But our computers aged the faces and identified your father and two brothers. You and I both know all three died in the past month."

His eyes didn't stray from my face. Father taught me to hide my emotions from clients by showing me a picture of the Mona Lisa, and making me imitate her. I assumed that expression now.

"Do you know the fourth person, Mylin?"

I leaned back on the hard chair and crossed my arms over small breasts that men seemed to worship once they tasted them. I looked Carr straight in the eye. The concrete cell without music urged me forward.

"Men lie to me all the time."

"I'm not lying," Carr said. "The FBI can change your future. How do I prove that to you?"

"Should I have my lawyer here?"

Bain shook his head vigorously, but Carr spoke. "Better the lawyers don't hear this conversation. You can always decide not to help us later." He paused, his jaw shifting. "Or let us help you."

"I tell you things. You leave. I go sit in my cell."

Carr nodded. "Agent Bain, would you excuse us for a moment?"

Bain's eyes widened in surprise. Then he frowned, closed his notebook, and stood.

"I'll be in the hallway."

The door clicked closed behind him. Carr stared at me in silence.

I unfolded my arms and let them drop to my sides.

He reached to the floor and lifted a thin briefcase. From inside he brought out a yellow pad like the lawyers had written on during the interrogation following Shen's death. I smiled inwardly at the memory of shooting my brother between the legs first, wanting him to feel the bullet, not die instantly.

Carr's blue ballpoint scratched across the page. He turned the pad toward me.

There are microphones, but no cameras.

I nodded my understanding and said, "Why did you ask your friend to leave?"

He wrote as he spoke. "He looked like he could use a break. Sometimes the tension gets to him." Carr pushed the notebook over to me.

My previous partner was shot by a sniper in Fort Mason. You were there. Graham had a gruff style, but was a good man. I want to bring his killer to justice.

I held out my hand for his pen. I said, "I was frightened when they brought me here. I don't understand America." I wrote: *Shen shot your friend. He was trying to impress...*

I paused, fearful, trying to foresee the future. I wrote: *others,* and pushed the tablet back.

His body sagged. "You shot Shen."

Not a question, but I nodded, since there were no cameras in the room.

Or *maybe* there were no cameras. Men often lied to me.

He wrote: *I must find the others. Including the fourth man in the photo.*

"Why?" I asked. "Do you wish to kill them too?" I waved my hand for him not to turn the tablet; I could easily read it upside down.

Something is missing. I need to know where it went.

I smiled. "National security?"

It's important...for the world.

Men saving the world, as if their puny efforts could make a difference before the gods.

I want to bring them to justice.

"Whose justice?" I asked.

Carr smiled and wrote: *Whoever gets there first.*

The air felt thick around me; this was a *race*. I must get there first. I said, "The fourth man is my Uncle Gan, my father's brother. We girls were not allowed to pose for pictures that day. Only the males."

Carr showed the hint of a smile. "Thank you. Can you tell me anything about the picture?"

I remembered the day clearly. I had played Bach for Father and Uncle. They applauded and smiled, and told me I had a great future ahead of me. I thought they meant as a violist.

My mind floated back...

"I was nine years old. We were visiting Uncle. The moon waxed and waned many times. My older sister Pé and I took music lessons from a stubby man with unruly white hair and nicotine-stained hands we called Professor Fingers. He would give us hugs if we played well, and spank us when we didn't. I practiced viola two hours in the morning and two in the afternoon, not counting the time I played with the string quartet. That was another hour, sometimes more."

"Where?"

The memories of a little girl poured from my lips. "An island of waterfalls, statues, beaches of silky sand so soft my tiny feet would sink and disappear. And a bridge, a red bridge, with giant white figures of humans and dragons molded into the side. It seemed to go up into the sky and disappear." I gazed at the blank wall and saw the island. "It's called Jeju. Uncle made me promise to work hard so the family could continue to live there always."

"That's Korea," Carr said.

I blinked and shook my head, then brushed my hair forward to cover the left side of my face.

"No, it's a wonderful part of China."

"You were living in South Korea." He began writing then apparently changed his mind. "Where were you born, Mylin?"

"I only know what I've been told."

"Hospital records? Photographs? Birth certificate?"

Loneliness filled my heart; the urge to cry returned. I beat it down with the willpower I had learned all the way back on Jeju. I whispered, "I don't know."

"I'll look into it." He sent a message from his phone. In a moment Bain was back in the room with a slim, black laptop computer. He placed it on the table and typed for several minutes. Finally, he shook his head. "That search we initiated, still hasn't found any public or criminal records."

Carr said, "Were you born in a hospital?"

I shook my head. "Father talked of an upstairs room where Mother would be safe from government informers. Sometimes, when he drank, he would grow angry at her spirit and throw saké cups across that room. I would clean up." I hesitated, remembering times I'd rather forget. "He would call me a slow worthless whore."

Carr squinted and took a slow breath. "He was angry at your mother?"

"Very. For dying when she had me."

The black man sat up very straight, his body radiating strength. "I'm sorry, Mylin. Grieving people can get angry in unusual ways."

"He wanted another son. After the ultrasound, he told her to get rid of me. Maybe he knew even back then that Shen would be weak." I paused. What did these men really want from me? I looked down at the table. "You came here just to show me that picture?"

They both laughed.

"No Mylin," Carr said, "we came to save you." He looked to Bain, who nodded agreement to an unspoken question. Then he looked at me as if he could see into my soul. "Help us, Mylin, and the charges against you will fade away like the mist over one of your Chinese rivers at sunrise."

CHAPTER 2

QIGIQ STOOD AT ATTENTION beside his motorcycle on Virginia Street in downtown Reno. Early October sun baked the back of his neck and glistened from the bike's polished green and white paint. The sky was the brilliant crystal blue famous in the Sierra Nevada mountain range. Cloudless. But it brought him no uplifting joy.

Qigiq had counted twenty-eight so far. Despite his best effort, tension cramped his shoulders as the twenty-ninth black vehicle rolled by a few yards away. With only Lilly, Jaio, and Mylin still alive, a total of thirty-nine hearses would pass before the day ended.

This procession existed because a local entrepreneur named Bear had the presence of mind to pass the hat through the thousands of people attending the Street Vibrations Fair. The thousands of people who had witnessed the explosions—and seen the orchestra members die.

The prepaid cell phone in the pocket of Qigiq's gray suit vibrated. A precaution. Was the FBI still monitoring him, or had they lost interest since their informant was dead? He moved slowly toward his bike so as not to disturb the hundreds of people lining the street watching black Cadillacs roll by. Text message.

We have been summoned.

Qigiq knew his partner Kandy was observing the same funeral procession. She was parked a few blocks to the north, doing exactly what he was doing: acting as an honor guard for dead girls while mourning their passing. Wishing he could punish someone, even though the perpetrator had already been shot dead. Wishing the world worked differently than it did. He caught himself grinding his back teeth, looked up at the thirty-third car, wondered what instrument this girl had played, and turned back to his phone.

Where?

Captain wants us to visit a prison. ASAP.

He stepped forward to his position on the street and stood tall to honor the memory of the thirty-fourth woman whose life had been cut short by an ambitious young fool. For the moment, he forgot about next steps and meditated on the deceased. Eventually the taillights of a pair of Reno Police Harley-Davidsons at the rear of the procession disappeared around a left-hand turn. A sigh escaped from deep inside Qigiq's chest. He returned to his bike. His thoughts drifted to the young woman he had failed to stop from shooting her brother. He had been there. Only a knife throw away.

* * *

Qigiq pulled his bike up behind Kandy's icicle-white Volvo. It was stopped at the gate to a compound of two-story buildings dropped onto the desert floor like giant Tetris blocks. A guard checked their IDs against a smudged computer screen: Qigiq, one name only, Alaska license. Dreeson, Kandy, San Francisco resident. SFPD homicide detectives. He directed them to a parking lot near a building that had three barrel-sized red pipes running up the side like stripes on a race car.

Qigiq dismounted and hung his helmet over the right grip.

Kandy appeared around the rear of her car.

They stared in silence at white buildings arranged in a semicircle. All were made of featureless concrete block cut only by horizontal strips of dark windows. Two fences twenty yards apart topped with razor wire surrounded the compound. Open desert lay beyond, except for a single stand of trees to the south planted in even rows as a windbreak.

Kandy said, "SFPD detectives staring at a Nevada county

prison. What do you think is on Captain Jasik's mind?"

"Getting rid of us?" Qigiq smiled, but his heart wasn't in it. It was still back in Reno with thirty-nine dead girls.

"Can't do that. He needs us to entertain him." She headed for the nearest building.

Inside, cool air and another identification check welcomed them. The checker led them to the closed door of a conference room, knocked, and stepped aside. The door was opened from the inside by a man Qigiq had never seen.

"These them?" the man asked.

"Detectives Dreeson and, uh, kah-jeck," the guard said. "Sent up from San Francisco." The guard looked them up and down. "We don't really need San Francisco to help us."

Kandy said, "We're not here to help."

The guard left without responding, but he wasn't smiling.

"Ki-jeek. Short I, long E," Qigiq said, extending his hand.

The man studied him for a moment, then held out his hand. "Agent Bain with the Bureau. San Diego office."

"Far from home," Kandy said.

"Special circumstances."

"Did you ask for us?" Qigiq said.

He shook his head. "No, we didn't." He slipped out the half-open door and stepped into the hallway, pulling the door closed behind him. "We're working a complex case. I thought we had it figured out until a couple of minutes ago." He half-smiled.

"We?" Kandy said.

"Agent Carr and myself."

She looked Bain square in the face. "David Carr is part of this?"

"He's the driving force. No, that's not right. He was selected —" He stopped. His eyes darted from one face to the other. "Do you two have security clearance?"

"We're lowly homicide detectives," Kandy said. "I doubt we have clearance for anything in your world."

"Would you please wait a minute," Bain said, and moved

down the hallway with long strides.

Kandy said, "Kind of a sensitive guy."

"Captain called you, right?"

Kandy nodded. "Which means someone called him."

"But that someone didn't update our new friend Agent Bain?"

Kandy shifted from one foot to the other. Looked up and down the empty hallway. Glanced at the closed door. Lifted an eyebrow in Qigiq's direction. Then she knocked twice.

The door was opened by a tall black man in a well-tailored suit.

"Hey," he said.

"Hey back. Your buddy Bain has us cooling our heels."

"He likes to dot all the I's before crossing a T. Come on in."

Qigiq followed Kandy into a room containing a table with two chairs on either side—one occupied by a thin Asian woman in prison garb. Her face revealed the kind of tired that sleep couldn't solve. Qigiq might not have recognized her, but straight dark hair obscured her left eye in a way he had seen before.

"Hello Mylin."

"Hello Qigiq. Hi Kandy. They really called you?"

Kandy kicked a chair leg; the chair didn't move. She scowled and slid onto the chair opposite Mylin.

"We did," Carr said. "Mylin insisted. She won't give us anything."

"You mean she doesn't trust the big mean guy from the FBI?" Kandy said, laughing. "Have you tried tapping her phone?"

"Funny," Carr said. "Of course she doesn't trust me. Hell, I hardly trust me."

"What about Bain?" Qigiq asked.

"By the book, but solid."

"Are we going to wait for clearance?" Kandy said. "I've got a plane to catch."

"You flew to Reno?"

"Metaphorically."

Carr's laugh was short but loud.

Mylin said, "Mr. Carr wants me to work for him."

Qigiq backed up until he reached the wall, then leaned his shoulder blades against the coolness, remembering meeting Mylin for the first time at Throckmorton Theater.

"You trying to make her a rat on the inside?" Kandy asked. "Could get her killed."

The room was silent. Qigiq counted three breaths.

Carr finally said, "We want her out. There's a larger imperative than her brother's murder."

"Is this the part where we need clearance?" Qigiq asked.

"It would be better. However, Mylin is the real key."

Mylin looked straight at Qigiq. "I will only do this if you help me."

Qigiq hesitated. "Mylin, I'm just a city cop. Fairbanks. San Francisco. Not even really big cities."

A tap at the door was followed by it swinging inward and Bain's face. "What are you talking about?"

"The life of a city cop," Qigiq said. "Lots of crimes happen in cities."

Bain looked to Carr. "No clearance on short notice. It'll take at least until morning." His shoulders drooped. "Maybe longer."

"Trail gets colder and colder," Kandy said.

Bain reacted. "What trail? What has he told you?"

"Relax, Thomas," Carr said. "I haven't told them anything."

Kandy and Qigiq nodded agreement.

"Good," Bain said.

"But I'm about to. So if you don't want to be part of the fallout, you might want to leave now."

"They don't have clearance."

"Right. And my partner Roger Graham is dead. Graham, like the cracker invented by a minister to suppress carnal urges. I teased Roger a lot about that." He stopped. His eyes drifted with a memory, then turned to Bain. "Sniper. Laser. One shot.

We both know where that rifle came from. So I'm moving forward until something stops me."

Qigiq wondered how he would feel losing Kandy, then pushed the dark thought away.

"But—"

Carr held up a hand. "Save it."

"Are you still on leave?" Kandy asked.

"No, they gave me this project." He half-smiled. "Okay, I walked in and demanded this case while every other agent was trying to get as far away from it as possible."

"Not Shen's murder. Not Graham's murder. So...what case?" Qigiq asked.

Carr addressed Bain. "You going or staying? Better if you stay, then I won't have to bring you up to speed later. But if these two don't get clearance, you were in the room and should have stopped me."

"Dammit David. Why do you put me in a position like this?"

"Because the FBI moves like frozen molasses. We don't find what we want fast, the case drops into a cold file, and we're sitting at a desk watching Russian ice freeze because of that rifle." His hand gripped the table like he was trying to crush it. "And I don't get...and justice isn't served."

"Can we speak in hypotheticals?" Bain asked.

"Sure. Drag this out for a week. A month even. Phone it in. Pretend we're making progress, fill out some paperwork." Carr sat down and turned toward Mylin. "But we're not going to. Mylin agrees to help us, I'll have her on a plane within forty-eight hours."

Bain slid down the wall, sat on the floor, and instantly looked more relaxed. "Okay, I know you're right. I just hate violating rules."

"There aren't any in this game, Thomas. Let's just do it."

"Just do it. Nike, the goddess of speed," Kandy said, laughing low.

"Yeah, speed," Carr echoed. "Let's see how *fast* we can do this." He sat up taller and took a deep breath. "Okay, everybody, we're in the middle of a top-secret, class-A firestorm. It's coming from everywhere: the past, the present, and the future if we fail. What do we do?"

"Paddle up river," Qigiq said.

"Correct. We go to the source and eliminate it. That's where Mylin comes in."

Mylin lifted her dark eyes and blinked. "Me?"

Carr studied each person in turn. He pointed at Bain and shook his head.

Bain removed a device from his pocket. "You're really not going to record this?"

"You bet I'm not. This team is going dark. We already have one body on a beach."

Qigiq glanced at Kandy. She gave him a nearly imperceptible one shoulder shrug he took to mean: *I have no idea what's going on either.*

Mylin said, "Someone else is dead?"

Carr nodded. "We'll talk about her later." He turned to Qigiq. "Mylin has agreed to help me if and only if you and Kandy are on the team. She has trust issues." He laughed, but it came out more madman than jokester. "You two know this is personal for me. However..." He reached into his briefcase and pulled out four 8-by-10 photographs, then spread them across the table so they faced Mylin. "This mission is broader and deeper than a dead FBI agent and his enraged partner. That's why San Diego sent Bain up to help me."

Qigiq recognized the paintings; he had rescued them. "Are those from a house in Sausalito that burned down?"

Bain said, "All but one. It was recovered from an art gallery."

Kandy's shifting feet caught Qigiq's eye. He was thinking about Mylinian too. "Those paintings are important?"

"Are they ever," Carr said. "Without them, we wouldn't be here with the three of you."

"None of whom have clearance," Bain added.

Carr laughed again, genuine this time. "How are you going to get security clearance for an illegal alien arrested for murder? I'm lucky they're letting me try this gambit." He looked from Kandy to Qigiq. "But it gets more complicated by the day."

"You're going to tell us how, right?" Kandy asked.

"They don't have clearance," Bain said.

"I'm not waiting. These are police officers sworn to protect and serve; they're not going to leak information about our mission." He closed his eyes and took a deep breath. "Should we move to a larger conference room or is everyone okay?"

"This is fine," Kandy said. No one disagreed.

Carr took a moment to compose himself. "Okay. What I'm about to tell you is beyond classified; it stays within this group. If details show up on Wikileaks, it'll be over for all of us. Don't talk to *anyone,* including," he paused, "maybe especially, people in your management chain. Assume you are under surveillance. Don't use official equipment. No phone calls. No text messages. Use codes. Write notes...then burn them."

Carr looked at Bain with a question in his eyes.

Bain nodded. "Yes, I put the prison's recording system for this room into lawyer mode; we're privileged and confidential. Only my password will switch it back on. They'll realize it eventually, but since the *FBI* is using it, no one seems to care." He smiled slightly. "They don't like us much."

"Thanks, Thomas. Allow me to work backwards in time—it'll make more sense." Carr cleared his throat. "The Chinese have an organization whose name changes from time to time; let's call it The Strategy and Acquisitions Office."

Kandy said, "Sounds like a division of Google."

"Maybe not so different," Bain said from his spot on the floor.

"This organization has a mountain of money and one charter."

"Something simple I bet, like Beat America." Kandy said.

Carr grinned. "The office is generally run by the wife of a high-ranking official." He glanced around. "Does that surprise anyone?"

Kandy said, "Do they order plate settings for the Chairman's dining table?"

"Not quite. Their charter is to acquire military technology *by any means possible.* You're all aware of Chinese hackers finding their way into American corporations. And you might recall Kun Shan 'Joey' Chun, naturalized U.S. citizen, 19-year FBI veteran; violating his security clearance to feed secrets to officials of the Chinese government."

A vent fan kicked on. Air moved against the back of Qigiq's neck. He said, "Those paintings carry that language the professor developed, don't they?"

Bain's eyes shot up.

Carr said, "Yes, they do."

"And the Strategy Office," Kandy added, "wants to acquire them. That means American military secrets. The paintings are being used to smuggle info out of the country."

"How can you know that?" Bain said. "This material is classified."

Qigiq smiled from his position against the wall. He preferred watching and listening; it gave him more space to think. Including about the knife injury to Mylin's leg.

Carr sighed. "Thomas, they're detectives. They deduce from available evidence." He aligned the photographs carefully on the table. "Mylin's father was an FBI informant. We let him operate a moving brothel in exchange for intel on human trafficking. Then we decided to trace the paintings shipped from his art gallery, thinking they had more value than was being declared. Turns out they were folk craft being sent overseas to towns in northern China, an island off the Korean mainland, and Russian cities I've never heard of."

"When did you figure it out?" Kandy asked.

"When you found that canvas of chicken scratch in the lab worker's safe."

"You're welcome," Kandy said with a wide smile.

"So, a secret is in play," Qigiq said. "You need Mylin to help get it back. She wants Kandy and me involved because she trusts us."

"The crux of the matter," Carr said. "Although, *get it back* might not be exactly what we need to do."

Mylin said flatly, "You can't."

"That's awfully pessimistic," Bain said.

"Can't what?" Carr asked.

"Go after it. Get it back. Stop them. They have spies like the eyes of a thousand invisible dragons." Qigiq watched Mylin's gaze roam the room and land on Carr. "You will end on a beach like the woman."

Carr took a deep breath. "Agent Shirley Sun was raped and tortured before being dumped in the ocean."

Mylin shook her head vigorously.

"What?" Carr asked.

"Uncle Gan is not careless."

Kandy said, "Mylin means that the body wouldn't wash up on a beach unless someone wanted it on that beach on that day."

Mylin nodded. "If he didn't wish for you to find her, you wouldn't."

"He's sending a message?" Bain asked.

Mylin answered. "Maybe this message is not for you."

Carr sighed. "We go after whoever received the paintings."

"You still have the paintings," Kandy said.

Qigiq said, "The Gallerié Electra had been open for months before it burned. Shipped out a lot of paintings."

Mylin shook her head slowly. "You will die."

Carr tapped a tattoo with the tip of his middle finger on a dent in the table. The metal top resonated.

No one spoke.

A chime sounded three times, rising in pitch. Bain stood and left without a word.

"I hate waiting," Kandy said.

Carr's shoulders hunched forward. "You and me both, Detective."

"Do you have a plan?" Qigiq asked.

"I had one," Carr said. "But Mylin tossed in a monkey wrench. She wants you two on board."

"Don't know what I'm getting on board for," Kandy said. "I like this conversation. But it's not clear how homicide detectives contribute." She glanced at Carr. "Can you tell me more about what's on those paintings?"

"No!" Mylin shouted. "I must not hear. Knowing brings danger." She looked down. "I already know too many things."

Carr leaned back in his chair and texted on his phone.

Qigiq studied Mylin, wondering about living life in constant fear.

Car slipped his phone away and leaned forward. "Okay, Mylin, just to be super clear. If Kandy and Qigiq are officially assigned to this project, you agree to help us?"

She nodded emphatically. "I am trapped. If I remain silent, your courts kill me. If I help you..." her voice trailed to silence.

"How old are you, Mylin?" Carr asked.

She blinked back tears. "Nearly twenty-one."

A knock interrupted. Carr opened the door. Two female guards entered.

"Mr. Carr, can you make them give me a viola?"

"I'll try." Carr stepped close to Mylin. He laid one hand on her shoulder and stared down at her. He whispered, "Pay close attention every minute. Whatever is going to happen, will happen fast."

She nodded slowly. The guards led her out. The door slammed shut.

Carr leaned his bulk against the door as if blocking out an intruder. "I understand if you two don't want any part of this case. They gave it to me because no one else will touch it."

Kandy spun sideways in her immobile chair. "That bad?"

"Worse. Government employees. Top Secret security clearance. Hyper-advanced projects. Makes Snowden's leak seem like schoolgirl gossip."

"All transferred to a Korean island?" she said.

"I'll do a touchdown dance naked if the paintings are still on that island," Carr said. "We might be able to contain the leak." His jaw moved back and forth sideways, like it was coming loose. "Right under our noses while we worked the informant on the sex trafficking angle." He shook his head. "We even provided weapons."

Qigiq remembered a detail of a conference with the FBI. "Operation Calm?"

Carr looked up. "Man, the FBI is getting worse and worse at keeping secrets. But yes, we thought we could track the guns and reveal trade routes in the process."

"Didn't you guys try gunwalking before? In Mexico?" Kandy said.

"Yeah, Operation Fast and Furious with the Alcohol, Tobacco, and Firearms people. Didn't end well. An agent was killed and our weapons were found at the site. We have better safeguards this time."

"Bad guys died," Kandy said. She hung one arm over the back of the chair, emphasizing the obvious strength of her biceps in the sleeveless shirt. "Your report card is improving. You got more weapons out there that we should watch for?"

"Yes. The rifle that killed my partner was likely the same model that launched the RPG into the hospital room."

"One weapon?" Kandy asked. "So a good guy died from it, too?"

Carr said, "One *kind* of weapon, multiple copies. All prototypes."

"I don't really want to know," Qigiq said. "But for completeness, how many did Wu have access to?"

"Three."

"I don't want to know either," Kandy said, "but how many have you recovered?"

Carr paused. "One. From the hospital explosion."

"Is this special rifle the top-secret thing Mylin has to help us retrieve?"

Carr crossed the room and took the chair Mylin had vacated. "Extra credit if we recover the rifles. If they're used on an American Embassy, or worse, one of our ally's embassies, the politicians will go berserk."

"The same politicians who green-lighted Operation Calm?" Kandy said.

Carr hesitated. "They didn't exactly green-light it."

"If that's the extra credit," Kandy said, "I can't wait to hear about the feature presentation."

Carr waved a hand at the pictures on the table. "These four are the tail. We have to find out where the dog went."

Qigiq said, "You think Gan is feeding your puppy?"

Carr nodded solemnly. "I think he's standing in a huge pile of—"

A knock on the door was followed by Bain entering. "Got the call. These two have clearance for Operation Igloo."

Carr smiled in a small way. "I wonder what happened?"

"Easy," Kandy said. "Someone called our boss. He made suggestions a rapper wouldn't quote."

Qigiq said, "Igloo?"

CHAPTER 3

I LAY ON THE FOAM MATTRESS wondering how the dragon gods decide who gets to be happy in this life, and who are abused and tossed aside. They had smiled upon me with musical talent that filled my heart with joy, and then put me in a family that cared about trivial things. Stacks of money, power to bend the will of others, secret backroom talks with men—always men—who wished to build or destroy empires. I begged the gods again to please make men leave me alone so I could play my music. It seemed such a small thing to ask.

A few weeks ago, they had begun to answer.

Elder brother killed Father. Younger brother killed elder. I killed younger. That left only father's brother: Uncle Gan. I drifted toward sleep whispering to myself:

I am almost free.

* * *

I awoke to morning imprisoned in a country whose laws wished to kill me for putting bullets into my abusive brother. Or maybe they would lock me up and let me play patriotic music in a prison orchestra like the ones in the re-education camps Grandma Chong talked about. That life would have beauty in it.

Uncle would never allow it.

His spies will find me. He will decide if I live or die surrounded by these gray walls of man-made stone. Or he might bribe those who can set me free. My heart skipped.

Was Agent Carr working for Uncle Gan?

Carr had arrived quickly...and knew so much.

I rolled over on the thin mattress and pain pierced the knife wound in my thigh. I sought the solace of my tiny sunbeam; it hadn't arrived yet. My eyes roamed gray wall to a calendar provided by my lawyer showing a picture of a lonely blue orchid. Monday. I had slept in this room for nine nights in a row.

The detectives would never help Uncle, even if they were my friends. But they might assist the black man. Unless they were like me: told what to do from above.

Would Uncle Gan break me out and sweep me back east? Or would he silence me the way my evil brother Shen silenced our orchestra? There was only one way to know if Uncle had ordered us killed: Ask him and watch his eyes speak the truth.

And if he had?

If the gods helped me, I would kill him too.

Footsteps beat against a hard floor. Stopped close.

"You have a visitor."

"Again?"

"Your grandmother."

I shot upright. "Here?"

"No, on Mars. You're going to teleconference through a NASA satellite." The guard laughed at his own silliness and unlocked my cage.

I fluffed my hair and straightened my prison clothes, but it made no real difference. I was a skinny girl in an oversized uniform that managed to be drab, even if it was bright orange.

The guard led me to a small room with two chairs and a tiny table. His eyes roamed over my body as if I were naked. He said, "You must have connections, pretty girl. Prisoners don't get a conference room unless their attorney demands it in writing."

I sat at the table. I worried over which connection was awarding me privileges. What they would demand in return. The door opened. Grandma Chong shuffled in alone, her thin body hunched forward. The door closed behind her.

I stood and bowed.

She wore a blue dress and a cream lace shawl; I was certain

she had made both herself. She moved slowly, still recovering from being hit by a motorbike. Another reason I was glad Shen was dead; he had been the rider.

She didn't speak, so out of respect, I didn't either. I came around the table and helped her into a plain metal chair, which this time wasn't bolted to the floor. I sat facing her. Her eyes fixed on me and revealed much sadness.

"Mylin." She lifted her right arm and stretched it across the table toward me. I took her fingers into my left hand and squeezed gently. For the first time in memory her hand wasn't cold. She smiled and said, "You're the only grandchild I have left."

The thought frightened me. I had been so concerned about myself, I hadn't considered what the deaths of the past weeks would mean to Grandma. I forced a smile to match hers, but remained silent.

"We must protect you. So you can make babies."

I stopped smiling. "I cannot make babies in prison, Laolao."

"Gan contacted me."

I sat up straighter against the hard chair. Uncle must have fewer options than I thought.

She said, "He has a message for you."

I glanced up at the corner. There wasn't a camera in this room either.

"We must not speak," I said. "Not even in Chinese."

Her lips curved into the lovely glistening-eyes smile that for years had hid what she was really thinking. She removed her hand from mine, reached into her purse, and came back holding a smartphone. She pushed it gently across the table and retrieved earbuds. I inserted them. The app on the screen showed two buttons: *Play* and *Shred*. I touched Play. My Uncle's voice, a voice I had been shocked to hear just weeks ago at my concert in San Francisco, spoke to me:

"Hello Mylin, I trust you are safe and well cared for. It is unfortunate for your future that you interfered with your brother. However, his actions far exceeded his position. Perhaps it is best that

you stopped him. I have arranged for the two surviving musicians to return home. By the time you hear this message, they will be safe in international waters. You, however, present a unique problem."

The voice cleared its throat. I didn't like being thought of as a problem. The death of my sister Pé entered my mind. Father had solved *problems* in horrible ways.

Uncle continued, "You are in the hands of Americans who wish to extract information, as they have for many years at their prison on the Cuban bay. Their psychologists are skilled at many forms of torture. You know secrets, even if you aren't aware of their importance. Among them are the identities of the men you have...entertained. These men continue to work for us. These men must not be captured. Hold out your right hand."

I put out my hand.

Grandma reached out and placed her wrinkled hand over mine. She gave it an affectionate squeeze and something touched my palm. I closed my fingers around two capsules.

"If the Americans torture you," the voice went on, "use these. Your passage to our ancestors will be painless. Do not reveal the secrets of our network. It must continue to operate or decades of painstaking groundwork will be lost. Your work. My work. The work of your father." The voice coughed. "Be proud that you have been key in many important endeavors."

I pushed my hand into the pocket of my baggy uniform. Would they search me before taking me back to my cell? Where could I hide them?

Grandma stood and shuffled around the table until she was behind me. She leaned over and hugged me as she whispered in my ear in Chinese. My eyes grew ever wider as she explained that the sticky tube she was hiding under the collar of my jumpsuit was to be used immediately. It contained the future of the family. With good luck, I would bear a boy with an inner dragon. If it failed, she would return with another.

Uncle's voice continued, "Listen carefully to your grand-mother. If we are fortunate and the Americans do not torture you, you will be free to perform this great service for your family. Be strong, Mylin. Whatever the future brings, make your family proud of you."

I longed to spit on the graves of Shen and my father for the pain they had caused me. Then, like a foolish schoolgirl, I surged with pride that I had been key to many endeavors—though I didn't know the details.

But impregnate myself? Who was the donor? *This, I knew, I would never be told.*

"Shred this message now, Mylin. It will not be able to be recovered even by the best people at the American NSA who think they are so clever."

I pulled out the earbuds and pressed *Shred.*

"Did he have kind words?" Grandma asked.

"Didn't you listen to it?"

She shook her head. "This is not my business. Gan say, take to Mylin. Those are my instructions."

I wanted to ask about the capsules. Surely Grandma could guess. But then, perhaps not. It took a special kind of mind to understand Uncle Gan. And Father. They made decisions that seemed beyond belief on the surface.

"Will you come to visit me again?"

Grandma was still for a moment. "It is a long bus ride from San Francisco. But I will try."

"Oh, Laolao. You must rest and grow strong again."

Her smile revealed teeth faded to yellow. "Lovely little Mylin. I am too old to grow strong. You grow strong for both of us." She leaned across the table and brushed back the hair back that I always combed down on my left side. Then she kissed my temple on the mark I carried. She held my face in both hands. "All of you is beautiful my dear granddaughter. Do not let anyone convince you otherwise."

I smiled weakly, and touched the side of my face where I had placed the tattoo of a dragon swallowing its tail. Destruction and rebirth were present in all things.

"Yes, Laolao. As you say."

Tears glistened in her aged eyes. She rose to leave. At the door to the room she placed her hand on the knob and stopped. She didn't turn to face me. She was still for several quiet chants. Then she departed in silence.

The door hissed itself closed.

The sound like a last breath made me realize I might never see her again.

I fought tears and held the capsules in my palm, thinking about the two paths to the future that had just been delivered. The door was fully open before I realized it had moved at all. A tall man in a blue uniform, dark greasy hair flopped over his forehead, stared at me. He said nothing, only looked straight at me for a few seconds. Then he stepped aside and pushed a prisoner into the room.

The door slammed shut.

I kept my hands on the table, studying the new arrival. The hair had been shaven to a stubble, the skull showing white under the tubular lights. The face was smooth, young. Dark eyes, almost black with a hint of...plum.

I gaped.

The prisoner pressed a finger to her lips. Her body was covered by a jumpsuit like mine.

I swallowed hard. "Why are *you* here?"

"Grand theft auto." She grinned. "I wanted something faster than my little Ford. Just for a minute, you know, so I could drive like Kandy. A chubby dude in a tailored suit left the fob for his Tesla while he went to the restroom. That super-electric acceleration seduced me."

"I mean here. This room." How could I explain? "I am poison."

"I bet super-secret software identified us on the pier after your San Francisco concert. They arrested me, but started asking questions about you." She paused, an otherworldly look in her eyes. "A *lot* of questions."

I covered my mouth with my left hand. Jilly had helped me escape that night the FBI agent was shot. Carr's partner. Carr had visited just yesterday.

"Oh Ji—" I stopped myself, unsure if I should reveal her name. "What kind of questions?"

"How long have I known you? What do you do for a living? When was the last time I saw you?"

I kept my hand holding the capsules on the table. I wanted to hide them, but was afraid to move.

"They want you to question me?"

"Not exactly." She reached inside her orange top, pulled out a newspaper, and unfolded it onto the table. The headline read *Sister Murders Brother* over the subtitle: *Governor says: "Deport Illegals!"* "Politicians are making a big deal out of an illegal alien shooting another illegal at a family festival. With a gun not licensed to anyone."

"I don't want to go back. They..." I blocked thoughts from my mind—not wanting to revisit the past, not wanting to be recorded, not wanting the recording to reach Uncle Gan.

"Forget that headline. I'm here about a plea bargain. You explain how your orchestral sex party worked and give them a list of customers. They let you off the death penalty and promise no more than twenty-five years, with possible parole in fifteen."

Fifteen years. I would be thirty-five. With many more years to play music.

Uncle Gan. Capsules. If I revealed secrets, how long before...

"That wouldn't be safe."

"They figured you'd say that. So they're offering to hide you in witness protection from the very beginning."

"Witness protection in prison?"

Jilly shrugged. "I bet they have ways." She held out her hand and flipped her palm upward.

I frowned in confusion.

A powerful knock shook the door.

"Got to go, they only gave me three minutes." She stood and added in a loud voice, "Think hard about cooperating, it sounds like a good deal to me." She turned around. By the time she reached the door it had been pushed opened from the out-side.

Her hand, why had she...the article was still on the table. I flipped it over. Tiny gray letters had been carefully penciled down one side:

I spoke lies. 1:04 AM tonight. We're leaving. Be ready.—JK

A tiny LCD clock attached to the paper with clear tape glowed 9:23 AM.

CHAPTER 4

"TONIGHT?" QIGIQ ASKED.

Carr reached across the table for a bottle of ketchup standing on its white cap. "We have to move fast. It's been over a week since the...uh...incident. The trail grows colder as we sit and feed our faces."

"An army travels on its stomach," Kandy said.

Carr glanced at her plate. "Do you always have burgers for breakfast?"

"Only after ten. And when you buy real meat—like here at the Squeeze. I usually have to settle for San Francisco foo-foo."

Qigiq sipped a decaf. They had stayed overnight at a place called Circus Circus, and though luxurious by his standards, he missed the quiet of his floating home on the Bay. He said, "How can we possibly be ready by tonight?"

"First part of the plan is in motion," Carr said. "The rest is up to you two."

"Lot of risk," Qigiq said.

"Total unknown," Kandy added.

"I can provide backup while you're in the U.S. But if you leave...well, I'll follow, but international resources are harder to come by and slower to deploy."

Kandy said, "You don't have offices in Asia?"

Carr squirted ketchup over his potato wedges. "Not that we talk about." He paused the red stream. "And not that they'll give me if there's a chance of discovery."

"Political fallout?" Qigiq said.

Carr nodded. "We're dealing with enough secrets to keep

Fox News busy for months."

Kandy tapped her fork against a pickle wedge lying on her plate. She asked Qigiq, "You ever done this kind of work before?"

"Went after a dealer years ago who used sled dogs to smuggle drugs. He invented a way to absorb it into their fur like a dye. Chased him to Minneapolis. I also followed a high-ranking military official to Asia once. That didn't work out so well."

"Sure it did," she said. "You're alive and got to move to San Francisco. Sounds like a win to me."

Qigiq smiled and said, "You mentioned a plan in motion."

"Got a man on the inside now."

A group of Asian men came through the door talking and snapping pictures. One held his phone up and panned slowly, like a cameraman on a TV crew.

"Is this place that special?" Carr asked.

"Check out the décor," Kandy said. "A kid's sled hanging from the ceiling, bicycles, chrome stools. Graffiti everywhere. Americana at its finest."

Qigiq considered his half-eaten eggs and tried to organize the past twenty-four hours. The FBI and Mylin were asking for his help. A secret had leaked. Someone had a good reason to find it, or the FBI wouldn't be putting up cash for the search.

"How important are scribbles on a painting?" Kandy asked. "Or is this really about retribution for Graham?" She paused, watching Carr's eyes. "Or is something going on that I don't understand."

"For me it's payback. But not for the Bureau." Carr paused, looked from Kandy to Qigiq and back. "There's something else going on."

Qigiq read tension in Carr's neck. He said, "And it's better for Kandy and me to stay in the dark?"

"This mission is flying fast under the standard-protocol radar with a big red *National Security* tag on its toe."

Kandy bit into a burger taller than a hooker's high heels. The Squeeze Inn was famous for them, yet they seemed impossible to eat.

"Should we ask?" Qigiq said.

"If you want," Carr replied. "But if I answer, you'll be going into the field with deep knowledge you couldn't have obtained through standard channels. Knowing things you shouldn't is a dead giveaway." He ate a red potato wedge. "Sorry, that was insensitive." He laughed.

"So we go in blind?"

Carr shrugged—his jacket wrinkled and flattened. "You know what you know: Wu's girls were prostitutes, he informed for us, the orchestra was both a cover and a client magnet." He glanced at the potato on his fork. "Government research labs compromised at undefined levels. This intel works against you if the opposition thinks you know too much for your official story."

"Damned if you do and damned if you don't," Kandy said. "Are you sure this isn't going to mess up my vacation?" She grinned. "Last case sure did. I didn't get to enjoy Burning Man."

"Your Captain is on board to move in whatever direction you choose. Budget being tossed his way may have swayed him, but he seems like a do-the-right-thing kind of guy."

"You mentioned tonight," Qigiq said.

Carr nodded. "Correct. Or we need a plan B."

"What about the eyes of the dragon that Mylin worries about?" Kandy said. "If we're followed, the whole thing falls apart."

"Agreed," Carr said.

They ate and deliberated in silence.

Qigiq tried to imagine how to locate something when he didn't know what it was, where it was, or what it was being used for. While protecting Mylin. And staying alive.

"I suspect you have a bigger plan," Kandy said. "I've never met an FBI guy that didn't have at least one." Her chest shook as she laughed.

Carr wagged his head. "Are you always so insightful, Detective?"

"Taught me that at cop school." She glanced at Qigiq. "You have a plan, too, don't you?"

Qigiq said, "Still trying to think of one that avoids more bodies."

Carr waved for a waitress. "We know we have two things Uncle Gan wants: Mylin and the paintings. Unfortunately, the other two girls have already disappeared."

"You snooze you loose," Kandy said.

"Should we find them first?" Qigiq asked.

Carr shifted his jaw in thought. "Not a bad idea. We have their faces from the surround cameras at the concert. Our recognition software is way better than anything Facebook uses. Never know, we might get lucky."

Kandy said, "There's a story about a blind pig and an acorn here somewhere. I'm a detective, I can sense these things." She returned to her monster burger.

"Does Gan want her?" Qigiq asked.

"Mylin?" Carr nodded. "Oh yeah. He wants them all. They're a liability. Someone had to be mighty scared to destroy an entire orchestra." He glanced to his left where a red and white polka dot bicycle hung on the wall. "Can you imagine making that decision? It's like a war zone maneuver."

Kandy's eyes tightened as if she were trying to bring a blurry object into focus. Qigiq guessed the funeral procession was still fresh in her mind, too. They had both been there when the stage exploded.

Kandy said, "Let's go with what you smart FBI guys call an operational assumption. Mylin has secrets. People, places, details. This info will put Gan on the radar of one or more nasty governments, which destroys his business and gets him arrested. However. She's linked to us. And we have his paintings. Wait, I have to eat this while it's still hot." She took a bite of her burger. "Does he know we have his paintings, or does he think they went up in smoke?"

"Best guess?" Carr said. "No, he doesn't know we have them, unless he has a mole in the Bureau."

Qigiq considered the implications of a leak from within the FBI. He knew secure communication was crucial to effective action, but the countries of the world seemed to be in a race to eliminate it.

Carr continued. "Let's assume Gan knows we have the paintings."

Kandy said, "How badly would he want them?"

"And entire orchestra and two FBI agents," Carr said. "On a scale of one to ten, I vote ten."

Qigiq leaned away from his plate and glanced at the polkadot bicycle again. "Mylin is the connection. He'll react if she disappears."

Carr nodded. "I'm counting on it. People in a hurry make mistakes. We're behind the curve here. We need that mistake."

"This big plan you have," Kandy said, "who's executes it?"

"Our informant is dead. For the Bureau's upper management, it ends there. But my boss lost an agent, she wants to know what's going on. So she's providing bags of money with no strings attached."

"I want to know about those paintings," Kandy said. "How about we free associate? I say a phrase. You say a word back."

"I only know what the test team and Professor Pemberly told me," Carr said. "I can't read that language at all."

"Okay, here we go. Biochemical weapons."

"Touchdown," Carr said.

Kandy stared at her burger. "Damn."

"Hydroelectric power."

"Funny," she said. "Money laundering."

"Dry cleaning."

Kandy pointed at Qigiq. "You try."

Qigiq rubbed his index fingers together like a magician distracting his audience. "They have the death chemical, old news. Those five computers in the penthouse had been working for a long time. More old news. These paintings haven't been delivered. Therefore, they must contain something brand new." He closed his eyes and saw an outdoor stage go up in flames. What could be so important? His fingers froze. "Military."

"Bingo," Carr said.

"*Our* military," Kandy added.

"Give the lady a stuffed Panda."

Qigiq opened his eyes. The waitress Carr had flagged down earlier arrived. Carr said, "Chocolate milkshakes all around. My friends and I are celebrating. I'm buying."

Smiling, she said, "Save some for my tip."

In a few minutes they were sipping rich shakes served in a tall glass accompanied by the metal shake-making container still half full.

"This mission is well above my pay grade," Qigiq said.

Kandy said, "There is no pay grade for this stuff. We do it because we love it." She huffed her low laugh and made the straw gurgle sucking air. "I love that sound. Takes me back to being a kid in a diner."

Qigiq shook his head. "You spent a lot of time in diners?"

"I was hired security. My job was to watch for kids stealing from the candy display by the cash register. They'd run, and I'd catch them."

"And take it back?" Carr said.

She nodded. "After administering instant karma."

"Anyone ever outrun you?"

"Once. Tall guy. Smart enough to have a couple of friends get in my way. I lost his trail. But he only got away with it once."

"Because?" Carr asked.

"Next time he came in we made eye contact."

They waited. Kandy poured the second half of her milkshake from the metal container into her glass. "What?"

"That's it?" Carr said. "You made eye contact?"

"That's all it took."

"Nothing happened after that?"

"Didn't say that," she said. "I said he never did it again."

Qigiq looked at Carr, who looked at him. They both

shrugged.

"Is that where you got the name Kandy?" Carr asked.

Kandy smiled. "Anyone care to summarize?" No response. "OK, analysis is not my forte, but here goes. The bad guy is into secret Department of Defense tech. We don't know how deep. We also don't know what it is, or what he's done with it. Just for clarity I should add, we don't know for sure if he's the bad guy or a middleman that leads nowhere." She glanced into the metal milkshake container. "How am I doing?"

"They don't pay you enough," Carr said.

"I'm quoting you on that. But that's only problem one. Problem two: our photo and knowledge of the general where-abouts of Gan are both a decade old. Problem three: no way to approach. His spies see us coming, evidence vaporizes. The target has already sacrificed an art gallery, a house, and an or-chestra. Makes him psychotic and dangerous in my book."

"You ever get tired of thankless detective work, come be an analyst," Carr said.

She stuck her straw in the metal container and continued, "This is where Mylin comes in. She knows Gan's nature. She can guide us. More important, she can get close without set-ting off alarms." Kandy took a long pull on a huge white straw with a red stripe winding up it. "However, she wants this guy," she pointed a thumb at Qigiq, "to go with her."

"She wants all of us to go," Qigiq said. "She's alone, needs people to trust. But three law enforcement officers flying in for holiday? It'll never work."

"Does she trust us?" Carr said.

Kandy said, "Problem four: Do we trust her? How do we know she isn't working *for* Uncle Gan? This call for help could be a trick to recover the paintings Qigiq stole." She grinned.

Qigiq shook his head. He had rescued them from a burning house, and kept them. A bit like stealing. Except now they were evidence in an active case.

Kandy continued, "He and I end up as...what do you smart guys call it? Collateral damage?"

"Only Army generals say that," Carr said.

"And the FBI? What do you call it?"

"Whoops." He laughed.

"Who else has been in to see Mylin?" Qigiq said.

"Her grandmother visited this morning," Carr said.

Kandy stirred her shake with the straw. "The woman where this all started visits a county prison in Reno, Nevada. All the way from San Francisco. Why would she do that?"

Carr said, "To visit her granddaughter who has no one else left in the U.S."

"Or?" Kandy said.

"To deliver a message from Gan," Qigiq said. "But that visit happened *after* Mylin asked for our help."

"Maybe she was anticipating instructions, laying ground-work," Kandy said.

"Are you two always so trusting?" Carr asked.

Kandy said, "Trust gets you killed."

Carr pushed the inverted ketchup bottle to the edge of the table. "What does your gut tell you?"

"You go first," Kandy said to Qigiq, leaning her chair onto its back legs.

Qigiq considered the soft-spoken viola player capable of pumping three pistol rounds into her brother at close range.

"Unpredictable."

"That's hard to work with," Car said.

"Your boss has bags of money," Kandy said. Carr looked her way. "Who do we get to help? We go through the Bureau, it leaks like a Snowden cone." She laughed. "We go through SFPD, who knows how long it takes, what we get, or who learns about it."

"You have a suggestion?"

"Depends on what we need to do," she said.

"How about using civilians?" Qigiq said.

Carr looked dubious. "Untrained people in an unknown situation?"

Qigiq said, "People known to Mylin who have specialized

skills. I have a photographer in mind."

"They would blend in better than cops," Kandy said. "Hey, I've got a sixty-four-million-dollar question. These paintings that are going to bring the world to an end, do we use the originals or make copies like Qigiq did for the Dragon Lady who date-raped him?"

"You were date-raped?" Carr asked.

"Drugged in a restaurant while the lady ran off with evidence from a victim's safe."

Carr blew a stream of air. "You think we should risk the originals?"

Kandy shrugged. "Only way to play it. If we ever get the chance to show one to the art-collecting uncle, it had better be real."

"The FBI keeps copies," Carr mused. "I guess, since we've already analyzed them. Still, if those get into the wrong hands..."

Kandy laughed.

Qigiq smiled. He knew Kandy's style after months of working together.

Carr looked back and forth between them. "What?"

Qigiq said, "I believe my partner is suggesting that we are strategizing because they are *already* in the wrong hands, and we're sitting here trying to find a way to put the genie back in the bottle."

"Subtle, isn't she?" Carr said.

"Only when she's not hungry," Qigiq said. "How about we take one small picture? Prove we actually have something in our possession. Claim the others are safely tucked away."

Carr was thoughtful, then nodded slowly. "Yeah, I can sell that idea."

"When can we have it?" Kandy asked.

"You'll need it tonight before showtime. Where do we meet?"

"We'd better get back to the city to pack," Qigiq said. "We need a place Gan's spies can't find."

Carr smiled. "I know just the place." He placed twenties on the check and stood.

"Wait, Mr. Moneybags." Kandy dropped her chair forward. "We need plane tickets to—" She froze, head tilted slightly.

Qigiq thought she was looking at him, but her eyes were focused somewhere over his left shoulder.

She leapt up, sending her chair sliding across the floor on its back. "I am so insulted," she shouted. "I *never* want to see you two again."

She sprinted directly toward a group waiting to be seated. They tried to step aside, but she rammed into a man on the left holding a plus-size cell phone. The tourists erupted into rapid-fire speech in a foreign language. Then the rammed man yelled in English, "Hey, that's mine. Come back." And started off after her.

Qigiq looked at Carr. "Kandy or the little guy?"

"Kandy. You know the area."

Qigiq stood. "We'll never catch her, but let's make it look good. Angel's Speed Shop."

"Got it," Carr said, and started toward the main entrance.

Qigiq felt a dozen pairs of eyes on him. He smiled, saluted politely, then ran after Carr.

Sunlight smacked his brain hard.

Through half-closed eyelids he saw Kandy a half-mile away running west on Las Brisas Blvd. The Asian guy had tossed his suit coat aside and was giving chase, blue tie flying over his left shoulder, gaining slightly. Carr ran behind the guy, hanging back, looking like he was on an afternoon jog in Central Park.

No guns in sight.

Qigiq fired up the frost blue BMW Angel had arranged for him while she repaired his crashed Guzzi. It had vintage style but a modern motor. He rode up Las Brisas and caught Carr in less than a minute. The trio was still running west. The Asian guy was slowing. Kandy turned right onto a trail that led to an open area kids had turned into a dirt bike track. Kandy loved running on dirt.

He pulled to the side of the road and pretended to make a phone call, in case eyes were on him. The guy stopped, doubled over, panting hard. Kandy had his cell phone; he was in trouble for losing it. He was likely chastising himself for shouting in the restaurant and informing his companions what had happened. Fabricating a good lie would now be difficult.

Carr ran past the guy and onto the dirt trail heading north. He wouldn't catch Kandy either, but at least it looked like he was trying.

The guy straightened up—and chased Carr.

Qigiq took off, reached the trail in seconds, and headed onto the dirt. He was on street tires, but dry dirt smoothed by hundreds of motorbikes was easy to ride. He pulled to a stop when he saw Carr standing with the Asian guy, who was now talking on a cell phone.

Qigiq guessed *Carr's* cell phone.

Of course Carr would be friendly and loan his phone to make a call. Of course the guy would delete the call log. But the FBI could likely retrieve that.

Qigiq spun one-eighty, rode back, and pulled out of sight around the edge of a building that formed an L-shape with the Squeeze Inn. A triangular lot for fifty cars covered the area behind the buildings. He shut off the bike and counted the windows on a Mercedes bus parked sideways across the back of the lot. Six down each side: dark, reflective. Empty driver's seat.

Make a call from a stranger's phone? Who would be so important?

The guy came plodding into the lot with his jacket slung over one shoulder and his sweat-soaked shirt stuck to his body. He walked directly to the Mercedes and ducked inside.

Qigiq texted details of the situation to Kandy.

He held his eyes on the bus.

A low-slung Japanese coupe entered the lot and parked behind the Mercedes. Its windows were nearly black against the vehicle's glistening white paint, including a tinted windshield, illegal in all fifty states.

Qigiq crouched to put his bike and forty feet of empty asphalt between himself and the car. The guy came out of the bus, his jacket again slung over a shoulder, and slipped into the car's shotgun seat. The engine revved a throaty roar for such a small machine and backed up violently. The car moved in rocket-like spurts, barely slowing for a right-turn-on-red, then shot south on McCarren Blvd.

In one motion, Qigiq stepped over the bike, started it, and dropped it into gear to follow. The bike easily keeping pace with the tuner car as it accelerated up a ramp to the Interstate. He hung back. A rider was easy to distinguish in traffic. A rider with a cop helmet could be seen by drivers for miles.

The car cruised in the left lane slightly over the speed limit.

Tailing alone would get him spotted. Approaching alone was too dangerous. But he hated giving up; it was so final.

Traffic grew lighter as they traveled south away from Reno. If he waited, he'd be noticed. He studied the low car, dark windows, jittery moves, performance exhaust.

Tuner boys lived to race.

Qigiq accelerated to close the distance between them. When he was within a few car lengths he checked his mirrors, mashed the throttle open, and swerved to pass on the right-hand side. He knew the manufacturer claimed this bike could top 125 mph stock.

But this machine wasn't stock; it had been touched by Angel.

Qigiq was ten car lengths past the white car before its rising exhaust note reached his ears. A glance in the mirror confirmed his evaluation of the driver: no lowly motorcycle was going to beat him.

That meant he was thinking about racing, not being followed.

The speedometer climbed as the open highway blurred beneath his front wheel. In seconds the car pulled alongside. The passenger sat stiffly against the headrest, eyes forward. Beyond the dark glass the driver smiled from ear to ear, ready to drag race from 90 mph, either not recognizing the cop helmet, or concluding Qigiq couldn't possibly be a cop because nothing else about the bike was right: no bags, no radar, no huge wind fairing, no colored lights, and riding twenty mph over the limit.

Qigiq leaned forward onto the gas tank, downshifted, and pegged the throttle.

The car stayed with him.

Qigiq held even for a count of twenty, then eased off so the guy would win. In short order, they were both back to the speed limit, the driver slapping his steering wheel and waving his right arm in shouted conversation with his passenger. Qigiq dropped back and followed casually. Racers were easy; they loved winning. And loved to talk about how awesome fast and unstoppable they are.

The car drove to The Chinese Duck House on Virginia Street and pulled to the curb. Qigiq slowed and gave the driver a thumbs up without looking at him. He stopped at a red light and watched his mirror. Both men walked into the Duck House, the driver gesticulating wildly and the passenger, shoulders slumped, maybe thinking about who he had to tell about that lost cell phone, ignoring him.

Qigiq was tempted to sneak back and poke around the car and restaurant. Kandy wouldn't approve; she hated missing action. And he had no backup. He circled the block, debating. He memorized the license plate number of the white tuner. He rode up the alley. Two Asian men wearing white aprons stood on the back steps of the Duck House smoking. They both held their eyes on him as he passed.

* * *

Angel's was a converted gas station with side-by-side overhead garage doors. He entered through a glass side door into a room that once sold snacks and cigarettes. Now it housed an ancient cash register and a scratched desk. Angel wasn't there. He opened the door to the back room where she remapped fuel injection systems and performed magic tricks on the ECU's that controlled modern gasoline engines.

"Did you get lost?" Kandy said as he entered.

"Had to show a guy how fast my new bike is."

A slender blonde woman in an orange tank top and black jeans looked up from a computer monitor showing the internals of a cell phone. "How fast?"

"Over the ton."

"Tsk tsk," she said. "It'll do that from the factory."

Carr stood beside Angel, studying the computer display.

Qigiq said, "What happened back there?"

"Got tired of that guy photographing my chest," Kandy said with a laugh. "It hit me he was recording us, maybe including our conversation. Not that it would make sense to most people, but names were dropped. I had the bright idea to grab his phone street-thief style. Switched it to airplane mode and let it keep recording so it wouldn't lock. Angel put it on a power adapter. We're getting a look inside now."

"Cloning memory and storage," Angel said. "If the phone locks up, we'll have the important stuff."

"Can it self-destruct?" Qigiq asked.

Angel shook her head. "Not physically. Erased remotely, yes. But only if we let it connect to a network. We're not going to do that until we're good and ready. Then we'll examine all the Wi-Fi networks it has ever attached to."

"And grab the encrypted passwords," Carr said. "So I can get to work cracking them."

"See?" Kandy said. "We're busting butt here while you're out joyriding."

"I got a little something. Nothing compared to the incredible work you're doing though."

"Keep talking," Angel said. "I'm liking you better all the time."

"Your guy walked back and waited in the tourist bus. A

tuner car picked him up. I tailed them."

"Was he fast?" Angel asked.

"I let him beat me. Wanted him to forget I might be following him for a reason other than to congratulate him."

"Which was?" Kandy said.

"Chinese Duck House."

"Great food," Angel said. "Love their dim sum."

"I almost went in. But figured if Kandy missed the action, she'll stop being so nice to me."

"You figured right," Kandy said, stretching both arms over her head. "What did phoneless boy do?"

"Shuffled in the front door like he was headed to the woodshed."

Carr leaned away from the display. "Ah, someone important lives there."

"At least more important than our boy," Kandy said.

Qigiq said, "Why lives?"

"Chinese restaurants often have living quarters squirreled away. Makes it easy to hide illegal people. Food supply, place to sleep, a job. Don't need much else."

"Personal experience?" Kandy said.

Carr nodded. "I've been chasing foreigners for a long time."

"When he got in the car, I think he borrowed the driver's phone. Who did he call?" Qigiq said.

Carr said, "Someone who could give him advice on how to approach the man he knew he needed to tell about the missing phone. A brother or wife. Someone directly affected if his honor gets tainted." He sighed. "I'd like to send these passwords to the crypto folks soon. Maybe they'll lead somewhere."

"Like a private Wi-Fi at the Duck?" Angel said.

"That'd be a great start. But if I send them to the FBI's lab, I don't know how long before Gan's spies see them."

"Use our guy," Kandy said. "You've been to his apartment."

Carr turned. "Who? Oh yeah. Bearded guy with the skinny girlfriend. I confiscated his computer."

"Never gave it back either," Kandy said. "He'll remind you. He's good with numbers. Has a private lab at home. Works magic."

"I need magic," Carr said. "How do we get the info to him?"

"We're going back to the city today. Hand delivery is secure."

"Unless you're followed."

Qigiq said, "Have you seen her drive?"

Angel straightened and turned around. The front of her orange top was emblazoned with a strategically place V-twin engine under the words *Angel's Speed Shop*. "OK. That's all I can do with this equipment. You've got everything that was in his Android system. It's a couple of revs back. Might even be the version that came with this phone."

"Executive summary?" Kandy said.

"This phone had been cleaned. Someone handed a blank slate to your photographer. There's nothing on it except pictures from...let's see, it's almost noon...he started shooting a little after six this morning. No email account, no browser history. Nothing, except it's ready to connect to a whole list of Wi-Fi networks in addition to CDH, which we might assume is Chinese Duck House."

"Hmm," Carr said. "GPS?"

Angel nodded. "These pics carry coordinates. Whoever receives them will know precisely when and where they were taken."

"Can we tell if they've been transmitted?"

Angel shook her head. "No digital breadcrumbs that I can find. Leggy Reno girls in miniskirts. Kandy's shirt. I think your boy was planning to review these before sending off the ones that were part of his job."

"How much does he have on our discussion?" Qigiq asked, wondering how many times he had been recorded in public and had no idea it was happening.

"Pretty much everything you did or said while he was in the restaurant. Including Kandy's hissy fit. Good acting, girl."

Angel smiled.

"Should we give the phone back to him?" Kandy said. "I'm sure the FBI can hack and track it."

Carr looked up at the ceiling as if seeking inspiration. "Let's wait a couple of days. Then I'll post a lost phone notice on Craigslist, see if he claims it. By then our conversation is old news."

"He's seen our faces," Kandy said.

"Hey," Angel said. "You might dig this." A picture of two Asian guys with the flared sun logo of the Squeeze Inn behind them smiled from the computer screen. "That your guy?"

"Sure is," Kandy said. "On the left. Who's the friend?"

Qigiq studied the faces, closed his eyes. "Not the tuner driver."

Carr leaned in close. "Good shot. We can use that. Any chance you found a name?"

Angel shook her head. "Nothing. I even checked free memory to see if he left deleted bits lying around. He's a careful shredder."

"Not an amateur?" Carr said.

"Maybe the photographer is," Angel replied, "but not the guy who set up this phone."

"How?" Kandy asked.

Carr turned to her. "You know those thousands of surveillance cameras the British government put all over London?"

"Yeah. Do you have cameras in China we can latch onto? Catch this guy hanging out in a hot tub?"

"Don't need them," Carr said. "The NRO has capability."

"Who?" Angel asked.

"National Reconnaissance Office. They run our spy satellites. You know their motto? *We Own the Night*. Nothing stops them from collecting data."

"What kind of data?" Qigiq asked, aware the government managed hundreds of satellites. China managed satellites. Russia managed satellites. Satellites were being developed to attack other satellites. The U.S. had even created an independent branch of the Armed Forces called the United States Space Force.

"You name it," Carr said. "But we want the optical photography from their giant mirrors. It's like a Hubble Space Telescope pointed at the ground."

Kandy said, "Sounds like a Vegas magic show."

Qigiq's eyes moved between the screen and Kandy. "Think those mirrors can find Gan?"

"On Jeju?" Carr inhaled slowly. "Maybe. At least South Korea is an ally."

Angel laughed. "Do we still have allies after Wikileaks revealed we were hacking their cell phones?"

CHAPTER 5

I READ THE NEWSPAPER article that called me a murderer. Americans would learn nothing about the real me, but would hate me all the same. The digits of the mini-clock taped beside the article changed: twenty-eight minutes since Jilly left. I was still alone in the tiny conference room.

The door to the room swung inward without a knock. Two guards entered and led me to my cell. Neither spoke. The metal door clanged behind me. A black rectangular pack with shoulder straps stood on my cot. Its shape implied only one thing.

My spine melted while my heart hoped.

I unzipped the pack. The viola didn't have a single fingerprint on it, and the bow's horsehair was new. I lifted it gently, tucked it beneath my chin, and played pianissimo. It was nearly in tune. I peered out my door, worried about being too loud. Although I couldn't see them, I knew there were other prisoners. I decided to risk it and cherished the warm vibrations of wood under my chin. Simple scales, played thousands of times by musicians over the ages, made the sun rise inside my cell.

The case had pockets.

I placed the instrument on my cot and moved a zipper that ran along the side of the case. After checking over my shoulder to be sure I wasn't being watched, I peeked inside.

I inhaled slowly, struggling to control my nerves.

Hundreds and fifties and twenties in tightly wrapped stacks. I squeezed the case. What should have been padding to protect the instrument was actually...

Who would send such a thing?

I yanked the zipper closed and stared at the object that was now more than a case. I added in my head. A thousand dollars, ten thousand, maybe even fifty thousand?

My heart beat presto.

Small pockets around the pack were held closed with Velcro. All were empty save one; it contained a folded sheet of paper and a fortune from a cookie.

Keep your friends close, your enemies closer.

The wisdom of Sun Tzu. Few knew that his birth name was Sun Wu. That's why my father had chosen the name Wu—to remind us that we were warriors first. My chest tightened until I could barely breathe. I felt the presence of energy; spun to look behind me. Nothing. Holding the paper close, I shuffled across the floor to stand directly beneath the window. I carefully unfolded it, wanting and not-wanting to know how it would affect my fate.

A pencil sketch showed a row of cells inside a building. A dashed black line twisted and turned as if leading to buried treasure. X's marked along the line had times written beside them. The first, 01:04 AM, was right next to my prison cell. Across the bottom a human hand had written:

Timing critical. Proceed no matter what happens. No going back.

I refolded the paper and slipped it inside my jumpsuit. My heart thumped against it. I gazed out the high window at blue sky and a lonely white cloud. I sat on the bed, stroked the shiny wood, and finally played the droning melody from Beethoven's Nocturne in D for Viola and Piano. Everyone knew Beethoven as a master composer. Many knew him as a pianist of astonishing virtuosity. But very few knew that when he was a boy he played viola in two orchestras at the same time to support his younger brothers after his father turned to drink.

My breathing slowed.

For the first time in...forever...I had no one to guide me.

I played until they took me away to eat. Then played again.

Then lay down to sleep. Jilly's clock showed 11:11 PM when I awoke with my heart fluttering from a dream of flying.

I sat on the bed, feet flat on the floor, and stared out the window into the stars of the night sky. Every few minutes I fingered the capsules in my pocket and rechecked the time. Then I shifted my leg, attempting to find a position in which the wound didn't ache.

Until 1:02 AM.

I strapped the pack onto my back and stood, repeating Sun Tzu's words in my mind, wondering who was who. Friends and enemies looked so much alike.

The steel door to my cage stared back at me. I waited.

The numbers on Jilly's tiny clock flicked to 1:04 AM.

I heard nothing. Saw nothing. Smelled nothing.

My being felt the lonely darkness of the starry sky. I had expected something to happen; a sign to show me that now was the time. I reached out and touched the door.

It opened.

No alarm sounded. No footsteps came running.

I checked my treasure map: I had three minutes to get to the second X.

I stepped out and eased the door closed. The cell block was dim and quiet, like a concert hall just before the first note. I squeezed my hands around the straps of the pack and felt strength from the viola on my back. At the end of the hall, a wide security door with a small window in it blocked my way. It was painted the mint green of the first dress I had ever performed in—many lives ago. I waited for three breaths, then pushed.

The door eased open and I stood in another hallway. The map indicated a right turn. I walked carefully, found the indicated stairwell, stepped in: 1:06 on Jilly's clock. The stairwell smelled musty, like it was rarely used.

I sneezed.

The sound reverberated up and down the hard walls of the concrete stairwell, sounding like thunder against the silence.

My heart raced.

One minute remaining.

I ran up a flight of stairs. A white metal sign screwed to the wall to my right read: *Roof Access. Do Not Enter. Alarm will sound.* Rust had dripped from a screw across the word *Not.*

I realized I was panting. The number 6 flipped to 7.

Lights flickered in the naked stairwell for a few moments. Then went black. The sound of timpani rose around me. I leaned my shoulder against the emergency bar.

The door swung outward.

No alarm.

I had no light to read my map, but had stared at it for a thousand seconds. I was to go up.

I could see nothing in the blackness, so I closed my eyes and pressed one hand against the cool concrete wall. My shin banged a metal step. I climbed and climbed. My cheek bumped something solid. My hands roamed it, found the bar. I placed both palms against the cold metal surface and pressed hard.

No alarms. I opened my eyes.

The door slammed shut behind me.

I was standing on a gravel roof under a million desert stars beside a red tube as high as a bus. Golden fireworks flashed above the building to my right. To the left, a bright moon glowed on a pair of tall gray fences. The fences should have been lit by floodlights like every other night, but weren't. I tilted my face up to take in the stars, then down at my map.

The dashed line ended where I was stood.

Silver boxes around me were silent, no longer pumping desert heat from the prison cells.

Aloneness drizzled along my nerves. I should have felt afraid, but was so confused I didn't know what to fear. I moved away from the door to hide in the moon shadow of a silver box and asked the dragon gods for protection from Uncle Gan's anger. A gunshot startled me.

I turned toward the fence, but could discern nothing in the

darkness.

With no warning a hard object the size of a cello landed on the gravel to my right, bounced against the red tube, and exploded in a shower of sparks. Octopus-like tentacles reached out and raced across the roof, grabbing at anything they touched. The door I had used flung open and a person wearing an orange suit darted out carrying something in their arms.

I wanted to run, but my instructions were to wait on the X.

The runner had almost reached me before I noticed the mask. The slender fingers of a woman held up a second mask. I closed my eyes. Hands yanked the thing onto my head like a helmet. When I opened them, the world was visible through a narrow horizontal slit.

"Face recognition cameras," a female voice said. "We're taking no chances."

Relief raced through me as I recognized the voice.

She unzipped my suit and reached her arms around my body, encircling me with a black strap. She yanked it tight before pulling the zipper back up. A hook the size of an apple protruded from between my breasts.

Jilly touched my hand and whispered, "Let's go."

I squeezed my hands tight around the straps holding my new viola to my back.

We ran past the cello thing to the edge of the roof. A fat black rope extended from the top of the building, over the double fence, and into a copse of scraggly trees that seemed out of place in the desert. The ground was stark gray under moonlight. A mountain of sparks erupted behind us.

"What's happening?" I asked.

"We're leaving. Sit. Hang your legs over the side." She clipped a short rope to the big rope, then clipped the other end to the hook on my chest. "Hold tight." Jilly pushed me off the roof.

I fell. A scream caught in my throat.

I wrapped my arms across my chest. The hook tightened the strap around my back, lifting me like a trampoline. Flying through space, I realized I was dreaming and would wake up in my cell with no viola.

The moon swung wildly in the sky. The sharp teeth at the top of the fences raced toward me. Wind rattled my prison suit and whipped my hair as I flew like a dragon across the sky. The world became a black forest. Shadows on the desert floor closed in. My feet dragged against hard earth.

Bodies emerged from the darkness wearing masks. Hands grabbed my arms. The hook was removed. They carried me to the passenger seat of a car that shone polished pewter in the moonlight. Within moments too small to count Jilly appeared behind the steering wheel.

The car was already running.

Headlights popped on to drill twin tunnels through the night. The car lurched forward on a dirt road, tossing me like a rag doll around the luxurious front seat, banging the viola against my back. In the outside rearview mirror, the prison lit up, the way it had been every night before this one when I would gaze out my window at the stars. We reached a concrete highway and were soon sailing along at tremendous speed.

Jilly said, "Are you okay?"

The tension inside me released and I started laughing.

She glanced my way, still wearing the flat mask with only an eye slit.

"I'm not hurt. But so much...I don't know if I'll ever be okay."

She peeled her mask back over her head and grinned. "We had to get you out of there in a way that won't raise suspicion."

I lifted off my mask. It was made of flexible rubber and reminded me of a terrifying New Year's Eve concert when I was eleven where all of the guests had worn masks until midnight. It had been like playing to a roomful of evil puppets.

"Who would suspect a foreign girl who murders her brother?"

"Your uncle."

"You want him to think I'm still in prison?"

"Or figure that you and I broke out on our own. Just so he doesn't think you were released and are helping people he doesn't want helped."

"For my protection?"

"For everyone's protection."

"Uncle doesn't trust me anyway. I'm a woman."

Jilly was quiet for a moment. Then, "What if he thinks you're working with the FBI?"

"Dragon eyes will see. I will be punished." I hesitated. "That's what Father would do. Uncle Gan is in charge now, I'm not sure what will happen."

"So he'll use you either way?"

I nodded. Father had always used me; I saw no reason things would change.

I said, "Where is Qigiq?"

Jilly shrugged. "They only told me my part of this job."

The shiny car flew through the night and the feeling of traveling down the fat rope remained inside of me. My knees banged the dashboard as I struggled out of the straps. I placed the viola case gently on the back seat and buckled my seat-belt.

"What's your job?" I asked.

"Deliver you." She glanced at a clock in a clear pocket on her sleeve—just like the one she had given me. "We're heading for the coast, should make our rendezvous before sunrise."

Floating along in luxury, my head resting against supple leather, thoughts of playing duets with my sister Pé came to me. I hated Father for murdering her. Now he was gone too. And both of my brothers. I tried not to think about my uncle. Instead, I filled my head with the sounds of my fingers coaxing Bach from my new viola in an open air concert filled with people and space and freedom so far from that tiny concrete block that had held me only minutes ago—and fell asleep.

The world quaked. Someone called my name. I opened my eyes. On the other side of the passenger window buildings hovered above me. Jilly was shaking my shoulder with one hand and driving with the other, wearing only a purple bra and panties.

"Where are we?" I asked.

"Almost there, take off your clothes."

"But…"

She pressed a finger to my lips. I unzipped the jumpsuit and peeled it down over my shoulders, baring my breasts. I slipped my hand in the pocket and wrapped it around the capsules.

Jilly said, "It's the middle of the night. The city is empty."

I kicked off my black prison slippers and peeled the suit down to the floor. Hers was rolled like a duffle bag on the back seat.

"We take the clothes with us," she said. "Not leaving a trace. But no one can see them. An orange suit screams *convict* around here."

I rolled the orange suit into a ball on my lap, tossed it onto the back seat, and put the capsules in a pocket of my viola case. At that moment I remembered what Grandmother had placed under the collar. In my rush to follow Jilly's map, I hadn't done it. I stared at the clothing, my mind racing through Uncle's orders and my own desire. The possible paths into the future began to unfold in my—

Jilly turned right, tossing me onto her shoulder. Our eyes met. She stopped in the parking lot of a marina filled with boats lulling in the moonlight. She switched off the engine.

I said, "I don't have shoes."

"Go barefoot, it's not far." She smiled. "If anyone sees us, they'll think we're going swimming." She flipped over the edge of her bra to reveal her tiny clock. It read the same as the one in my hand: 3:48 AM. I tucked it into the edge of my panties.

"I don't want to complain…"

"You need a ladies room?" Jilly said. "Me too. In a minute. We're not supposed to arrive before 3:55." Jilly reached over and squeezed my hand.

"Why are you here?" I asked.

"They thought you wouldn't go with a stranger."

They were right; my world was spinning too fast. I had spent hour after hour accepting a life in prison. Then suddenly...I am here, naked, surrounded by the floating toys of rich Americans.

"Have you ever been on a boat?" Jilly asked.

I nodded. "A ship on the ocean. And a fishing boat to cross Lake Erie."

"This will be more like Lake Erie." She looked at her clock. "Okay, be ready. I'll come around. You take the suits." She reached into the back seat, got out, and dashed around the car. When she opened my door, she was holding my backpack.

I stepped out onto rough pavement. Cold night air caressed my legs. I slipped the pack on. Lifting the suits from the back seat, I squeezed the orange bundle to my chest.

"This way," Jilly said.

Small stones on the pavement pressed into my soles as I followed her. Soon we were on a dock made of concrete. Then another of wood. We walked directly under bright security lights illuminating the harbor. I kept my face down, wishing I was still wearing the mask. We turned right, and right again, passing boat after boat with names scrawled on the back in large letters: *No Pain* (a boat with a tall tower), *Winner*, *Something Special*, *War* (blood red deck on a sleek black sailboat), *Delicious* (shaped like a missile).

She stopped. "Delicious," Jilly said. The sides of the boat were the bright red of painted lips, the deck a gleaming pearl-white.

"This?"

She soundlessly pulled the boat closer to the dock, stepped on, took my clothes and viola, then helped me aboard with two hands. The deck wavered from our added weight. The breeze again touched my body.

"We're traveling first class," she whispered.

A low door opened between two white seats the height of bar stools. A woman came up wearing a red bikini under a long white jacket. Her body had the curves of a Roman goddess. She was barefoot.

"Welcome to my delicious world, ladies. Everything you need is below. I guessed at sizes."

The woman hopped into the seat on the right, pressed a button, and the growl of a tiger came from below. The deck vibrated tingles into my toes. She jumped up to the white deck and walked along its edge with practiced strides.

I said, "She's beautiful."

Jilly stared after her. "Qigiq didn't mention that. Let's get dressed." She took my hand and led me through the little door down into a room covered in wood and light gray fabric. It had a kitchen and multiple beds.

"Are we going to live here?"

"For a little while." Jilly pointed. "There's the bathroom. It's called a head. You go first."

When I came out Jilly was placing clothes on the bed: jeans that looked short even for me, sandals in pink and yellow, and colorful shirts. She held up the jeans. "Try these." She tossed them to me, followed by a pair of white panties. "Put everything you wore at the prison with the jumpsuit. We're going to ditch the evidence."

"They're too short."

She laughed. "Try them on."

I changed panties and slipped into the new jeans while Jilly used the head. The pants reached just below my knee, and clung and stretched so easily I still felt naked. I turned around.

Jilly's purple-contact eyes moved up and down. She sighed and tossed me a shirt. I pulled it over my head and it came past my bottom.

"Perfect," she said.

"Is this how sailors dress?"

"Only if they're trying to look casual and sexy."

Jilly stripped and hopped into an outfit much like mine, except her pants reached her ankles, and her shirt was yellow where mine was white with blue stripes.

"Your friend bought all this?" I asked.

"I never met her before. But yes, I think so."

The woman stuck her head into the doorway, her brown hair cascading down around her face. "We're casting off. Come on up and have a seat."

With Jilly and I together in the left chair, the woman in the bikini backed out, drove between rows of boats much like hers, and into the open bay. She pushed two handles, the front lifted, and we flew across the water.

In minutes we were surrounded by slate gray water that vanished into blackness in all directions. My mind was pulled back in time *to a naive girl in a storm on Lake Erie. I am one of four girls in a fishing boat roaring across open water taking us into a country we have only ever seen on the one television Father allowed in our house. The man driving the boat stares ahead as windshield wipers fail against the onslaught of rain and waves. He glances at me. His hands hold tight to the wheel. I do not learn until later that I have been chosen.*

Now I am riding with two beautiful women, sneaking away from the very same country I was smuggled into.

"Where are we going?" I called to Jilly through the swirling wind.

She shook her head. "Don't know. My job was to get you on this boat." She put her arm around me. I leaned into her slender body, the feeling of the prison cell still inside of me.

The boat settled into a straight line. A giant orange-gray bridge hovered far above us as we passed beneath it. The woman motioned for us to come near. We crowded behind the steering wheel.

"We're clear of ears, so we can talk now. I'm Karen, a friend of Qigiq's. He said you two needed to get out of Dodge. Your names had better be Jill and Mylin, or we're in big trouble." Her laughter mixed with the sound of the powerful engines.

I bowed. Then Jilly and I each shook Karen's right hand while she held the wheel with her left.

"Where are we going?" Jilly asked for both of us.

"Up the coast." Karen pointed at the dashboard. "I put the waypoints in the satellite thing. We just follow them."

"How far?" I asked.

"Hour or so. You can nap if you want. And there's food in the fridge."

White foam sprayed over the windshield. Karen ducked, but Jilly and I got our faces wet.

Karen laughed. "There are towels below too."

After we dried off, I found a small refrigerator stuffed with sandwiches. Jilly and I sat at a table and ate while the floor moved like a giant rocking chair.

"What will happen next?" I asked.

She gazed at me for a long time. "They didn't tell me. Probably best if I don't know. I might say something to the wrong person." She paused. "I wouldn't want to put you in danger."

I smiled at the thought. "I cannot escape danger." I reached across the table and touched her hand. "Jilly, what happened? Back at the prison."

"Agent Carr hired me to go inside as an auto thief. He's using civilians like Karen and me to keep everything on the q.t."

"And tonight?"

"He arranged failures. Delayed the back-up generators. That's why it was so dark when we zip-lined out. The fireworks were electric sparks."

"He did this for me?"

She grinned sideways. "He did it to get you out. You agreed to help him."

"He hasn't said what he wants me to do."

"I bet you can guess."

"Find my uncle?"

She shook her head while biting, the sandwich flopping back and forth. "More. Secrets and paintings. Your dad had an art gallery, right?"

"Yes. And an orchestra." Sadness washed over me. I silently asked the dragon gods to protect my friends on their journey through the cosmos. Then I asked myself which would be worse, sitting in that cell playing my viola or working for Uncle Gan.

* * *

After eating, Jilly fell asleep on a curved mattress that reached all the way to the front of the boat. My brain was buzzing; I couldn't even close my eyes. The roaring engines chased me up to the chair opposite Karen. We watched the bow rise and fall. She held the wheel with only two fingers, like a lover urging the machine forward over the black waves. She talked about fashion, and boats, and how many hours she spent lying in the sun to maintain the golden skin tone that I had been born with.

She talked about men. And desire.

In this I had experience. Unlike mine, her stories ended with man's desire filling her bank account. I had known many men, but little money. Karen used the word "capitalism." And seemed to adore it.

Her breasts rose and fell with the ocean swells. She glanced at numbers on the dash that told her where we were on the water. I had worn an ankle bracelet for years, never realizing that my father could look at numbers and know exactly where to find me.

Now my ankle was bare. Uncle Gan would be angry.

Karen leaned close. "Where are your prison clothes?"

"In a drawer below. Should I get them?"

She nodded.

I stepped carefully backwards down the stairs and found the clothes Jilly and I had taken off in the car. My panties dropped onto the floor. I grabbed them, tucked one bundle under each arm, and made my way back to the cabin.

Karen slowed the boat and released the wheel, yet it continued straight through the darkness.

"Lay them on the floor like you're wearing them."

I spread the orange clothing on the deck and assembled it like a store display with the panties inside.

"Shoes?" she said.

I pulled the prison slippers out of the pockets and placed them below the four legs. The clothing made me think of the outlines the police draw around dead bodies.

"Good," Karen said. She opened a plastic bottle and poured blue liquid on each item.

I looked forward at a silver splash of moonlight glistening on the water. There was much about the world I didn't know, including how a boat could steer itself to an invisible destination.

Karen said, "When I slow down, pick up one person at a time and throw them off the middle of the stern."

I met her eyes but didn't move.

She touched my shoulders and guided me to a padded seat across the back. "Stay here." She handed me Jilly's clothing. I thought of her sleeping below and that I might never see her again after this night. I kissed the bundle in my arms. Karen slowed the boat more and motioned with her head. I tossed everything into the air.

The jumpsuit floated with arms outstretched like a man leaping from an airplane. It landed on the churning water behind the boat and was pulled under. After a few seconds, it resurfaced midst swirling white foam. I turned to face Karen. She nodded, so I knelt and scraped together the clothing I had worn for over a week while isolated in a stone room like a political prisoner.

I tossed the second bundle; it fluttered, fell, and disappeared.

When I turned around, Karen was accelerating, jacket flapping in the wind. She appeared to me a goddess of such strength that no man could bend her to his desire. She turned around and looked into my eyes. Her smile reminded me of the joy music made me feel.

The boat hit a fat wave and shuddered. I grabbed the side with both hands and made my way up to Karen.

"What did you put on those clothes?"

"Something big fish like."

I imagined my suit sinking into the ocean while dozens of fish sniffed at it like puppies wanting food. But she had said...

"How big?"

"Sharks. Which technically aren't fish, but..." She shrugged.

I moved closer until our arms touched. Karen took one hand from the wheel, put her arm around me, and pulled me close. The touch of her bare skin sent heat through me like the night Joe the photographer had held me in his long white truck.

"Are there sharks here?" I asked.

"Thousands. You better stay in the boat." She laughed a pure, rich sound. How could anyone be so relaxed racing across an ocean full of sharks?

"Don't worry," she said, "I've never heard of a shark jumping into a speed boat." She squeezed my shoulder. "You want to drive?"

"Me?"

She pushed me behind the wheel. "Boats have white, red, and green lights on them. Look out across the water. If you see lights, call me and I'll take over." She pointed at the dash. "That's your compass heading. Steer so it stays close to ten degrees—almost due north."

I put both hands on the wheel. "We're going north?"

"For a while longer. Then we head to the beach."

"Are there sharks on the beach?"

"There sure are, but we aren't going swimming." She touched my hand. "Relax your grip. *Delicious* won't run away from you."

I tried to make my fingers soft. The number was down to eight, so I turned the wheel and it went down to six. I turned it the other way and it went to fifteen. I wiggled the wheel until the number ten showed. Then I remembered I was supposed to be watching ahead for lights and looked up.

Dark gray water undulated under a splatter of stars as if the whole earth had become molten. Roaring wind filled my ears.

Karen's powerful motors vibrated my bare soles. I checked the compass again and again. I watched the water. I learned to flex my knees when a wave came and let the boat rise and fall as it zoomed over the top. I smiled without meaning to.

Karen touched my shoulder. "You're doing great. Do you want to sleep?"

I shook my head, feeling like I was on a journey to an enchanted land.

"I'm going to grab some food. Shout if you need me."

I gazed wide-eyed across the water and played Mozart in my head. The wind tossed my hair haphazardly, but there was no one to see the mark, so I didn't care. Holding the wheel filled me with a sense of power. The speed felt like drinking too much wine. I wondered if this was why Americans owned such extravagant toys. And then from nowhere, worry arrived: Were Jilly and Karen in danger for helping me? Joe Roberts had secretly taken my picture, was he safe? The fun I had performing with the rock musicians of Magnetic Fusion— until my brother...

What would Uncle Gan demand?

A number on the dash blinked yellow. I turned the wheel left and right but it wouldn't stop. I called out, "Karen." She was beside me in seconds.

"You did great," she said. "We have to turn soon. When a new number comes up, steer to the right until your compass matches it."

"OK."

"Be right back." She disappeared below.

I searched the water for colored lights and glanced down every few seconds. The number went up to twenty. Then thirty. I nudged the wheel right. The boat tilted and straightened as it hit waves from the side. The wheel felt momentarily heavy and then light in my hands. The number 80 glowed green on the dash.

I was falling in love with this machine; its thrust and roar made me feel like I could do anything.

Karen's head popped up. "I'll take it in a few minutes. You want anything?"

"I want to drive forever."

She laughed. "I bet you're thirsty." A minute later she came up with a sealed bottle of water. "You'd better hydrate. I'm sure Qigiq has plans for you."

I held the wheel with my bow hand and drank with the other, the way I had seen Karen do it.

"You look like a pro," she said, standing beside me and putting her arm around me again. The warm feeling came back. She gave me a squeeze, then went below.

A hint of yellow light appeared in the distant sky. My heart leapt thinking I might get to see the sun rise on my first morning of freedom. I must not forget that it was the first Tuesday in October.

The dark spot became a shape. The shape grew larger.

"Karen!"

She was on the deck in a flash, reaching around behind me and pulling two levers backward. The boat sighed into the water. Emptiness filled the space inside me where our boat had been. I wanted to cry.

"We're almost there," Karen said. "That dot is a barn. We're still miles out."

"Do you want these clothes back?" I asked, having only been given gifts by men who wanted favors from me.

"No, those are for you. There's a black jacket down there too, so you're not easy to spot. And boots, since I don't know what you'll be walking through."

I went below. Jilly was still sleeping. I knelt beside the bed and kissed her cheek.

I whispered, "Goodbye, my friend, I hope to see you again someday."

I sat on the floor and pulled on black boots with four-inch heels. They came up over the short pants. I stood. One of Karen's stories was correct; tall felt powerful.

I slipped the jacket over the striped shirt and zipped its

bubbly surface tight around me. Only then did I realize my body was shivering. I climbed back to Karen. She navigated *Delicious* into the mouth of a river. Angled shadows through the fog must have been more buildings, but no light shone from them. The slender craft burbled as it glided through smooth water at a walking pace.

"We're early, just the way I like it." Karen grinned. "There's nothing worse than being late with no way to drive faster." She consulted a smartphone and compared its numbers to the ones on the dash, then turned off the motors. The world became a mass of insects arguing. The boat drifted on a paper-smooth surface so different from the water hills we had just crossed.

I said, "Where are we?"

"Rivers flow to the sea. We're on one those rivers. Let's not talk about which one in case anyone ever asks you."

"Are you a cop too?"

Karen laughed, then covered her mouth with her hand because the sound had filled the night. "No way I would ever work that hard. I met Qigiq when he was taking pictures of my, uh," she pointed up, "radar. He was on a case. Qu is quite the unique guy."

Qigiq had come to meet me in Mill Valley. Chased me to Burning Man. Attended my San Francisco concert. Had been on the pier when the agent was killed. And was there when I shot my brother. My left hand drifted down to massage the leg where his knife had tried to stop me.

I said, "Yes, he is."

"He asked me to go for a joy ride tonight. And take passengers. Sort of like ride-sharing for fast ocean racers."

"Thank you."

Karen's gaze roamed over me. Her lips, hips, those blue eyes clear as crystal, filled me with an unexpected sensation. She said, "Then you two show up naked. Rendezvous coordinates were hiding in an envelope tucked under the windshield wiper of *Delicious*. They lead to this decrepit dock that hasn't seen a boat in ten years. Cops don't normally operate this way." Her gaze settled on my face. The boat drifted with an unseen current. The numbers on the dash changed slowly. I didn't know if we were getting closer or farther away from our destination.

"What would you like to know?"

Karen leaned against the sloping side glass. "I would *like* to know everything. Are you running to or from something? Are you a good girl or a bad girl? Why is Qigiq helping you? Who is this Jilly character you travel with? However..." She glanced at the dash, then stared out over the water. "That's our dock." She crossed her arms and tilted her head back to gaze straight up at the stars. "Man, are we ever small and meaningless."

We drifted to the chorus of insects. I said, "However?"

"Hmm. However...our cutie Qu suggested that for my personal safety I had better not know anything. He assured me you weren't dangerous. Though he mentioned you can handle a handgun if the need arose."

"I'm not very good."

"Not good is better than never have." She looked up and down the river. "We seem awfully alone out here. I'm not expecting much action."

"I shot my brother," spilled from my mouth.

Karen examined me with those blue eyes again. "I bet you had a hell of a good reason."

My face grew hot. I was sure I was blushing. "Many."

She nodded as if I had just explained everything. "Men have a way of messing us up, don't they?"

I smiled. She was beautiful *and* smart.

"Now you're in deep legal trouble and Qu is helping you get out?"

"That's part of it."

"You know, saying that is like pausing a movie in the middle. I get to see the first half, but not how it ends. I hope Qigiq realizes he's torturing me here."

"I have an uncle."

"Ah, the plot becomes raspberry Jell-O. I bet your uncle is a troublemaker."

I smiled inwardly at her wisdom. "Yes."

"Let's get over to that dock. We have to creep in or we'll knock it down." She started one engine and sent me to the front with instructions to loop a rope she called a line over the dock post. I knelt on the hard white deck. Fog clung to the black river. We floated like the lug-sailed junk in the mist in a painting we sold at the Gallerie Electra—before it burned down. Bubbles boiled the river water behind us.

"Now," she called out in a whisper.

The nearest wood post was black with tar and cracked down the middle. I slipped the loop over the top. The engine spoke louder; the boat slowed; the engine stopped. Jilly popped up through the half-door wearing a confused expression. I sat cross-legged on the deck and listened through the silent mist for the voice of the dragon gods.

Karen and Jilly conversed in tones too low to decipher. My consciousness hovered, telling me to prepare for the next step, even not knowing what it was. This languid river was many worlds away from that concrete cell. Such beauty within arm's reach; yet humans stuffed themselves into dirty cities and fought over nonsense. I was being given a mission. Why? I foresaw paths to the future, something—

The boat bumped the pole I had lassoed.

Karen gestured for me to come back.

I crawled carefully along the rail, afraid of falling and meeting Karen's sharks.

"Be ready for anything," she said. "I had instructions to get you here by 5:05 AM. That's less than ten minutes from now."

I went below to retrieve my viola; voices floated down from above.

"What about me?" Jilly asked.

"We play it by ear. I'm happy to have help running the boat back if you're not part of the game plan."

I removed the capsules Laolao had given me from their hiding spot and slipped them into the pocket of my new pants—in case someone took my pack away. I strapped the viola to my back and went up on deck. The air hung damp and motionless. Karen and Jilly were watching the shoreline where a narrow road followed the curves of the river.

I whispered, "Do you hear that?"

They turned to me, then back to the shore. Both shrugged.

"Purring."

Karen touched the dash and the lights on the boat went out. I didn't think it possible, but the night grew darker, the shore more visible. Two trees had managed to grow side by side. Beyond them tall grass hung its head in gray sorrow. A dot moved far to the left.

"Do you see it?" I asked.

Jilly nodded. "It's following the river."

"Small for a headlight," Karen said. "Noisy for a bicycle."

"Should I go ashore?" I asked.

"It's five sharp," Karen said. "Better go ahead. Be super careful on that rickety-tickety dock. I don't want to have to fish you out of the drink." She laughed softly.

I wished I knew how to laugh as much as Karen. Maybe if I had her life...or her body.

I pulled on the rope until the boat bumped the post, stepped onto the dock, and turned around. I waved weakly to my friends—felt tears rising, wanting to jump back on the boat and hug them goodbye.

The purring in my ears grew louder.

By moonlight, I shuffled my new boots forward along cracked and gritty wood. Missing boards left gaps large enough for my entire body to drop through to the sharks. The purring became the soft rumble of an engine's exhaust.

Halfway to shore I stopped and looked toward the sound. A motorbike bearing a lone rider approached. I hurried to the end and stared down into the water separating me from the shore. A reflection of the moon waved up at me. The old dock didn't connect to the wildflowers that had bloomed long ago.

How far could I jump?

I removed my pack. Hoping the money would protect my viola, I tossed it with both hands. It landed flat and slid toward the road. I made my way back along the dock three paces, turned around, and considered the wide boards that were likely older than me. I planned a spot for each high-heeled footstep and lifted my eyes across the chasm to the muddy shoreline. The rumble grew louder. I counted a tempo in my head, then took quick steps and leapt.

My feet were going to fall short.

I landed on my chest, suddenly couldn't breathe, and slid toward the river. I clawed the hardened dirt I had thought was mud to stop my descent. A motorcycle pulled onto the gravel shoulder. I lifted my head, panting. The rider was wearing a white helmet, black goggles, and a maroon scarf wrapped over his face. Strips of black tape blocked the headlight except for a narrow, horizontal band in the center.

He beckoned with a gloved hand.

I forced myself to my knees and strapped the pack on. The bone between my breasts screamed each time I gasped for air. I crawled toward the bike, worried I had destroyed Karen's new clothes.

The machine was the color of fog. A blue and white emblem glinted in the moonlight. The rider held the bike upright with both legs and tapped the seat behind him. I struggled to stand and lift my leg over the bike. A black helmet appeared in his hand. Before I could buckle it, we were moving.

I said, "Hello, Qigiq, I'm so happy you're helping me," but my voice was lost in the wind.

CHAPTER 6

WHITENESS FROM THE HEADLIGHT hit thick morning fog and splattered into a gray morass. The road hugged the shoreline so tightly that progress was tedious. Karen would wait, but the longer she sat at an isolated dock, the more opportunity someone had to see a bright red boat on a quiet river and wonder what it was doing there.

The Scrambler's tires had no trouble with the cracked and potholed river road. A switch to kill the headlight and ride by moonlight would have been welcome, but Federal laws had removed it years ago. Taping over part of the headlight the way soldiers did in World War II would have been a good idea. Rounding a left turn, the outline of a lopsided dock emerged from the mist. The boat tied to it appeared pewter in the moonlight. Two heads bobbed behind the windshield. Twisting the bars pointed the headlight directly at the boat for a split second, signaling his arrival.

The dash clock showed 5:07 AM.

A minute later a slender shape standing where the dock ended six feet from shore emerged from the fog. The last section had been removed, or more likely, collapsed. Even in the fog-glare from the headlight one thing was clear: the figure was pointing a gun at him.

He flicked the bike's kill switch and dropped low to the outside in one motion, coasting toward the dock. He peered below the handlebars and recognized Jill Kiner, the girl who admired Kandy enough to use KD as her alias at Burning Man.

He stopped the bike and shouted. "Jill, it's Qigiq. What's

wrong?"

The gun lowered slightly.

He took off his helmet and stood slowly. The higher he got, the lower the gun fell.

"Qigiq?"

"Sorry I'm late. The fog slowed me down."

"But." Jill turned toward the boat, and back. "But."

He moved closer, aware he was exposed at the river's edge. "Is Mylin okay?"

Perhaps it was the moonlight, but Jill's face was ghost white as she stared at him.

"She's gone. A motorcycle picked her up. We thought it was you."

"How long ago?"

She glanced down. "Seven minutes."

In fog, maybe thirty miles per hour, three or four miles if they stayed by the river. Once they reached an Interstate though...

"What kind of bike?"

Jill tossed a cell phone into the air; he caught it with one hand.

"I shot video. Looks just like the one you're riding. It was even silver."

As he was watching the video Kandy's white Volvo crunched to a stop behind him. Jill was right: silver BMW Scrambler. The bike reminded him of the café racers in his last case...and a club called the Ton Up.

Kandy stood by his shoulder.

Karen arrived beside Jill on the dock. She called out, "What's wrong? Where's Mylin?"

"Someone scooped us," Kandy said. "I'm taking a fast drive. When I catch them I'll break radio silence and give you the location of Grandmother's house." She ran to her car and was gone with a screech of tires fighting for traction.

"Can you put out an alert?" Jill asked. "Get everyone looking for her."

"Carr wants this whole operation super quiet," Qigiq said. He sat cross-legged on the dirt to think for a moment, remembering the spies Mylin was constantly afraid of.

Karen said, "Can Kandy catch them?"

He shook his head. "Difficult in this weather."

"How did they find us out here?" Jill asked.

He admired her energy. He said, "They watched the prison."

"It's my fault," she said. "They followed me."

"No, it's our fault," Qigiq said, "for not protecting you enough. We had cars following you and watching for a tail. No one reported anything."

"Then how?" Karen asked.

"Lots of ways," Jill said. "A drone with a camera. A bunch of guys parked along the road with binoculars."

"That's how they tracked *Delicious,* isn't it?" Karen said.

Qigiq stood. "Maybe. Spotter. Dead reckoning to estimate your position. It wouldn't be hard to guess you'd come to shore at some point. They just needed to have a rider ready."

"Why?" Jill said.

"Kandy and I visited the prison yesterday. Easy guess. Plus..." He turned and studied his loaner bike. "Newer model. Anyone could locate one if they knew what Carr got for me. But beyond that...this was the plan they executed. We have no idea how many plans they had, or how many people we're up against."

"Dragon eyes," Jill whispered, as if conjuring a spirit from a Ouija board.

Carr's team was being tracked in more detail than Qigiq had suspected. Every country from China on down now monitored digital traffic and analyzed it with AI supercomputers. Then he remembered that *We own the night* satellites could see a face from miles up in the sky. Maybe even *his* face and the location of his motorcycle. He sighed...technology was still ahead of him.

Footfalls brought his mind back to the shoreline. Jill flew through the air, landed on the bank with both feet, and fell forward like an Olympic long jumper. He caught her with both arms.

She said, "I lost her. I want to help find her."

Her face showed the kind of determination he was seeing in the mirror less and less often.

"We have to ask Carr. It's his case."

"Take me with you. Karen, says she can handle the boat."

"You'll need a helmet, I brought an extra small for Mylin."

"What are the odds we'll be in an accident the few miles I'll be riding with you?"

"Murphy's Law says nearly a hundred percent."

Karen called from the dock. "Take this." She tossed a bright red object from the dock. "It's for waterski racing."

Jill strapped the helmet over her blonde hair, waved to Karen, and yanked on the sleeve of Qigiq's jacket. "Let's go, the dragon guys are getting away."

* * *

An hour later, after miles and miles of intense searching, Qigiq sat on a concrete road leaning against the front wheel of his bike, empty-handed and short on options. Orange and red streaked the sky. Jill paced circles around him and the bike. She repeatedly pulled out a smartphone, stared at it, then put it away. Kandy sat on the hood of her car facing east. No one had spoken for five minutes.

Kandy said, "Annoys me."

"Miles of roads. A lone bike," he said. "The guy could pull into a garage and hide for days while we knock ourselves out trying to find him."

"Or roll the bike into a van," Jill said.

"Annoys me," Kandy said.

Jill stopped pacing. "I hear a plane."

From the south, an aircraft approached the Petaluma Municipal Airport: the primary rendezvous point, the culmination of planning that now added up to zero. No, not zero. They had put Mylin into the hands of the enemy: a giant negative.

"This should be one interesting meeting," Kandy said.

Qigiq had learned an enormous downside to foregoing electronic communication: it allowed for surprises.

The executive jet's tires puffed blue smoke as they smacked concrete. The plane taxied within a dozen yards of their position before the whistling engines wound down. A door swung to become a stairway and reveal FBI agent David Carr wearing black from head to toe. He waved a greeting, motioned for them to board, then stepped back inside.

"I'll tell him," Qigiq volunteered.

"Was there ever any doubt?" Kandy said, laughing her alto huff.

"He already knows," Jill added. "The moment he saw my hair."

The stairs wobbled as they boarded the plane in single file —Kandy, Qigiq, Jill—and entered a luxurious cabin of woodgrain and leather. The interior smelled like a new car; made Qigiq wonder why new motorcycles didn't smell like that.

Carr was alone.

"You guys travel cheap," Kandy said.

"The Bureau gets the dregs. You should see the NSA stuff."

"Don't show me," Jill said. "I'll have to seek asylum."

Carr looked her way. "Funny girl." He sat down at a table for four built against the starboard side of the aircraft and motioned for them to join him. Jill slipped onto the soft leather chair beside him. Kandy and Qigiq sat opposite. Carr studied their faces.

The door to the aircraft whirred and thumped closed.

"Did Mylin stop in the powder room?"

"Grabbed off the shore minutes before I arrived," Qigiq said. "They used a motorcycle. Possibly the same model as mine."

Carr turned his head and looked out the window at the red sky. "Don't that just take the cake. We bust her out of a high-security prison and poof, she's gone."

"Heavy fog. I was a couple of minutes late."

Jill added, "The air was like gray cotton candy."

"Yummy," Carr said. His placid eyes moved from one to the other. "So much for Plan A." The room was quiet. Unintelligible voices leaked from the cockpit. A jet engine whined like it was getting excited. Carr started laughing.

The others looked one to the other with blank expressions.

Carr's palm slapped the smooth grain of the table. "Fantastic! They're paying close attention to the one remaining musician. What *incredible* luck."

"Luck?" Jill said. "We lost her."

"If we hadn't, we would be guessing. Are they watching? Will she be welcome? Do they care what happens to her? But not now. Now we know for certain. She's important."

The plane jerked and began to move.

"Hey," Kandy said. "My new car is on the runway."

Carr waved a hand. "We'll take care of it." He dragged a stack of papers from the overhead compartment and flopped them onto the table. "Buckle up, we'll be in the air shortly." He flipped through the pages and unfolded a sheet that covered the entire table. "Our original plan where Qigiq and Mylin go in together needs a remodel."

"Do we still try to sell him a painting?" Kandy asked.

"Absolutely. We locate Mylin, all accidental like, so she and Qigiq can rekindle their love affair while Uncle G's cameras watch."

Jill's eyes flicked between Kandy and Qigiq. "You had an affair with Mylin?"

"The FBI plays fast and loose with the English language," Kandy said. "We saw her at a concert in Mill Valley. Qu let her father know he wanted to meet her. The plan was to understand the inside of the orchestra business by masquerading as a customer. It never panned out."

"Correct," Carr said. "But that gives us history, which is important to building trust."

"A cop hiring a prostitute?" Jill asked.

"Oh, *that's* never happened." Carr laughed and leaned over the map. "We land in fifteen hours, plenty of time to rest."

His finger traced a line across the table. "Our first stop is here: Hotel Shilla."

A siren wail filled the cabin. Kandy's head shot up. Qigiq considered reasons a siren might sound in an aircraft rolling across a runway.

Carr held up one hand and reached for his cell phone with the other. He read for some seconds. "We have been smiled upon twice in one day." He stood and reached into the overhead again. This time he came back with a laptop armored to survive the Apocalypse. "Just got a message from the Air Force, they have spotted our boy." He opened the computer and navigated for a moment. "Here."

He spun the machine around.

An Asian male wearing a charcoal three-piece suit and black sneakers had been photographed mid-stride stepping off the deck of a sport-fishing boat. An orange rectangle enclosed the man's face. His black hair showed streaks of gray.

"Is that Uncle Gan?" Jill said.

"Expensive computers think so," Carr said.

"Remarkable picture," Kandy said. "But it's not the best you can do, is it?"

"Sorry, can't answer that," Carr said, smiling.

Qigiq said, "No one on the planet is safe from you guys, are they?"

Carr hesitated, then replied, "I hope not."

"Hey," Jill said. "How did you get that picture if we're not using communications?"

"Internal private networks."

"And those are safe?" she asked.

"Safer," he said. "It's also where I got these." He spread pictures of a beach, a hotel, a campsite in a forest, and a busy city street across the table.

"More satellite pics?" Kandy said.

Carr shook his head. "Joe Roberts."

Qigiq remembered Roberts, he had kidnapped Mylin and taken her to Burning Man. By the time Qigiq caught up with them, her father was dead. "You have Roberts instrumenting the island to augment your satellites?"

Carr grinned. "They aren't *my* satellites."

"You plan to track him electronically," Qigiq said, "so Kandy and I don't have to tail him."

"Bingo."

Kandy said, "Qigiq is getting better at this tech stuff."

Qigiq smiled slightly. He might be getting better, but the problems were getting harder.

"Won't Gan's spies detect the signals from those cameras?" Jill asked.

"We're using consumer grade stuff so we look like civilian traffic: home webcams, security cameras, that sort of thing. Except for the encryption, that's special NSA sauce."

"So," Kandy said, "They won't find you because you don't stick out, but if they do, they won't be able to read you."

"That's what the super-geeks tell me."

"In the meantime," she said, "we get spotting reports on Gan. That siren was the first one."

Carr nodded. "It helps that he's on an island, or we'd be searching all of China, Korea, Vietnam, and half of Russia."

"Does he know?" Kandy asked.

"I doubt it, or he wouldn't constrain himself so much."

"Why?" Jill asked.

"Trade-off. The more he plays like a mosquito, the easier it is for him to have defenses in place. But also, the easier he is to follow. Once you find him the first time."

"He really doesn't know we're following him?" Qigiq said. "Even with hundreds of dragon eyes?"

"I can't be sure. We only know about Jeju because Mylin told us a story during an interview at the prison."

"So long as she doesn't tell him she told us," Jill said. "But why?"

"Why use Jeju? So far, we have ten hypotheses."

Kandy said, "He doesn't want to be on the Chinese mainland because they intercept Internet traffic."

"That's one of the ten."

"The natural protection of an island," Jill said. "He can see the enemy coming."

"That's one too."

"His brother had four kids during the Chinese one-child policy," Kandy said.

"That could have been the original motivation to move to South Korea."

Qigiq spread the fingers of one hand across the map, estimating distance. "Because there are multiple ferry boats each day."

"Not on the FBI's list. Why do ferries matter?"

"As a teenager in Alaska, I shuttled mail between island villages in a kayak. Sort of a pony express on water. Gan communicates without electronics by moving paintings with hidden messages."

"Speaking of communicating." Carr shuffled the papers beneath the map and retrieved an article with Reno Gazette on the masthead. "This will be printed in today's edition. It describes what happened at the county prison last night."

Kandy said, "I know Mylin busted free and you guys cheated me out of the action."

Qigiq thought about the missed rendezvous, and how being late had created an opening.

Carr spoke without consulting the article. "The power station beside the prison exploded. Of course, prisons are designed for outages, so two backup diesel generators tried to kick in. Only one did. The article reports that the other had a problem with a fuel pump that wouldn't bring line pressure high enough. That said, the entire prison can work off of a single generator."

"How long were the lights out?" Kandy said.

"Four and a half minutes."

"So the second generator..."

Carr continued, "Wouldn't come on line. It was running and ready, but the switch that automatically connects it to the internal grid got stuck."

"Murphy's Law," Qigiq said.

Kandy laughed. "Yeah, David 'Murphy' Carr, saboteur incognito."

Carr smiled, looking guilty.

"Did anyone escape?" Jill asked softly.

He tapped the page. "The article is very clear that there were no security violations."

"Yet two people are no longer inside," Qigiq said.

Kandy said, "There are two empty cells. Public records clearly indicate those cells were empty before the outage. Don't they, David?"

Carr only grinned.

"But Mylin had been arrested. There are lots of records," Jill said.

"Yes, there are," Carr said. "All now classified."

Kandy said, "In twenty-five years, some enterprising reporter will use the Freedom of Information Act to figure out what happened."

"I'll be retired. They can take it up with the poor slob who gets my job."

"So Mylin and I don't exist?" Jill asked.

"Not in the prison records. I cleaned everything. And added a few tidbits."

"Do I want to know?" Kandy asked.

"You'll recognize them if they show up."

Qigiq glanced out the window; they were over open water. "Speaking of showing up. How is it that a pair of hard-working homicide detectives can arrive on an island paradise, in a private jet, on city-cop salaries?"

Carr folded the newspaper. "That's precisely the question Uncle Gan will be asking himself when we walk off this plane."

CHAPTER 7

JOE'S EYES FLICKED BETWEEN surf-washed sand a hundred yards from his Premier Grand Deluxe hotel patio and the screen of his laptop displaying the front door of The Spa at Shilla. A middle-aged Asian woman had visited the spa three times in as many days. Each time, she was inside for fifteen minutes, timing he verified with recordings from surveillance cameras. Cameras he had hidden after Carr sent the location of a yacht. A satellite had recognized a face.

Fifteen minutes seemed like a short spa treatment.

The consistency bothered him. He couldn't say why.

He was supposed to be watching Gan So Wu's place, not the spa at the fancy hotel the FBI was paying for. He reminded himself to appreciate every minute of living so far above his pay grade as a fine art photographer.

He switched cameras: The Shilla's private beach house. Two women lying in the shade of an umbrella, both talking. Americans.

Something gnawed at him.

He switched. The Asian woman was standing in front of the spa doing nothing, not even looking around. He had been taking clandestine pictures for years; rarely had he seen anyone do nothing. However, for the first time ever, he was well-funded. Cameras, computers, wireless links, anything he wanted. Even a white Mercedes van to drive around to gather data like a Google car mapping the universe.

All thanks to the FBI. And a dynamic guy named David Carr.

The woman walked directly toward his lens.

Joe stood and stared at her face. She looked a bit like Mylin, though decades older.

He set his smartphone to mirror the laptop and raced to the elevator. As he stepped off at ground level, she was descending brick-orange stairs. From his rounds placing cameras, he knew them to be the Terrace Stairway that led to Soombi Garden.

He walked fast, eyes on phone, mind on Mylin. She had haunted him ever since that random photo in Michigan of her, a cigarette, and the moon. He longed to be near her, help her, know her. But her life was...insane. He wasn't sure he would ever see her again.

The woman passed out of camera range.

Joe memorized the indigo dress, beige heels, dark hair touching her shoulders. The way she moved when she walked. Then he ran through the hotel and down the Terrace Stairway. At the bottom he turned left, away from the hotel. He glimpsed her dress in the distance.

He closed the space between them with long, quick strides, trying to hurry without appearing to. As he reached the top of narrow wooden steps labeled *Stairway to the Sea* she exited at the bottom and disappeared. He took the steps two at a time, then scanned the beach.

Nothing.

He walked toward the sea, squatted, then turned around to examine the entire beach.

She stood two feet away, looking down into his eyes.

"Why are you following me?"

Not *Are you following me?* But *Why?*

"Uh, I was..." Joe stood slowly to give himself time to think. Up close, mid-forties. She crossed her arms. Her beige heels dangled from her left index finger. With her feet in the sand she was barely five-foot-two. Close up and not on a flat screen, she looked even more like Mylin. Or maybe he was just obsessed. He said, "This will sound utterly stupid, but you look familiar."

She swung the shoes by rocking her shoulders. "This is the

best pick-up line you have?"

He smiled. "No really. You remind me of someone back in the states."

"You mean, we all look alike to American male."

He hadn't meant that, but it held a grain of truth. "Yes, you're all beautiful."

Her lips quivered as she fought a smile. "You did not deny that you were following me. Don't they teach denial in American schools?"

"I wasn't following you—you were attracting me. It's not the same thing."

This time she smiled, met his eyes, and said, "So what was your plan after catching me?"

"I hadn't thought that far ahead."

"Another American trait. What are you doing on our lovely island? Do all Korean women attract you?"

"I'm...um...taking pictures."

She studied his face, took two steps back, and said, "Take my picture."

A test.

He moved in an arc until the afternoon sun was at his back and the ocean lay behind her. Her eyes tracked his every step. He took a few shots with his smartphone, dropped to one knee in the sand, took more. Then he walked directly toward her, holding the phone far above his head. Her body seemed to radiate energy. She looked up to see what he was doing. He released the shutter repeatedly, trying to capture her face surrounded by a blanket of sand.

"Let me see."

He held the phone out and flipped through the pictures.

"Impressive...for an American."

He ignored the veiled insult, pleased he had her picture, though he didn't know why. She was merely a woman who went to the spa.

"Would you like to have them?"

She hesitated.

"Not impressive enough?"

Her dark brown eyes glimmered. "It's not that…"

"You would have to explain where you got them?"

"Something like that."

"And who took them."

She hadn't backed away. He did what he often did in an uncomfortable silence: he lifted his arm and took a close up.

She laughed. "Would you leave them for me at the spa?"

"Sure.What name should I give them?"

She called back over her shoulder, "Show my picture, they know me." She stopped, slipped her shoes on, and headed up the stairway. He listened to her sandy soles scuff against wood steps. She was halfway up before he realized that two men had been waiting nearby, both wearing black tunics despite the heat. They stared at him for half a minute, then followed her up the *Stairway to the Sea.*

Joe slipped the phone into his cargo shorts fully aware that if a package didn't arrive at the spa, one of the tunics would find him. He made his way to the Shilla gift shop where he tried to buy a thumb drive but had to settle for a SIM card and tweezers. Carr had said no electronic communication. And told him about the U.S. government hacking the entire Internet with projects like STELLARWIND and OPTICNERVE, including the formerly secure open-source Tor network. Even searching for the term "Tor" would put his IP address on a list.

He'd do this old school.

Back in his room Joe gazed out at the surface of the infinity pool where it blended into the ocean, feeling like a tiny fish in a large aquarium of predators. He wanted to contact Carr for permission to deliver the pictures, but Carr had insisted: no digital traffic unless necessary. He drew a tall curtain completely across the window. Then connected two devices with a cable and copied the pictures of the mystery woman from the phone to a laptop. A DuckDuckGo search assured him that nothing on a SIM could identify him or his laptop.

He used the tweezers to push the brand new SIM card into

the computer. No fingerprints. Then copied the best photos of the woman in blue...one at a time.

Using the tweezers, he carefully slit the overwrap protecting a complementary white comb and slipped the SIM card inside. He rolled the combo inside a fresh hand towel, reasoning that a comb for a woman shouldn't attract suspicion. He walked to the spa where he was greeted by a round-faced Korean girl in a tight green shirt whose lilting, accented English was not only musical but easy to understand.

He smiled, unfolded the towel, and slid the comb package onto the marble counter.

She stared at it, then looked up at him.

"Would you please deliver this to..." He pulled out his cell phone and swiped to the first picture of the woman in the blue dress.

The girl's sparkling black eyes told him she not only knew the woman in the picture, but was terrified of her. She nodded vigorously, picked up the comb, dropped it into an envelope, dabbed the flap with her tongue, and pressed it closed. She scribbled the date, glanced at a white-faced clock, carefully recorded the time, and wrote: *Please deliver to M. Win.* The envelope disappeared into the cash register. She slid the drawer closed and met his eyes.

"Would you like to schedule an appointment? Our therapists are among the best in the world."

Joe smiled, everyone pitched Americans as if it were the island's national sport. As he shook his head no, he glimpsed a row of doors. "On second thought. Does..." he gestured toward the envelope, "have a favorite?"

She blinked three times, glanced left and right, leaned toward him, and whispered, "Nashi."

"Does Nashi have time available today?"

Her dark eyes went to a computer screen he couldn't see while he hoped the spa wasn't booked weeks in advance.

"Available for what?"

The woman's voice from behind surprised him. He turned.

The glass door of the spa was swinging closed behind a woman in a skintight white razor top and white athletic pants. Her blonde hair hung straight, touching shoulders ready for an Olympic gymnastics competition. Based on the accent and six-foot frame, he placed her somewhere between Serbia and Moscow.

The girl in green said, "This gentleman would like a massage."

The woman stepped behind the counter and stood beside the round-faced girl. They studied the hidden computer screen. Joe fidgeted with the hand towel, dropped it onto the counter, and pushed one hand into a pocket. A vacationer shouldn't appear nervous. *But he was.* He had been on the island for days and was still waiting for Carr to show up. The special cameras were in place. The van was parked where it could act as a communication hub. All cameras had passed his laptop test, which is what he had been running when he stumbled upon M. Win.

"Sir?"

He refocused. The Russian woman was staring at him.

"Are you a hotel guest?"

He nodded. "I have a beautiful suite overlooking the pool."

Her eyes seemed to grow bluer. "I see."

He didn't know what she saw—maybe the Premium Deluxe room had special privileges. Or she thought he was wealthy: a grandiose miscalculation.

"I am Nashi. I can take you now if you like. I have one hour before my next appointment."

He fingered the hotel key in his left pocket and slipped his phone into another. They were the only things on him: no wallet, no car keys, no ID. Carr's instruction had been specific.

"Now would be fabulous."

She curled a finger and led the way along a corridor of closed doors. Photographs hanging between them showed a school of fish, then a volcano, and the Hotel Shilla itself. The images had been created on a beach with multiple colors of sand, the pictures taken as these artistic expressions were being washed away by a rising tide.

She stopped beside the last door and held it open for him.

He entered.

The narrow room contained a table covered with pale blue sheets and a granite sink in the corner that could pass for a wet bar. A panorama of white mountains glowing beneath ceiling-mounted LED lights, as if the room were an art gallery, covered the entire wall to his right from floor to ceiling.

"Do you miss the mountains?" Joe asked.

"The sea is beautiful here," Nashi said. "I swim every day." She turned back the top sheet and adjusted a circular pad protruding from the end of the table. "Let us begin face down."

Swimming explained her strength, but she had dodged the question. "Have you ever seen those?" He indicated the panorama. "Or does the hotel put that picture in every room?"

She smiled, showing perfect teeth save one: a twisted eye tooth on the left. "That's my picture. I took with cell phone."

He moved closer to examine it. In the dim light of the LEDs, it was plenty good. The snow even reflected icy blue in places, like her eyes. "It's beautiful. I take pictures too." He bit his tongue too late. He was showing off to impress her, but he had just given away real information.

"Everyone does. The machine does the hard work. Even foolish American can take a good picture now." Her smile grew.

"Good thing or I'd be helpless."

She patted the table. "What kind of massage would you like today?"

"The one you would get for yourself." She tilted her head. He read disapproval in her expression. He added, "Wrong answer, huh? I'm not strong enough for that level of pressure, am I?"

"An honest American? I thought you were extinct. Macho men come in and ask for deep hard massage. Next day, cannot walk and never come back. Do you know what Nashi means in

Russian?"

"Giver of crippling massage?"

Her laughter was as alluring as the mountains. "It means nothing. I made it up. It's short for Natasha. Too many Russian girls named Natasha."

He started unbuttoning his shirt. "How about a massage that makes me want to come back and see Nashi again?"

"Hmm." She turned and left the room, pulling the door closed quietly behind her.

He kicked off the barefoot running shoes he used for sneaking around because they helped him feel subtle variations in the ground, then fought the urge to frantically search the room. What did he expect to find: a connection to M. Win, a false bottom in a drawer, a secret code? He unbuckled his pants with one hand and slid open the small drawers beside the sink with the other. The second one contained a book with a black leather cover and gold-edged paper.

Do not leave fingerprints.

He stepped out of his jeans and lifted the corner of the book with a fingernail. The front page had been inscribed: *Nashi +8819-OX3-4706.* He flipped it open: a standard week-at-a-glance calendar. Appointments in pencil. Plenty of erasure marks. He wanted to take pictures; instead, he memorized the number and carefully turned to today's date. Three entries, including one for M. Win. He backed up to the previous week: nothing. The week before: M. Win at a different time. The week before: nothing. He started for the previous week but the doorknob rattled. He dropped the book closed, spun to face the door, bent over to pick his pants, and simultaneously pushed the drawer closed with the back of his thigh.

Nashi pulled back when she saw him. "Sorry."

"That's okay, come on in. Had a knot in my shoelace." He hopped on the table and slipped between the sheets.

"I wear sandals on the island," she said. "Feels more free."

Wordless music resembling ocean waves whooshed from hidden speakers. He wished he could see her face, instead of facing the floor with a padded ring around his cheeks.

Her palms gently pressed his bare back. His neck relaxed. His breathing slowed. Down his arms, hands, along each finger, pressure against each fingertip. The next hour disappeared into a dimension of fresh tactile sensations, while he silently repeated: *8 8 1 9 0X3 4 7 0 6.*

CHAPTER 8

I WRAPPED BOTH ARMS around Qigiq's waist and squeezed, pulling us together against the forward rush of the bike and the chill of fog. The feel of his body against mine made the isolation of the prison more vivid. I nearly wept with the joy of freedom. We leaned together following twisting pavement, the still black water of the river always to our right. We rose into hills. A burning sky welcomed us, pushing the jail cell deeper into the recesses of my mind.

This was my third ride on a motorcycle.

My first had been with Joe Roberts. He kidnapped me away from a man who'd hired me for the evening, foolishly thinking he could alter the path of the gods. Joe and I flew for hours and hours on a buzzing machine that swooped through turns like a giant mechanical bird. That ride ended with the death of my father.

My second ride had been with my brother Shen after he dragged me away during a Bear Naked Orchestra performance with a rock band. That ride ended with three bullets in his body.

I smiled under the helmet wobbling on my head. Shooting Shen had set me free, even as the police locked me away with my sunbeam.

Now I was riding with my arms tight around Qigiq, the first cop who had ever helped me.

We rode the silver machine for an hour in the predawn glow, its engine thumping between my legs like the wings of a flying dragon. Another river came into view, or perhaps the same river in a different place, as wide as ten rice paddies. Two container ships sat by the shore and a bridge hovered far above us like a concrete rainbow. We exited the highway on a smooth ribbon of gray.

Potholed streets welcomed us to a city. A sign zipped past announcing Sacramento Marina. White-hulled boats beneath tin sunshades floated still as a cemetery. The air smelled of seawater, fish, and exhaust fumes. I closed my eyes and for a fleeting moment wanted the safety of my prison cell.

Qigiq parked the bike at the end of a row of boats. He held the machine upright and motioned me off. My stiff legs and sore back welcomed the movement. The engine stopped. Silence enveloped me like Joe's arms that first night in his truck.

Two men with sun-wrinkled faces wearing light blue overalls walked off a dock and turned toward us. Qigiq lowered the dark scarf he was wearing to protect his face from the wind.

My chest became weightless. This man was the right size, he was on a motorcycle wearing boots, leather jacket, white helmet. Everything outside said Qigiq. But inside, he wasn't Qigiq. He was a man with black eyes and an empty gaze.

A voice behind me called out in Chinese.

My legs started to run before the thought reached my brain. Stiff from the ride, they responded slowly, yet no hands grabbed me. I gathered speed. My vision filled with white yachts, glistening water, sunshine, cracked pavement. I turned onto a dock and raced along a row of boats. My mind flashed back to the prison that held me in, but also kept men away. The beating dragon wings of the motorcycle came closer. I struggled to understand the maze of docks to avoid being trapped. Feet pounded against wooden planks, the sound, echoing from the roofs, coming from everywhere at once.

I twisted my head left, right, the helmet moving with me. I ran toward the sun. Back to pavement. The dragon approached. Something struck my arm, tilting me off balance. My hip hit the ground. I rolled.

The dragon flew away.

Downward pressure on my backpack. Voices chattering excitedly in Chinese. I was lifted by my arms and shoved into a shiny yellow boat shaped like Karen's. The hatch closed with the finality of my cell door.

I was sweating, gasping, crying.

I removed my pack. *What had gone wrong? Who? How? Why?*

Engines came to life. The boat vibrated. A dock receded on the other side of a narrow window near the ceiling of my little room. I tried to deepen my breathing to calm my heart. Sunbeams streamed at me from the right side of the boat. I watched the little clock Jilly had given me. I brought out my viola. After 30 minutes, the boat slowed and a lonely, tilted dock made of almost black wood came into view.

The hatch opened. Instant brightness made me squint. This was the moment when men would come for sex before delivering me to my destination. I hoped they would settle for my mouth.

No one descended the ladder.

I put my viola away and thought of holding Jilly's hand... and Karen's arm around me...how I had felt safe. I slipped the pack onto my back. Wherever I was going, it must go too.

A man shouted Chinese words down at me.

I climbed into sunshine. The two men who had dragged me to the boat were conversing with a gray-suited white devil with a brush-shaped mustache. He was sucking on a black stick that glowed green on the end. He removed the stick, exhaled white vapor toward me as I stepped onto the deck, reached into his jacket, and withdrew a photograph. He stepped from the tilted dock onto the boat, came to me, and pushed away the hair that hid my left eye. I forced myself to remain still, knowing that a reaction might provoke violence. His eyes made three round trips between the photograph and my face before he said:

"Hello, Mylin. Did you have a smooth trip?"

I bowed slightly.

"Good. Onward to the next phase. Follow me."

He stepped on the deck, then onto the dock. The two men who had brought me stood at the back of the boat, watching. Neither moved to help me, so I mimicked his movement until I stood beside him on a wooden dock that wavered under our weight. My eyes barely reached his chin. Up close he appeared scrawny, as if his family were very poor.

He reached into his jacket again and handed an envelope to the two men. No words were exchanged. The men started the boat's engines and backed it into the river. The scrawny man walked along the dock, avoiding the missing boards.

I wanted to jump in the water and swim to the other side. But the yellow boat was floating in the middle of the river, growling its low voice, not moving.

Unlike Karen's, this dock reached the shore. A long black car like movie stars ride in awaited. He held the door to the back open. Leather seats and red velvet invited me inside. I removed my backpack, ducked in, and sat on the far side of a curved seat that was softer than most beds. I tried not to think, to keep my head clear, live in the moment; but my mind abandoned me to:

The motorcycle rider had just sold me.

The buyer got in after me and closed the door. The car moved. He sucked on his black stick and blew mist into the air. I squeezed the viola between my legs, as if it could protect me from being raped.

"You are very pretty."

"Thank you," I said, not from gratitude, but training.

His hand disappeared inside his jacket and came out holding an envelope. He leaned over and held it out to me.

I stared at it.

He urged it toward me.

I took it. A gob of wax imprinted with an ornate *M* sealed the flap.

"You had better open it now. This is as far as my instructions go."

The car sped up.

I broke the seal with my thumb. It contained a letter, a passport, two hundred dollars in American paper money, and a boarding pass for a flight scheduled to leave today. It also held a headband with a bright green lightning bolt embroidered against the black cloth. I unfolded the letter.

Speak these words to the man you are with: "International Terminal, United Airlines."

Cover your left eye with the lightning bolt.

I said, "International Terminal. United Airlines."

The scrawny man nodded and repeated the words to the driver, who bowed his head. The car moved even faster. In minutes I was standing at the curb holding my case in one hand and the envelope in the other watching the rear bumper of the long black car as it drove away.

He hadn't touched me.

I turned around slowly. I was in front of a tall building of glass and steel with a thick curved roof that made me think of a giant eyebrow. As I realized that I was leaving, my mind filled with memories of America: Jilly in her little green car, Joe Roberts gazing at me in the back of his truck with something like love in his eyes, Kandy summoning a tattooed man to help my bleeding friend Lilly. I wanted to be with them. But someone with power had plans for my future.

I crossed a sidewalk as wide as most stages. I stopped near the giant wall of glass and used it as a mirror to tie the lightning bolt headband around my forehead, pulling hair over my left eye as always. Then I turned around and squatted against the smooth wall of the building, watching rental-car busses pass, wondering what one girl alone could do against such forces.

I reread the boarding pass. Hong Kong.

A man in a charcoal suit with a crisp crease in the pants leg stood to my left, his eyes watchful. A shorter one to my right, dressed identically, stood stock still behind nearly black sunglasses. I got to my feet and made my way through the terminal to the security line.

Both men followed me.

I had almost fooled myself; I didn't have any choices.

A lady in a dark blue uniform looked at my ticket, pointed, and said, "Use the Premium entrance over there, honey. It will go faster for you."

I bowed and thanked her. The man with the black glasses followed me into the Premium line and through security. I thought I would be led to a barren room and strip-searched, but nothing happened. Everyone smiled and waved me through as my backpack containing my viola and secret packets of money lumbered along on a moving belt like a loaf of bread at a grocery store. A security worker asked me to remove the boots Karen had picked out for me.

But that was all.

Then I was inside a secure area in the United States of America: a place I had never been. I had never been through customs before. I had never flown. Not once in my entire life.

I hoped I wouldn't be sick.

The man with black sunglasses was ahead of me now, glancing back over his shoulder. I followed him to a waiting area filled with hundreds of people. He stood at attention between a large gray pillar and a thin statue made of iron.

I visited the ladies room.

When I came out he was beside the door. He followed me back to my departure gate.

I waited standing up.

Soon, the flight number on my ticket was called for boarding. I stood in line, checking over my shoulder. My watcher had not moved. I shuffled down a tilted tunnel with hundreds of other people, unable to run in any direction, imagining myself a cow ambling toward slaughter.

While I waited in a luxurious leather chair sipping orange juice, a thick door swung shut, trapping me inside a long bus-like tube. Then I was lifted into the sky by roaring tigers. On the other side of the scratched window beside my seat, the earth receded into a new kind of beauty. I became a falcon gone hunting, seeing far, seeing much, knowing people were in those buildings below. Small. Insignificant.

I heard music in my head. No particular piece, just a viola improvising new melodies from a place deep inside of me. I was given food on a tray. It tasted much better than the prison food. I slept. More food. More sleep. Without warning, the blue-white outside my window disappeared, and a magic city of stone and lights and color spread out below me.

We bumped on the ground.

Another tilted tube took me out of the magnificent airplane. A different man in dark glasses awaited me. Onto another flight: smaller plane, fewer people, but the same beautiful views. I flew above blue water that was glorious and powerful and angry.

And then.

I stepped through the thick doorway in the side of the plane and into sunshine and down metal stairs onto concrete. Another long car awaited: steel gray with black windows. I don't know how I knew it was for me, but as I approached, the rear door swung open. I stepped in and again held my viola between my knees. Perhaps *this* was the important man; *now* I would be raped. I leaned over and pulled the door closed. The interior became black. My eyes adjusted bit by bit. At the far end of a couch running along the side of the vehicle, the outline of a woman formed. She wore round dark glasses despite the lack of light. The car moved.

She remained silent. I felt her eyes on me. I reminded myself that only I knew the FBI man's money was hidden in my case. I must not let anyone take it from me; it was my ticket back to America. I smiled. I now possessed a passport. I could travel anywhere like a dragon with wings.

My right hand slipped down and gently stroked the two capsules in my pocket.

The woman shifted on the pale leather seat.

The car settled into a highway drone.

In a thin voice like tearing paper she said, "You're not as pretty as your pictures."

CHAPTER 9

QIGIQ STARED OUT THE WINDOW at a two-layer traffic-control room perched on a tower of white. A city of modest skyscrapers glowing in the sunshine stretched along the foothills just beyond. The place looked crowded, except for orchards surrounding the entire area.

"Oranges," Carr said, "and mandarin."

"Impressive. I was expecting a dirt runway maintained by goats." He wasn't entirely joking; bush planes in Alaska landed almost anywhere.

"This airport has one of the busiest airline routes in the world—nonstop to Seoul."

"Smart location," Kandy said. "Easy to hide movement inside loads of movement."

"In this haystack we're going to find a needle named Gan?" Qigiq asked.

The plane touched pavement and bounced. Jet engines whined their slowdown cry.

Carr spoke above the roar. "We found him once."

The executive jet that had been their home for the day taxied toward four similar planes.

"You think he'll turn up again?" Kandy said. "Might have been freakish luck."

"Roberts is here setting up surveillance equipment for us."

"And?"

"We don't have secure communications, so he's sitting tight until I contact him."

"Life is hell without cell phones," she said, laughing. "Ask any teenager. You really think Gan's spies can see us?"

The plane rocked to a stop. The seatbelt sign went out. Carr unbuckled and stood, stretching his legs one at a time. "That was long."

Kandy extended her legs across the neighboring seat. "You're just too tall for this plane."

Carr grinned. "I requested a Dreamliner, but it was in the shop. To your question, I don't know what dragon eyes can see, but they grabbed Mylin right from under my nose, so they see plenty." He popped the overhead compartment open. "The dragon we can deal with. The invisible moles..." He shook his head.

Qigiq turned away from the window and his effort to fix the layout of the city in his mind. "Inside the FBI?"

Car shrugged and brought down a hard-shell briefcase. "I don't have specifics, but look at the criminal element we're dealing with here: people who can steal government secrets that my boss writes a blank check to get back. Think they might have inside access?"

"They were watching the prison," Kandy said. "Obvious and easy. The breakout surprised them. That's why they didn't grab her until after the boat ride."

"How'd they know what bike?" Carr asked. "Or a bike at all?"

Qigiq thought back. And back. "Mylin is an important asset. They've probably had her under surveillance since she came across Lake Erie. That means they know I contacted her in Mill Valley."

"How'd they know Qigiq was picking her up?" Kandy said.

"Good guess?" Carr suggested.

Qigiq shook his head. "Kandy and I visited the prison. That's when they ID'ed us and started the tail. They tracked me riding north. If they were watching the boat and me at the same time...one plus one."

Carr said. "So, if Gan has eyes everywhere? Did they see this plane take off?"

Kandy said, "Absolutely. But they don't know where we went. Unless the dragon can see our flight plan?"

Carr considered before saying, "The NSA monitors a lot of stuff, just read Snowden's book *Permanent Record*." He smiled. "International flights? I vote yes. Someone decodes it. Eventually the dragon eyes report that we're in Jeju."

"Eventually?"

"Takes time to crack encryption," Carr said. "Time we can use." He opened his case.

Kandy glanced at Jill still asleep across the aisle and popped gum into her mouth.

The motion made Qigiq think of cigarettes and the number of weeks since he had smoked: still in the teens.

She said, "You're telling me the dragon is watching us, our own guys are watching us, and the dragon is watching our guys watch us?"

"At least," Carr said. "I'm worried one of our guys gets a paycheck from Gan. And those are only the people we know about."

"You're implying there's someone else?"

"At least one."

Cracking gum filled the quiet cabin. "I'm not going to ask."

"You're no fun," Carr said. "Whoever bought the intel." He paused. "Or is going to buy it. They have eyes out too."

"How's a city cop supposed to get work done with you techno-mammoths stomping around?" She didn't laugh.

"Street smarts," Qigiq said. "You and I stay under the radar, the Internet, cell phones, and anything else that can track us."

"That leaves face-to-face on planet Mars," she said.

"And paper and pencil." Qigiq wiggled his fingers. "And hand signs."

"How about smoke signals?" Carr added as he reached into the briefcase with both hands. "And these." He lifted out a stack of shrink-wrapped black boxes.

"I love new toys," Kandy said.

"The newest." He handed each person a phone, including

Jill Kiner, who had just woken up.

"You turn yours on first, Qigiq," Kandy said. "I don't trust these things."

"Are they secure?" Jill asked.

"Secure is a relative concept," Carr said. "But we have a few things going for us. These are prototypes of a next generation phone."

"You stole them?" Kandy said.

"Didn't have to. I have a friend in the Bureau's test lab working directly with the manufacturer."

Qigiq said, "You're installing a back door so the FBI can crack them anytime it wants."

"That's the NSA's job," Carr said. "We're trying to make these devices un-hackable so we can use them within the Bureau."

Jill said, "And be confident that no other government agency is spying on you."

Kandy rolled her unopened box around in her hands. "You three-letter agencies need more bad guys, so you don't have to fink on each other."

"My friend was assigned to do a live field test."

Kandy broke the seal on the package.

Qigiq said, "So we're guinea pigs?"

Carr nodded. "Precisely. What we have here is a group of brand new hardware devices that form a Sealed Circle. Only my friend knows we have them. Unlike a standard Silent Circle that encrypts communications within the group, a 'Sealed Circle' means these devices only communicate with a list of IP addresses stored internally. Peer-to-peer. To any other computer in the world, these devices don't exist."

"The guinea pig likes it so far," Kandy said.

Qigiq had no opinion of the new devices, but he was sure that the need for them was complicating his world.

Carr continued, "We believe the bad guys haven't cracked them because these devices are being carefully allocated."

"You mean the manufacturer doesn't field test with bad

guys?" Kandy said. "Seems like a shortsighted marketing strategy."

"We're the first to get more than two."

"Do they do anything else special?" Jill asked.

"All the standard Silent Circle stuff on Blackphone. But we're not going to use it."

Kandy said, "Because…"

"Technology in broad circulation might already be cracked, so we would be revealed even though we have the new high-price spread."

Jill flipped her phone over and back, the screen blank. "So what does this Sealed Circle do?"

"Lets us message and talk securely among this set of devices. They won't respond to any IP address other than the ones they already know about."

"So no one can talk to us except us," Kandy said.

"Like the Choctaw and Cherokee code talkers in World War I," Qigiq said.

Jill turned the package round and round in her hand. "Can we talk to anyone else?"

"That breaks the seal. Once we do that, we're back to consumer level vulnerability."

"How do I stop enemies from reading over my shoulder with the optics on a sniper rifle?" Jill asked. "Or from listening to my conversation with that machine that measures wall vibrations and converts them to speech?"

Kandy said, "Good thing we're not paranoid."

"Only the paranoid survive," Qiqiq said. Kandy lifted an eyebrow. "Saw that on the cover of a book at the airport in Fairbanks. I was heading to the Pentagon."

"Valid points. Yes, the bad boys can read over your shoulder. So, we build another layer. That layer is prototype software built at the FBI by the friend who got these phones allocated to us as a matter of national security. No one else has it. I mean *no one.*"

Jill said, "I've heard that obscurity is the best form of security."

Carr nodded. "A profound insight. If the bad guys don't have access to the tech, they can't crack it."

"Do I want to know how this layer works?" Kandy asked.

Qigiq watched his phone. "It's translating."

"That's correct," Carr said. "It has internal maps of Jeju Island and San Francisco, which I knew would be familiar. The specific relationship between locations is changed at random intervals synchronized by internal clocks. Tap in a Jeju location and it translates to a San Francisco location. If someone intercepts the photons emitted by your screen, they see messages about San Francisco with Pacific time zones."

"Intercept the photons?" Kandy mumbled, nudging Qigiq. "Listen to that FBI talk."

"Someone will see me put it in," Jill said.

"Here's what they see. A map of San Francisco pops up. Touch a key location, and the phone will speak the Jeju location into your earbud. Tap the one you want and the text goes into the Sealed Circle message app. It sends something like 'Coit Tower.' The receiver sees Coit Tower, but hears Hotel Shilla. Same thing happens with time of day."

"So we use a combination of encoded maps, text, and audio, and hope they can't figure out what's going on?" Jill asked.

"On top of a hyper-secure device that very few people have in their possession."

Qigiq touched the map on his phone. "Better than public phone booths, which is what I thought we were going to do." He grinned.

"You can also use the GPS coordinates of the phone's location. It will map those through to San Francisco too."

"What about our names?" Jill asked.

"They know about the four of us. They might be aware of Joe Roberts, he's been near Mylin for weeks."

"So they know who we are and probably what we look like," Qigiq said.

"Just not what we're doing...or where," Jill added.

Carr nodded. "We have to assume they have this entire island under surveillance."

Kandy said, "The guinea pigs had better lay very low."

Qigiq gazed out the plane's window at a city that looked like any other city, though the buildings were not nearly as tall as in San Francisco. His new phone showed: 4:03 PM Wednesday. A day had disappeared. The phone vibrated in his hand. A message arrived.

Cyril Magnin Suite of the Mark Hopkins on Nob Hill. 8:15 PM.

* * *

Qigiq watched the door swing away and stairs unfold from the side of their aircraft. Kandy left first, crossing the tarmac with bold steps. The Mark Hopkins was the rendezvous point. All parties would arrive by different routes and modes of transportation. Kandy, of course, would drive the car.

Jill Kiner departed next. A slender girl with dyed blonde hair barely over five feet tall, she moved with powerful strides like a mini-Kandy, which is exactly what she aspired to be. She was to master the public transportation options.

David Carr had arranged for a hardened SUV. He would be picking it up at a nearby U.S. military base that was still under construction.

Qigiq shook the FBI agent's hand—Carr's grip was strong and encouraging. Their eyes met. Neither spoke. Carr's face showed what Qigiq felt: Confidence in themselves and their colleagues, but acute awareness that for this hodgepodge team, international espionage was uncharted territory.

Qigiq stepped out of the multimillion-dollar aircraft into Mediterranean weather: sunny sky, seventy degrees, light breeze. An ideal day to ride a motorbike to the sea. He descended, entered the terminal through glass doors, and stopped at an information counter. Two smiling Korean women provided him with directions to the natural wonders of the island and walking maps of the historical sites. They were briefly stymied by his request for the location of the nearest motorcycle rentals, but went to work on a computer and came up with several: Yo Sung Motors, a language mashup called OuiRentScoot, and Mr. Lee's Bike shop. Mr. Lee's was closest.

Qigiq typed 2452 Orail-Dong into the Blackphone's map system.

A tiny yellow taxi with a chain-smoking driver picked him up at the curb and cruised on the left side of the road into a dense urban area. Qigiq assembled a mental map. A road sign announced Seogwangno just before they reached Hanguk Hospital. The cab turned right on Seosaro and passed an office building occupied by the Halla Daily News. Signs pointed off to the Jeju Athletic Stadium just before the driver stopped abruptly in front of a low white building. A row of scooters and small displacement motorcycles sat out front. One scooter was covered in white plastic, as if it had not yet been unwrapped from the factory. A four-wheel ATV was parked sideways amid the bikes.

The cab pulled away trailing blue smoke, leaving Qigiq standing in front of a building covered with a dozen signs. He could read two:

mr. Lee's Bike Shop (Rentals in English)

and

Bridgestone

A Japanese tire company. He wondered if the small "m" had hidden meaning or if the sign painter had made a mistake. To his right a multi-story building housed perhaps a dozen apartments. The chipped white paint suggested it was at least a few decades old. HVAC ductwork ran down the outside on the wall facing the bike shop. Behind the shop the peak of a house poked above the mr. Lee sign. Everything was eggshell white, except the bikes. They were the usual red, black, blue, and green.

After riding his Guzzi hot-rodded by Kandy's friend Angel, he hoped for something fast. Not because he normally rode fast, but because he chased criminals. He strolled along the sidewalk evaluating the machines. Soon a slightly overweight and cheerful Korean man of about thirty arrived wearing a white suit with a powder blue shirt open at the collar. He introduced himself as Mr. Lee. After a bit of negotiating in careful English, Qigiq decided it would be easiest to rent a bike for a full month.

Could their search possibly go on longer than thirty days?

Mr. Lee pointed out the relative merits of each machine before recommending a dark red Yamaha with one big cylinder and new tires. Fresh rubber would require breaking in, but then would provide great traction.

"Please sign here," Lee said.

Qigiq read the English side of the contract, which pretty much said he was responsible for everything. Given that they had flown in on a private jet, the price of buying the whole bike would be lost in round-off error in Carr's budget, so he printed his name, and signed.

"Key Jeek?" Lee said carefully.

Qigiq nodded, and smiled at having found someone outside of Alaska who could pronounce his name.

Lee stared at the contract as if reading it for the first time. Then he pulled out a cell phone, took a picture, and said, "For records." He handed Qigiq the back copy of the contract, which was barely legible, but would hopefully satisfy the local police in a traffic stop.

Qigiq folded the contract and slipped it into his black jeans. Then he took it back out and made sure he could read the date. On the back he sketched a crude map of where he had seen the hospital relative to the bike shop.

"Do not ride on sidewalk," Lee said, holding his hands wide. "Big fine."

If the time came that Qigiq needed to ride on a sidewalk, he'd do it. But he nodded.

He bought a pair of aviator sunglasses with impact-resistance lenses for a fraction of their U.S. price. Lee handed him a silver key and a black helmet that was part of the rental, and grinned widely when the bike fired up on the first try. They shook hands and Lee was back inside the shop before Qigiq had buckled his helmet. He stepped onto the bike to adjust mirrors, test brake and clutch levers, and verify that the lights worked. He was about to pull away when he noticed a girl approaching, boots up to her knees, tight pale green pants. She was wearing round sunglasses and walking fast.

Hair covered her left eye.

The rental bike had its rear tire against the building, so he would have to cross the sidewalk to reach the street. He let the bike idle.

She came closer but didn't look his way. He called out, "Mylin?"

The girl glided past, her dark lenses pointed straight ahead.

His eyes followed her; he became more convinced.

Mr. Lee might shout at him, but he idled down the sidewalk. Her profile, that he had seen a dozen times while she performed, made him certain.

"Mylin, it's Qigiq. From San Francisco."

She turned toward him, her eyes hidden behind dark lenses, then spun away and climbed stairs to the front door of the apartment building beside Lee's shop. He swung the kickstand down. The door slammed shut. He considered the odds of Mylin randomly walking past as he was renting a bike.

Astronomically low.

He hustled and stopped just inside the main door of the building. She wasn't climbing the stairs and she wasn't partway down the hallway on the first floor. The door banged closed behind him. A hand grabbed his arm above the elbow and dragged him forward. He began to break free before realizing it was the girl from the street. She pulled him along the hallway and into the elevator. After pressing "6" for the top floor, she stood with her arms folded across her chest, facing the closing doors.

She said nothing.

They reached the sixth floor with no stops. She guided him

to a narrow stairwell. At the top they exited onto the roof where she hid near a roaring AC unit and yanked on his sleeve to pull him close.

She whispered, "They are after you."

He took off his new sunglasses, but was still wearing the rented helmet.

"Mylin, what's going on?"

"They want to know why you follow me."

"I didn't even know you were here. I came to talk to your uncle."

She touched a finger to her lips. "They listen." She held her hands a foot apart. "Elephant microphone."

He smiled. "We're not telling secrets. What happened to you?"

She glanced left toward tarpaper roof and sky, then right at more roof and the low buildings opposite mr. Lee's Bike Shop. She reached up and removed her sunglasses, then brushed strands of dark purple hair away from her face. The tattoo erased all doubt. She spoke rapidly.

"The prison exploded. I flew through the sky on a rope, then rode in Karen's boat. At the river, I thought it was you on the motorbike."

"We guessed you were kidnapped, but we couldn't find you."

Her eyes studied his. "You look for me?"

"Jill told us what happened. Kandy took off to catch you, but there were too many roads." He hesitated. "We couldn't risk bringing in the police."

Mylin released his sleeve and brushed her hair down over her eye. "You are the police."

"I'm working with the FBI agent who came to the prison. You promised to help him if Kandy and I were involved."

Her "Thank you" was barely audible. "But you must leave, they will trap you."

He shook his head. "Can't leave, we have a job to do. How did you find me?"

"Only a few motorbike rentals on the island. Show picture around, give name, promise reward for information. Mr. Lee called. I come and walk by."

He had let himself be predictable, not a good habit for undercover work. "So I would see you?"

"So they can trap you. I tried to get away, but you followed me. You must leave."

"Who grabbed you?"

"We must leave. They will come. You will be caught." She started for the stairwell. He followed. As the doors to the elevator squeezed closed she turned to him. "Do you remember that day you came to the café?"

"A woman drugged me."

"And my brother tried to shoot you." Mylin stepped out of the elevator. "You are not safe from her."

He needed to get a message to Kandy before they grabbed him. He also needed someone to lead him to Carr's missing secrets; the lady from the café would be a good start. He reached out and held her arm gently. "Will you set up a meeting?"

Her eyes grew wide. "Why?"

"They have something we need."

She shook her head. "You will never get it. Please go away."

"You asked us to help you."

"I wasn't sure I could trust the big dark man. If you agreed, I hoped..." She turned away.

He released her arm. "Leave a message for me at Mr. Lee's."

She ran toward the front door.

He considered following, then imagined trained fighters a decade younger than him standing on either side of his bike. He pulled out his Blackphone and headed toward the back of the building. He touched the icon for LookingGlass and wondered how he was supposed to find Mr. Lee's on a map of San Francisco. The obvious struck him; he lifted the phone and said:

"Mr. Lee's Bike Shop."

A red pin dropped onto a map of San Francisco, then the

phone switched to the Signal messaging app with an address for a Starbucks on Third street. As he ran past the closed door to the first floor apartment, he entered:

found mylin here. being followed

When he reached the rear door he stopped. Even amateurs would cover the back exit. After they saw Mylin exit, one guy would enter from each end. He ran up the stairs and down the hall on the second floor to the front of the building. When the guy came in the front door, he would look up the stairs, just as Qigiq had done. He went back to the elevator, waited for it, reached in, pressed 1. With luck they would waste time riding up.

In his rush to catch Mylin, he had let himself be boxed in. He went to the door for the second floor apartment on the bike shop side, let himself in with the edge of his knife, verified no one was home, hustled to the bedroom, and worked the window open. He had noticed outside ductwork. Now he used it to climb down onto Lee's roof and make his way to the front of the bike shop. He set his Blackphone to record video and edged the camera around the corner of the apartment building as he watched the screen. His bike hadn't been moved, and no one was near it.

Qigiq worked his sunglasses on under his helmet.

A woman towing a child in a yellow dress passed from left to right, leaving the sidewalk below empty. He let himself hang down over the slanted storefront of Lee's shop, dropped his feet to the seat of a tall scooter whose shocks swooshed louder than he wanted, and hopped to the ground.

Now he was committed.

He dug the bike key out of his pocket, took a breath, ran straight to the rental bike, shoved the key in, and thumbed the starter. When the engine fired the front door to the apartment building swung open. He dropped into gear, swerved into traffic, and didn't look back.

He looked forward to meeting the woman in the café again. The painter of secret art. The thief of his canvas.

This time, he wouldn't drink the tea.

CHAPTER 10

"YOU FOUND THE RED MAN?" the woman asked.

I stood before a wide desk with sides of cherry wood and a gray sandstone top and nodded. The woman behind the desk had met me in a limousine after my journey from America. She had Aunt Win's slightly pointy nose and the same distant look in her brown eyes. But my aunt died when I was a child. Her face showed tension that made me think she was angry with me—yet we had just met.

She held a thin cigarette. Smoke rose straight up, then whirled like an inverted waterfall. The aroma reached me. The fourth and fifth fingers of my right hand twitched. I longed to hold a cigarette as I had during countless hours of practice as a teenager. Inhale, play a phrase while exhaling, inhale again. With no time to put the cigarette down, I had held it in my bow hand as I played, the smoke painting patterns of rhythm in the air. A moonlit night came to mind; a night I smoked by a pillar; a night when a man named Joe captured me with his camera.

I stared into the woman's brown eyes, flecked with the cheap gold of fake jewelry. My aunt Win had eyes like that. Eyes men worshipped for their uniqueness.

She said, "Why is he not here?"

"I told him you wished to see him." I hesitated, afraid. *I told him to run away.* "He believes he has met you before."

Her thin red lips around the cigarette crawled into a smile. "But he wouldn't come with you?"

"He asked me to arrange a meeting."

She nodded so slowly the cigarette smoke remained undisturbed. "He wishes to prepare. A wise one." She pointed with her free hand. "Your hair."

I frowned, confused.

She flicked the fingers of her free hand. "Push it away from your face."

I sucked in my breath, lifted my arm, and pushed my straight black and purple hair behind my left ear.

She tilted her head. Stood. Leaned forward over the wide desk. "Come closer."

I shuffled forward until my thighs pressed against the stone edge of the desktop.

"A tattoo on your temple."

Not a question.

I rotated my head right so she could see the mark I hid from the world.

She tilted her head in the opposite direction. "A dragon devouring its tail."

"A sign of destruction," I said, explaining something that didn't need explaining.

"That is one interpretation. Is it yours?"

I nodded slowly.

"When did you get it?"

"Years ago." Her expression told me she wanted more. "After my aunt died."

She straightened and walked around the desk until she stood by my left side. She was slightly taller than me, but was wearing high heels.

"This aunt...she was important to you?"

"She and my Grandma helped raise me." And were the only ones who protected me.

"Oh?" She brought the thin cigarette to her lips.

I wished she would remove the temptation of tobacco; I had stopped when my sister Pé died. The smoke in the room conjured Pé's spirit rising to meet our ancestors and was confusing my thoughts.

"My mother died."

"How sad," she said.

"I killed her." Emptiness filled me. "Being born."

She reached up and outlined my tattoo with an icy fingertip. "I see. You are the destroyer. There is a white mark beneath."

Of this I never spoke. Only my father knew I had been scarred in my struggle to enter the world. Some days, I wished I hadn't bothered and had died on the table with my mother. The urge to run back to the Nevada prison where I could be safe rose in me.

I said, "It's nothing."

"You lie to yourself. There is a pockmark. Lighter skin color reveals it. But you hide behind a tattoo for an aunt."

"Forceps. Father said the doctors worked very hard to save me." I hesitated. "And my mother. But they failed her."

The woman returned to her chair and drew on the cigarette, studying me with careful eyes. I took several breaths before she said:

"This burdens you?"

I hadn't thought of it as a burden. "It defines me."

"The destroyer," she said.

I touched my temple with the flat palm of my left hand, hiding it. "Whatever touches me."

"You take a great deal of responsibility for the forces of the Universe."

I pulled my hair back over my left temple and felt instantly stronger. "I only know what I see."

"And you saw your aunt die?"

"No, I saw an urn. Felt her leaving. She had been ill for most of a year."

"That's when you got the tattoo? And your father allowed this?"

I shook my head. "He didn't know for many months."

She tapped her cigarette over a perfectly clean tray of jade. "And then?"

"Then he didn't care because he was already selling me. He said the tattoo was better advertising than a scar."

She leaned far back in her chair and lifted her chin. "What was your aunt's name?"

"We kids called her Win Win."

The woman smiled. "A common Chinese name. It is also mine. What was your mother called?"

"I do not know. After I was born, speaking her name was forbidden in my father's house."

She leaned forward and ground the half-used cigarette out against the pale green stone as if crushing a dangerous insect. Without looking up she said:

"Her name was Ko. Of the Li family."

CHAPTER 11

"WHY ARE WE IN A TENT?" Kandy asked, poking a finger at the stiff white fabric of a makeshift structure on the elaborate grounds of the Hotel Shilla.

"Glamping," Carr said. "Glamorous Camping. Keeps us away from other people. Pretend you're on an African safari with Hemingway."

"Where are the locals to carry my luggage?"

Carr poured sparkling water from a clear bottle. "You don't have luggage."

"I could go shopping," Jill said. "Use your sugar-daddy budget. Jet planes can really excite a girl."

"Uncle Sam is your sugar daddy. I only take out the trash."

Kandy pulled out her Blackphone for the twentieth time, stared at it, then stuffed it back into her dark jeans. "Qigiq is never late."

"Could be lost," Jill offered.

"We're on a volcanic island." Kandy said. "He'll ride straight over the mountain, just for fun."

"You're thinking someone recognized him?" Carr said.

"I'm thinking he's late. He's never late. Ergo…"

"Something has happened," Carr finished for her. "Given our circumstances, something less than ideal."

Kandy reached for her phone again.

"You could strap that to your wrist," Carr offered.

"Why didn't you bring me a secure Black *watch* gizmo? Hey wait." She read. "Qigiq found Mylin. He's under surveillance near a motorbike shop."

"They found him?" Jill asked.

"Qigiq in a bike shop. Who would ever guess that?" Kandy laughed.

"Requesting assistance?" Carr asked.

She shook her head. "No. Updating me. Are these delayed?"

"Blackphones only use comm channels they like. Can take minutes to get a message through."

Kandy placed her phone face up on the marble table at the end of the beige couch. "What's vehicular traffic like over the volcano?" She tested the couch cushion with her hand, then sat down.

Jill tapped her own phone. "Let's see…commute hours on a Wednesday, eight hundred people per square mile on the island, only a couple of roads go over Mt. Halla. Buses travel around to the west."

Kandy's phone vibrated. She leaned forward. "On road. Pumping gas. Stop worrying."

"How long have you two been partners?" Carr asked.

"Going on four months."

"Newlyweds." He laughed.

"Do we have a plan?" Jill asked.

"Step one was to locate Mylin," Carr said. "Only been here an hour and we nailed it."

"What's next?"

"Mylin leads us in," Kandy said. "Then all hell breaks loose."

Carr said, "Are you always so optimistic?"

"Comes naturally."

"You are correct though, we have limited intel on what we'll find. The situation could go south in a hurry."

"Sorry if this is poor timing," Jill said, "but your partner who was shot. How is that related to this?"

"You ask a lot of questions."

"I'm a student, that's my job." She pushed the orange streak in her blonde hair behind her right ear and tossed him a smile.

Carr looked from Kandy to Jill and back. "How did I ever end up with a team like this?"

"Luck," Jill said. "You have the intersection of people you trust, Mylin trusts, and who aren't being tracked by your big bad spy machine."

"Given those constraints," Kandy said, "you're lucky to not be a solo act."

Carr crossed the hardwood floor of the tent and dropped into a puffy chair opposite Kandy, his smooth features creased by a deep frown. "My partner was shot. I'm going after the people responsible. But I'm currently backing up an agent following a container on a ship named *Changqing.*"

"How do you follow a container?" Jill asked.

"He's going to say *very carefully,*" Kandy said.

"You steal my fun," Carr said. "Shirley Sun hired onto the ship as a communications specialist. Basically, a radio operator. That was her job in the Navy before joining the Bureau, so it wasn't much of a technical stretch for her."

"How many are in the know?" Kandy asked.

"That's tricky. Her immediate supervisor, me, and a partner who was supposed to be her contact."

"Not liking that word *was,*" Kandy said.

"He became ill two days before the *Changqing* was scheduled to sail." Carr looked pensive. "I wish Graham would have caught a cold and not been on that pier."

No one spoke for most of a minute.

"Speaking of partners," Kandy said. "I notice my buddy Bain isn't here."

Car spoke quietly. "He's a good guy, but strictly by the book. We had a long conversation. Detectives. Civilians. Foreign country." He shook his head. "Not something he wanted to be involved in. Even though our official role is purely observational, you and Qigiq have clearance, and the kids are just technical consultants, not Blackwater-in-Iraq military contractors, I think Thomas still views this mission as a career-ending move."

Kandy nodded, stroked the side of her phone, and stared into space. "Back to Shirley. You had to find a replacement.

You picked someone with experience you knew to be trustworthy. But you needed approval from his or her boss, and budget approval, and who knows what else to make a reassignment happen."

"Have you worked for the FBI?" Carr said.

"Government bureaucracy is government bureaucracy. Yours is just bigger than mine."

Carr's grin was lopsided. "You're on the right track. They picked a guy named Rodney Arnold. Over twenty years experience, has done a ton of great stuff."

"Where's Rodney now?" Kandy asked.

"On vacation. He took it pretty hard."

"Think we should bring him in?" Jill asked.

"We can, but I have the transcript of his debriefing. One second Sun was on the radio confirming weather information with another vessel, the next the radio was silent."

"Ship security grabbed her," Kandy said. "Accused her of being a spy."

"They didn't arrest her," Jill said. "Or drop her at a port. She never made it to the final destination, did she?"

"You must get good grades," Carr said.

Kandy pushed her phone into a front pocket. "You have a working hypothesis?"

"Computer transaction," Carr said. "Every major government monitors Internet traffic." He paused. "Even though we do our best to hide it. I think someone sniffed a packet that identified the *Changqing*."

Jill searched on her phone. "It's based in Hong Kong."

"How did they get her off?" Kandy asked.

"Can only guess," Carr said. "But based on when the radio stopped and where she was found, probably a chopper."

Kandy sighed. "Happened fast?"

"Yeah," Carr said. "A naval vessel was sent to intercept under the guise of routine inspection BS. No sign of her when they searched."

"Hard to search a whole container ship," Jill said. "Satellites indicate anything?"

"No. But as you know, it was possible for Malaysian Air to lose an entire commercial aircraft."

"So a chopper, or even a small fast boat, might go undetected," Kandy said.

"We'll eventually find out how they did it."

"Maybe too late to help Agent Sun," Jill said. "That's what they counted on. You couldn't respond fast enough without blowing cover on a hundred other assets."

"Maybe not a hundred," he said.

"Poor woman," Kandy said. "What about her backup on the boat?"

"No one heard a thing, including a chopper."

"They're all still alive?"

Carr hesitated. "We think so, yes. But we hesitate to communicate out of an abundance of caution." Carr chewed at his upper lip. "Thus, these Blackphones. I have no idea how deep this goes, or who can hear what."

"What a way to run a railroad," Kandy said. "Is there more?"

"A body with ID washed up on a Chinese beach."

"I don't get it," Jill said.

"A warning," Kandy said. "Or message."

Jill sat up straight. "You mean the body of an FBI agent on a particular beach is telling someone something?"

"They could have dropped her anywhere," Carr said. "Or nowhere. She could just disappear."

"But she didn't," Jill said. "They used her to communicate." She checked her phone even though the screen was dark.

Kandy said, "They're not going to scare the U.S. Government with one body. Even if they piss us off, they can be confident we're not going to admit to spying on a Hong Kong vessel. Hong Kong is a hot potato with China."

Jill stood and paced between the screen door and a potted plant in the corner holding maroon flowers. "So they're telling someone else what's going on?"

"Correct," Carr said. "Someone who needs to know, but

didn't hear it from us."

"Chinese beach," Kandy said. "You have a hunch."

Carr nodded. "I do. They were letting the buyer know how close the USA is to their game. Probably via prearranged proceedings."

"One question," Kandy said. "Why is the FBI involved in international spook stuff?"

Carr leaned back and squeezed the soft arm of his chair. "It's complicated."

Kandy stared at him.

"OK, goes like this. An agency gets a lead on a domestic problem. Clear jurisdiction for the FBI. Things happen. A clue points here or there. When does the project get handed off? How do people from multiple agencies cooperate fast enough to keep up?"

Kandy nodded. "Someone makes a judgement call. When to pursue the bad guys versus when to bring in other agencies. Yeah, that spells complicated."

"What's that sound?" Jill said.

They stayed quiet until Kandy said, "He made good time."

Qigiq stepped through the tent's split-screen masquerading as a main door while unbuckling his helmet. He removed his sunglasses. "Mylin says we'll never find what we're after, go home while we can." He looked around. "We're sleeping in a tent?"

"FBI glamour," Kandy said. "What are we up against?"

"Two guys bucking for promotion to ninja, Uncle Gan, and possibly the woman from Café Rent."

"I shouldn't be surprised," Kandy said, "but I am. Same team as San Francisco. Where do we stand?"

"Mylin is terrified. Told me to go home now, they know I'm here. I asked her to set up a meeting with the lady." He glanced at Jill and Carr. "Sorry I'm late."

"We were just discussing a plan," Carr said.

Qigiq pulled off his helmet, massaged his head, and brushed his dark hair into less of a mess. "We have the paintings." He crossed to a chair in the corner covered with a dark green cloth. "Can you put a tracking device in the one we brought?"

Carr shrugged. "We could. But my organization would know it had been tagged."

"Not if we tag it ourselves," Jill said.

Kandy stood, stretching her right leg, then her back. "Won't they throw it into a vault and wait?"

"Depends," Jill said. "How important are its secrets? If they need them fast, they'll decode it right away."

"Probably using a hunched-over Chinese guy with an abacus in a shack lit by a couple of lanterns," Carr said.

Qigiq pulled off his left boot. "Good. Let's ID that guy, watch him. Who he talks to, how he communicates. Maybe unravel a bit of their world."

"Before or after they snatch one of us?" Carr asked.

"Who do they know about?" Jill asked.

Carr pointed. "Qigiq for sure. Maybe Kandy. Probably Kandy."

"Not you, me, or the photographer?"

Carr shook his head. "Unless they've connected me with Graham." He glanced at Jill. "My late partner for whom I seek retribution. But I've seen no indication."

"That means Qigiq and I go in," Kandy said.

Carr shook his head. "Awfully dangerous."

Qigiq said, "How else do we offer to sell the painting?"

Everyone was quiet.

"It's the original," Jill said softly.

"We tried the duplicate trick back in San Francisco," Kandy said. "How about a GPS transmitter?"

Carr shook his head.

"Radio signal?" Jill suggested.

"They'll scan it."

"What if it only broadcasts once an hour? Or a day?" Jill said.

Carr nodded. "Better."

"What if it only listens?" Qigiq said. "And talks to us when we ask a question."

Carr nodded.

Kandy cracked the knuckles of her left hand. "What if we have Joe put a camera in it? And broadcast only when we ask?"

"Won't they find it?" Jill asked.

Carr slid down in his puffy chair and stared at the toes of his dress shoes. They were shiny enough to reflect moonlight. "Likely."

"Perfect," Kandy said. "First, we sell a painting to this woman who might be the lady in the café to prove she's interested in secret codes. Then our original painting disappears and we can't track it." She reached over the end of the couch and patted Carr's shoulder. "Great plan."

CHAPTER 12

QIGIQ UNDRESSED AND STRETCHED out on a full-size bed two tents and fifty yards from where the team had met. Insects chirped incessantly. Different sound than in Alaska. Here, there were more of them. And they sounded bigger. His superphone showed 4:04 AM local time. The flip of day for night from California time made him restless. Kandy was likely out doing martial-arts exercises to release pent-up energy. The peaked ceiling of the tent carried his thoughts to small cabins made of hand-hewn lumber strung out on a chain of islands—an ocean of food nearby. Alaska had been a pleasant place to grow up and learn how to stay safe in the natural world. Someday he would go back, see what it might hold for him now. Today he was immersed in a digital world he couldn't touch or smell. Sometimes he wondered if it really existed.

The night grew quiet.

He let his right hand drop to the boots beside the bed to retrieve the knife that had been his companion for most of his life. Silence was a warning. The insects were unhappy.

Three thumps shook the zippered tent closure.

He reached to the night stand and pressed the remote control. Across the room, a glass enclosed fireplace came to life, flooding the interior with lush orange light. He grabbed his phone and texted to Kandy:

I have visitors.

He slipped off the bed and crawled along the soft wall away from the entrance to a screened window. Flickering gas torches provided enough light to reveal three bodies standing outside. None were tall enough to be Carr.

Three more thumps shook the zippered door.

The tent had the disadvantage of a single exit. He pressed the tip of the knife into the wall. The material separated slightly.

The zipper on the tent began to rise. He should have locked the zipper to the tent.

His phone lit up: *on my way.*

He moved away from the bed in case the first act was a gunshot at the pillow.

A hand parted the door, followed by a black sleeve, then a man dressed like a secret service agent down to the coiled wire from ear to collar. A black shirt replaced the white shirt and tie. He walked to the far side of the fireplace and stood with his back to the wall. His clone followed and took the near side. Neither searched the tent with their eyes.

A woman wearing a lacy gray shawl followed the glowing ember of a cigarette. Beneath the shawl, a dress, black from shoulder to waist and a white marble pattern from waist to knee, clung to her body. She stopped beside the fireplace and surveyed the interior.

"You have a lovely room, Mr. Qigiq. Excellent feng shui."

He rolled the knife in his palm, wishing he had taken a moment to pull on pants over his briefs.

"Welcome. I apologize that I'm not prepared for visitors."

"I will avert my eyes. Don't mind these gentlemen, they see nothing."

He inched upward. One hand covered her eyes while she smoked with the other. Remaining behind the bed, he pulled on pants, boots (slipping the knife into its spot), and was halfway into a shirt when she lowered her hand. The moment he saw her face—he was certain. He stood.

"How is your painting these days?"

She smiled. "Not many commissions of late."

He motioned to the L-shaped couch facing the fireplace. She sat in the heel of the L. He took the end where he could watch the men who saw nothing, turned to her, and said, "The very reason for my visit."

Her face remained passive except for a slight arching of the left eyebrow. She drew on her cigarette and exhaled toward the fireplace.

"You require an artist?"

"For a special project. One who can locate a buyer for the finished piece."

She surveyed the room. "You are close to nature here."

"And away from others." He asked himself how she had found him. Mr. Lee's shop had seemed so ancient, he hadn't checked for a GPS tracker. Hadn't told Mylin where he was staying. Did this woman have eyes inside the Shilla?

"You prefer isolation?"

"I'm from Alaska. We measure distance in light years."

She laughed a soprano squeal that put his nerves on edge. "Tell me, Mr. Qigiq Flying Hawk from Alaska, how does a lowly city detective arrive on our beautiful island in a private jet?"

She must have half the island on her payroll. "Please call me Qigiq." He shrugged. "Airplanes can be leased." He glanced at the two men and back to her. "I'm sorry I have nothing to offer you. Shall I call room service?"

She met his eyes. "Perhaps they have tea?" She laughed again and waved her hand. "Don't bother, I shall only be a moment. Yes, easy, but not inexpensive."

"I have...supplemental income. Detective work merely provides excitement." He paused. "And access."

She tilted her head, considering him through the smoke-screen of her cigarette.

He felt the urge for tobacco. But he had smoked his last cigarette in Fairbanks and wanted to keep it that way. He crossed his left ankle over his right knee and busied two fingers with the leather edge of his boot—just above the knife.

A rustling sound preceded a shadow passing across the wall of the tent.

The woman frowned and jerked her head. One man headed

for the unzipped door.

Qigiq preferred the new odds.

"You collect art with this other income?"

"Ms....um...I'm sorry, what shall I call you?"

She smiled and flicked ashes on the wood floor.

He nodded and continued. "I gather artworks in my travels and resell them."

She watched smoke from her cigarette swirl toward the peaked roof. "How, may I ask, did you come by this particular painting?"

Back in Fairbanks, he had gone undercover to hunt for illegal gambling. He recalled advice from a colleague who specialized in undercover work: the right information at the right time. No more—no less.

"I rescued it from a burning house."

Her eyes flashed to his face, then darted away—an involuntary response. They settled on the flames slithering behind glass. He had surprised her. She must have assumed the Sausalito fire destroyed everything. A new can of worms was now open.

"A fire? Wasn't that dangerous?"

He shook his head. "Foresight."

Her eyes became glassy, distant. "What kind of buyer would you be looking for?"

"One who understands that seven figures is a bargain."

She crushed her cigarette out on the marble top of a small table beside the couch and interlaced her fingers on her lap. "This must be a very beautiful painting indeed."

"A hazy landscape of greens and blues. Too much sky for my taste. But for the right buyer..." He shrugged.

"May I see it?"

One of the risks of improvising—painting oneself into a proverbial corner. The picture was on the plane. How to show it and walk away alive?

"A good faith deposit perhaps? Say a hundred thousand U.S.?"

She smiled slightly, stood, and crossed to where he sat. Standing close, his eyes level with her breasts under black cloth, she lit another cigarette with a slender silver lighter that encased a single pearl visible from both sides. She smoked with her right hand and brushed the dark hair across his forehead with the fingertips of her left, gazing into him all the while.

He felt her probing for truth. He tried not to blink.

"You're not of the white devils. Why do you work with them?"

"Opportunity," he said, which was absolutely true. He had gone to San Francisco to experience technology. But that wasn't the opportunity he wanted her to think about.

She stopped stroking. Her hand disappeared behind her. The man by the fireplace moved.

Qigiq's hand lowered toward his knife.

Her hand returned holding two thick envelopes. She dropped them on the couch.

He said, "There are other paintings."

"How many?"

He smiled without taking his eyes from the flecks of gold in her irises. "More than one."

She sat down beside him on the couch, the two envelopes between their thighs. She said, "How shall we do this?" But she seemed to be asking herself.

CHAPTER 13

JOE ROBERTS' HEAD RESTED against the padded back of a chair bolted to the floor of Uncle Sam's Mercedes van. The computer monitor showed 11:47 AM Thursday. He was daydreaming about the touch of Nashi's hands when Jill Kiner poked his arm.

"Hey new partner, how come we have to sit here and do nothing?"

"Is that rhetorical?"

"Not if you know something I don't."

He worked himself upright. "All I know is Carr's orders, and I quote, 'You are civilians. Observe only. No contact unless you are in immediate danger.'" Joe thought about the woman in blue and Nashi's phone number. Important? Or melodrama.

"I'm *observing* a mile-long stretch of crappy sand with nothing on it but lily-white tourists from foreign lands. I left a five-star resort for this?"

"You left to monitor cameras. We are Big Brother. Um, and sister." He smiled. "We have to cover the whole island. Establish a presence. Carr wants locals to see this truck, so they won't remember it later if things get weird. Personally, I think we're emotional support pets for Mylin. He needs her a hundred percent engaged."

Jill stepped forward and put both palms down flat on the narrow desk. Above it hovered an array of eight monitors covering the inside of the vehicle like wallpaper. "The only reason we're here is because Carr couldn't get anyone else." She studied each monitor in turn. "Nothing is happening."

"Nothing is supposed to happen."

"So I'm stuck in this tin can?"

"We have a fridge." He grinned.

"What is it with men and food?" She turned full circle. "Look at this place. A zillion computers, drones, rifles I don't know how to shoot, laser guided grenades that I *might* be able to launch in a pinch. And bicycles. Why do we have bicycles?"

Joe resisted the temptation to spin his chair around to face her. As soon as he did, something important would fly past one of the cameras. Not that the system needed him, the computers were analyzing the camera feeds too.

"Same reason cops use bikes, so we can go places the van can't. Plus, you can ride to a station if we run out of gas."

"We'll flip for that," Jill said. "Unless you want to arm wrestle." She paused. "Why the war equipment if we don't get to play?"

"Secrecy, I'd say. If Carr keeps these toys in his hotel room, or rents a storage unit, someone will find them. This way they're hidden in a delivery van."

"Carr thinks local cops will never look inside a delivery van?" She shook her head.

"I've been studying this contraption for a week. Watch this."

He dug the key fob out of his pocket and pressed the button for the rear doors three times, paused, three more, paused, one. The van made sighing sounds as sheets rolled from the roof down either side. The table dropped and folded. His chair shook so he stood, then it collapsed into the floor.

He and Jill now occupied an empty van.

"Slick," she said. "Why didn't you tell me it did that?"

"Carr gave me the code just this morning. He said to use it if we get stopped by anyone at all, 'even locals thumbing a ride.' I hadn't tried it until now."

"At least it's a trick tin can. What else can it do?"

"Carr claimed that it's faster than it looks. And gave me this." Roberts removed an iPad from a duffle bag. "Electronic

Documentation on how to run everything. I've only looked at my specialty—cameras."

Jill took the device and paged through it. "Diagrams. Use case scenarios. Classified stamped all over it. Do you have clearance?"

"If you mean an official background check by spooks in Washington DC, not that I know of. Carr just handed it to me and said, 'Don't lose it.'"

"So it's OK for me to read it?"

"I doubt it. But I'm not going to arm wrestle you for it."

She grinned. "Show me why you stare at TVs all day, Mr. Roberts."

"Surely, Ms. Kiner." He punched the code into the key fob again. More sighing resulted in the monitors sliding out of the walls. He offered her the one chair.

"Thanks, I'll stand. You be the super spy. What are we really doing here?"

Joe sat and scanned the monitors. "These show eight cameras at a time. But the system monitors over a hundred. The computer analyzes all of them for activity and shows us the interesting ones."

"Man, if these are the interesting ones, the others must be watching golf. Did you set this up?"

"The van was parked at the hotel when I arrived. I've hidden cameras for years as part of my business. Installing them around the island wasn't much different."

"Business?"

"I'm a photographer. I take pictures of people who don't know I'm doing it."

"Sounds creepy. You're not a spy?"

"No. I'm a starving artist. That's how I met Mylin."

Jill grew quiet and focused on the monitors. Eventually she said, "So what are we looking at?"

He pointed. "In front of our van. Behind us. That beach runs for a couple of miles. Those pictures are from a drone flying at a thousand feet with the camera pointed straight down."

"Won't all this video communication lead the bad guys to us?"

"According to Carr, the drones use a pulsed-laser system. Limits them to line of sight, but makes them exceedingly hard to listen to."

"I saw a laser at an astronomy talk. The lecturer pointed a bright green line into the sky to explain different constellations."

Joe shook his head. "I haven't seen laser traces. All I know is: pulse for a few milliseconds, then silent, then pulse. And they're smart enough to relay from one device to the other until the signal gets to the van."

"OK, we have electronic eyes. What are we looking for?"

"Whatever Carr wants. He hasn't asked for anything yet."

The video on #6 froze: a still frame of a man's face and torso. Beside it, #7 switched to a stored photograph of four people. The computer drew a red circle around a man in the back row.

"Who's that?" Jill asked.

"Facial recognition match on document DR-252-89. If this thing knows a name, it's not sharing."

She leaned in closer. "Asian. About fifty. Suit fits like he bought it in Milan. Got more pics?"

Joe worked a keypad that was more television remote than computer. A second screen showed four pictures taken with increasing zoom.

"Now we're talking," Jill said. "I'd guess he's sixty-eight inches tall, is loaded with dough, and has a three shot handicap on the links."

"You get his handicap from a picture?"

She pointed. "Golf green in the corner. Flag for the eighteenth hole. If this was taken on the island, we can find that course." She gestured at a building in the upper right corner. "Carr's super-spy computers wouldn't show this to us if it weren't relevant. The stone construction verifies that it's the building those guys are coming out of in that first pic. Looks expensive to me."

Joe studied the picture. A sense of something hidden that he of all people should be seeing went through him. He said:

"How does that building tell you his handicap?"

"Deduction. An old guy has a lifetime to refine his game. He's walking out of a posh club on a paradise island. The guy beside him is short, pudgy, and if you'll pardon my subjective evaluation, a tad ugly, so he must be important. A Chinese businessman never plays golf with someone important unless they themselves can make a decent showing. The entire country is hyper-competitive, maybe even more so than the Japanese, if that's possible."

"And from this arm-chair analysis you conclude?"

"Our target is rich, rubs elbows with a person we want to know more about, and plays a mean round of golf—although he lets the fat guy win most of the time. Not always, of course. If he always lost, the fat guy would know the man was throwing games and lose face. That would be bad for everyone."

"I'm about to ask you how you come by your incredible insights. But first, who won today?"

"The fat guy. Look at that smile on his face."

"How do you know they didn't just ink a business deal, and the, uh, short guy, is feeling good about it?"

Jill shook her head, orange flashing midst her blonde locks.

"No way. They would both be stoic, each thinking he had bested his opponent. They would each let the other poor sucker save face. For sure these guys were playing golf. But, of course, talking about more important matters between shots."

"You've studied the business practices of the Chinese?"

Jill twisted toward him wide-eyed. "You're psychic. That was the exact title of the course I took at the University of San Francisco: Business Practices of the Chinese. It only covered the last fifty years. I wish it would have gone back and shown how things have changed over millennia."

"You think things change?"

She smiled. "Back then there was no golf." She turned to

face the close up.

"Something bothering you about his face?" Joe said.

Jill nodded. Slowly. Like she wasn't sure of her answer.

Joe held a button on the controller, then lifted it and spoke. "Mylin close up. Facing thirty degrees stage left."

Jill met his eyes. "You see it too?"

"Maybe. However, I'm obsessed. I see her everywhere."

Mylin's picture popped up beside DR-252-89. Joe had seen a lot of faces through a viewfinder in his time—this was a long shot.

"Related?" Jill asked.

"I vote yes. I think we found Mylin's uncle. Unless she calls all male authority figures uncle."

"We didn't," Jill said. "Carr's face-recognizing computer did. So why is Uncle playing golf with fat boy? And..." her eyes fixated on the two faces. "What do we do now?"

"Are you sure you wouldn't like to sit down?" Joe asked.

She shook her head. "Too nervous."

"We wait until Carr contacts us. He was extremely clear that the lowly civilians should take absolutely no initiative."

"Yeah," she laughed. "He thinks we'll end up in hot water, and he'll have to ride in and save us before we tarnish his shiny FBI badge."

Joe could see the tension in Jill's jaw; waiting didn't suit her. He, however, was accustomed to it. Sometimes he waited for hours for a photo op to present itself—like the shot he had taken of Mylin in Ann Arbor that started this crazy journey. Patience was important when doing surveillance. Patience was a virtue. A job requirement. But mostly—it was boring.

"What do you like to do, Jill?"

She turned. Straightened. Seemed lost in thought. "May I have that chair now?"

Joe laughed. "Thought you would never ask." He stood and stepped aside. "Please don't touch the controls until you've read the classified manual that you didn't get from me."

She dropped into the chair and spun it like a kid meeting

office furniture for the first time. She stopped it facing Joe.

"Let's follow Uncle."

CHAPTER 14

QIGIQ PLACED TWO ENVELOPES on the dark wood table in Carr's tent.

"From our lady friend who wouldn't give me a name. I'm to wait for a message via Mr. Lee at the bike shop."

"How close is Lee?" Kandy asked.

"Not close," Carr answered. "She's smart enough to use a random islander. We grab him, he can tell us exactly nothing."

"She must trust him," Qigiq said.

"He could rat on her," Kandy said. "But he has to live here. If he gets clever, she'll make his life miserable. I vote he delivers a cryptic message he doesn't even understand, if and when she decides to talk to us." She gestured toward the table. "Think those have GPS trackers in them?"

Carr rotated the envelopes with the tip of a blue Hotel Shilla ballpoint pen. "We might as well assume they do and behave accordingly. How much did she give us?"

"I haven't opened them, but I mentioned a hundred thousand good faith deposit."

Carr tapped the table with the pen. "Why would she trust you with a hundred grand?"

"Speculation?" Kandy asked. No one objected. "Two reasons. One, whatever is in those paintings, she wants desperately."

"Man, I wish we knew," Carr said. "Any word from your computer guy?"

"Ferdinand and the professor were hard at work when we flew out, but they hadn't found a translation." Qigiq stared at the envelopes. "When they do, they don't have a secure channel to reach us."

Carr chewed his lower lip.

Qigiq felt like the hunter becoming the hunted in a dime novel.

"We either bring the science geeks here," Kandy said, "which exposes them to discovery and risk. Or we pull them into our Sealed Circle and hope it stays secure across an ocean."

Carr tapped an envelope. "Of those two options, I think our work would go faster if they were here. But they'll need lab equipment."

Qigiq crossed to the entrance of Carr's tent, which was currently zipped closed. "And a security force to protect them."

"Agreed," Carr said. "We need to protect that student and the photographer too." He took a breath and sighed it out. "But I don't have people. We're here under the radar, fact-finding. If we find interesting facts, we might get help. Maybe."

"OK," Kandy said. "I'm officially nervous, which is not a place I generally inhabit. Let me review, you guys tell me if I've lost my mind."

"You're really going to let me tell you that?" Carr said, smiling.

Qigiq located Shilla stationary in the drawer of the corner table and found a four inch pencil with the name of the resort embossed in gold.

"I'd rather know I'm confused before I hurt someone," Kandy said. "First, something is missing. Mylin is supposed to get us close to the people who made that something go missing."

"Right," Carr said, dropping the pen to the table as he leaned away from the envelopes.

"However," Qigiq added as he wrote with the stubby pencil, "this something is so sensitive that Carr's boss is concerned about security—inside and outside the Bureau."

"Right again," Carr said. "No FBI involvement. I've been told to get this back because I had the relationship with the informant—and now with the informant's daughter. Along with responsibility for popping her out of prison."

Kandy said, "The hot potato is in our lap."

"Exactly."

"Bottom line," Qigiq added. "Our job is to uncover sufficient information so other parties can take action—without causing new problems."

"Preferably," Carr said.

"Which brings us back to Ferdinand," Kandy said. "How can his magic bag of science tricks help us if we can't bring him in?"

"How about an all-expenses-paid vacation," Carr said, grinning. "I'll send our plane back for him."

"Let Ferd decide. But I vote he'll jumps at a vacation like this."

"Where do we have secure meetings if our plane is gone?" Qigiq asked.

"I'll get another one. Better yet, I'll order up a supply plane and sneak the science team onto it. They'll need the extra space, it'll be harder for anyone to know who's on it, and I can keep sleeping in our plane where I feel safe." He looked around at the walls of the tent.

Qigiq sat down beside Kandy. "I agree so far. This woman wants what we have badly enough to put up money in advance."

"We think," Carr said. "We haven't opened the envelopes yet."

Qigiq nodded. "What's the second reason?"

Kandy said, "Tracking. If that's a hundred grand in cash, she knows you aren't going to keep it in a tent. So what *will* you do with it?"

They were quiet for a moment.

Qigiq said, "They're watching me, correct?"

"All of us," Kandy said. "And I don't like it. I'm supposed to be the detective watching other people. On this island, I'm off home turf, don't know the customs, or the language, or any informers..."

"A lot can go wrong," Carr said.

Qigiq stared out a clear windowpane. It would be easy for someone to hide out there with binoculars or a rifle scope pointed at the tent. He reached up, poked the flexible plastic, and said:

"Dragon eyes are everywhere."

"Exactly," Carr said. "So where should we lead them?"

CHAPTER 15

I STOOD ON THE SECOND FLOOR near a tall narrow window framed with cherry wood. Sunlight fell on the sheet music that had been on the stand waiting for me. Gray bands as wide as my finger striped the page: shadows from black steel bars over the window. The woman who shared a name with my aunt Win said the bars protected me from intruders. Local residents resented foreigners on their island including Chinese from the mainland and the Japanese who had invaded a hundred years ago. But those bars also made sure I couldn't leave—something I would do the moment I had a place to go. A place that wasn't a concrete prison cell in the Nevada desert.

The room wasn't extravagant, but felt spacious after prison. It even had a bath with a shower covered in tiles made from the sands of the island. And a kitchen where I could prepare duck dishes—if I could locate a duck. Metal screeched as a key turned an old lock.

The door to my room glided inward.

I stopped playing—wishing I would be left alone to work on this Beethoven. I was hesitating on the dotted rhythms, sounding like a student who didn't practice.

Win entered, her red silk gown with a dragon from neckline to hem flipping around her ankles. Her movements brought my aunt to life in my mind. She traversed the room with eyes fixated on me, sat on the side of the bed, and crossed her legs. It was a high bed, with white posts and golden sheets that shimmered in the striped afternoon sunlight.

"Come, Mylin," she patted the spot beside her, "we must

speak. There is work to be done."

I returned the viola to the blue fur of its case.

"Leave it open," Win said. "The grain of the wood adds a natural accent to your room." She swiveled her head to take in a space that could hold four prison cells. "This room needs more accents to be welcoming."

"You've done so much for me. Please do not trouble yourself with more."

Win met my eyes. A slight smile touched her red-painted lips. She brushed her hair back with one hand revealing gray hairs that proved she was no longer young, though her body was slender, and her manner confident.

"My dear, I am not concerned about you. Quickly now."

I left the lid upright, then stood and faced this woman I had only known for a day.

"Remove those silly American rags. We must fit you with something appropriate."

I was still wearing captain Karen's gifts; they and my instrument were my only possessions. I hesitated, even though my experience told me that I had no choice. I drew inside myself and removed the striped shirt, the high-heeled boots of smooth leather, and the jeans that stopped below my knees. I folded and stacked everything beside my instrument. Sunshine warmed my back as I stood beside the music stand, unable to read the slightest emotion in the eyes that seemed to swallow me.

"I see why you were the popular one in the orchestra."

My surprise must have seeped out despite my effort to remain poker faced.

"Your uncle follows your activities carefully."

"Thank you," I said softly, not knowing what my dead father had told my uncle. I was simply the violist in the orchestra (and *The Geisha Quartet* an internal voice reminded me).

"Let us choose a dress for you," Win said. She stood and began to turn, but stopped. "Mylin, your feet!"

I looked down at the same feet I always saw: my second toe slightly longer than my big toe. They were flattened against the cool bamboo floor.

"We must wrap them in white so they appear less...monstrous. Come."

Win watched while I shaved my legs and washed my hair using shampoo and soap that smelled of blossoms and honey. She passed a fresh razor to me. I removed hair from between my legs until she was satisfied. Then she sat me on the side of the bed naked and proceeded to wrap my feet from toe to ankle with a soft strip of white cloth. The material was comforting, almost like a massage, though very snug.

She glanced at a round watch on her wrist, glittering gold in the afternoon sunshine. She spun the rim and the face displayed a message I couldn't read, and the time, which I could: *PM 1:07.*

She stood. "We must guess at the color. Tell me Mylin, what did you wear in America?"

I wondered at the correct answer. The gun and prison and flight to this island and time zone changes had muddled my mind. Did she want information? Was Uncle Gan testing me?

"Whatever I was told to wear."

She smiled. Slowly. Like it was rising from a deep place that she rarely visited.

"Of course. But tell me, what colors seem to suit you best? Not red, I will be wearing red, and we must not appear as equals."

I thought of my favorite dresses. Of the request from the tall man with the curvy convertible he claimed had been handmade in England. I remembered the sensation of those dresses clinging to my body, gazed into the distance, and recited his words from memory:

"The green of emeralds polished a thousand times, the blue of the southern sea under a blazing sun, the blackest black of midnight on the run."

She stared with unconcealed anger in her eyes. Finally, she

said, "You have been trained into an enticing woman. I think for the afternoon we shall choose green."

Father was finally dead; yet others were still making decisions for me. I chastised myself for being ungrateful. Shen was dead, that much had changed. He would never abuse me again. I felt the hot memory of the trigger of Uncle Gan's pistol on my fingertip.

Win nodded, believing I agreed with green.

The dress she brought from the walk-in closet was indeed the color of emeralds. She gave me lacy lingerie in snow-capped-mountain white. Too much lace, but Win insisted. The dress reached below my knee and was snug along my hips and thighs. She wriggled high-heeled boots of deep-gray leather and fine mesh onto my feet, just tall enough to cover the ankle wrapping. I crossed the room so she could examine me.

"Perfect," she declared.

She added dangling silver chain earrings, each tipped with a tiny star of black onyx.

"Yes," she said, apparently satisfied. "Stay here." She headed out, swaying in her red gown. In the doorway she stopped and turned. "Practice while you wait. Remember, how you behave tonight is very important. Your uncle does not waste time on trivial matters."

The door closed. The old lock scraped. The sound was small, but as final as the clang of the steel door in Nevada. I squatted to retrieve my instrument, my toes three centimeters above the floor. Standing, I stared out between the bars, arms at my side, the bow dangling from my fingertips. Sunshine warmed my chest.

Where was I?

Jeju Island, yes. Fifty miles long. It had seemed gigantic at the age of twelve: already years older than Mozart had been when he toured Europe to play for kings and queens. I smiled. Mozart I was not. I could barely do justice to his compositions when performing them; I had no hope of composing such sublimity. Of course, no one else in the hundreds of years since his death could compose like Mozart either.

The world two stories below my window appeared...frantic...like an ant colony kicked by a mean little girl. I tucked the instrument under my chin and began the Beethoven, playing from memory the music on the stand to my left. Its flowing energy provided counterpoint to the street: a taxicab honking as it swerved; two girls in short skirts and tall shoes like mine crossing a street waving cell phones; a man with a white cane moving left and right like a metronome; a woman in a maroon hat and gray skirt towing a child in American blue jeans and a T-shirt with Hello Kitty on her chest; a fat man in clothes the color of rain clouds stepping from the back of a limousine like the one I had taken from the airport; and lastly (I reached the dotted rhythms that confused me and let my fingers find their way), an old man in a crumpled hat shuffling slowly, hunched forward, a hand on his left hip, carrying a sack in his hand that I would bet was filled with groceries.

So many people.

So much Qi life energy.

So many ways to be free.

I wanted to be down there, one more ant struggling among them.

Three sharp knocks startled the bow out of my hand.

I picked it up and returned the instrument to its case, my mind returning to the room, the present moment, the words Win had spoken about the woman I had become.

What will they demand of me?

I stopped at the mirror and brushed hair down over my tattoo. The tiny black stars on my ears danced at the end of their chains. "I too am chained," I whispered to them carelessly, wanting to dream of being free—but having no time for silly self-indulgence.

My feet, stuffed inside of foot wrapping and new boots, barely obeyed me as I made my way to the door. Why would she knock after having locked it from the outside? I rotated the knob and pulled.

The door didn't budge.

I touched the keyhole above the doorknob. There was nothing to turn without a key.

The sharp knocks repeated.

I took two steps toward the dresser where I had examined myself in the mirror. Without a key, I was trapped. I opened and closed drawers, searched for a jewelry box, ashtray, jar—anything that might hold a key. I went to the center of the room and turned in a circle. Win said I had been trained well. Where would—?

I ran my thumb along the neckline of my new dress and into the lace decorating my bra. My fingertips touched hardness. I had the key in the lock and turning when the knocks came again. By the time I yanked the door open, I was breathless.

A rotund man in the hallway stood eye-to-eye with me. He was Chinese and wore the cloud-gray suit of the man I had seen exiting the limousine. He was alone. His smile showed misaligned teeth.

I bowed my head.

"At last we meet," he said in English, returning my bow. "Who I am is unimportant. You may call me Long."

"I am Mylin. It is a pleasure to meet you, Mr. Long."

He stepped through the doorway without waiting for an invitation.

"I have known of your beauty for many months. And what a fine musician you are, as I heard through the door." He walked past not looking at me, but gazing toward the window. "I see you have received my gift of the Beethoven score. Are you enjoying it?"

His gift?

The sound of the people on the street reached me through the window. I slowly removed the key from the lock with my left hand. A feverish desire filled my legs.

"Yes. It is filled with beauty and technical challenges. You are very wise to have chosen it for me."

He held a squarish black case like doctors carry in American Westerns. I had watched many such movies on TV in silence while a man snored beside me in the days when the orchestra traveled across the United States. I inhaled slowly to hold back tears. My dear sister Pé was dead. Thirty-nine musician friends burned alive. My father, my elder brother. The feverish energy reached my heart.

"You will play it for me," Long said, turning to face me.

I held out my right hand American-business style.

"It would honor me to play for you."

His eyes dropped to my hand, and came up smiling. "She said you had traveled to the West, so I should be ready for surprises."

He raised his hand to clasp mine. The weak grip of pudgy fingers felt like half-cooked noodles.

Fever filled my lungs.

I bowed and squeezed with all my strength.

His eyes locked onto my face. The instant I relaxed, he yanked his hand away.

I leapt and slammed my elbow into his chest. He fell backwards onto the bed. I raced to the door and jerked it closed behind me. I held my breath as I struggled to insert the key into the upper lock with my left hand. The knob began to move in my right.

The key turned. I pulled it out.

And ran.

CHAPTER 16

"*WHAT DOES SHE LEAST EXPECT?*" Qigiq asked.

"Us to disappear with her cash," Carr said. "But if we do, she'll chase us until she gets a look at that painting. In the end, we might not even have what she wants."

"All this drama for a No Sale," Kandy said. "You guys are cheering me up."

Carr paced the length of the business jet between window shades pulled all the way down. Low interior lighting suggested an aircraft about to land.

"What would make her happy?" Qigiq said.

Carr stopped. "We stash the paintings in a safe spot for her to pick up, then disappear."

Kandy shook her head. "She'd sense a teaser. The clever Americans hide the good stuff and hold out for a bigger payday."

"We sort of are." Carr laughed and examined a food tray he had conjured from the Shilla, found a slice of meat, and popped it into his mouth.

"If we deposit the cash in a local bank," Qigiq said, "her spies will take note."

"Why would the clever Americans use a South Korean bank?" Kandy asked.

Carr said, "Avoid getting get caught carrying that much paper into the U.S. Use the bank to launder an international transfer."

Kandy watched Carr at the food tray. "Doesn't seem secret enough. What kind of bad guys use banks to move money with tracking a government pastime?"

"Corporations." Carr moved along the tray. "They do tricky stuff every day. Remember the Panama Papers? Billions of dollars hidden in offshore accounts. Or how about that island nation of Nauru where anyone can set up their own bank for twenty grand? I've seen reliable intel that the Russians moved a hundred billion through a shack with a computer in it when the Soviet Union collapsed."

"What does she want to know?" Qigiq asked.

"If this Qigiq guy is the real deal," Kandy said instantly. "And does he have the goods? If he does, her hundred grand tells me she wants them." She paused to glance at Carr still poking at the food tray. "And fast. Which is good, people make mistakes when they're in a hurry."

"She's the painter," Qigiq said. "We met in San Francisco when I gave her that canvas from Birk's safe. That means she knows we know about Birk."

"And she knew Shen," Kandy said. "He was in the back room when she drugged you. Think dragon lady has spies in the U.S. too? And knows he's dead?"

Carr nodded vigorously. "It's been weeks. If they tracked Mylin's breakout close enough to grab her, they surely know about the dead brother."

"I say they want to know if Mylin's tongue's been wagging," Kandy said. "Do you think they can trace that hundred grand?"

"They'll trace the bank transaction," Carr said. "See where it leads."

"And where do we want it to lead?" Kandy asked.

"A mistake." Carr said, smiling. "They'll trace it for sure if we spend it on the island." He paused in thought. "We could bribe her spies, maybe find one who doesn't much like the lady."

"Or...do nothing," Kandy said. "That might convince her we're connected in ways that let us fly into the U.S. and walk a hundred grand through customs."

Qigiq drummed the table with a finger, the steady beat

helping him concentrate. Without stopping the rhythm he said, "This may sound wishy-washy, but what if we attack her defenses on multiple fronts? Spend twenty grand extravagantly. Show her we don't really care about such small potatoes. Then I talk to Mr. Lee, have him put the word out that I'm paying for information related to the Dragon Lady."

"Feels like action," Kandy said. "Gets my vote."

"We also put thirty grand into a bank for local financial support."

"And we hold onto fifty thousand to take back with us," she said. "Buy me a new car as a reward for sitting around doing nothing."

Qigiq said, "You just got a new car."

"Planning ahead." She grinned. "Did you see what the FBI makes me drive?"

Qigiq inched a shade upward and squatted. A black sedan was parked in the gray shadow of the maintenance hut. "Looks fast."

"V-six, no turbo, four-speed automatic. I'll be lucky if it will climb the volcano so I can gawk at the pretty red lava."

"Hallasan," Carr said. "Highest in South Korea. Visible from everywhere on this island. It's only 6,400 feet, you'll be able to climb it okay."

"Not fast though," she complained.

"I like your idea of taking a chunk of cash back with us," Qigiq said. "Prove that customs point you mentioned."

"Who wants what?" Carr asked.

"I'll take Mr. Lee. He's already met me."

"And ratted on you," Kandy said. "I'd kill the banker. They move like robots with dead batteries. Can I have the extravagant party option?"

Carr chuckled. "Sure. I'll take the bank. Far as I know, they don't have my face yet. That might encourage them to trace the cash."

"I thought we were saving the cash for Ferd and the nerd crew," Kandy said as she stood.

"We'll leave half untouched. The forensics people can study the fifty thousand we'll be smuggling into the U.S." Carr pointed a finger back and forth between the two envelopes. "Eeny, meeny, miny, moe. Catch the dragon by her toe—"

"Give me cash, and let me go," Kandy said.

"Which one?" Carr asked.

Kandy and Qigiq moved to the table and stared down at the two manila envelopes. Same color, same size, sealed with a metal clasp taped over with clear fiber-reinforced tape.

"Any chance there's something in these besides money?" Qigiq asked.

Carr flipped one over with his ballpoint. "Anthrax powder. Tracking device. Explosives."

"Thanks for the warm thoughts, Agent Optimist. What do you really think?" Kandy said.

"She'll play it straight until she gets what she wants. After that, all bets are off."

"Any markings?" Qigiq asked.

"They're identical," Carr said. "Right down to the length of tape used to secure them."

"Guys, just open one at random. I'm dying of inactivity here."

Carr pressed his elbow down on the packet nearest him and slit the end open using his ballpoint.

Nothing happened.

He upended the envelope; packets of bills tumbled to the table.

Kandy leaned forward. "Fifty thousand *won* notes?"

"Common denomination," Carr said. "The exchange rate jumps around, but it's worth about fifty U.S. dollars."

Qigiq counted twenty packs, maybe fifty bills in each. "Issued by the Bank of Korea."

"Sounds impressive," Kandy said.

"Twenty packs at twenty-five hundred dollars per pack. Fifty grand," Carr said. He pushed the packs around with his pen. "How about you each take five? I'll deposit the other ten."

He hesitated. "In fact, let me go first. The bank will check. If this stuff is counterfeit, you might have to bail me out."

Kandy stuffed packs into her nylon jacket. "You think she wants us to get caught passing funny money? That'd create a public relations problem for Uncle Sam."

"The thought crossed my mind."

"Keeps us out of the way until she swoops in and saves us. Improves her bargaining position."

Carr gathered up ten packs. He popped open an overhead compartment and brought down a thin briefcase, dumped a sheaf of papers and a pair of pens out of it, and inserted the money. "I'm going to play this loud. Walk into the bank and find whatever they call a vice president, and demand that he check every one of these bills before I accept them as payment in a business deal. If these are fake, the bank will probably call the cops. The cops will confiscate my property and ask lots of questions."

"And what'll you do?" Kandy asked.

"Show them her picture and wait for their reaction." He grinned.

"When did you get her picture?" Qigiq asked.

"Leaving your tent last night. Joe Roberts has infrared cameras all over the island."

"Robot eyes watching a dragon." Kandy said, stuffing money into the back pockets of her pants. "Agent Carr, I like your style."

CHAPTER 17

JILL SAT CROSS-LEGGED and barefoot on the narrow desk that popped out below eight monitors. She alternated between meditating with her eyes closed and staring at two displays, one above the other. They showed the software's choice of every building or road deemed important. Her boots stood in the corner of the van beside the iPad she had been using to read classified documents. She inhaled a huge breath that filled her slender body from navel to throat—then let it out through her nose to a silent count of ten.

"Why don't you read more about guns?" Joe said. "You seemed to be enjoying that."

Jill spoke without opening her eyes. "I can only take in so much abstract instruction without firing an actual weapon." She popped one eye open to study the rightmost monitor. "It's too quiet in here. We need an explosion."

"I could pop a balloon when you're not looking."

"Cute." Jill scrunched her mouth in thought. "We're on an island fifty miles wide, and this is the best action your super-spy cameras can find? How do we know this system is working?"

"Does that manual say the super-spy AI is looking for action?"

"Not in so many words. It said something like, um..." She closed her eyes. *"Analyzing visual data relevance as defined in the current project profile parameters."*

"There you go. Adjust your project profile parameters."

"I'm afraid to mess—" She stiffened. "No way! That's Mylin!"

Joe shifted in the chair. "What? Where? You're blocking the screen."

Jill leaned away so he could confirm she wasn't hallucinating. "Exiting that three story building. A hotel—or a mansion. Our super computer has a lock on her face."

The picture swiped left. A woman in a green calf-length dress was running along the street, the dress confining her to small, quick steps.

"She shouldn't run in those boots," Jill said. "She'll break an ankle."

"Or fall and break her arm. Then she won't be able to play. And might never recover full use of her hand."

"Wow, your glass is half-empty."

"I worry about her," Joe said. Their eyes met. The picture cut to Mylin half a block down the street, her body partially obscured by a girl in a pink helmet riding a blue motor scooter racing in the opposite direction.

"Is this delayed?" Jill asked.

Joe moved close to the monitor and checked his watch. "Ten seconds."

Jill spun off the desk, her feet thudding hard against the metal floor. "You mean she's running right now? Not like an hour ago. And your spy system just told us?"

"*My* spy system?"

"You're the peekaboo photographer. Let's go help her."

The screen cut to Mylin bent forward at the waist, no longer running.

"What makes you think she needs help?" Joe asked.

Jill pulled her left boot on. "When have you ever known Mylin to not need help?"

Joe hesitated. "Uh, when she's performing."

Jill stopped halfway into the boot. "Point taken. But this isn't that."

The image expanded to the leftmost monitors. Then updated.

"She's taking off her shoes," Joe said.

"She wants to run faster. I told you she needs help."

Jill zipped the boot up over her ankle and reached for the other one.

Joe scrambled for the remote control. "I recall reading about a panoramic mode—"

The eight screens became a single giant image covering the side of the van like a monitor array at an all-night rave. Mylin was two-thirds of the way to the right with a shoe in each hand. She had hiked up her dress and was running with the long strides of a sprinter pressing for the finish line.

Jill hopped up to Joe's side, still zipping her second boot. "That guy is chasing her." The picture updated across all monitors. "OH NO! It's the ugly guy from the golf course. No wonder she's running. Let's go!"

"Jill, Jill, we can't. Carr told us to *remain invisible* until we heard from him."

Her eyes flashed between Joe's face and Mylin's pursuer. "We can't let him catch her."

Mylin stopped behind a dozen pedestrians waiting for traffic to clear an intersection. In the next update, she was gone.

"We lost her! Where are these pictures coming from?"

Joe worked the remote. Numbers popped onto the screen. "GPS location." One monitor changed its display. "Aerial view of the neighborhood."

"Chase her with your drone!" Jill said.

"These are *satellite* aerials, that's why the delay. The system will try to auto-track her."

"A ball in outer space can see a face on the street?" She scowled at him. "We can't," she said softly. "We can't just do nothing. Let's drive over there."

Joe stepped between Jill and the wall of monitors that were showing the fat guy plodding along the street. He made her meet his eyes.

"Jill. How is chasing Mylin with a white van remaining invisible? We can't do anything that jeopardizes the mission. If this fails, Mylin goes to prison."

"But...but...I want to help. We can stop him. Distract him. Look at the weapons we have."

"But...but...we don't know who he is, or what's going on. Did you see her feet wrapped like she's been hurt? We have no idea if we would be helping the situation or making it worse. And if our faces get recorded, we're of no use at all."

Jill took a deep breath. "Carr will send us stateside, won't he?"

"Unless he makes us swim for being stupid. Our presence is a gargantuan liability for the mission. Case in point. We see Mylin on a surveillance screen, and have no idea what to do."

Jill stood silent, eyes darting around the huge display. "I want to see what's really happening."

"Grab the manual. Let's send a drone."

Jill reached for the manual. Joe changed the display to Command Center, found the launch section, and entered the GPS coordinates of the last picture that showed Mylin.

"It takes off from the roof," Jill said. "The manual says, 'Take precautions against the drone launch being seen by bystanders.'"

Joe accessed a satellite image showing the dark rectangular shape of their truck. "Feels strange looking down at ourselves."

Jill stepped up beside him. "A hundred-million dollar mirror in the sky and me with no makeup." She touched a finger to the screen. "How about that alley? It's only a couple of turns away. More private than this street. Can we launch while we're moving?"

"I'll be shocked if this rig can't do something that simple." He held out a key. "Are you okay driving?"

She took the key and moved toward the cab. "If I can handle my Ford compact, I can drive this itty-bitty thing." She laughed and disappeared into the cab.

Joe raced through flight options: surveillance altitude, airspeed, weapons, cameras. He chose no weapons and two cameras for redundancy, even though it lowered the top speed, while worrying that the guy would catch Mylin and pull a handgun. Or a knife. He hurried while hyper-concentrating to avoid mistakes, hoping the second camera for close-ups was a good decision and not just his paranoid habit.

The truck made a right turn. Joe pressed a hand against the desk for stability while he worked through the launch protocol. After another right the van slowed and wobbled.

He reconsidered arming the drone.

It would cost more top speed. He gritted his teeth; Carr wouldn't want him using weapons except as a last resort. And maybe not even then—civilian, U.S. citizen, international incident, living out his life in a Korean prison.

He confirmed NONE, deciding he would sacrifice the drone like a kamikaze fighter if the time came. There was, after all, only one man chasing her.

He checked himself.

Only one *so far.*

Only one *they knew about.*

The ready button glowed; a low whine emerged from above his head. The truck rocked and rolled. He checked the satellite; they were moving along an alley with tar-paper-roofed buildings on one side and overflowing trash containers on the other. A section of the truck's roof glided back like a sunroof.

He crawled to the front and cracked open the door to the cab. Jill was gripping the steering wheel with both hands, knuckles white, staring at the broken road ahead like she was driving through a minefield.

"Ready back here."

"No one in front, nothing in the mirrors. But those dragon guys hide."

"Feeling time pressure." Joe hesitated. "I'm worried what happens if he catches her."

"Let's do it."

Joe took two quick steps into the dim interior and one last look at the satellite image. Then he entered the ID Carr had made him memorize, saying it would operate anything the FBI wanted him to operate. The roof vibrated. On the satellite image a tiny dot lifted away from the van.

The sunroof slid closed.

The center monitor switched to the drone's #1 video camera. The van shrank on the screen. Numbers popped on and ratcheted up until the drone was moving 100 mph at an elevation of a thousand feet. Joe dropped into the chair thinking about what the drone would find, and realized he didn't know enough to form an accurate worry.

The van swung left and stopped. Jill crawled in. "We're on a side street." She stood behind his chair. Pictures slipped past in a spotted blur, like standing under a waterfall looking up.

"It's fast," she said.

"Let's hope fast enough," he said softly. "Two minutes since our last visual of Mylin."

Digits labelled TIME TO CONTACT spun toward zero. After what seemed like hours the door of the building where they had first spotted Mylin came into view.

Jill said, "We've lost them both."

"Maybe," Joe said. "The drone has access to the super-AI, and it's faster than we could ever hope to be in this van." He rewound the pictures of Mylin until her face was visible, then marked it as an area of interest.

"Now the handsome guy," Jill said.

Joe marked the face of the middle-aged Asian man whose droopy eyes suggested overworked bureaucrat. Then he guessed how far Mylin could run in the minutes since they had first seen her, set the search area to one point five miles, took a breath, and switched FLIGHT OBJECTIVE to auto.

The image tilted and flowed as the craft swooped to search for two faces among hundreds on the street.

"Can we use the satellite too?" Jill asked.

"I never stopped it. Those images," he waved a hand at the other monitors, "are from the satellite. But the drone can peek into windows, up alleyways, change angle. If no one shoots it down, it might find something."

"How big is it?"

He frowned. "You know, I have no idea. I've never seen one. All I saw was a dot come out of our van."

Jill leaned her palms on the narrow desk. "I can't see crap. The pictures are hopping around like a GoPro strapped to a kangaroo."

"Give it a minute."

"Hey," Jill said. "It's hunting. Watch how it stays near the sidewalk."

"The AI knows it's looking for humans. I bet it knows a bunch about where humans go, how they move through a city." He pointed to the time readout. "Six and a half minutes. It knows how fast humans can run too."

Jill's voice shattered the small space. "That's her!" The jittering ceased as the image settled on Mylin's dark hair and turned in a semicircle around her. "Mylin, he's right behind you!"

"We're supposed to be quiet."

"I want to *do* something. My heart is pounding like I'm the one running." She dropped to her knees so her eyes were level with Mylin's. "Where is she?"

A hundred-foot-high three-tier temple came into view. Gray steps running the entire length of one side suggested an ancient craft floating on a sea of stone.

Mylin still had one shoe in each hand, but had released her dress and was moving with small, shuffling steps. She hopped up the lowest step and spun to look back, her chest rising and falling. The drone marked a red rectangle around Mylin's face that immediately switched to green: positive identification. A second monitor changed to the long range camera. The camera zoomed until it landed on a man's face. A second red rectangle became green. The man carried a boxy briefcase in one hand, the other held his left side as he hobbled after Mylin, cheeks puffing.

Mylin ran up the broad steps toward pillars painted brilliant red-orange. The white cloth around her feet was blackened on the bottom. The wrap on her left foot trailed like a kite tail.

She disappeared behind a pillar.

The bureaucrat hobbled up the steps, leading with his left foot and following with the right.

"Stop him," Jill said, kneeling before the wall of monitors as if it were an altar.

Joe took manual control of the drone and guided it toward the entrance of the temple.

"He'll see it," she said.

"I'll hover, then follow him in. He's exhausted and focused on Mylin. With luck, we can hide in the architecture of the temple once we're inside." He glanced at the iPad lying face down on the floor. "I wish I knew what we're flying here."

"Would it matter?"

"I don't want to ram him with a Matchbox helicopter. On the other hand, if it's a meter wide, hiding won't work."

Jill spun on her kneecaps and grabbed the tablet.

Mylin had disappeared inside the temple.

The man had stopped halfway up the expanse of steps. A young Asian couple descended toward him, glanced his way with a hint of disgust, gave him a wide berth, and glided silently past.

Jill said, "It has a self-identify feature. Put it back on auto."

"OK."

"Talk to it. Using your ID code."

Joe lifted the remote, spoke his code, then said, "Self-identify."

A diagram popped up on the monitor in the lower left-hand corner.

"Hey," Jill said. "It looks like a Star Wars fighter. But they always spin in the movies."

As she spoke, the 3D image began to rotate and the sides fell away to reveal the infrastructure of the craft. Numbers scrolled up the right side of the diagram.

"There," she said, leaning in close. "It's five centimeters high." She turned to Joe. "Is that really what it says?"

"Yes. And with two cameras, it weighs half a kilogram."

"It's puny."

"We can't stop him with this. He'll swat us out of the sky."

The drone display went black.

Jill groaned. "We've lost contact."

The screen flickered gray, spun, then showed the inside of a room as tall as half a dozen circus performers standing on each other's shoulders. Three gold Buddhas guarded one end. A pair of pillars in front of the Buddhas were home to coiled, mustached dragons whose eyes glinted jade.

"It has a stealth mode." She held up the flat screen; Joe followed the instructions. The floor receded as the drone lifted to the ceiling, remaining locked on both targets.

Mylin reached the center Buddha and twisted her head frantically.

Jill pointed. "She's trapped. Is there another way out?"

"A public space should have a fire door. But I don't know if she'll find it before—"

Her pursuer moved into the frame.

Mylin turned to face him, her back to the Buddha, a green-eyed dragon inches to her left. She stretched her right arm back, a heeled shoe dangling from her fingertips.

CHAPTER 18

"ENOUGH!" THE MAN calling himself Long shouted.

My body became rigid, as if my nerves had short circuited.

My boot swung from the fingers of my bow hand like a pendulum. Perspiration dripped down his puffy cheeks. He had chased me all the way from Uncle's house to this temple; yet he was smiling.

"You are of the lineage of the Tiger Woman as promised. Soon I will put that energy to good use. Now, end this game. Bow to the Buddha and thank him for my patience."

I released my boot-like shoes; they clunked on the hard floor. Two women admiring the Buddha far to the left gawked at me. I faced this plain man. His eyes told me he carried a heavy load in his world. The rebellious energy that had overcome me in my barred room swirled away like water down a drain. The soles of my feet burned. My body sagged against the scales of the dragon beside me: a sculpture four times my size. I reached out and stroked the skin carved by a master artist. Had he chosen his life as a carver of dragons, or had someone chosen for him?

Mr. Long wrapped a pudgy hand around the back of my neck. He said, "Bow to your Buddha," and pressed until I was kneeling upright on the cold floor. Then his hand twisted my face toward the twenty-foot high statue of the smiling fat man towering above me.

I did not resist. He pressed forward.

I bowed until my forehead touched the lava floor of a temple built before I was born. Maybe even before my father was born. My third eye embraced the polished stone. One of my boots stood upright inches from my head. The straps, the high platform, even the shiny leather and translucent mesh, representing servitude. Madame Win had been shocked by my size seven and a half feet, and attempted to make them more pleasing by binding them.

I didn't care if my feet pleased anyone. I only cared…

A chant popped into consciousness from my childhood in Sela Valley. I hummed it softly. I couldn't recall the words, or if it was a chant of praise, or wishing, or maybe even desire. Only the naked melody came to my mind, from a time when temples were a comfort for a child whose world was being twisted by adults.

Male adults.

A voice joined mine. A baritone. A voice that knew the words for this fragment of melody that had arisen from my past.

Keeping my forehead pressed against the smooth floor, I moved only my eyes. Mr. Long was kneeling beside me, the deep chanting coming from his round body. The briefcase he had been carrying since I met him stood on the floor between us. I mimicked his words and soon realized that I was asking the Buddha for help adhering to and understanding the path life had placed before me.

More voices joined ours.

I couldn't see them, so I imagined the women I had seen earlier bowing to take part in our impromptu choir. Mr. Long stopped singing. The high female voices drifted in the cavernous space like a breath of wind. He stood. I finished another round of the chant and lifted my torso, but remained on my knees. Two women continued to sing. A young man some distance away, who could only be an American tourist with his scruffy beard, colorful backpack, and starry-eyed girlfriend, began singing quite beautifully.

Mr. Long retrieved his briefcase and gestured toward my shoes. I gathered them up.

Then his arms were on my body, lifting me from the floor with surprising strength. I squeezed the shoes to my breasts as he pulled me to his chest, carrying me like a bride across a threshold toward the exit.

The chanters continued.

The American couple applauded softly.

Mr. Long carried me outside and seated me gently on the very top of the massive row of concrete steps that led to the earth below. He carefully rewrapped the cloth that had unraveled from my left foot, then held his hand out toward me, palm up.

I stared blankly, fatigued from the strain of running, and confused by this Asian man with the Western-style briefcase. His hand moved slowly toward my breasts. Without thinking I pulled away.

He smiled his crowded-tooth smile and wrapped his fingers around one of my boots.

I released it.

With great gentleness he slipped it on, buckled a strap across my foot, and a second around my ankle. Then he held out his other hand.

I placed the second boot on his palm. What did he want of me? He had called me 'Tiger Woman,' which meant he knew of *The Ways of the Plain Girl.* Perhaps he had even read her teachings. But I had never read a story of a man kneeling on temple steps to place shoes on a woman's feet with his own hands.

Mr. Long finished buckling, stood, and held out his hands to help me up. Wearing the boots and standing a step above, I towered over him. As I gazed down into his black eyes, I again felt powerful...though this time I didn't have Uncle Gan's shiny gun to assist me.

He picked up his briefcase in his left hand and lifted an elbow toward me, expecting me to slip my arm under it and allow him to escort me down the steps. I giggled as the memory of a movie from childhood came to me. In it a tin man, a scarecrow, and a lion locked arms with a silly American girl who thought she could go home along a fancy road instead of following her destiny into the future.

Mr. Long smiled at my giggling and gestured with his elbow. I wrapped my fingers into the crook and he led me down dozens of temple steps, guiding each movement, shifting his eyes between my face and my feet as if both were equally important.

We reached the last step.

He said, "You ran quite far."

I cast my eyes to the ground. "Forgive me. I am a silly girl."

He guided me along the street slowly. "Forgive you? I wish to thank you. I have not been so energized in many years. We will have much joy together."

The height of my heels sent pain into my arches. How far had I run to reach a temple I hadn't even known was there? A mile? Two?

Miles.

I had been in America so long I was thinking in the obtuse English system they stubbornly adhered to even after the rest of the world had moved on.

"Do your feet hurt?" Mr. Long asked. "I will carry you if you wish."

My eyes widened in surprise, but I remembered to smile. "The house is much too far."

"Nonsense. I carried provisions heavier than you, and much farther, while serving our beautiful country."

His arms swept under my legs and once again I was pulled against his broad chest. I was careful not to struggle. How many years, or decades, had passed since he had served a country? And which one? Under what ruler? Perhaps I hadn't yet been born in the days he carried those provisions.

"Mr. Long, you mustn't," I protested. "Please conserve your energy for more important things."

Pedestrians on the street took notice. A scooter beeped a tinny little horn and the riders waved to us. Everyone smiled at the boyish antics of this businessman.

"Do not worry, Tiger Woman. You have given me great strength."

"But you make me feel guilty for being so weak."

He laughed. "Do you take me for a fool in these matters? I know when I am being tested. You will see. I will exceed your expectations, my lovely Mylin."

I rested my head on his shoulder and allowed myself to be carried, knowing better than to argue with a man who felt his masculinity was being challenged. American men were just the same.

Perhaps all men were the same.

By the time we reached the house he had given me his case to hold to my chest, and his jacket to drape over my arm. Perspiration speckled his forehead and he needed a fresh shirt.

"Please stop here," I asked. "I would like to climb the stairs by your side." I winked. "And we can ride the elevator to my room together."

He lowered me gently until my boots touched the sidewalk. He smiled. I suspected he was as happy to be rid of my weight as to honor my request. We ascended together, his arm around my waist. I clutched his jacket and case to my chest. Once the doors closed us into the tiny elevator that served the house, I faced him and met his eyes. With my arms crisscrossed over his briefcase, I moved closer.

He was perspiring heavily, but the privacy of the small car must have tempted him. Reaching out, he wrapped his pudgy hands around my upper arms and pulled me to him. He was clearly battling to restrain himself and be the suave seducer—and just as clearly failing as his mouth devoured mine. By the time the elevator dinged to announce the third floor, his manhood pressed firmly against my thigh through the silk of my emerald dress.

The doors clunked open. I took his sweaty palm in my hand and led him toward my room, where I expected Madame Win to be waiting with punishment for the foolish prostitute who ran away. As we approached the room, I removed the key from my bra.

But it wouldn't be required.

The door stood open, wrenched into the hallway like a net ready to entrap me. The frame where I had turned the deadbolt was splinters. The shaft from the lock had bent and hung from the edge of the door. Hinges were torn away from wood.

"I apologize," Mr. Long said. "I became impatient. I considered calling Win, but feared she would be too slow to keep the energy you had created within me alive. I will, of course, pay for the repairs."

Win was going to be angry with me, but I focused on immediate concerns. I turned to Mr. Long, now eye to eye thanks to my boots, and said:

"You are very strong."

His smile reminded me of a sheep. "I was filled with the energy of the hunt. I heard your footfalls moving away. Of course, I could have called for help. But then, what kind of man would I be?"

I pushed the door with my elbow and scraped the largest of the wood fragments into my room with the side of my boot. Mr. Long manhandled the door closed behind us. With his help, I turned the deadbolt so the door would remain closed, though it was far from secure.

We faced each other, his briefcase now heavy in my arms.

"Thank you for coming to visit me, Mr. Long. Welcome to my humble room."

He laughed and began removing his shirt. When it was fully unbuttoned he held out his hand.

I hesitated, confused. Then I extended his case. He took it without a word and disappeared into the bathroom. In a moment, the shower began to make its hissing-snake sound.

I stared at the shattered frame and dislodged hinges.

I was tempted to make another escape attempt, one that might take me all the way back to a jail cell. Instead, I hung Mr. Long's jacket in the closet and undressed. The water was still whooshing when I finished, so I asked myself what the Tiger

Woman in Mr. Long's mind would do.

She would hunt.

I found matches in the nightstand and lit the jade-green candle standing on top: a candle as big around as my leg. I pulled the shade over the barred window, creating an afternoon darkness much like dusk. I reopened it and wrapped my fingers around the bars and shook as hard as I could.

The black steel laughed.

I pulled the shade low again and picked up the flickering candle.

The shower was still running.

I eased the bathroom door open slightly. Hot vapor floated into my face. I slipped an arm in and found the light switch. To Mr. Long's credit, he didn't call out when the room went black. I glided into the mist and placed the candle on the counter near the shower. Men like light. They always wish to see a woman's body, rather than just feel it.

I slid the fogged glass door open. The flickering candlelight revealed Mr. Long almost ready for me. Together we reviewed *The Teachings of The Plain Girl* until I was seated on the mirrored dresser with him standing before me. My legs encircled his plump body in what some call Padlock Pose: bodies joined together like a lock and key.

His belly protruded over our private parts. I held my gaze on his sagging eyes. The sad eyes of a man who knew his power in life was waning, and was doing his utmost to fight the inevitable decline. In the moment he reached ecstasy he did indeed look happy—his smile seeming to contain all of the work the Tiger Woman had made him perform to reach this apex.

He lifted me easily and dropped us together onto the bed. I expected him to fall asleep as most others had done, but he requested his briefcase. I fetched it and knelt on the floor naked. What could be so important that he carried everywhere and wanted now of all times? I shuddered as a cool rod of recognition filled my heated body. Uncle Gan had given me a box. A beautiful box containing a beautiful handgun that changed my life. Perhaps this? He must have sensed my mood.

"Relax, my Mylin, you will like what I have inside. But first you must understand what is happening around you. Understand so that you can play your—" He stopped and stroked the sides of the leather case. "No, so that *we* can play our roles precisely. And quickly, for there is little time. As always in these endeavors, there is much at stake—though it is quite impossible to predict exactly what until it has been done and the dust settles in far off lands."

He paused for a long time, his hands stroking the case as if it could feel his touch.

"Secrets run the world, Mylin."

I held myself in the stillness of the last fading note of a concerto as fear rose in me. If his eyes hadn't been half open, I might have thought he had fallen asleep after all.

He sighed long, like he was trying to expel a poisonous gas from inside his lungs.

"I wish to see you again. I do not know when that will be possible. Much depends on—" He studied my face. "Much depends on your friend Win. She must deliver what has been promised. And do so with great haste. Now that I have met the true Tiger Woman, I cannot know happiness unless she is near me."

He gestured with fingers that had been inside of me minutes before, then gave me the briefcase.

I placed it on the bed beside him and continued to kneel. He turned it toward him and worked a pair of numerical locks. Clasps popped free. He did not open the case; instead, he rotated it to face me.

"Your friend and I are doing business. By delivering you, she has fulfilled phase one. Now we must prepare for phase two." He flicked a finger. I touched the case with both hands and began to lift. As the aroma of leather reached me, I paused.

Mr. Long nodded for me to continue. His face showed me nothing as I swung the hinged top upward, afraid to look, afraid what I would see, afraid of the new world it would carry me to.

"Go ahead," he said.

I lowered my eyes to pictures of a woman I didn't recognize. She had the serene face of an artist. I didn't guess, because guessing led to errors, but the paper had the intricate ornamentation of money. But what kind of country would put a woman's face on money?

"Korean won," he said. "Take two."

"I cannot."

"You refuse me?"

I was trapped. "I beg your forgiveness, Mr. Long. It is only that...I...I have never been the one in my family to care for money."

"Exactly." He smiled. "Now remove *four* packs from the case, Mylin."

I did so, stacking them with my left hand until they formed a brick. A brick of money I didn't understand, yet the stack of paper made me dream of where it might take me. And reminded me of the padding in my viola case. Who owned it? And when would they come to take it?

"That is for you, my Mylin. Place it where no one can discover it and take it away from you. It is enough for you to hide in a small apartment on a corner of this island where no one will find you for years. If they even bother to look for you afterwards. Promise me you will keep it safe. I will rest easier knowing I have cared for the Tiger Woman, and may one day visit her again."

"Thank you," I whispered, my voice shaking. I had never in my whole life had my very own money. I wasn't quite sure what I would do with it—except to hide it from Win.

He said, "I want you to hide the rest, too."

My eyes widened. "All of it?"

He reached out his hand and pulled my wrist until I crawled onto the bed and he could kiss my breast with his full lips. "Yes, Mylin, all of it. I will take that fine case with me when I leave and protect it. Those who have been observing me will assume that it remains full—including our mutual friend. No one will think for a moment that an experienced business-man from the Chinese mainland would entrust a large sum of money to a lady of the evening. Only a fool would do such a thing."

"But you trust Mylin?"

His smile wasn't all smile.

"I trust no one, lovely tiger. But you have touched me, so now I must trust a little. I know you won't run away with my money. Not only would I hunt and destroy you, but now you have money of your own. And you will not give it to Win unless I order you to, because you are wisely afraid of which one of us will kill you first." He waved me away. "Go, my dear, sweet tiger, hide your treasure. I have much work to do."

I lined my four packs behind the Beethoven score on the black metal music stand, ensuring they were invisible from every direction. Most everyone ignored sheet music. Mr. Long sat on the bed and removed a notebook from a pocket inside his briefcase. He leaned against the padded suede headboard and began to write with a silver pen.

I counted three layers of packs—three across, and four down. Thirty-six minus my four left thirty-two, each the size of a smartphone, but thicker. I only had this room, which wasn't even mine. Where? Where could they hide?

Mr. Long stared at the ceiling, either daydreaming or deep in thought. I could usually tell with men, but his opaque ex-pression blocked my instincts.

I made a tall stack and carried the tower between my palms as I walked slowly around the room searching. They would fit in my viola case, but then where would I keep my instrument? If I left it out, Win would ask questions. Or perhaps try to put it away herself.

Madame Win knew much more about money than me. She would know where to look. But maybe Mr. Long was right: she wouldn't think to look. No one would expect Mylin to have money. I only earned money. Father had said I earned large sums of money. But never for me. Always for the family.

So no one would look.

Therefore, it didn't matter where I hid Mr. Long's money, so long as it wasn't discovered by accident.

I carried the stack to the closet. Dozens of pairs of fancy shoes lay in a tumble beneath dresses. Men liked shoes, especially high ones. Even shorter men like Mr. Long were excited by a woman wearing high heels—something about the aesthetics of a dancer on her toes. Or maybe, as some claimed, it really was because a girl couldn't run away as fast.

I knelt and leaned forward to reach the boxes behind the footwear. They were stacked in perfect columns and contained more shoes. I poked until I found an empty one.

How clever should I be?

As clever as possible, the dragons suggested. You are a stranger in this new land. You are in the hands of a foreign woman. Your friends from America are near, but you have known them only a short time. And Uncle Gan. Where is Uncle Gan?

I dragged a box toward me and removed the lid to find brown shoes and yellow paper. I lined the bottom with a row of money, carefully covered it with paper, then replaced the shoes and top before pushing it to the bottom of a stack of boxes. If the money were found, I would simply deny knowing anything about it.

I stood and calculated that six more boxes were needed before Mr. Long's case would be empty. I took two steps; a gurgling sound stopped me. The entrance door was broken—

I silently released my breath.

Even if Win found the won, it was Mr. Long's money. At least I thought it was his money. Perhaps he had robbed someone, and I was helping him hide the booty.

The sound again.

I poked my head out from the closet. The candle had gone out. Mr. Long was flat on his back, jaw dropped down. His briefcase stood open. His hands were folded on his chest as if he were on display in a funeral parlor. A folded slip of paper protruded from between his fingers.

I moved closer. My name was written on the paper.

The business he *needed to attend to* was a note to me?

I forgot about my hiding-money job and floated my hand across the bed with great care. His chest rose. As it fell, a rattling sound emerged from his throat that explained the noises. I waited for the next rattle and wriggled the note out from between his fingers.

His expression didn't change.

The sheet of paper had a ragged edge along one side. His notebook was back in the pocket in the open briefcase. I stared at my name in the darkness. Surely he had intended to give it to me, but had fallen asleep before doing so.

Should I read it?

Fear tempted me to put it back between his fingers and wait for him to awaken. He might wish to witness my reaction. But what if it was an important instruction that he wanted me to carry out while he rested?

I sat on the floor and leaned my back against the bed. Life was more confusing without Father to make decisions for me. Yet the Buddha had taught: *Confusion precedes all understanding.* Maybe that hadn't been the Buddha. It might have been the professor who wrote love letters.

The paper swished as I unfolded it. My throat tightened.

If Mr. Long had written these words, that meant...

It meant too many things for me to fathom. First, I must...

The day had turned nearly to night outside of my barred window. I raided his notebook for a sheet of paper. I couldn't find his pen, so I went to the bathroom and found a pencil used to enhance eyebrows. There, on my knees at the counter, I worked in the darkness, afraid to turn on the light for fear it would awaken him.

I strained my brain to remember all that the sweet Professor Pemberly had taught me.

And began to translate the Mylinian words Mr. Long had written.

CHAPTER 19

QIGIQ FLICKED THE KILL SWITCH; the engine sputtered to a stop. The second ride around the volcano had become more exhilarating as he learned the personality of the rental bike and the change in elevation cooled the air. He removed his helmet and hung it on the handlebars. Living on this island paradise might beat Alaska and San Francisco put together. Although he would miss snow…one day.

Before he could dismount, Mr. Lee emerged from the shop. This time the white suit was accompanied by a pale pink shirt and brown wingtips that had been recently polished.

"You no like bike? No refund on long-term rental. We speak about this before. No refund."

Qigiq held up a gloved hand. "The bike is excellent. I will recommend your shop to my riding friends in America."

Mr. Lee stood more upright, his face showing surprise. Then he smiled broadly.

"Yamaha is very good bike. Big. Powerful. I know you would like it."

Qigiq moved toward the shop door and placed a hand on Mr. Lee's shoulder—two comrades joined by the love of two-wheel adventure.

"Mr. Lee, let me thank you for the very capable machine. I have been up and down your volcano twice, and it has carried me to great joy." It had actually been weak at the higher altitudes; the carburetor could likely be jetted better for the island. But it hadn't stalled. To Qigiq, any bike that kept running to its destination was indeed a joy.

"Great joy?" Mr. Lee echoed, his smile held in place as if by mechanical assistance. Then he repeated, "Yes. Yamaha build very good bike."

Qigiq had the distinct impression that no matter which bike one rented from Mr. Lee, it was always a *very good bike*. But as much as he enjoyed them, he wasn't there to talk bikes.

Qigiq sat down facing the small desk where he had filled out the rental paperwork. Mr. Lee rounded the desk and repositioned the worn office chair with green metal legs and only four of five wheels.

"A friend of mine wishes to contact me through your shop. I wonder if perhaps you have heard from her?"

Mr. Lee's shifting eyes indicated that he heard many things. Perhaps even some not intended for his ears. "A friend?"

Qigiq almost laughed. Like any middleman, Mr. Lee would surely do his job to extract money wherever possible. This was opportunity number one.

Qigiq removed a 50,000 won note from his pocket—one of many from dragon lady's advance—and laid it on the desk. He placed his palm over the bill.

"I would be grateful if you would pass along my friend's message."

Mr. Lee had ceased smiling at the first question, but now started up again.

"There may be something. Let me check with my assistant who answers the phone." He stood and disappeared into an attached garage.

On his first visit, Qigiq hadn't noticed any other employees. And he didn't see or hear any now. Alone in the shop, he relaxed and paid attention. Not to anything in particular, but to the surroundings, as if his brain were recording the environment for anything that might be helpful to the case in the future. A case that gave him the odd sense of racing forward and standing still at the same time—like riding a motorcycle in a fevered dream.

The shop made impressions: the smells of gasoline, oil, and

180 | JOE KLINGLER

fresh rubber tires; a cork board filled to exploding with bike porn of chrome and slender Korean girls; a poster for the band Metallica alongside one of Robben Ford playing a gold guitar, beside Yanni at the Acropolis; a beat-up olive green filing cabinet containing probably nothing but rental receipts. No telephone. A safe made of an ancient green block of concrete a meter square with a combination dial set into the top.

Too heavy to steal.

What would Lee need to protect? Cash and check payments until he could get to the bank? Maybe some cash on hand to be ready to jump on the purchase of a used bike—nothing out front was less than ten years old. Qigiq's eyes glided from the safe to a rear entrance that opened onto an alley. Nothing but pavement and a few bushes. Solid doors that swung inward appeared to be made of steel.

Mr. Lee's voice reached him from the other room. He couldn't tell if Lee was on the phone, or mumbling to himself. A call from tourists on a shoestring budget negotiating a scooter rental?

Maybe. Maybe not.

Mr. Lee came through the doorway from the garage at a brisk walk. His face had taken on the pale patina of a person with a grave illness. He dropped into his bargaining chair behind the desk and began opening and closing its small drawers.

The 50,000 won on the desk remained untouched.

He found the drawer he wanted and extracted a yellow legal pad filled with doodles. He shuffled through pages to a fresh sheet and wrote with a bright red pen. Then he leaned far back in his chair, visibly relaxed, and gazed at Qigiq with renewed interest.

Qigiq reached for his money. Mr. Lee's arm shot forward with the speed of a martial artist and swept it away.

"You have a message," Lee announced, pocketing the bill.

"From?"

"A woman."

"Her name?"

Mr. Lee shook his head. "This is a small island, my motor-bike friend. Population is barely half a million. It is like your San Francisco, but without the fog." He grinned. "Many of us are third and fourth generation who go back to the early twentieth century when the Japanese tried to steal our island." He tapped his yellow tablet. "We have no need for names." He leaned forward and adjusted the height of his chair. "Besides. She said you would understand what this means." He rotated the legal pad 180 degrees and pushed it to where the 50,000 won had been.

884173900808

Qigiq thought phone number, ISBN number for a book, credit card number, bank account. But why would the Dragon Lady say he would know?

"Of course. May I?"

Mr. Lee nodded.

Qigiq tore off the sheet, understanding now that Lee had memorized the numbers while on the phone. He hoped they were accurate. He stood. "Thank you for the message. Perhaps you could help me learn more about your island."

Lee's shoulders relaxed. "Certainly. What do you like? We have hundreds of kilometers of beautiful seashore filled with the loveliest women in the world. Our volcano is highest in all of South Korea and has a crater lake at the top. Perhaps something unique: a mile-long lava tube or a dense forest that provides water for the entire island. We are one of the Wonders of the Natural World. Islanders have known this for centuries, of course, but recognition helps the tourist business." He grinned again.

"Those sound fascinating. But I'm interested in two things. First, where is the most challenging riding?"

"For the street rider, there is nothing better in all of Asia than the curving roads climbing from the sea to the Hallasan Crater. They are like your Tail of the Dragon in Tennessee." He paused. "I would love to ride your dragon one day." He lifted a finger. "But beware, twisting asphalt has claimed the lives of many. The road is stunning, but heartless to those who fail to show respect."

Mr. Lee loved to talk, so Qigiq said only, "And?"

"The trails in the rainforest. Unpaved and unforgiving." Lee considered him with a squinted eye. "Please remember that your insurance is invalid for off-road riding. You are responsible for all damages."

If he were forced to ride the rented Yamaha through a tropical forest, insurance would be the least of his troubles.

"I'll remember. And will take good care of your bike."

Lee smiled.

"Since you've been on the island for years, perhaps you can help me with this." He unfolded a picture Carr's security camera had taken of his late-night visitors. Without explanation he slipped it onto Lee's scratched desk with 100,000 won beside it.

Mr. Lee didn't move, but he wasn't enough of a poker player to hide the fact that he knew the face and was mentally calculating how much he could safely reveal.

"Everyone knows her."

"Has she lived here long?"

Lee rolled his lips inward and back. "Long is relative."

Qigiq decided to simplify.

"Does she live on the island?"

"Yes," Lee said. "And no."

Qigiq laughed. Waited. Glanced down at the money and back up to Lee, Waited. Lee filled the silence.

"She has a residence here. I may have heard it is in the south, but I am not sure anyone knows exactly where. She floats in and out like a ghost." Lee spread his hands on the desk. "She is everywhere...she is nowhere."

Not much help. Yet, Qigiq felt slightly closer to the mysterious woman who wanted his paintings. "She has been on the island for years?"

Lee nodded.

"How might I find her?"

Lee shook his head. "You leave a message, like you are doing now. And she finds you."

Qigiq didn't want to be found on her terms. He took a chance.

"How is Gan these days?"

Lee's eyes narrowed. His face became almost comical, like a game show contestant trying to lie.

"You know this man?"

"He visited the U.S. recently, but we missed each other. I was hoping to see him while I'm here."

Lee frowned. "If I meet a man of this name, I will mention the American rider visiting our island."

Except for the numerical code, Qigiq had learned little. But he had tossed money around as planned. He stood and picked up the woman's picture his friend Mr. Lee had been careful not to touch. He left the cash and folded the picture slowly while watching Lee's eyes gravitate toward the money. Qigiq made a decision, pulled the roll from his pocket, peeled five more bills, and placed them on the desk beside the two already there.

"I appreciate your help. I will stop back soon," Qigiq smiled, "to let you know how the Yamaha is running."

Lee's face confirmed that he was happy to work verbally. He stood and met Qigiq's eyes. "You must visit our Buddhist temple. It has the largest open worship space of any temple in all of Asia. And though it is not ancient, it is...profound."

Maybe Lee *was* on the inside. Maybe even more inside than the Dragon Lady knew—bikers had ways of connecting.

"What do you ride, Mr. Lee?"

Lee grinned widely and wiped the 350,000 won off the table in a single stroke.

"Come, my friend."

Qigiq followed the spotless white suit to the repair area, past half-assembled bikes, and to a wall with swinging doors that were latched and secured with a padlock.

"I do not let everyone see. They do not understand. I think

you, however. You will understand."

Lee spun the dial, removed the lock, popped open the hasp, and turned his back to the swinging doors. His face showed the anticipation of a magician about to make a woman disappear.

Lee swung the doors open and stepped aside in one motion.

An LED spotlight popped on overhead.

Qigiq stared at the last bike he had expected: a red-framed V7 Moto Guzzi Sport as clean is if it had just come out of the Lake Como factory in 1971.

CHAPTER 20

THE RIDE BACK FROM MR. LEE'S shop put the orange ball of sun behind and long dark shadows on the winding blacktop ahead. Between curves he had plenty of time to contemplate the ways a 12-digit number could be used. He considered her last words to him: *How should we do this?*

We? She and her colleagues? She and Qigiq?

She had entrusted a great deal of money to him. But what *this* did she mean? Not the blank canvas with Pemberly's language on it; she already possessed the copy he had given her in San Francisco. If she wanted the secret hidden on that canvas, she already had it.

He swept left and climbed, the bike still breathing well.

Did she want to see the first canvas as proof that he had others?

Only this one road led up the great Hallasan volcano. Cars passed opposite heading down into the setting sun. Rearview mirrors revealed no vehicles following him. He glanced at the sky, searching for a drone. Carr had checked the bike for a tracking device, but found only a weld from a crash.

Alone and riding—one of the best feelings in the world.

The digits could be an international phone number, but that could be traced and recorded. Why would a woman who ran informants on multiple continents be so careless?

It could be a reference: a book, address, location, a code that would reveal the name of a town.

Qigiq reached the airport on the eastern shore. Carr's flashy jet hadn't moved. Parked beside it, gleaming in the golden light of dusk, sat a red SUV with a lifted suspension to accommodate monster-truck tires. It looked angry enough to drive right through a volcano.

Visitors?

The shades were drawn over the jet's windows. He parked behind the maintenance shack where he couldn't be seen from the plane and contemplated what he might be walking into.

No messages on his secure phone.

The plane's stairway had been drawn up. Light glowed from the cockpit, but no one was visible. The air temperature was easily 80 degrees Fahrenheit, but he felt the frigid isolation of a caribou hunt. He reached into his boot for the knife and rolled the ivory handle in his palm. Checked the time on the phone.

Waited.

At 7:31 footfalls approached: a fleet-footed runner moving fast. Without warning, yellow and red ground lights lit up at the far end of the runway, their glow creating a hazy dome of light pollution. The runner drew closer. Qigiq inched deeper into the shadows behind the shack. The footfalls stopped as a person reached the SUV. He eased his head right for a better view.

Kandy stood beside the machine, fumbling with keys.

"Psst, psst," he hissed.

Kandy froze.

He whispered, "The snow precedes us."

"Hi, Qu, come on out. We've got problems, but not here." She opened the driver's door. The interior light from an older model Chevy Tahoe glistened on her skin. She ran often, but ran farther when under stress, using her feet the way he used a motorcycle.

He hustled to the passenger side and ducked inside. She pulled her door closed, blanketing them in darkness. He stared out at the parked plane.

"New problem," she said.

"You accidentally locked us out of the jet."

"You could pick the lock." She scratched her nose with a bent index finger. "I received a truncated message from Carr. 'Cash is genuine. Cops here. I think they're going to A R R.'"

"The locals nabbed him?"

"They probably think he's a drug lord from Los Angeles smuggling cash into their country."

"Small potatoes for a dealer," Qigiq said. "Besides, it was won, not dollars."

"Maybe they think he's dealing here."

"Lots of competition from the Chinese," he said. "Plus, it'd be hard for Carr to blend in on this island."

"It'd be hard anywhere, except maybe a Navy SEAL's convention." She gazed at the plane. "Are you thinking what I'm thinking?"

"Only if you think our lady with dragon friends was involved."

"Or Uncle Gan has joined the party."

"She left a message for me." Qigiq pulled out the paper Lee had filled with red numbers and passed it to Kandy. "Just that. No hello or goodbye."

"Too short for a credit card, so we can't go shopping. Got a guess?"

"Code telling me what to do next. And a test. If I'm not smart enough to figure it out, she doesn't want to do business with me, even if I'm not a white devil."

"Criminals testing each other. Old concept." Kandy gestured toward the plane. "I locked up the luxo-jet when I left for my therapy run. It's empty."

"I dropped won on our Mr. Lee. He insinuated that the Dragon Lady is a ghost-like presence who can appear anywhere on the island. His eyes told me that he also knows Uncle Gan, but his lips wouldn't move."

Kandy stared at the plane. "Give him a little time, see if his memory improves. I want to know what she's really after. Do you remember the people Shen tried to eliminate: financial whiz, communications CEO, kid stealing secrets from a government lab?"

"Leaves the door wide open, doesn't it?"

"And now we have an FBI agent in a Korean jail who is very angry about his murdered partner."

"Should we go spring him?"

Kandy shook her head. "Would love to, it's my kind of action. But we walk in, they grab us as accomplices."

"That'd shut down Operation Mylin."

"Except for the two civilians."

"Jill and Joe are smart, but untrained. And we're on the Dragon Lady's turf."

"Severe disadvantage," she said. "They also don't have our official channels for support. Or Carr's money."

"Which leaves us where?"

She handed his paper back. "Sitting in this toy I rented to show how extravagant we are. Five-hundred horsepower Corvette engine, paddle shifters, 8-speed transmission, and a suspension that will go anywhere."

"Anywhere?"

"Well, it doesn't float."

Qigiq held up the paper and put his thumb over four digits.

Kandy squinted at the numbers in the darkness. "GPS coordinates?"

He nodded.

"Why block those last four digits?"

"I think the message is: this place, at this time." He removed his thumb.

"Oh-eight hundred tomorrow morning?"

He thought about when that phone call had come into Lee's shop. "She was talking to Lee a couple of hours ago. Lee didn't have anything to write with, so he ran back to his desk and didn't speak to me until after scribbling down these numbers."

Kandy worked her lips in thought. "You think we're dealing with sloppy civilians?"

"I think the dragon is careful. But my biker buddy is just

a shop owner. She could have said eight minutes after eight o'clock tonight."

"Only he forgot to tell you."

"Yeah. Because he didn't actually *tell* me anything. He just made this note. He was even careful never to touch the paper with his finger—only the marker." Qigiq recalled the moment. "He didn't hand it to me either. The tablet was lying on his desk, he spun it to face me. I tore off the page myself."

"Your friend is paranoid."

"Helps bikers stay alive. But you're right, he became uncomfortable the moment I showed her picture."

Kandy pressed a button and the night filled with the rumbling growl of a mechanical predator. She pulled out her phone. "Nineteen forty-four. Not much time to get to where we're going and plan an entrance."

"She'll want the original of that blank canvas. It's on the plane."

The truck took off with a gravel burst from the tires. "I didn't have anything to do after I beat you back to the plane, so I loaded a few things into my new toy."

"Do I want to know?"

"Your secret scroll. Food in case we stake out her place." She glanced across at him. "And if you decide to break your smoking ban, don't stand too close to the back of the truck." She huffed her low laugh, spun the truck around the edge of the shack, and bounced it onto the two-lane pavement he had ridden in on.

"Did you get a nav system with this?" he asked.

"Sure did. Also disabled the Internet connect so nobody snoops our position." A flat display glowing blue rose out of the dash like a zombie from the grave. "Old school. Whoever built this Franken-truck borrowed that from a Volvo. I have one just like it. The remote is in the glove box."

Qigiq dropped open the glove box. The control was laying on top of two handguns stuffed into leather work gloves.

"A matched pair of Glocks, should you need one," Kandy

said. "Spare change is in the back with your picture. I bought a bit. It was on sale."

"You purchased ammunition here on the island?"

"Don't want them to think we're amateurs. If they think that, they'll make stupid mistakes we have to compensate for."

The dash spoke: "Left turn in five hundred feet."

"Will do, kiddo," Kandy said. "How come these things always talk like an anemic girl who's out of breath?"

"Market research," Qigiq said.

The truck swung a hard left without slowing. They were heading due south.

He said, "Care to guess?"

"Somewhere on the coast. Limit the attack vectors and provide an escape route, assuming they have a boat waiting. That's what I would do."

"We need Karen here with *Delicious*," he said.

"Good idea, red bikini as cloaking device. The dragon eyes will be on her while we find out what's going on."

They cruised the uneven two-lane road as fast as Kandy could push the truck. Qigiq held on with both hands. He said, "Do you have a working hypothesis?"

"Bits and pieces. Only thing I'm sure of is the Dragon Lady wants what you've got."

"Maybe. Let's see what happens after she inspects our original."

"And if she likes it?" Kandy said.

"We cut a deal for the rest of the paintings. And figure out a way to follow them."

"Risky," she said. "Speaking of which. After we finish our drive along the beach, we're going to end up someplace we've never been."

"Advantage, dragon."

"How do we go in?"

"SWAT team on one side and Navy SEALS on the other if we're going where I think we're going."

"Which is?"

Qigiq said, "The map Carr showed us suggests the city of Seogwipo, population 150,000. It's a port on the southern end of the island."

"Complicated," she said.

Qigiq touched his Blackphone, hoping no one could track what he was about to do.

Kandy said, "I don't see how she can not like a blank canvas. So let's assume the Dragon loves our painting."

"She'll want to see what else we have for sale," he said, his head down as he tapped.

"Agreed." Kandy rolled down her window. "Nothing but surf."

"Feeling lonely?"

"Listening for tire noise or a revving engine trying to keep up with me. It's weird being out here by all this water on our own. Even San Francisco cemeteries aren't this quiet."

"You thinking ambush?"

"Great stretch of road for it," she said. "But why bother? We're driving right to her."

"What do I tell her? We have a dozen paintings, but Ferdinand has identified only three with Mylinian inscriptions."

"So far," she said.

"Do we offer the entire dozen for a single price? She'll never believe we don't know what's on them."

"But we don't," she said, laughing. "Show her the collection, let her pick the ones she wants."

"She plays art collector, we're the dealer?"

"You're the dealer. The less anyone knows about me, the better."

"We'll need a gallery." He glanced at his watch, the tachometer on its face reminded him to think like a champion. "And we have ten minutes to build it." The vehicle slowed. Qigiq looked up. The horizon was glowing the orange-yellow of light pollution. "You're right. It'll get gnarly fast."

"You could stand her up. But then you fail. Some girls don't give second chances." Kandy slowed more. "Ferd has a Secure Circle phone, correct?"

Qigiq made the call.

Carr moved fast, apparently Ferdinand had already converted the cargo plane into a flying laboratory. By the time the anemic voice was directing Kandy to the harbor in Soegwipo, Qigiq had two dozen new pictures in his phone. While swiping through them, memorizing the order, he gave a play-by-play:

"Ferdinand sent us a full-frame image of each painting at a low resolution he's confident can't be used for translation. He also provided a close-up of a small section of each one. If she selects paintings other than the three we know have writing, she knows something we don't."

Kandy nodded. "OK partner, we arrive in two minutes. Time for tactics. I've got floodlights shining on an arched pedestrian bridge to the right, four cranes for loading containers at the far end of the dock at center, a white warehouse to my left that's probably locked, a row of blue boxes beside it that look to be more containers, ship, tugboat, and ferry on the water." She stopped at the end of the row of cars waiting to board. "I wonder where that ferry goes?"

"South Korean peninsula. Looks too small for a run to Japan."

"Since this line isn't moving, let's leave the truck here in plain sight. It'll confuse people."

"Think her spies have identified your stealth vehicle yet?"

"I paid extra to keep the rental quiet. Told the guy my boss would be pissed if he found out I was playing off-road when I was supposed to be doing marine biology research on slimy crawly things. Then I reminded the young gentleman he was the *only* person who knew I had rented it, I had an excellent memory, and I always paid my debts."

Qigiq said, "He assured you that he was going to forget he ever met you and couldn't recall who had rented the red truck, didn't he?"

"Are all Alaskans psychic?" Kandy used her Blackphone to

take photos of the area. She was nearly finished when an incoming message interrupted. "It's Jill apologizing for breaking silence. Says Carr hasn't contacted her as planned."

"Think they took Carr's phone?"

"He'd self-destruct it before giving it up. What do you think?"

"Involving civilians is a bad idea," he said. "Slightly worse than having no backup."

She smiled. "You have me." She reached across to the glove compartment and removed the pistols, handed one to Qigiq, gave him a spare magazine, and took everything else for herself.

"You got anything for range?" he asked.

"Toy chest in the back. Let's try not to need it."

"I thought you liked action."

"I'm more of a hand-to-hand girl. This waterfront, unknown adversary, Rambo stuff is stimulating, but makes for fewer sweet dreams."

"The civilians?"

Kandy rolled her lips inward and popped them apart. "Joe's good with cameras." She stared out the windshield at a row of cars with KIA logos and a stake truck loaded with brown boxes. "Jill is a quick thinker, though a tad aggressive. Yeah, I know, the pot calling the kettle aggressive." She laughed. "How about we send the GPS coordinates, have them send a drone to watch over us, but stay far away so we don't have to rescue them. If they need help, try to contact Carr directly." She tapped the wheel. "And hope he's not tied up."

Qigiq sent the message and the coordinates of the harbor from Lee's scribbles. That reminded him of his own notes for this project.

Kandy pointed out her door. "Carry your picture that way, toward the container ship at the end of the dock."

"Can you make out a name?"

"The ship?" She squinted, then reached in the back seat for binoculars. "Conning tower in the rear. Deck full of containers looks like a rainbow of steel. Looking...the Qung-sin Ru."

"Mean anything to you?"

She continued to scan with the glasses. "Not military. Not U.S. Not Russian. Not Her Majesty's Ship." She paused. "It's big, but not supertanker humongous."

"I wonder if Carr's connections could tell us where it's been."

"Sure. If he'd stop sitting around eating donuts with his Korean cop friends and get to work."

They made their way to the rear of the truck. Qigiq put Kandy's loaner pistol in the outside right pocket of the leather jacket he had worn on the volcano ride. She handed him the painting, still wrapped in the blue bubble wrap they had taped around it in California. Kandy held out her hand; met his eyes. They shook like business partners consummating a billion-dollar deal.

Kandy said, "Bring me back a big fish."

Her grip was warm, firm, and welcome: something solid to hold onto in this slippery mission that by all reasonable accounts, shouldn't even exist.

She released his hand and moved silently away along the row of autos, their drivers waiting for a peaceful ferry ride to the mainland.

* * *

Qigiq gazed across the harbor. A lone crane in a row of four was lifting containers from the far end of a ship onto the shore. Hundreds of steel containers of various colors, narrow ends facing him, created a thick wall. What did the people on this island want that could fill so many?

He consulted his phone. It told him to walk south, which put the long white building and six freshly painted containers to his left and the working crane directly in front of him. He headed for the crane, phone in his left hand, bubbles under his left arm, and his right hand in the pocket of a jacket that was a bit heavy for the 70-degree air.

He and the crane were the only things moving.

The rubber soles of his riding boots thudded softly. The grip of Kandy's pistol warmed in his right hand. He reached the warehouse, its white paint reflecting the overhead lights onto the cracked concrete dock. His phone continued to indicate south. He reached the far end of the warehouse. Three workers in blue jumpsuits and white hard hats exited it through a swinging door. They traveled a path parallel to his. He heard voices, but didn't understand the language.

The three walked a dozen yards to his left and disappeared behind a rusty red container sitting askew on the dock. His eyes were on the container when they emerged from behind it. By the time he recognized her, they were within a car length.

No one spoke.

The woman who had visited his tent, and who Carr's computers had yet to identify, was in front. The other two were likely the bodyguards who had been with her, but the harbor lights cast too many harsh shadows to know for sure. She came to a halt before reaching the working crane.

Qigiq stopped.

The nearest man handed him blue coveralls. She held the bubble-wrapped package while he slipped into them. The same man handed him a white hard hat. While he adjusted the band and slipped it on, the man stepped up and faced him.

In English she said, "Let him keep his toys. He's not fool enough to use them." She motioned with two hands and a slight twist of her wrist. Both men stepped back.

"These are my shadows," she said. She smiled. Her teeth would have been considered straight before the invention of orthodontia. Up close her face revealed lines around her eyes. Forty-five. Perhaps fifty. Her expression gave away nothing but confident power. Standing alone with him on the pier, even knowing he was armed, seemed of no concern.

"How is Uncle Gan?" Qigiq asked.

A slight flicker of surprise touched her eyes before her

mouth settled into amusement. She would guess that he was fishing, trying to establish a connection he only suspected. Yet she couldn't be certain of everything that Mylin had revealed—or what he and the FBI had discovered.

"I hear he is well," she said, admitting essentially nothing.

Qigiq suspected she heard many things; dragons also had ears. "I will tell Mylin when I see her."

Another flicker. Then she nodded, handed the painting back to him, and walked away.

He followed, feeling like another shadow.

She walked dangerously close to the operating crane and stopped in the open. He stood beside her. The crane lowered an enclosed yellow mesh basket. She opened the door and stepped inside; he had little choice but to follow. She latched the door and waved her hand. The basket lifted and swung toward the wall of containers. He lowered the painting to the toe of his boot and held the steel mesh with both hands as the crane swept them skyward.

She turned toward the approaching wall of steel, putting her back to him. It would be trivial to shoot her. Or slit her throat. She must know this. And also knew it was a fool's errand that would achieve nothing—especially not Carr's goal of discovering the destination for secrets they couldn't define.

The basket swung close to the wall. When it aligned with the end of an orange container stenciled with a black number, it stopped rising. They were hanging one row from the top.

She leaned over the mesh of the cage and knocked on the end of the container. The split door creaked open. With seeming disregard for the multi-story drop below their feet, she clanged opened the door to the basket and stepped across the chasm into the metal box. She turned around. He handed her the painting, then forced himself to stare straight into the blackness of the box and step in after her. The basket swung away. A stocky Asian man pulled the double doors to the container closed from the inside.

She had successfully isolated him, with no way out.

As he waited for his eyes to adjust to the darkness, he considered what Kandy had witnessed from the outside, and what her action-oriented mind would do about it. She would monitor the bodyguards and keep one eye on the container, as long as her patience lasted.

He said, "I bet you don't get much cell coverage in here."

She smiled. "Mr. Qigiq, this is my colleague, Mr. Long. He is an exceptional chemist. We have worked together on several successful projects."

The man bowed. Qigiq returned an unpracticed bow; no one bowed in Alaska.

To Long, she said, "This gentleman is in possession of artwork that I am considering acquiring. We would like you to authenticate his claims."

Mr. Long bowed again, more deeply this time. "I am honored."

A row of LEDs strung along the ceiling filled the container with the eerie red glow of a photography darkroom. A table with folding legs sat in the center of the space beneath a black box the size of a snare drum. A brown sofa across the far end had a beige blanket strewn across it as if someone had taken a nap. A white cabinet at one end of the couch held a camp stove and a ten-gallon container filled with clear liquid. Behind it sat a low chemical toilet of the type used on small watercraft.

Qigiq concluded that Mr. Long could live in this container for days, perhaps weeks, if necessary.

Long placed Qigiq's package on the table and filled the room with echoes of crinkling plastic as he removed the bubble wrap. He ran his fingertips across the entire canvas, systematically back and forth, the way a robot vacuums carpet.

"Is good," he announced.

The red lights went out.

A blackness deep as an Alaskan winter settled on them. Qigiq's eye sockets began to ache. The floor became an undulating ocean swell. He closed his eyes.

The floor stabilized.

He wrapped his fingers around Kandy's automatic and focused on sound, preparing for an uncertain future. His eyelids changed shades of black. He opened his eyes.

The box above the table glowed midnight blue.

Lines on the surface of the painting showed white-silver. Rows and rows of curves and shapes: a language Qigiq didn't understand, but was beginning to recognize.

"Good," Long said. He bent over the twenty-four-inch canvas, obscuring much of it. He now wore black-framed glasses and held a notebook close to his face with his left hand, scribbling in it with his right. The woman's shadow touched the wall. She breathed slow and easy, almost a meditation. She didn't speak. Instead, she clicked her tongue, the sound like a metronome marking largo on a student's piano.

The blue light went out.

Qigiq's eyes ached again, but he held them open and facing the source of the clicking.

The box became the pink hue of a child's cheeks on a chilly day.

Markings on the painting glimmered the rust-red of dried blood. These marks were in rows like the previous ones, but shaped differently. This was a revelation: the canvas had multiple layers of writing. Ferdinand had discovered only one. Did the woman realize that Long was educating him, or figure Qigiq for a dumb cop who had no idea what was happening?

"This is a beautiful canvas you have, Mr. Qigiq," Long said. Still scribbling in his notebook, he added, "I hope you will be able to acquire it, Madame."

No name. Qigiq had been hopeful for a fleeting moment.

The pink light faded away.

Of course. These layers didn't exist in the copy she had taken from him in San Francisco. So her deposit was already paying off. She not only had confirmation that he possessed the original canvas, she now knew what was encoded on it.

Her tongue clicked slightly faster.

A lime green light came on that made him think of fire flies swarming in a swamp. The painting was covered with Chinese characters. Qigiq couldn't read this language either, but the movement of Long's pen said that the man was having no trouble.

She moved up beside Long and gazed at the canvas.

"This too is good," Long whispered.

"How many more?" she asked.

Long twisted his neck to stare over his shoulder at Qigiq, as if seeing him for the first time. He answered, "Several."

"Are you convinced?" she asked.

"Completely. Too accurate for forgery."

"I would be a fool to bring a forged painting to you," Qigiq said, attempting to sound insulted at the very thought.

"And even more of a fool to sell it to me," she said.

The green light went out. A long row of white LEDs snapped on and pierced Qigiq's eyes like lightning at midnight. Long scribbled in his notebook. The woman moved toward the end of the sofa away from the camp stove, sat down, and patted the brown cushion beside her.

So he sat.

She clicked her tongue.

Long's pen scratched across paper.

Finally she said, "You have other pictures I might acquire for my museum?"

"Yes."

"You desire to sell such precious works for what reason, Detective?"

He should have assumed she knew. It wasn't hard to trace people these days, especially from a photograph. He didn't use social networks, but there had been the occasional news story in the Fairbanks paper. Still, the word "detective" coming from her lips made him feel exposed.

"I prefer liquid assets."

She smiled knowingly. "Your skin is not as white, but you have the greed common to all Americans. Materialism is the kind word for it. Tell me, do any of you care about things beyond financial wealth?"

"Some care about fame," Qigiq said, and laughed.

"I see." She clicked her tongue twice. "But fame is a burden. Tell me about these paintings you wish to convert to money to fuel your American dream."

"There is another reason."

"More powerful than money? To an American capitalist? No such reason exists."

"Others have shown interest. But I wish for a connoisseur to possess them, rather than an amateur like myself. I prefer to focus on simple things that I understand—like motorcycles."

"You fear the power of this art?" She laughed aloud. "Yes, fear can be a great motivator."

The LEDs switched back to the light of blood. Long scribbled.

"Tell me about your pictures," she said in the darkness. "Mr. Long's judgement has guided me well in the past."

Qigiq stepped into the opening. "I have twelve more, each more beautiful than the last. A few are smaller, but most are much larger."

"You must have a great deal invested." She clicked once. "And on a detective's salary."

"Enough that I'm motivated to sell." He paused for emphasis. "To the right buyer."

"Ah, you speak of your fear. But you really mean 'at the right price.' What do you have in mind for these marvelous works?"

"I've had difficulty locating someone to provide an accurate appraisal. And there is an additional problem." Her face, tinted pink by the light, wasn't pleased at his last word.

Long mumbled softly to himself, like a student making a math calculation.

She said, "Could this problem prevent my acquiring your collection?"

"Perhaps." He let the word ring in the steel container. "Your deposit has run into trouble."

She was either genuinely taken aback or an excellent actor.

"How surprising."

"I sent a colleague to make a deposit in a local bank."

"And your *colleague* ran off with your money?" Again she laughed at him, seemingly amused by this whole affair.

"No. As he was opening the operating account, he was arrested."

More surprise. "Whatever for?"

"They refused to accept his explanation of the source of the funds."

She leaned forward. "What did he tell them?"

The pink light went out, leaving them in darkness so complete Qigiq couldn't even see the couch he was sitting on.

"That the money was a deposit on an art purchase."

"They arrested him for that?"

"Holding him for questioning. They suspect he's moving illegal drugs onto Jeju Island. The cash is evidence."

"He had better not be. Powerful people will be upset if your friend infringes on their business."

He waited, giving her time to contemplate. Then he said, "Might you know someone who could clear up this misunderstanding?"

She remained silent for half a minute. "You wish this person released?"

"And forgotten. No records. I'd also like my account set up, but that's a bank matter, not police business."

"They're not as far apart here as in some countries. Where?" Her voice disappeared into the blackness.

"The bank in Jeju City."

A shifting of the couch cushion told him she had stood up. The white LEDs came on, less bright than before. She walked to the doors where they had entered and opened one side. The ambient light of the docks silhouetted her overalls in the doorway. She pressed a cell phone to her ear.

Mr. Long went to the end of the couch and adjusted the camping stove.

Since the woman was standing, Qigiq rose to show respect.

He wondered absently if the container or his tent were higher on the "glamping" scale.

She pulled the door closed and returned, touched his forearm, and pulled him down to the cushion with her. "The interrogation was gentle. Your friend will be released later tonight. Now, tell me more about your collection."

Qigiq extracted the Blackphone from his pocket. "I have photographs for you."

Long's head jerked toward them. The water he was heating spilled over the edge of the cup and sizzled on the stove's steel.

CHAPTER 21

"HOW MUCH DID SHE AGREE TO?" Carr asked.

"I started at a million each," Qigiq said, "hoping she'd focus on the one or two that she really needed. Didn't work. She refused to split the collection."

Kandy stretched her legs across the aisle of the plane. The stairs were up and locked, the shades drawn down. "So whatever dragon lady wants is spread across the whole shebang."

"Could be," Carr agreed. "Or it's a smokescreen. She doesn't want us to know which one is important."

"She's doing a good job of confusing me," Kandy said.

"And me," Carr said. "I don't know how it helped her to spring me out. She's never even seen me."

"Probably so she can tail you," Kandy said. "You're one more source of information. Plus, it takes the local cops out of the picture. Always a good thing." She laughed.

Qigiq said, "She agreed to two point six million. She got to two million quickly, but took her time after that."

"Protecting her profit margin," Carr said. "I bet she had a buyer before the accident that killed our informant." He hesitated. "These paintings were in that house the day it was torched. The deal must have been in the pipeline for months."

"That means the buyer is waiting," Qigiq said. "His deal is behind schedule. Now that she believes I actually have them, she's in a hurry. She would have driven me over to pick them up if they had been on the island."

"OK," Carr said. "What have we got? She pays us two-point-six in U.S. cash. It'll be tough to track that to its source."

"She has a bag of tricks," Kandy said. "Meets in a container. Uses magic lights to reveal codes. I bet that container is on its way to Russia by now, so we can't put a forensics team on it."

"The lady is careful. But she did get me out of jail."

"Only because she hasn't met you." Kandy laughed and glanced at a wide black elastic wristband with a watch attached. "Ferd is here with the goods in an hour. If we sell this stash to Dragon Girl and she blows town, what do we have except a pile of retirement money we're going to need after we all get fired?"

"Uncle Sam will want payment for these planes," Carr said. "Don't plan on retiring soon." He turned to Qigiq. "Walk us through it one more time."

Qigiq pressed flat the sheet of notes he had taken after stepping out of the basket and being left alone on the dock. Then he had located Kandy parked in the lot for the arched walking bridge that reached far into the harbor.

"We agreed to phases. She pays for one painting at a time, sends GPS coordinates, we deliver it. Neither side is ever exposed for more than one-twelfth the total. If either of us is dissatisfied, they can withdraw after any transaction, no questions asked." His eyes moved from Kandy to Carr. "I think she asked for that clause in case she doesn't like the merchandise."

"Yeah," Kandy said. "Or if cops get close and she needs to get out of Dodge."

"We *are* the cops," Carr said.

"Yep. But we're not acting like cops. We need to arrest someone. Or at least fire a warning shot."

Carr turned to Qigiq. "Is she always like this?"

"No. She's on good behavior trying to impress the FBI."

"I don't like it," Kandy said. "We collect a pile of untraceable cash, and she disappears into the mountain mist with our goodies. We'll never find out what's really going on."

"Or who's doing it," Qigiq added.

"You two are cheery," Carr said. "Let's work on fresh strategy. Ferdinand will be here by midnight."

"There are only the three of us," Kandy said, "plus two civilians and a super nerd. We haven't even talked with Gan or Mylin yet. If I were a gambler, I'd be putting chips on the Dragon Lady, which I have to tell you, completely ruins my week."

Carr said, "We need to change the rules of engagement. Create a variable we can control."

Qigq stared at a new food tray, wondering where Carr was getting them. He was hungry, but not in the mood to eat. Which made him feel like two separate people. He said:

"You mean like tracking weapons?"

Carr jerked upright, then relaxed. "I see what you mean. The Operation Calm variable is still out there, so we should watch for references. I was thinking of something more direct."

"What's our desired outcome again?"

Carr answered, "Find out who wants those paintings you rescued on a hunch, and why. Stop them from doing whatever nasty thing they have planned. Figure out their supply chain, disrupt it, and throw the bad guys into a federal penitentiary."

"You always fantasize at work?" Kandy asked. "There's one you missed."

"I'm trying not to let it fog my thinking. Yes, I want to know for sure who killed Graham. And for what reason. But let's not talk about it now."

She nodded. "OK. I don't like twelve deliveries in twelve unknown locations. How can we possibly prepare for that?"

"The Dragon Lady doesn't want us prepared."

"Speaking of dragons." Qigiq got up and headed for the food tray. "Does it bother either of you that we know nothing about this woman? We can't even find out her name."

Carr's eyes followed Qigiq to the tray. "I'm trying, but we're in a trust-free zone. If I start the FBI's data-mining software searching through archives of faces—"

"Someone watching is going to tell her," Kandy finished for him.

Carr sighed. "It's a difficult two-way street. The more information we generate..." he shrugged, and wasn't smiling.

Kandy chimed in, "...the more about us there is to find, the more likely our mission leaks to the wrong people. Therefore, our best bet at remaining invisible is to generate no digital trail at all."

"Really hard," Qigiq said.

"Almost impossible," Kandy said. "Look at this big nasty FBI guy. He's got satellites that can tell how fast I'm driving. What else can they know?"

Carr said, "A lot if we log into the system. So let's stay out." He turned to Kandy, who was still stretched sideways across a couple of seats. "You'd prefer one big delivery?"

Kandy nodded. "I think our chance of success goes up if we don't have to get lucky twelve times in a row. Deliver one package, with mini-steps to drop payments if you don't want all that tempting cash in one place."

Carr's cell phone squawked like an enraged hawk.

The three of them were together. Qigiq knew that Jill and Joe were on radio silence. And Ferdinand was in the air. So who was calling?

"Head office," Carr said. "My official phone, not the Circle." He stared at it. "If I answer this I open up the possibility that someone will track the metadata to Jeju."

"It's really hard to be invisible," Kandy said.

Carr turned off his phone. "Let them leave a message in the cloud."

"Can you retrieve it from your Blackphone?" she asked.

"Not without breaking the security of our Circle."

"How about going old school and calling your voice mail from a pay phone?" Qigiq asked.

"Doesn't help. The computer will note my voicemail number being accessed, then it will track the location of the incoming call to the payphone."

"Whose phone number isn't the mysterious T.H.E.Y. watching?" Kandy asked.

Qigiq assembled a ham and cheese mini-sandwich between

two wheat crackers. It crumbled into four pieces as he bit into it, which gave him an idea. "What if you call our colleague Molly from payphone Carr-One. Then she walks to the coffee shop and retrieves your messages from payphone Molly-One. After that, she walks down the street to the laundromat and calls you from payphone Molly-Two to payphone Carr-Two here on the island. Use different prepaid cards each time. Could they track something like that?"

"Qigiq, you crazy guy," Kandy said. "Did you tap dance in Alaska?"

"The watcher would wonder why I retrieved voicemail from a San Francisco pay phone."

"You're based there," Kandy added. "Maybe you forgot to charge your cell."

Carr stared at the dark rectangle he still held in his hand. "These things have hidden powers."

"Yeah," Kandy agreed. "And they leak like a paper funnel flowing transmission fluid. Yes, I speak from experience." She crossed her legs; her boot shook with nervous energy. "What do you think is in that voicemail message?"

"Something important enough to bypass our security protocol. Or—" He turned the phone over and sideways, read the serial number. "A mole inside wants to know where I am. A simple misdialed number would let him or her find out."

"Good thing we're not paranoid," Kandy said, "or we'd never get anything done."

CHAPTER 22

I WAS SQUATTING IN THE DARK closet beneath Win's dresses. I knew I shouldn't touch Mr. Long's money, but my desire to know had drawn me like a human magnet the moment he departed. I had counted two billion South Korean won so far, according to my stacking method. Nearly two million U.S. dollars. My share was tiny, but it was all mine. The idea of packing up my money, walking out the door, renting an apartment, and practicing all day long overpowered me more than if Mr. Long had injected a drug into my brain.

I continued counting.

Partway through a pack I came upon a brown envelope that fit in the palm of my hand. A golden wax seal—with an embossed letter M—protected its contents.

My initial.

I shook it.

Scraping sounds suggested it had rice inside. But why would Mr. Long carefully seal an envelope of rice? I bit the tip of my tongue while turning the envelope around and around. The opposite end was a simple glued seal.

I licked back and forth to moisten the glue, then carefully peeled the paper away. I tilted the envelope upward over my palm. Stones slid into my hand: ruby and blue and emerald and a clear white one that glistened even in the dim light. I tapped the envelope. Colorful particles the size of salt crystals floated onto my palm.

I had seen such gems on the ears and throats of American women at after-concert parties.

Mr. Long was hiding riches within riches.

I had promised myself I would count the money and not foolishly run away again. Not yet. Not without a plan. But gems suggested great wealth and were easy to hide. The temptation to run grew.

"Borrow?"

The word came clearly through the wall near my head. A man had shouted. I listened without breathing.

"We only need...minutes Long...is no...millions of dollars purchasing..."

A muffled woman's voice was barely intelligible.

I worked the stones back into the envelope, careful to include the colored salt. It too might be worth great riches. Perhaps more than all of the won surrounding it.

A man replied, his voice deeper, less shrill. I couldn't make out his words. I inched across the floor of the closet and pressed my ear to the wall. Magically, as if a curtain had been lifted, every word became distinct.

"It is dangerous," the man said. Uncle Gan! I hadn't seen him since arriving on the island. And now he was so close. I brought the envelope to my tongue and moistened it.

"Everything we do is dangerous from six directions," the woman said. "This is simple. What we desire will be in a perfect package. And we know when."

He was talking with Madame Win.

"You lead enemies to us," he said. "What if they come to this house?"

I smoothed the flap on the envelope. Unless someone looked carefully, they would never know I had gazed upon the beauty inside.

"This house? Why, Gan, such an idea. I shall invite them myself. There is nothing to find here, nothing at all."

My neck hurt from twisting to keep my ear flat against the hard wall. I rotated my head and pressed my opposite ear to it.

"Have you forgotten that Mylin is here?" Uncle said. "We must protect her. She is ours."

"She brought the white devils. She must satisfy Long. After he succeeds, she can make the devils go away." She paused. "We will be more powerful than ever."

Mr. Long had promised. If things went wrong, he would tell me where to meet him. Now Madame Win had plans for me. Others always had plans. But no one ever asked what I wanted.

You are a woman, Mylin, born to serve.

In my head Father's voice telling me I should be *honored* to serve the family that protected me. But my family had shrunk: one, two...three...four dead. Only Grandma back in San Francisco and Uncle Gan remained. Without them, I would be alone. I had never been alone. Not for a moment.

"They will not leave without achieving their objective," Uncle said. "Americans are fools, but they rarely give up."

"We must learn what they truly seek," Win replied. "Then we satisfy them."

A door opened and closed on the other side of the wall. I imagined my uncle seated behind the wide desk of cherry wood I had seen when I first met Win. Surely it was his desk—it couldn't possibly belong to her. She was only a woman too.

The outer door of my room creaked.

Crouched in the closet holding the packet of gems, I shivered with instant fear. Stacks of won notes surrounded me. I scooped them into my arms like a lost lover and crawled to the shoes. I shoved all of the packets into a box for boots, placed the envelope along one side, and pushed the lid on as a woman's voice behind me said:

"What are you doing down there, Mylin?"

I was barefoot and wearing clothes I had found in a drawer: tight American jeans and a loose blue T-shirt with the logo of Yamaha—three tuning forks in a circle that reminded me of Da Vinci's painting of man. "Looking for purple shoes," I said, promising myself that I would return the moment she left to hide Mr. Long's money so no one could ever find it.

"Why would a Chinese girl ever want purple shoes?"

I buried the money box in the lowest row and tossed shoes

in front of it before crawling backwards into the center of the closet. I reached to the back of my head, grabbed a handful of hair, and lifted it to reveal the dyed layers beneath. I said cheerfully:

"To match my hair."

Win laughed a snide sneer that let me know she thought I was a stupid little girl, which is what I wanted her to think so she wouldn't snoop into the boxes and find enough money for ten lifetimes.

On my knees, her feet, at least a full size smaller than mine, glared like warning beacons. She wore red shoes with delicate paintings on the sides depicting not a dragon (as I expected), but the back of a woman's head and the faint yellow umbrella she held to protect her skin from the sun.

"Come Mylin. Your uncle wishes to see you." She stepped back, pointed at my bare feet, and scowled. "Cover those."

She crouched to reach for a pair of shoes for me. Panicked, I grabbed the first ones my hand touched.

"Well, at least they're not purple," she said, before turning and strutting out of the closet.

I glanced at my hand. Lime green sandals with chunky wood heels dangled from my fingertips.

They matched nothing.

I put them on, smiling as if I loved them, and walked out of the closet straight and proud to show them off.

"Must you be a walking billboard of American capitalism?"

"Yamaha is Japanese. They make wonderful musical instruments. And I enjoy wearing a tuning fork—I wish it could play a note."

"Don't worry, Mylin. A silly company in America's valley of silicon will one day make that shirt play concert A for you." She opened the broken outer door and left with no further comment on why Uncle wished to see me. It wasn't as if he were asking and I could say yes or no. But I wanted to calm my mind to prevent word of Mr. Long's money slipping from my lips.

I followed with my head bowed.

As I walked, the sandals pinched the pinky toe on my left foot. We made our way along a hallway with carpet so thick my clunky sandals made no sound. We passed below a golden chandelier the size of a cherry tree. We reached a doorway in a house even larger than the one in California where the orchestra had slept.

Win stopped.

Two men stood at the top of a stairway farther along the hallway. We did not approach them. Instead, she knocked near the edge of a door whose wood had been stained so dark it was nearly black. A row of red rectangles down its center, each the size of a human face, divided it into equal halves. The second time she knocked directly on a rectangle.

The door opened. Win entered. I followed. Uncle Gan rounded the desk. He stopped beside the high-backed chair behind it. Its supple leather attracted my eye and made me wish to feel its soft texture against my body. I shook my head to clear away the thought.

I would never touch it. Not without permission from Uncle.

Win stopped in front of his desk and remained standing. I stopped near her, one step back. The desk held a black computer to Uncle's left and an empty black marble ashtray to his right. The sight of the black stone brought a taste to my tongue and craving to my chest.

Bad habits hung on like moss in the jungle.

At the edge of Uncle's desk sat a cardboard box whose tape seal had been split down the center. A box could mean anything, or nothing. Perhaps it was simply a new dress for Madame Win.

"Hello, Mylin."

I bowed.

Uncle seated himself but said nothing more. Eventually Win said, "I will go ensure that all is ready."

"Thank you," Uncle said.

I swallowed and tried to think of how often a man had ever thanked me for anything. Well, for sex, yes. After. But they never meant it. They were merely thanking the dragon gods for providing my body to service their carnal desire. They weren't really thanking Mylin: the girl who had performed, the girl who had been used, the girl who preferred her viola. Except for Mr. Long. His words carried hidden truth. And he had backed them up by secretly giving me money of my own.

Or perhaps Mr. Long was merely a good actor.

Uncle waited. The door latched closed behind Madame Win. He stared at my face. I had learned to detach myself from the eyes of men wandering over my body—but it wasn't working with my uncle. He looked too much like my father. But at the same time, he was different. Calmer. Controlled. Comfortable in a way Father had never been. The way I felt when playing music.

He said, "Would you like to sit down?"

Standing in the sandals was killing my toe; I longed to sit. But I said, "If it pleases you."

"It does. I would like to see you relaxed."

To my amazement, he rose and walked to the entrance to fetch a straight-backed, four-legged chair: the kind that wasn't overly comfortable so visitors would be on edge and not stay too long. It was covered with the same oxblood leather as his chair, though less of it. As I bent to sit, he slid the chair forward to meet me. My palm touched the supple, cool leather of the seat. It instantly made me feel like a born princess, even like the leaders of China themselves. It was impossible to believe this had once been a cow.

"Thank you," I said meekly.

He stood behind me and stroked my hair like I was a lost puppy. My experience with men touching me sexually caused me to remain very still. Father had only touched me to punish me. I swept my mind for a memory, but couldn't recall Uncle Gan having ever touched me, even when I visited the island as a child to study music.

My body shivered, confusing me. I tried to stop it.

"Why do you color your hair so oddly?"

The words from my mouth were an automatic reaction to any question about my person. It was the answer Father preferred. "Men find it attractive."

"But no woman naturally has hair the color of the darkest grapes of the winemaker."

"I think that is why they like it." And was also the secret reason that I did—it made me unlike anyone else. "This color makes me otherworldly...unique."

"Ah," he said, leaving my side, "of course. Man's desire to possess that which no other man has. This one irresistible desire explains many of the woes of the world."

He returned to stand behind his desk, eyes still on me.

My throat tightened, thinking he had learned of Mr. Long's money. Or worse, the money Mr. Long had given me to keep. I vowed that no one would take it from me—though I didn't know how I would stop them. The Americans had taken the gun Uncle Gan gave me, after I used it to kill my brother. It was mine, not theirs. How was that justice?

Perhaps Uncle was upset that I lost his gift.

Or he was angry I ran away from Mr. Long.

Or perhaps he was angry that I killed Shen. But he had told me to protect myself and given me a weapon. So many questions filled my head, I almost didn't hear his.

"Mylin, what is it you most desire from this life?"

This question, Father had never asked. But I knew my answer, had known it for years.

"To play the music of the master European composers."

He smiled, revealing teeth yellowed from years of smoking tobacco. "I thought as much. However, our family has responsibilities that continue, even without my brother...or yours. Much now rests upon your young shoulders. Will you accept your role for our future?"

I do what is asked of me; I knew no other way. And I was punished if I questioned the decisions of men. Or disobeyed. I said:

"I have always done what was required of me."

His gaze didn't falter. "Of all the children who came to be because my brother left China and its one-child policy for this island; of all of them, you walk the path of our ancestors most carefully." He clasped his hands on the desk. "But the path will soon become steeper."

"Then I will grow stronger."

He laughed softly, then coughed the dry hack of a smoker. "Yes, Mylin, I believe you will." He reached to his right and flipped open the long box on his desk to reveal a smooth black case. He lifted it out. Even from my chair I could see luxurious leather, gold hinges, golden stitching.

"First," he said, "we must take care that you have your music." He walked around the desk, making me uncomfortable that he was now standing and I remained seated. This was not how I had been taught to honor my elders. But he had invited me to sit, and not told me to rise. He held the case in his upturned palms, bowed, and placed it on my lap.

The fingers of my bow hand stroked the surface. "It is the most wonderful viola case I have ever seen."

"Kangaroo skin, from friends in Australia. It is said to be stronger, lighter, and more supple than even the finest Chinese cowhide."

I thought of a happy kangaroo, hopping through a meadow, being felled as an archer brought it silent death so that this could be made.

"There is much work for you to do, Mylin. But first, music." He stepped back slightly and leaned against the cherry wood desk that I hadn't dared to touch. "I have arranged a special concert for you this weekend. Sunday at sunset, if arrangements proceed as planned." His eyes watched my hands holding the case. My eyes watched his as I wondered about a mysterious future that would begin with a concert. "An important dignitary will be visiting our island. This event must be unforgettable."

In my mind's eye a silly Asian girl sat in a prison cell practicing music with a chopstick.

"I am to perform?"

He laughed again, his eyes still on me. His hands came up from his sides and clasped together. At that moment white cuffs protruded from his charcoal suit revealing gold chunks that reflected light as brightly as the sun. Cubes. Burnished. Even my richest clients did not exhibit such finery. And my father would never have worn objects of such wanton greed and pride.

I lowered my eyes to the case.

"Mylin, you are the entire show. We will feature your favorite pieces, ones you have played often. And, of course, the Beethoven that Mr. Long is anxious to hear."

"But—" I began, before realizing that a negative reaction to such an honor would be an insult. I thought of my friends, all killed in one night, and said, "We have no orchestra."

He nodded thoughtfully. "Adjustments will be necessary. At first, I had thought we would hire a pianist. But there is a technical problem. And the piano is a bit commonplace. Then I learned that our esteemed visitor has a daughter, and solved two problems with a single modification."

"Do we not have a suitable piano?" I asked, hoping that the gold cufflinks meant there was money for an outstanding piano, which cost more in America than many houses.

"Several. But the stage has..." he rubbed his chin with one hand, "limitations. A piano is too heavy."

I tried to imagine a stage that could not support a piano. He said the dignitary was coming to the island. "Where will this concert be held?"

"That's a secret. We wish to surprise everyone. But I will tell you if you promise to reveal it no one."

I had no idea who I might tell, except Mr. Long. And he would be attending.

"I won't whisper a word."

"We are planning an outdoor concert at sunset. The

weather is pleasant, and shadows on the water, combined with your music, will enthrall the senses of your fans."

"But—" I stopped. I had done it again. Perhaps I had been in America too long. "What will we do without an orchestra or a piano? I have played solo, but my repertoire is small."

"In a South meets North embrace of the arts, you will be accompanied by Yon Kim, our honored guest's daughter...on the harpsichord."

My breath caught. The harpsichord made the music of angels—delicate and bright. Not nearly as overpowering as a piano could be when played by the wrong hands. I almost said "but." Instead, my lips stayed sealed. Then I asked:

"How will only two instruments be heard outdoors?"

He smiled. Uncle Gan always had an answer.

"I am having a special stage constructed." He gestured with a lift of his finger. "You must open the case, Mylin. See the gift your..." his voice drifted off. His gaze shifted around the room. "Your uncle has brought for you. But first. Mr. Long must be happy with our transaction. Tell me, is he happy, Mylin?"

Mr. Long had seemed satisfied with my body, yet distracted by the money and something *coming up soon* that might not work out. I had no idea what any of it could possibly have to do with a somewhat obscure Beethoven Sonata for the viola.

"Mr. Long has much on his mind. I did my best to help him forget. And performed everything he asked of me." Including hiding his money. I glanced down so my face wouldn't reveal my inner guilt. "Before he left, he asked me to undress and play the opening while he recorded me." My hand touched the gold latch I was growing anxious to open. I pressed my teeth together to help me wait.

"You are quite perceptive. Mr. Long has a great deal on his mind. I haven't heard from him directly yet...which I take to mean he is very happy. Now..." he gestured.

The latch clicked with a nearly musical tone. The lid hinged away from me. My eyes took in an aged viola that bore the markings of much use. A bow, similar in age, lay by its side.

"Mr. Long wishes me to play this for him?"

"Would you like to try it?" Uncle asked.

I placed the case on the floor and removed the instrument from deep red velvet. While still seated, I positioned it under my chin and played a long concert A.

I stopped.

I bowed a scale. Plucked notes pizzicato. Played the opening from Mr. Long's Beethoven.

Unasked for tears streamed down my cheeks.

"A seventeen thirty-nine Guarneri." He stared into my damp eyes. "It is all yours, Mylin."

Through distorted vision I watched my uncle open a drawer in the cherry wood desk. He removed a blue box with a gold ribbon around it, remarkably like the one he had given me after a concert in San Francisco.

CHAPTER 23

JILL'S EYES BURNED AS SHE again swiped left on the small screen.

"How long are you going to read that manual?" Joe asked.

"Until something more exciting comes along." She twisted away from the wall and stretched her body face down along the floor. It was metal and cold, but at least it was smooth. "I'm trapped in a sardine can and our airtight security prevents me from even sending a text. How, I ask you, is a young woman expected to survive without text messages in her life?" She laughed, but felt only frustration.

"We have pizza."

"Prepackaged food substance that might sustain life, though we have no proof."

"We're on a stakeout. We can't be seen exiting the van. There's other food if you want it."

"What I want," she rolled to her side, "is to hear from Carr like he promised. I've been running scenarios through my brain. So far, in every one I end up in a Chinese prison being traded to the North Koreans, or vice versa."

"You have an overactive imagination."

"Helps being female. Men can only fantasize about football."

He pointed at her tablet. "Learn anything?"

"Tons." She waved a hand over the weapons strewn on the floor around her. "I've flown drones and test fired every one of these in virtual reality scenarios, but I can't be sure that I'm doing it right."

Joe spun his chair and came to rest facing her. "You want to blow something up?"

"Don't tease, gets me all excited." Jill rolled to her back and stared at the van's roof. Then she slipped sunglasses over her eyes, even though it was permanent dusk inside the truck. "You do realize this vehicle is a drone delivery machine. We can launch half a dozen different kinds, even some with a bomb. The van is a drone too. It has self-driving gadgets. I thought those were just toys in Silicon Valley."

"Has good cameras, that's for sure. Wish I could use it for my artwork."

"Talk to Carr when this is over. He'll rent it to you for a week for a couple hundred grand." She laughed again, but there wasn't much energy in it.

"I wouldn't need the weapons," he said. "Maybe he'll give me a discount."

Jill touched the screen. "You know what else we've got?"

"You mean besides all the amenities of a good motor home?"

"According to these classified documents, we have anti-drone weapons."

"Is that up to date? We're blacked out. It can't check in."

"I'm pretending that when the FBI outfitted the gear in this van, they also bothered to toss a new file onto this tablet computer. Or maybe the truck got a whole new computer. Humor me."

"Consider yourself humored."

"This says drones are kind of stupid. And slow. And not highly maneuverable."

"Don't need much to take a few pictures."

"Right. But that makes them easy to shoot down. Especially —" She swung her feet around and sat cross-legged, facing him.

"Especially?" Joe said.

"If one is in possession of the anti-drone tags we have in our possession."

"Super. I'll send up a surveillance drone. You practice

shooting me down."

"Your days would be numbered. But this sounds cool. I want to play with it."

"Join the military. They would love to have you."

She was quiet for a moment.

"Sorry. Did I say something wrong?"

Jill shook her head. "No. I have a friend who was overseas at the wrong place at the wrong time. You made me think of her."

The van was silent; the equipment didn't even generate fan noise.

"Brave woman," Joe said.

Jill nodded slowly. "She is all of that."

A cell phone vibrated on a hard surface.

Jill said, "My prayers have been answered."

"Might be the pizza bill." Joe spun and glanced at his phone lying on the narrow table below the eight monitors. "Must be you."

Jill got to her knees and patted her pockets out of habit. She crawled around the floor moving rifles and scopes and objects designed to explode.

The vibration filled the van again.

Jill lifted a pizza box designed to both heat and serve. Her Blackphone lay face down on the desk.

"Message from Carr." She read. Scrolled. Read. "He got arrested at a bank. He's back at the flying ranch with Kandy and Qigiq. Wants an update. Says he has news, but not on this channel." She sighed. "I hate being out of the loop."

"Tell him about the guy chasing Mylin into the temple. And that we have the address of her location earlier today."

Jill's thumbs typed like they were in a karate match with each other. "OK, what else?"

"You told him all that?"

"You're a little wordy."

"Tell him about the guys coming out of the clubhouse at the golf course. Maybe he has a way of verifying who they are."

Jill's thumbs flew as she talked. "I'd sure like to know why one minute rotund boy is with a guy the computer thinks is Uncle Gan, and the next he chases pretty girl into temple and bows to the Buddha." Jill thought of her time with Mylin in San Francisco, the incredible concert, and the detached way Mylin talked about her family. Jill knew prostitutes existed, was even friends with a few. But she had always thought of it as a temporary job choice, like working at McDonald's, not a future your father managed.

"What do you think is really going on, Joe?"

Joe sat quietly for a moment before saying, "Given what we know of her past, Mylin is working. Though I don't see how running away fits in."

Jill swallowed a lump in her throat. "I bet it's a marriage ritual. You know, hunt the bride, bow to the Buddha together, bring her back for the main event."

"In a bright green dress?" Joe rummaged in a zipper pack beside the desk.

"We're a long way from Las Vegas chapels. This could be a solemn, month-long ritual."

Keep a drone on Mylin's building.

"Instructions from Carr," Jill said. "He instructs us to do the blatantly obvious and park a drone on the building where we last saw Mylin, which we did hours ago."

"Nice that management agrees with our brilliant operational minds. Anything else?"

"Two more. 'Avoid local cops.' Since we're avoiding everyone, that should be easy. The last one says, 'Follow Mylin.' I'd never have thought of that." She stared at her phone. Took a deep breath. Waited. Took another one. "New one. Carr says, and I quote, 'Protect Mylin, you have the means.'"

Joe stopped rummaging. He turned to Jill. "Does he mean what I think he means?"

"She's his responsibility. Can you imagine the approvals he had to get to spring her from prison. And…" she met Joe's gaze, "he's expecting trouble." Her phone buzzed. "There's more. 'Don't get caught.'" The situation was serious, and getting worse, but she laughed anyway. "Wait, he's typing again. This guy is wordier than you are."

They waited.

She read, "'Engage only as a last resort.'"

"Feel the trust," Joe said. "But he's right. I'm in over my head. I can take pictures, but this," he waved his hand across the floor, "is way above my pay grade."

Jill's eyes ran over the killing machines she hadn't seen before today. "You're right. Carr's right. I'm a lowly student doing a semester abroad." She ran her fingers along the barrel of an assault rifle. "I shouldn't touch any of this stuff."

She looked up. Joe met her eyes. She saw something in them that made her think of dying on this little island before she'd begun to live.

"Unless you have to," Joe said.

CHAPTER 24

QIGIQ LAY ON HIS BACK, floating in dreamless sleep, when scuffling movement startled him awake. His left shoulder ached from the reclined seat of the airplane; his hand reached for the knife. The bed in the glamping tent was better, but the jet was more secure. One unannounced visitor was one too many.

He recognized Carr's silhouette flowing past the in-floor emergency lights.

He glanced at the glowing hands of his Championship watch—3:31 AM.

Ferdinand arriving early?

The paintings could turbocharge this project, or lead to disaster. The Dragon Lady reminded him of a polar bear: attentive, powerful, nearly invisible.

Kandy drifted past. If they were both moving, he should be too. He sat up.

"Glad you're awake," Carr said. "Your colleague is due in a couple of minutes. Weather pattern change helped them out at the last minute."

"Can they land in the dark?" Kandy asked.

Qigiq inched a window shade up. No moon on this side of the aircraft. The runway lay in shadows under a sky of stars unobstructed by a single cloud. No runway lights. The wooden-shack tower, nothing like the modern white pillar at Jeju International Airport, was dark and empty.

"That plane can land itself in a typhoon," Carr said. "Its lights have probably been off for the last hundred miles. We won't see anything until it pulls up beside us."

Qigiq scanned the sky.

"Robot plane," Kandy said. "Is there a pilot on board?"

Carr shook his head. "Can't risk the security breach. That's why we came over without pilots."

Kandy twisted toward the cockpit and back. "I thought they were just staying out of sight."

"They're out of sight all right. Probably in a coffee shop in Miami wondering when their plane is coming back."

"You use robots a lot?" she said.

Carr grew somber. "My first time. The tech people assure me this plane can do anything necessary. We tell it the destination and when to take off."

"You tell me this before I've had coffee?" she said, searching for fresh grounds for the drip machine in the cramped galley.

"Would it have made any difference?"

"I wouldn't have worried about our pilot falling asleep coming across the ocean." She laughed. "Hey, look who's up."

"Good morning," Qigiq said. "So we're up to meet Ferdinand's robot plane?"

"Unmanned Aerial Vehicle," Carr said. "Autonomous drone. There are backup operators on standby if we need them." He hesitated. "But they know nothing about our mission."

"UAV with human cargo?" Kandy said.

"Cargo is cargo. It's classified as unmanned, not unoccupied."

Kandy found an unopened bag of Peet's coffee. "Didn't know anyone was flying this stuff yet."

Carr's smile was bright, even in the low light. "That's intentional." The coffee machine gurgled. "I figure we make face-to-face contact immediately. Find out anything they didn't want to put in the Secure Circle, and let them know what we know."

"Short conversation," Kandy said, holding her empty cup as the pot filled. "We have an Uncle Gan sighting, a guy we can't ID, and..." she pulled the pot out and filled her cup halfway, "the same guy has contact. with the players we know about:

Mylin, Gan, and Dragon Lady."

"Where does he fit?" Carr said.

"Employee?" Qigiq suggested.

"Why chase Mylin?"

Kandy said, "She was a bad girl and ran away. He was dispatched to bring her back."

"But he's the guy who analyzes paintings," Qigiq said. "Verifies authenticity. It wasn't clear if he could decode what he was seeing, but he seemed to be in command of the light required to see it."

Carr pushed a window shade halfway up and stared out at the runway. "High-tech lackey is one possibility. Any others?"

Kandy sipped. "Given that Wu ran a family business, probably a cousin."

Carr frowned. "Good thought. I need an agent in China to visit Gan's family tree."

"I like that idea. Shake out more bad guys."

"Risky. Start data mining from inside one office, and suddenly everyone knows about it. Computers are busier than usual, someone wants to know why. A notification pops up on a screen at the wrong time. There are countless ways for information to leak."

"And they find out about your secret team on Jeju." She paused. "So don't use an office."

Carr lifted his eyes.

"Use Ferdinand," Kandy said. "Or outsource. Masquerade as a civilian paying a genealogy company to find skeletons in your tree. Asians are big on ancestor worship. I bet they have more computers dedicated to it than the Mormons."

"The Mormons?"

"The Mormon Church has a giant data center in Utah trying to track anyone who ever lived. I was involved in a case of a guy hacking it, got to enter his apartment and confiscate the toys."

"Why would anyone hack a genealogy data base?" Qigiq asked.

"He didn't feel his ancestors were important enough in the church, so he tried to upgrade them."

The coffee stopped dripping. Qigiq started pouring into a ceramic mug; felt a slight vibration under his feet.

"Let's watch the landing," Kandy said.

"Black plane," Carr said. "At night with no lights. Dark runway."

"Glad I'm not landing it."

"Me too." Carr laughed.

"Is the runway clear?" she asked.

"The plane has sensors that can see a soccer ball from ten thousand feet. Let's grab ringside seats." He walked forward and opened the door to the cockpit. Carr dropped into the pilot's seat with Kandy to his right. Qigiq stood and studied the array of instruments surrounding them, but couldn't pinpoint the computer that knew how to fly.

"Nice chair," Kandy said. "I should have this in my office."

"See anything?" Qigiq said. "I feel vibrations."

"After riding that old Guzzi of yours, I'm surprised you can feel anything." Kandy laughed.

Carr placed his hand on the dash. "I can fire up the radar if we really want to know. But let's just watch a minute."

Kandy leaned closer to the windshield and gazed into the night sky. Qigiq noticed stars blink off and on. "They're almost on the ground."

Rubber squealing on pavement broke the silence.

"Impressive," Kandy said. "I see it now."

Qigiq saw it too: an aircraft triple their size moving on the far end of the runway. The roar of engine braking reached them.

"What does the FBI use for jet engines?" Kandy said. "That thing sounds like a Kenworth hauling steel up a mountain."

Motion arrived in the periphery of Qigiq's left eye. Years of riding motorcycles had trained him to pay attention to such nudges. He moved behind Carr and scanned the area from Kandy's jacked-up SUV beside the mechanic's shack clockwise toward the runway.

It was black. Moving fast. And so unexpected, it took seconds for reality to register. When it did, nothing good came to mind. He said loud and clear:

"Vehicle moving in from nine o'clock."

Carr and Kandy both whipped their faces left.

Kandy said, "Semi, dual trailers, loaded with cobblestones."

"Heading for the runway," Qigiq added.

Kandy jumped out of her seat, but didn't go anywhere. She typed on her Blackphone. "I hope these messages go through fast."

"Not much the passengers can do," Carr said, "that plane is already braking. The computer will react if it predicts a collision."

Qigiq tracked the vehicle. "An eighty-ton aircraft is aimed straight at that truck."

Carr turned. "That'd be suicide."

"Only if there's a human driver," Kandy said.

Qigiq was struck by the weirdness of autonomous machines approaching each other in the darkness—dueling computers deciding the fate of his colleagues.

Kandy shouted, "Do something!"

Carr pulled out his phone. "I'll put drones in the air."

"I'll go see for myself," she said, scrambling over the plush seat and out the cockpit door.

Carr called after her, "Take cover. If there's a—" His voice was lost to the screech of tires on tarmac.

Qigiq wished for a superpower to reach out and lift the truck out of the way. Then the question he should have asked first came to him: *Why was construction equipment on an airport runway at four in the morning?* Unable to think of a single useful action to take in the next few seconds, he stared out the windshield like a spectator watching a NASCAR crash, memorizing details.

The tractor-trailer rig was moving fast. He held out hope it would make it across the runway before the plane arrived.

Then it stopped.

It didn't slow, or swerve as an evasive maneuver; it came to a screeching halt that caused the trailers to jackknife into a V pointed at the approaching aircraft.

Qigiq stopped breathing. Blue smoke rose like steam from all tires of the aircraft, its nose bowing low under the extreme deceleration. Qigiq's body tensed, anticipating the impact.

The plane reached zero velocity 15 feet from the trailers, then lifted as the stressed suspension rebounded. Black smoke belched from the twin vertical pipes of the stationary truck, its engine idling after strenuous effort.

"I'm going out there," Kandy called out from the passenger cabin.

"Too close," Carr said. "Way too close."

Light reflected from a moving object near the edge of the airfield. Qigiq ran to the cockpit entrance and called out:

"Kandy, we have company."

From beside the stairs control panel, she stepped sideways, and raised a sunshade with one hand. With the other she flicked a circuit breaker. The interior went underwater black.

Qigiq turned around, "What have we got?"

Carr was staring at the runway. "Humvee's at seven, ten, and three o'clock, coming in fast. Cargo areas under canvas. They could be carrying anything."

Qigiq poked his head into the rear cabin. "Three Humvees. No head count. Weaponry unclear."

Kandy said, "A pair of nines and four spare magazines."

The executive jet shuddered as if flying through turbulence. Qigiq reached for the doorframe. He could make out Kandy's face near the window until she pulled the shade down. Next thing he heard was her voice near his feet.

"They backed a Humvee up against our stairway," she said. "How can I get out?"

"Emergency exit," Carr said from the pilot's seat. "But what can you do on an open runway?"

"Not get trapped in this flying bus."

Carr said, "There's a vehicle at Ferdinand's door too."

Qigiq squinted into the night. "Can we tell that plane to take evasive action?"

"Not in my skill set," Carr replied.

"Ferd will figure it out," Kandy said. An explosion lit the airfield. Its shock wave rocked the jet. "Escalation. Now what?"

A block of white light streamed outward from the side of Ferdinand's plane. A Humvee dragging a door on a cable made a U-turn in the middle of the runway.

"They blew off the door," Qigiq said. "They'll board that plane like pirates."

"Where's the third Humvee?" Carr asked. "I know I saw three."

An exit door clunked opened. An emergency exit slide hissed.

"She's going out there?" Carr asked.

"Unless you have a better plan."

"Let's move the plane."

A staccato pulse of gunfire erupted from the starboard side of the aircraft. Bursts were still being fired when Kandy crawled into the cockpit on her elbows.

"They shot up my slide. I could make the drop, but I'll be exposed to all that firepower. Can I sneak out the belly of this thing?"

"So you can get shot?" Carr said. "We don't even know what they want."

"It's not like they asked politely."

A Humvee backed toward Ferdinand's aircraft and covered the opening, plunging the runway into darkness.

Qigiq said, "Black truck. No lights, no markings, no plates. They're here to steal the paintings."

"And no one has shown themselves," Carr said.

"I'll fix that," Kandy said, and crawled away.

"She's not crazy, is she?" Carr said.

Qigiq shrugged. "Depends on who you ask. And when you

ask them."

Cracks of pistol fire preceded more automatic bursts.

Kandy returned. "Driver in a ski mask. I can't tell you anything except to check your phone, Jill is trying to reach us."

Two messages arrived on Qigiq's phone, each with a video link. He tapped *aerial* and the runway appeared as if he were standing on a hill overlooking a battlefield. A Humvee was parked up against each plane. A slide hung limp from the side of the smaller aircraft.

The port engine of the plane whirred alive.

"Can you fly this?" Kandy asked.

"Not directly," Carr said.

"The third truck is parked..." Qigiq gauged distance based on the size of the Humvee. "Ten car lengths east of us."

"Backup," Kandy said, staring through the windshield, her eyes just above the dash.

"Two pin us down, the third steals my art collection."

"And maybe takes hostages," Carr added.

Kandy didn't say anything, but looked ready to jump through the windshield.

Qigiq studied details of the video. The door lay on the tarmac. Two planes, three Humvees, and a tractor trailer were strewn like tossed dice. None showed lights.

"Ideas?" Carr asked.

"I need a weapon that will stop an armored Humvee," Kandy said.

"RPG launcher in the forward overhead. Remember, the skin of a plane won't stop bullets."

She dropped low and crawled away.

"What if we turn the airfield's landing lights on?" Qigiq said.

"We get a few seconds' head start while their eyes adjust."

"Grenade into the truck blocking our door?"

Carr shook his head. "What about the firestorm of bullets while we toss it?"

Qigiq touched the link in Jill's second message. This drone

was hovering in front of the cargo plane peering through the windshield and the open cockpit door into the main cabin. Ferdinand and Pemberly sat side by side with their hands on the tray tables in front of them. A black clad figure with his back to the camera was pointing a rifle at them.

"Armed guard on the scientists," Qigiq said. A body moved past carrying blue bubble wrap. "They're masked. And taking the paintings."

"There goes our leverage," Carr said. "Now the trail turns cold and we head home empty-handed."

"Haven't lost the trail yet."

An explosion lit the near side of the tractor-truck. The third Humvee inched toward the fire.

Qigiq said, "Test shot. Kandy is avoiding Ferdinand's plane."

"I hope she's making them nervous. I hate being the only one stressed out."

"In a few minutes they'll have all the paintings. Do they leave, or are they going to destroy the planes with us in the them?"

Carr turned away from the windshield and met Qigiq's eye. "Cheery thought."

"But why wait? They could have attacked this plane when they arrived."

"So you think they'll leave quietly?"

Qigiq nodded. "Makes the most sense. That Humvee is keeping its distance. And no gunfire in reply to Kandy's big hello. All they did was break down a door and rob us."

Carr stretched back and stared at the roof of the plane. "You're saying that team has grab and run orders? No one gets hurt?"

"Why else would they let us sit and watch?"

"OK, say I accept it. Maybe they know who we are and prefer to avoid an international incident. You're selling the paintings to Dragon Lady, why go to all this trouble?"

"Someone else wants my collection."

Carr sat up. "Let's find out who." He touched the dash. The

jet engine to his left howled, the brakes released, and the plane rocked forward. The tortured screech of bare metal dragging against metal filled the cockpit. An explosion erupted in front of the Humvee parked against Ferdinand's plane.

Qigiq switched to the overhead drone. "Humvee number three is on the move."

Carr touched a control and the plane's forward landing lights converted the tarmac to a white-washed landscape. The third truck passed in front of them. The one near the cargo plane followed. Carr accelerated to intersect it.

The screeching ceased.

Kandy came running up the aisle with a black nylon pack in one hand and the grenade launcher in the other. "Steps are jammed, won't go down." She spun and raced away.

Carr brought the plane to a rapid stop. Another slide hissed.

By the time Qigiq and Carr reached the exit, Kandy was running across the pavement toward her jacked-up SUV.

Carr leapt onto the slide.

Qigiq grabbed a weapon and jumped. When his feet touched concrete at the bottom of the slide he double-timed to the bike—two chase vehicles were better than one. He stuck his Blackphone in Mr. Lee's plastic GPS mount, put the pistol in his left pocket so he could reach it with his clutch hand, and almost had his helmet buckled when Kandy's red SUV roared past. Minutes ago he had been sound asleep, his mind far away. Now he started the bike holding onto a single thought:

The paintings are in the middle Humvee.

He dropped into gear and took off with one eye on the video feed from Jill's drone. The tractor-trailer hadn't moved. Three vehicles raced past a sign for the village of Bomok-dong. Kandy wasn't in the picture yet. He followed the ten-year-old headlight of his Yamaha along unlit streets, dodging ruts and rocks. The caravan moved steadily, implying the drivers knew precisely where they were going and how to get there.

He was riding alone, roaring down a narrow island road.

He slowed to clear Bomok-dong and accelerated into darkness.

On the video from the drone, the middle Humvee pulled out of line to take the lead.

CHAPTER 25

DID THE HUMVEE DRIVERS KNOW they were being followed? They raided the aircraft, but hadn't bothered to disable the SUV. Unless they missed it hidden in the shadow of the shack. The rented Yamaha had been there too. Perhaps it didn't rate as a threat.

Losing the paintings meant the end of the mission. When he caught up, he needed to know which vehicle contained the artwork, and the vehicles were now swapping positions in a Humvee shell game.

And if they had taken hostages?

Qigiq put his head down and accelerated. He heard nothing but wind and the single piston between his knees fighting to produce power. Minutes passed. Kandy's taillights became demon eyes a half-mile ahead. Gray pavement streaked below his aging headlight. He stole glances at his Blackphone. The overhead drone's night vision showed roads snaking around the mountain. He saw two options: take a series of bridges and intersect the convoy from the east, or veer off to ride the hypotenuse, shortening the distance to contact. The second option wasn't paved. The bullets at the airport convinced him that arriving from the rear on a motorcycle would achieve nothing.

Ride dirt.

One pass. The lead Humvee now held the paintings. With no warning, all three disappeared, one after the other, as if they had activated a cloaking device. He reached a fire control road with dark green foliage down the center and a brown rut on either side. He chose the left.

And stood up.

The bike shuddered but held its line. Within a mile the two ruts disappeared, leaving a single trail of scruffy grass inside a tunnel of green. That's what had happened: the Humvees drove under forest canopy and become invisible to the drone.

He pushed on; he, too, now invisible to Jill's drone.

He anticipated outcomes—either he would reach the intersect point first and have new options; or they would, and he'd be back where he started. He remained standing, wrestling the bike, his thighs beginning to burn with the effort. He kept his vision up as the single headlight converted a black hole to flying leaves, shadows, and a squirming snake under his tires. After a full minute of climbing, he crested a hill. In the distance, a black ribbon stretched across his path. He stopped, killed the engine, and doused the headlight.

The jungle enveloped him: rustling leaves, millions of insects, the intense aroma of thousands of flowering plants. The valley ahead was filling with predawn fog as the air temperature neared the dew point. Jill's drone showed four vehicles approaching from the south.

He had been fast enough.

Option #1: Stop the lead vehicle with a bullet from a pistol. Then stand against men with automatic weapons. Probability of success: low.

Option #2: Create an accident by tossing the motorcycle into the path of a multi-ton armored four-by-four. Likely outcome: crushed bike and hitch a ride with Kandy out of the jungle. With great luck, the Humvee would flip off the shoulder and disorient the occupants long enough for an attack. Probability of success: low.

Option #3: Follow the convoy hoping for a favorable location for an attack. Kandy was already executing this strategy.

Option #4: Don't attack. Carr didn't want the paintings back, he wanted to know where they were going.

Option #5: Follow from the front.

Two vehicles appeared through the forest of trees. The inside of the second was glowing pink. He pulled the clutch and coasted the bike down a trail that had been grooved deeply by rain, across a gutter lined with jagged black stone, and up onto the asphalt road. He pointed the bike north and coasted to a stop in the middle of the road. The rearview mirror showed him a straight, hilly road. Jill's drone showed nothing but trees as she worked to keep pace with the again invisible Humvees.

He paid careful attention to the jungle's version of silence—no exhaust noise.

He released the Velcro strap around his left wrist, pulled the glove off, then worked it down over the taillight protruding from the rear fender. He tightened the strap, leaving the fingers pointing into the air like they were waving goodbye.

He checked the switch for the headlight: OFF. He checked it again. He waited for the sound of approaching engines and was soon rewarded. The bike started on the second try. Twin white dots confirmed that the lead machine was closing the distance between them. He set off. Using the spacing between the dots to gauge distance, he rode fast through the starlit forest with two fingers resting on the front brake lever, anticipating randomness from the forest.

Humans saw what they expected, what they *wanted,* to see —or so the university had taught. At this time of night, the driver of the lead Humvee expected nothing but dark empty road in front of him—so that's what Qigiq would give him.

The rush of wind told Qigiq he was riding close to 50 mph. The drone was alternately seeing and losing the trucks as they moved through the rain forest canopy that covered the interior of the island. In front of him, the road ended.

He squeezed the brake lever.

A fork would have been difficult: a fifty-fifty chance of choosing the right path. But this was a makeshift roundabout where jungle trails merged. The road he was on went straight out the far side of the circle, but there were three other choices. Outside the circle, jungle undergrowth looked black under the stars. The interior was filled with tall grass gone to seed like an abandoned yard.

Qigiq idled into the circle—a circle not yet visible in the drone image.

He stopped on the far side and turned carefully toward the center, keeping his knees against the gas tank to limit marks in the grass. When he was dead center, he shut off the engine and lowered the bike to its side, hoping the dew-moistened growth was too wet to catch fire from engine heat. He sat down cross-legged beside the bike facing the road from the south.

White headlights appeared through the waving blades. He identified the distant sound of the Humvee over the ticking of his cooling engine. He didn't want to use it, and didn't think it would be effective, but he removed the pistol from his left pocket. The grip was cool in his bare hand. He moved the weapon to the gloved right.

The lights grew larger. Engine rumble reached his ears.

Committed.

Qigiq flattened himself to the ground. His phone, tilted sideways on the handlebars, showed the lead vehicle ten car lengths from the traffic circle. He placed his arm over the display to block the light. The teeth-like black bars of the Humvee's grille bore down on him. It slowed, raced halfway around the circle counter-clockwise, and continued on the main road.

The second vehicle came in even faster, its interior now black as the paint on its fenders. It veered right and headed east up a strip of pavement half the width of the main road.

Neither gave any indication they had noticed him.

The third approached with its interior glowing sky blue. It slowed but did not go counter-clockwise like the others. It turned left into the circle and immediately made a sharp left up a dirt road.

The Humvees had split up—knowing Kandy couldn't follow all three.

He lifted the bike and started it. Kandy flew through the circle and exited east, following the second driver up the hill. That left a decision: the glowing blue Humvee or the lead vehicle.

Glowing blue Humvee.

He took the rarely used dusty road and stood on the pegs to let the bike find its way. He watched tiny bouncing red taillights. Those lights led him to backstreets of Jeju City that tourists never saw. A third of the buildings had boarded windows. Broken glass glittered along curbs and uneven sidewalks. Graffiti was omnipresent. The only person he saw was asleep at a bus stop beneath a tattered green coat.

A different kind of jungle.

Continuous drone images from Jill let him tail the Humvee from a half mile away using parallel streets. He hoped another drone was guiding Kandy. And the scientists were safe in their aircraft with the missing door.

Qigiq rode north for most of an hour. Then the target vehicle turned into an alleyway near the waterfront. He pulled to the curb on the opposite side of the street, close enough to see into the alley. He let the bike idle and bent low to feign fiddling with the carburetor.

The Humvee stopped three buildings from the far end.

Qigiq circled the block, slowing as he passed the third from the end: 404 Island Way, one-story structure, glass display windows, three foot high Kanji symbols in brilliant red above smaller painted black letters that spelled out:

GALLERIE ELECTRA

CHAPTER 26

UNCLE GAN HAD INTERRUPTED my practice on the ancient instrument that I could not yet believe was mine. He had then given me a task in his store, where I now stood behind a glass counter. The case was filled with jewelry made from pearls. Pearls brought up from the ocean floor by haenyeo: the famous female divers of Jeju Island.

Friday—less than one week from my prison cell in the desert.

The clock ticked away seconds with its thin red finger. 10:01 AM. A palindrome. My friend Qigiq's name was one too. I worried he would be killed for following me; no one was safe from the eyes of the dragon. I unlocked the front door from the inside with a brass key and thought about the young girl I had yet to meet who would accompany me on the harpsichord.

On Sunday—two days from now.

I had arrived at eight-thirty, as instructed, found the twelve paintings in the storeroom wrapped in blue bubbles, and hung them on the walls. Deciding on ideal placement to make a sale had been difficult, my being a musician and not a visual artist or businessperson. I considered grouping them by color (blue hues here, red hues there, yellow and orange on the back wall). Then by theme: seascapes near the front door, buildings (especially the individual houses that seemed so sad to me without people) along the west wall. I even considered what grandmother Chong might say about proper feng shui, while wishing she were here to consult with me.

For a moment I fantasized about being a billionaire and

flying her to Jeju on my private jet. We would have fun mixing colors and trying new things—the way we did before I became a woman. Her absence saddened me. I worried about her, alone in San Francisco, longing to visit China before her death.

The pictures brought back memories of my friend Joe Roberts. I thought about how he might do it, and arranged them by size, the smallest near the door. This achieved showing the lower cost items first, so as not to frighten shoppers, and placed larger works at the back where they made a bold visual statement the moment a customer entered the gallery.

Satisfied, I returned to practicing my instrument whose magical voice was the most resonant of any viola I had ever heard. As I rehearsed from memory my gaze fixed upon the blue box with gold ribbon resting on the glass counter before me. I imagined my vision penetrating it to reveal a shiny silver handgun and a row of bullets—just like the gift Uncle had given me once before.

That time he had said: "Protect the family's assets."

I had failed.

Instead, I killed my brother and was sent to a prison I thought I would never leave.

I stopped playing and inhaled slowly through my nose. I didn't want another gun, fearing what I would do with it.

The dull clattering of bamboo brought my attention to the main entrance. I lowered my instrument and prepared to meet my first customer. His clothing was dusty, reminding me of the homeless people I had seen in Reno. Perhaps he had slept on the beach. Clearly not a Caucasian tourist. He moved to my right and examined the paintings just the way I had devised: small, larger, and larger still. He stopped at a picture of a blue house I had tucked into the corner of the gallery.

I hadn't seen many blue houses in my life; this one looked almost part of the sky.

I stooped to return my instrument to its case and adjusted the collar of my white blouse paired with a gray skirt that reached modestly below my knees. I straightened to greet—

"Qigiq?" I whispered. "What are—" I stopped my tongue. Stared. Smiled, though nothing inside of me felt joyful. My mind raced in a spiral. I forced my mouth to stay shut, I cleared my throat, and held the false smile.

"Hello, welcome to the Gallerie Electra of Jeju Island. Please browse, enjoy the artwork. I will be happy to answer your questions." I couldn't answer much, but those were the words that Win had taught me.

"Thank you," Qigiq said. "How long have you had this collection on display?"

"Today is the very first day. Is there something in particular that interests you?"

"I've met this artist. I'm hoping to collect another of her pieces."

I remembered—the woman I saw through the one-way glass in the little restaurant in San Francisco. I fired a gun that day too. "Where should we begin?"

Qigiq returned to the blue house painting.

The door squeaked and clattered. A chubby white man entered wearing a multi-colored shirt and the khaki trousers favored by tourists since I was a child. His beard reminded me of my friend Bear back in Reno, though this man wore thick black-framed glasses that made him look like an owl.

"Welcome to Gallerie Electra," I called across the room. "Are you looking for anything special today?"

The man walked directly toward me, stopped at the glass counter, and looked down at the jewelry in the case between us. He didn't answer my question. Up close, I sensed I knew him. But how? I was thousands of miles away from America and the rich men who had paid for my company.

He looked up.

Dark brown eyes of such intelligence...bushy caterpillar eyebrows...recognition flooded through me. My mouth moved before my brain could catch it.

"Professor Pemb—?"

He placed a finger to his lips, his other hand flat on the counter, and then bent over at the waist to peer down into the case. I bowed.

He said, "That silver piece interests me..." His palm shifted to reveal a small piece of paper on the counter, hidden from the security cameras by our bodies. "...the black onyx intermixed with pearls. It exhibits a special sort of balance that..."

The note was in Mylinian—a language he invented. Even though my uncle had paid him, it was still the most special thing anyone had ever done for me. I translated in my head:

Dear Mylin, it is my great pleasure to see you again. Your friends need assistance. They sent me in the hope the dragon eyes do not yet know me. May I ask a few questions?

"Thank you for visiting our gallery. We are always happy to welcome visitors to the island." I continued reading while he spoke.

"The pearls seem to be of extraordinary quality."

Are video cameras watching us?

"Oh yes," I said. "We watch for new artists all the time."

Is audio being recorded?

"I'm sorry, we don't carry recordings, but there are wonderful folk performers throughout the island. My uncle doesn't care for modern technology, so he keeps things simple with paintings and jewelry."

We require access to these paintings.

I thought and thought while the professor chattered about stones and colors and metals. The paintings were hanging in the gallery. The gallery had cameras. How could anyone access them?

I said, "The gallery closes at five-thirty," still bowed forward and gazing down through the glass so that no camera could not read my lips. I slid the case open from my side and pointed at one piece after another, wishing to put on a good performance for the electronic eyes.

An idea popped into my head. "I will be here tonight practicing. If you care to hear authentic South Korean folk music, I will play my viola for you."

The Professor placed his large palm over the note. I was glad that Mr. Long had given me practice with the language just recently. The paper disappeared between the professor's palms as he straightened.

"There are many stunning pieces here. Do you have a favorite?"

I thought of the heart shaped from wire wrapped skillfully around a green stone that my friend Jilly had given me for luck. That had been just before our first Bear Naked Orchestra concert.

"I am partial to hearts."

The professor again leaned over the glass. This time there was no note. He shuffled slowly along the counter. "There." He pointed into the case with a perfectly manicured index finger twice as thick as my own. I remembered how afraid I had been seeing those hands for the first time, thinking how clumsy they would be touching me, pressing into me.

I had been very wrong.

His hands had explored and exploded my body with great gentleness, as if it had been *they* who were afraid.

I followed his direction; my eyes landed on a row of necklaces from a local jeweler named Su Dokgo.

He said, "In the center."

I retrieved a silver chain holding small pearls in the shape of a heart. At the center was a black stone—likely onyx from mainland China—that had been polished into the shape of a heart. A heart within a heart. Or perhaps the artist had meant two hearts as one. It was delicate and quite beautiful. I placed it into his outstretched palm.

He looked in my eyes. "Do you like it?"

"Oh yes, it is exquisite. Su Dokgo does work of the highest quality."

"Could you gift wrap it for me?" he asked.

Wrapping paper brought to mind the blue box from my uncle sitting on the counter waiting for me to summon the courage to open it.

"What color would you like?"

The professor's eyes rested on my face for a moment.

"Do you happen to have purple?"

"Several shades. Do you prefer violet or grape?"

The front door clattered.

My dusty friend Qigiq had left. My sadness returned. Then I remembered how I had been brought to this island by men unknown to me. Men paid by my uncle. Perhaps it was safer if Qigiq didn't say hello to me. Perhaps we should never again say hello.

"Dark," the professor said. He gestured upward. "Like the color of your hair."

I smiled and crouched to reach the wrapping supplies in a drawer at the bottom of the display case.

The professor paid for the necklace with paper won and stood patiently while I wrapped his box.

"Ribbon?"

"Silver, like the necklace."

While I tied a bow with stretchy silver ribbon, he drifted to the paintings and wrote in a notebook the size of a pack of cigarettes.

"Ready," I said.

He returned to the counter, accepted the package from my hand, turned it over, and slipped a folded note under the ribbon.

"Would you please show me the bamboo wind chimes you have on your front door?"

I stepped out from behind the counter, walking carefully in the five-inch heels Madame Win insisted I wear to make me taller and show off my calves for the customers. "These are handmade here on the island using a combination of glass and bamboo rods." I opened the door so they would sound. "They are carefully tuned by ear for the most beneficial effect."

He stepped very close and looked straight up at the chimes. At the same time, something touched my free hand.

"They certainly make a delicate sound. I will order one

after I find a suitable bungalow on the island to purchase."

I moved my eyes to his face to judge his sincerity. But he had turned away and was already partway out the door. "Why would you purchase..." My eyes caught sight of the purple package and silver ribbon in my hand. I crossed my arms to conceal it and headed for the storeroom.

The door tinkled closed behind me.

I stood in the dark in a musty corner where a small statue of a nude woman that came up to my waist was stored. Turning the package over, I found the note, and translated:

Thank you, Mylin, for reawakening in me a love of life. If you ever need anything that is in my power to give, simply ask. I will return after 5:30 PM tonight. Please wait for me.

By the time I walked back to the long glass counter, my tears had almost dried.

CHAPTER 27

THE TRANSPORT AIRCRAFT THAT FERDINAND had converted to a flying laboratory was missing its forward door. The opening had been covered with a gray tarp and sealed with duct tape. Carr leaned on his elbows at a table stretching along the port side of the plane. Kandy relaxed on a couch Ferdinand had included in the flying lab for his power naps. Pemberly and Ferdinand discussed the photographs Qigiq had taken at the gallery. Qigiq poked around in a narrow fridge—lack of sleep making him hungrier than usual.

He found a nutty energy bar assembled on top of a layer of chocolate and swung the door closed. Then he sat and gazed out the window at the executive jet across the runway. Its exit doors were closed. Deflated slides drooped onto the tarmac from both sides.

Carr sat as if lifted by an invisible puppeteer. He was clearly fatigued from sleep deprivation and a rough ride in Kandy's SUV all the way to a dock where the Humvee rolled onto a ferry. Carr had called off the chase at that point, deciding foot soldiers wouldn't have much to tell him anyway. He had been gobsmacked when Qigiq told him the paintings were hanging in an island art gallery.

Ferdinand moved a narrow black box slowly back and forth like a t'ai chi master practicing. The green light being emitted from its base turned pink.

"It's only noon," Kandy said, leaving off *what am I going to do until the gallery closes at five-thirty?* that Qigiq knew she wanted to add.

Carr stood and walked the length of a plane designed to carry rows of Army tanks. He stopped beside Qigiq and whispered, "I have a new problem."

Qigiq bit into chocolate coated nuts, grabbed a bottle of water off a metal shelf, and motioned with his head. A problem that could make a guy like Carr whisper required privacy. He headed for the cockpit. Carr closed the door behind them. Qigiq took the pilot's seat, feeling odd knowing the plane had flown in with it empty.

"Before you hit me with the new problem, let me review what I think I know. We know where the paintings are. We have Jill and Joe watching the gallery with a pair of drones, so we'll know if someone tries to move them."

"Right," Carr said, remaining standing. "But we're not sure who attacked us. Or why. We also don't know the state of our deal with Dragon Lady." He shook his head. "We sure can't sell her something that's not in our possession."

"We could steal them back. But Ferdinand is more interested in finding out what the colored lights are for. He has a theory."

Carr managed a tired grin. "Scientists always have a theory. I have one too. We don't know what's happening, and if we lose track of those paintings, we lose our primary connection to —" He stared out the slanted windshield.

"To?"

"I was going to say, to the people we're trying to find. But I don't know if that's true. It's still possible this is just garden-variety smuggling."

"In which case, it leads nowhere in your big picture, leaving you and me holding a tome filled with unanswered questions."

Carr turned around. "Including this new one."

Qigiq bit into his bar. Chewed. Finally said, "I'm not going to like it, am I?"

Carr ran a hand through his hair, which was so short and curly that it barely moved.

"I don't know. In a way, it could be good news."

"That's in short supply."

Carr returned to staring out the windshield at empty runway. Eventually he said, "Remember I told you about Shirley?"

"Your undercover agent on a container ship sailing east. Her body washed up on a beach miles from a population center."

"Right, that's her. Only...it's not."

Qigiq stopped chewing. "The deceased wasn't your agent?"

"ID says yes. Clothing says yes. Height, hair color. But a preliminary DNA test says no, not even close. So we're not looking at a subtle interpretation error in a DNA lab."

Qigiq took a slow breath while gazing at the instruments. "That's two problems."

"At least," Carr said. "Now we have a Jane Doe on a foreign beach. Not our jurisdiction. And technically, not our problem."

"Except her IDs are real. You're about to tell me they are, in fact, the working papers issued to Shirley. So whoever arranged to put them on that body—"

"Now has Shirley." Carr turned to face him. "Or knows what happened to her."

"And you're wracking your brain trying to figure how this fits with our paintings."

Carr nodded and lowered himself slowly into the co-pilot seat.

"Got anything yet?" Qigiq said.

"Nothing I can act on. Just a feeling."

"Lots of answers start that way in our business."

Carr slid lower in the leather seat. "OK, Detective, speculate. Why wash a body up on a beach with an operating ID?"

"Same as before, send a message to someone. Only now I don't understand the message."

"I don't either. But I'm getting an itch that time matters. The perps had to know a country as technically sophisticated as the United States would figure this out."

"Two thoughts," Qigiq said, wishing for a bigger energy bar.

"First, if you think she's dead—"

"We won't look for her," Carr finished for him.

"Right. But you *will* look for how she died, where she had been, how she was caught."

"Of course. They motivate us to look at the past."

"Yes, backwards. Make us waste time and resources looking at all the places she was."

Carr sat up straighter. "Which means not looking at where she was going."

"They did something else too," Qigiq said. "They bought themselves time. Whatever Shirley found is long gone by now."

Carr's shiny black shoe tapped the steel floor. "We can do a lot with satellites." He paused. "I never said this, but cracking the operational computers of international shipping companies is well within our skill set. This administration finally understands the role of offensive cyberattacks."

"Is that like watching the metadata on who called who on their cell phones?"

Carr laughed a hearty sound that resonated off the windshield. "Didn't have to crack that, the communication companies gave it to us."

Qigiq tucked a thumb into his boot and rubbed the tusk handle of his knife like a worry stone. "So now we have three objectives. Our original of finding out who is receiving the information on the canvases." He pulled a slip of paper out of his pocket and wrote. "Second, where is Shirley? Third, what did she find that made her disappear?"

Carr said, "Can you wrap those up by tonight? I'm ready for a flight back home." Then he produced laughter with a maniacal edge.

Qigiq removed his hand from the knife. "Did the Dragon Lady grab the paintings to avoid paying? Or is there more to it?"

"She doesn't want the paintings. You saw the proof in the container, she wants what's hidden on them. Or this Long guy does. Or somebody we don't know about does. My question is: What is she selling? Information? Or paintings with a magic code? A million bucks is now hanging in plain sight. How many people are keeping eyes on it?" He returned to gazing out the windshield. "What I really want to know is what the hell is on them?"

Qigig said, "Let's brainstorm with the team this afternoon. We already know what we're doing at sunset." A thought struck him. "Did we get a Humvee?"

Carr nodded. "U.S. military base in South Korea. It's on the ferry covered in that white plastic used to protect new cars."

CHAPTER 28

JILL SAID, "WHAT ARE YOU DOING?"

Joe stretched both arms and cracked his knuckles. "Reviewing pictures from a security camera."

"I'm working and you're playing?"

He leaned forward so he could see her images coming from two laser-pulsed drones parked near the Gallerie Electra. One showed the glass front of the gallery, the other displayed the back door beside a garbage bin piled with brown cardboard and blue bubble wrap.

"You call that working? There isn't even anything moving."

"Something might." She spun a pizza box with the toe of her boot. "We need better food." She glanced around the interior. "And a bigger truck."

"Cabin fever? That happens to me when I stay in one place for too long."

"Carr never said helping Mylin would be this boring."

Joe sat more upright. "Have you seen any sign of her?"

"Not since the bearded guy left the gallery." Jill stood and bent over to touch her toes, held the position for ten seconds, then straightened slowly. "So what are you really doing?"

"Research."

She glanced at his monitor. "You're playing with blocks?"

"Containers. See that ship? They've been loading and unloading all day."

"Where?"

"A harbor town on the south of the island with a name I can't pronounce. Carr's update said Qigiq met the Dragon Lady there yesterday."

"Does she have a name?" Jill asked.

"Not yet, but I've been working on it. Qigiq sent this." He brought up a picture on a separate monitor.

"Hard hat and blue overalls." Jill pointed. "Not much of her face. Can you match it?"

Joe shrugged. "Maybe. If Carr would give us access to his fancy government databases."

She studied the picture. "Is this the person Mylin says has spies watching our every move?"

"That's the rumor."

Jill knelt, put her chin in her hands, and elbows on the desk. "Let me get this straight. Carr won't let us use government databases. So you're playing with blocks and ogling an old lady in work clothes."

"She's not that old. Maybe only twice your age." Joe laughed.

"OK, smart guy. What exactly *are* you doing?"

"Working while you get goggle-eyed hoping Mylin will come out again."

Jill pressed her lips together. "That obvious, huh?"

"Yeah, but don't worry. She's an easy person to…" He looked down. "Uh, she sort of gets in your head and doesn't leave."

"And now lives in South Korea, *six thousand miles* from California. Where I finally got into the academy."

Joe stared at the image of the gallery for a minute. Nothing moved. He finally said, "Let's focus on helping Mylin. First, who is this woman? Second, why did she summon Qigiq to the docks? I mean, yeah, to look at the painting. But why the docks, as opposed to say, a hotel room, or a dark basement?"

Jill watched a crane move a box the size of her San Francisco apartment. "I see loads of activity to hide in and open space. Land access from only one side. Easy to protect."

"What about escape routes? Dragon Lady had herself boxed in."

Jill shook her head. "Not if she has a boat like Karen's red rocket? If the Dragon took off in that, even our drones couldn't catch her."

"There's something else. I got to wondering how long containers sit around. Look." Joe traced a line on the screen with one finger. "This stack at the end of the pier is five containers high and ten wide. There's room on the dock for another ten wide. Five by twenty would be a hundred containers."

"A hundred places to hide," Jill said. "Is that what you're thinking?"

"Not counting the ship's deck sitting behind them. More containers. Four cranes."

She said, "Docks are where cultures meet. Many things are possible for the man with a little moola to pass under the table to the dock master."

Joe nodded. "Interesting place. I'm trying to find anything that doesn't fit."

Jill opened a metal folding chair and sat. "Why do we have only one good chair?"

"Budget-conscious Congress." He laughed. "Have you ever played Tetris?"

"That game where blocks fall from the sky invented by a Russian engineer? Yeah, I suck at it."

Joe tapped the screen. "I've been watching that crane. Just sort of staring at it unloading huge containers. I noticed a pattern."

"You mean like you and I wasting our lives in the back of a borrowed government van watching boring movies? With one hard chair?"

He smiled. "That too. But mainly I watched the containers. The crane guy moves them into stacks. Then unstacks them to make other stacks."

"Organizing them." Jill moved closer to the monitor. "Do trucks come to pick them up?"

"One container went out on a flatbed. I followed it to the ferry."

"Funny way to unload from one boat to another," Jill said.

"It probably makes weird economic sense with import duties and stuff. Or maybe it's faster than waiting for the bigger ship to head north."

"The Internet calls it *intermodal.* Trucks, trains, ships, all use the same containers. Saves a lot of handling. Maybe most of the goods stay here on the island. A couple of times a container was unloaded right on the dock into a bunch of small trucks. The empty was moved to one side."

The picture updated, as it had been doing every five seconds for hours.

"Do you think this island produces enough to fill the outgoing containers?"

"That's an economics question, I'm a photographer." He grinned. "If you want a guess, I'd say no way. But, like you, it got me interested. So I went back to the satellite feed we used earlier, the one where we found the guys playing golf. There are archives."

"All so you can play Dinosaur Tetris?"

"Madame Win used a container for her meeting with Qigiq. I was curious what else might be going on."

"Who?"

"What?" Joe said.

"Who is Madame Win? You said *Madame Win.*"

"I did?"

"Yeah. You called the Dragon Lady Madame Win, clear as day."

Joe frowned. "Natasha sent me a message. She calls herself Nashi. That was after...um...the girl at the counter—"

"Counter? *What counter?*"

Joe wagged his head. "Sorry, I've been staring at camera feeds too long. How could I forget something so obvious?" He took a breath. "Let me tell you the whole story. I was testing the surveillance cameras that Carr had me install around the island. I noticed a woman going in and out of the spa. You know how I think—I see everything as a possible photograph. So I took her picture at the Hotel Shilla. It wasn't important, it was just something I did because I'm a fine art photographer and do weird stuff. She, uh, caught me following her. A couple of guys with her looked like they could get nasty. She instructed me to leave copies of the pictures at the spa. When I did, the cashier recognized her in the photos and wrote *M. Win* on the envelope."

"And you're just remembering this now?"

"I thought I told you already."

"Nope. I would have remembered a tidbit like the *Dragon Lady's name.* Are you sure it's her?"

"My subconscious thinks so. But we don't have good pictures of the Dragon Lady. She seems to know where the cameras are and hides from them."

"Did you tell Carr?"

Joe sat quietly. Containers moved on the monitor.

"Well?"

"I'm trying to remember. I meant to tell him about the entire interaction, but we're in this 'Don't call us, we'll call you' communication lockdown. I sent him copies of the pictures I took, I'm sure of that."

"Maybe you should send him the name now, and how you got it. It's probably just a smokescreen for spa appointments."

Joe pulled out his phone and connected to the Secure Circle. He spelled out what happened in a brief status report.

Jill pointed at the chair. "My turn." After she was seated, she said, "Okay, super spy, tell me what you found out about these containers?"

"Let me show you." A time-lapse movie of satellite shots intermixed with drone photos played. Multiple cranes lifted and swung in a dance of steel. A small ship sailed. Later, a larger ship arrived. The sun rose and set, casting long shadows to the right, then short, then long again to the left. The ship's deck became crowded with containers. Trucks arrived and departed. The movie ended on the live frame from the drone.

Jill said, "Watching that makes Tetris look easy."

"It seems chaotic the first few times. But the computer can

track specific objects."

"And the punchline is?"

Joe leaned forward to point at a sky blue container three rows up from the ground in the huge wall of containers. "That one."

"OK. Play it again, Sam." She laughed.

Joe ran the movie again.

"There," Jill said. "That blue one just arrived."

"Yep."

They watched in silence.

Jill stood to put her face closer to the screen. "Hold a second. Back it up. Is that a basket? What's that for?"

"They move people and tools around with the cranes," Joe said. "Why?"

She shrugged.

The movie moved on and again stopped at the live image. The number three crane was loading a container onto the ship.

"It's still there," she said.

"Yep."

"And all the ones that came in with it are gone."

"Not quite. I think there's a second one. That beat-up brown one over there. It came in, and the contents haven't been unloaded."

"You could have them mixed up," Jill said. "The satellite angle isn't that great. And you only get a good look during daylight."

"I called POTUS and asked for a special satellite feed for Princess Jill. But he didn't call back."

"Haha. So you leapt to the conclusion that these two containers are significant because they haven't left?"

"Well…"

Jill held up a hand. "And…you believe that significance is connected to this Win woman you photographed, who is maybe the Dragon Lady. Is that your hypothesis?"

Joe laughed. "I don't have a hypothesis. But these containers seem worth watching to me, so I was watching. Which, if you recall, is the question you asked: 'What exactly are you doing?'"

"How do we get a peek inside?"

"That very question has been occupying me for hours." Joe's phone buzzed; he looked down. "It's a reminder to schedule another massage. I want to get Nashi talking about Win."

"I bet you call that *work*." Jill laughed, then focused on the drone image. "The containers of interest are up high. We could climb, but security cameras would see us."

"*We* could climb?" Joe said. "Let's rethink this."

"You're the master photographer. Can't you get a tiny camera up there to peek through a crack?"

"I can try. But containers are designed to float. And even if I could position a lens, there's no light inside, so we'll need a strobe."

Jill pressed her palms together and touched fingertips to her lips. "Can we see through the side with some sort of Superman X-ray vision?"

"Through steel strong enough to hold twenty tons of consumer goods? Not with any equipment I know about."

Jill studied the floor. "We could blow a door off."

He laughed. "No one will notice that."

"We could wait until someone opens them. But...well... waiting stinks. I don't even want to talk about it."

"Talk?"

She faced him. "This waiting is killing me."

He bobbed his head. "Maybe we can *listen* through the side. Let's check." He brought up the screen for setting up drone payloads. "Twelve camera options. Four microphone options."

It took only minutes to put a third drone in the air.

"Let's drive back to the Shilla," Joe said.

"Not yet. The drone will be there soon. Maybe we'll hear something really important."

"We don't have to stop listening. I just need to keep an appointment."

Jill leaned back in the good chair. "OK, but I get all the credit. Ha ha ha."

Joe crawled forward to the driver's seat and started the truck.

He called back to her, "Clear?"

"Good to go. Hey, Joe, when we get there, park where I can hear a pin drop in a container twenty miles away."

CHAPTER 29

THE GIRL BEHIND THE CASH register smiled as Joe passed through the glass entrance doors into the spa's waiting area.

"Hello again. You are excellent photographer."

Unaccustomed to attention, he stopped, "Uh, thanks."

She leaned forward. Light glinted off three silver rings in her ear as she whispered, "Madame Win like your photos. She give me big tip."

He nodded, understanding why she had remembered him in a sea of hotel guests.

She tilted her head. "Would you take my picture someday?"

He held up an index finger as if to ask her to wait a minute, then moved it sideways to his left. Her eyes followed. He lifted his phone up to the right in slow motion and managed three shots before she realized what was happening. During the next three her face showed surprise, then transformed into the fake smile everyone but children show a camera.

He lowered his hands. Of the six shots, two weren't bad, considering the low light in the spa designed to help customers relax as they spent wads of cash.

"You tricked me."

"I tricked Mad...our friend too." He turned the phone toward her. "Take a look."

She swiped back and forth through the photos and stopped on his favorite: eyes gazing off to one side, face peacefully expressionless. Her shyness returned. "I didn't know I could look so pretty."

"You do. All the time. It's just tricky to capture beauty in a camera." He slipped the Blackphone into his pocket, suddenly aware he was being his careless photographer self and leaving a trail of memories behind. This was not the low profile Carr wanted. "Would you like to have the pictures?"

Her eyes dropped to the floor. "I can't afford to pay you."

How could he help her feel comfortable? Men offering gifts often wanted something in return.

"Consider them a thank you for introducing me to Nashi."

A wide smile preceded, "I would love to have them."

He'd like to print a huge giclée that her parents could hang in their house. But he had no equipment in Korea. He pointed at his phone, then at her. She understood immediately and tapped her phone a few times. An icon popped up on Joe's phone. He dropped all six pictures.

Her "Thank you" was barely audible.

"Is Nashi in?"

She brushed her hair back with one hand, showing off the earrings in her left ear he had focused on for the pictures, and glanced at her computer. She lifted an arm to point.

"Room four at the end of the hall, sir."

When he reached it, the door with the gold 4 stood ajar. He peeked in, tapped with a knuckle, eased it open. The room hadn't changed since his last visit. The soft music even contained tubular bells.

No Natasha.

He stepped inside and left the door open. His fingers itched to search drawers, notebooks, shelves—anything to learn about Natasha and Win. But if he got caught, Carr would ship him stateside and he might never see Mylin again. He stuffed both hands in his pants pockets and wandered around trying to look innocent while searching with his eyes.

A voice from the doorway spooked him.

"It's nice to see you again. Was your last massage satisfactory?"

He turned around. "And beyond."

Natasha smiled under blonde hair whose tips touched an

indigo shirt stretched tight across her shoulders. It had three-quarter length sleeves and a low round collar that exposed cleavage tanned by sunshine. She floated into the room and lit the double wicks of a fat round candle. The aroma of a forest after rainfall surrounded him. She stretched one hand over her head to adjust the audio system to the sound of rain and sighing violins.

Joe's shoulders relaxed. He couldn't afford spas—especially not at the Shilla, perhaps the best hotel on the island. But Carr had been clear that information trumped budget.

"Same as last time?" she asked.

"Whatever the expert masseuse recommends."

She went to the doorway, glanced down the hall in both directions, then back at him. Her dark, fitted jeans had gold stitching, making him curious how much a massage therapist in Korea earned.

"If you aren't in a hurry, we should do a full ninety-minute session. That way I can spend extra time on your tight spots."

He felt guilty doing "research" while Jill sat alone in the van. But he had a secure cell phone if anyone needed his skills. Plus, he might learn something important.

"I have time."

She smiled.

He tried not to be seduced by her breathtaking Russian-athlete physique.

She said, "Excellent. We must work together for the best results." She stepped out, pulling the door closed quietly behind her.

He dropped to one knee, unbuckled his belt with his left hand, and reached for the brass handle of a low drawer he had missed on his first visit. The doorknob behind him rattled. He had no time to even remove his fingers before she was kneeling beside him on the cool slate floor. Her hair brushed his left cheek.

He wracked his brain for a good lie.

"Come quickly," she whispered, grabbing the hand that had

been undoing his belt. She pulled him through the door and eased it closed behind them, leaving the music floating in a sea of rain and the candle burning its double flame. Without releasing his hand, she led him through a doorway beneath a lit sign he couldn't read and up a metal outdoor stairway to ground level. At the top she released his hand and dove into the front seat of a black ragtop Jeep. He slipped in beside her, surprised that an iconic American rock-crawler had gray leather seats and was on an island in South Korea being driven by a Russian.

He buckled his belt.

She started the engine, slapped a long floor-mounted shift lever into gear, and blasted off in a spray of gravel.

He said, "Is this tour included with my massage?"

If Natasha knew Win, he should be concerned about where they were headed. But he was too excited to be going anywhere with Nashi to care. In that moment, he understood why magnetic women were used as spies during every war there ever was: men's brains stopped working.

Over the road noise she said, "Glovebox."

He unlatched the door by his knees. Two pairs of dark glasses fell onto the open door.

Her right hand shot toward him, palm up.

The sun was shining, but it was late on a Friday afternoon. He really didn't think glasses—

"Hurry."

He handed her the pair with round lenses the size of drink coasters, figuring them more feminine, and slipped the plain black frames on himself.

She said, "I'm never outside without them."

"Do you have sensitive eyes?"

Her face flicked sideways and back to the flat windshield. "Do you play the fool as part of your regular-guy disguise, or is America using amateurs now?"

Joe knew the answer, but also knew not to admit it. If Uncle Sam had drones and satellites with super-cameras in the air, of course other countries did too.

He laughed. "Oh, we're hiding?"

She glanced his way again, her expression serious. Then she laughed too. But she didn't remove the dark lenses that covered her sensual blue eyes and half her cheeks. She up-shifted until the Jeep was in fourth gear, steered with her left knee, and used both hands to pull her hair back into a tight pony tail, revealing sharp cheekbones he hadn't noticed. He wasn't sure what she was hiding from, but the eyes of a dragon came to mind.

Nashi said, "You are friends with Madame Win?"

Joe braced his elbow against the door as she flew up a wind-ing road passing through a meadow filled with tiny yellow flowers. Not what he expected to see on an island built by a volcano.

"We met once."

"You take pictures for her?"

"I'm a professional photographer," he said, aware he hadn't answered her question.

She drove a few miles in silence. The lack of conversation gave him time to think, but he didn't come up with much, ex-cept he should let Carr know where he was. Which gave him an idea.

"May I take your picture?"

She smiled with a mocking look he wished he could have photographed. "Don't be silly. We have things to speak about. But not here."

The Jeep's oversized tires ate up the road. He stared straight ahead to not look at her while struggling to get his brain back.

"Okay if I take pictures of the countryside? Or is that silly, too?"

"South Korea is beautiful, especially this island. Did you know it is one of the natural wonders of the world? I love working here."

She hadn't said no, so he brought out his phone. He took pictures out his window, careful not to point the camera her way, careful to capture any building or wall or tree that would help him find his way back if he had to, and extra careful to capture her reflection in the windshield or side mirror when possible.

"How do you like your Jeep?"

Her smiled held. "A practical machine. As you will soon see, it takes me anywhere: the coast, the volcano, the forest. And it is easy to park. This is freedom."

"Jeep should use you in a television commercial. You would sell loads of cars."

"I already have a job."

She whipped the Jeep off the pavement onto a dirt road that had the same yellow wildflowers growing down the middle. The Jeep sat so high it didn't even nick the petals as it raced over them.

"Soon," she said, answering his unasked question.

They traveled miles. He hoped he wouldn't be hiking back alone in the dark. The Jeep crested a hill and tried to lift off, charged down the other side, and landed in a gravel parking lot for a dozen cars.

"Short cut." She switched off the engine, grabbed a mesh backpack from the rear seat, and tossed a bottle of water at him. She said, "Can you run?" spun out of the vehicle and trotted off across the lot.

He twisted the cap off the bottle and chased her receding figure as he drank, keeping his eyes focused on the loose surface against the temptation of watching her body cast a long shadow.

She disappeared.

He entered a cave of black stone: walls, ceiling, floor. He ran faster. In a hundred yards he was beside her chasing a bouncing white circle cast by LEDs strapped to her forehead. They passed a family of four carrying flashlights going the other way.

"Lava tube," she said, speaking easily despite the feverish pace.

His feet pounded on a well-worn path as he perspired in the cool, damp environment. He was about to ask for a break when she stopped. He bent forward, taking deep breaths. "This isn't...as relaxing...as a massage."

The light on her forehead blinded him, but also cast shadows down her face, making it appear ghastly narrow and on the road to death. She stepped to the side of the trail to sit on a naturally formed bench and patted the black rock beside her.

"Come, let us talk."

Joe shuffled over and sat.

She turned off her headlamp.

The darkness was thick. The only thing he saw that wasn't black was the tiny specks of the family's flashlights in the distance. "What is this place?"

"A private office. Tourists generally tire before reaching my favorite chair. This tube is over a mile long."

"That's a lot of lava."

"Tubes form after eruptions. Lava cools and contracts, leaving air spaces and pillars like the one beside you. The size of this tube is highly unusual. Scientists claim it was formed after an eruption thousands of years ago."

"I bet it'd be beautiful if I could see it."

She laughed softly to his right. "We must be where no man can see us, hear us, or approach us. Drones and satellites are useless here. Long-range microphones have difficulty with the acoustics. Yes, I am sure. Plus," she paused.

Their breathing filled the space. The distant flashlights were no longer visible. He shifted on the rock seat, his cotton pants making a scratching noise.

She continued, "We arrived fast and will finish quickly, creating but a small window of opportunity." Since he didn't know what they were doing, he hadn't thought about leaving. But so far, going with her still seemed like a good idea. "As we spoke before, you know Madame Win?"

"Only in passing. I'm just—"

"A photographer, yes. I have reviewed your work." She paused as if studying his face. But he didn't see how she could be, it was too dark to see anything. "You take compelling pictures. Several of an Asian girl intrigue me."

His fingertips tingled. If Nashi knew about the *Smoking Girl* pictures of Mylin, then she had found his website, knew his name, bio, and probably more about his life than Google and Facebook combined.

"You didn't have to show me your lava tube to buy a picture."

"Acquiring a print doesn't interest me. Have you sold to Madame Win?"

"I haven't sold anything in Korea. I'm..."

"Just a photographer. I understand. Then let us talk."

In his opinion, they were *already* talking, although she was doing a good job of beating around the bush. The inky darkness made him feel like he was surrounded by enemies—clouds over the stars was daylight compared to it. Time ticked away. His heartbeat grew loud in his ears. To break the silence he said:

"I really enjoyed my last massage."

"Thank you. I have studied for many years. And during those years, I have made many friends around the world."

"What do your friends think of my pictures?"

"In the past forty-eight hours, they have contacted me repeatedly. Madame Win is offering something for sale. We wish to buy it." She didn't continue.

Was he supposed to guess? "Is there more to your story?"

"I was hoping you could tell me."

"Madame Win doesn't talk business with me. I'm just..." He laughed.

"Yes, I know," she said. Then laughed with him before saying, "This something my friends wish to acquire, she is offering to another party."

"That happened to me with a camera once. I hate being scooped on a deal."

"We would be very unhappy to be...*scooped.*" He counted seventeen heartbeats before she added, "But you can help me."

He noted the friendly first person. "Would you like me to take your picture?"

"Oh, my photographer friend, you can be so silly. My deepest desire, the very thing Madame Win chooses to sell elsewhere, you are providing to her."

He ran back through the conversation in his head. It occurred to him that Nashi must think he had given Win something important in the envelope he left with the cashier. It had been a SIM card, and could contain anything digital.

"Those were impromptu pictures that I shot outdoors."

Nashi may have nodded; he still couldn't see her face. Talking to a voice without a body made him feel like he was on a video chat with a bad connection.

"Pictures?" she said.

"Yes, in the envelope. On a SIM card. I took them with my cell phone."

"I see." Silence. "You will be making another delivery soon?"

He wasn't privy to Carr's plan, but he doubted it included Joe Roberts, amateur spy, delivering anything to anybody.

"Probably not me."

Joe felt pressure on his palm. He closed his fingers around the strap of her backpack.

"My friends would like you to have this. Remember, they are profoundly interested in what Madame Win is selling, but prefer to buy directly from the artist."

The pieces fell into place like a Tetris win. She wanted whatever Carr had and was making a move to cut out the middleman and the competition in one tactical maneuver.

"I'm the photographer. I can't make any promises."

Her hand gripped his thigh firmly in the darkness and slid upward.

"I understand. I am just a masseuse."

CHAPTER 30

"HOW DID YOU MAKE THIS RECORDING?" Ferdinand asked.

Jill spoke at the roof of the plane from her supine position on the couch. "Joe set up two drones. We flew them to the harbor. I pressed a couple of buttons and they stuck themselves to the steel sides of the containers like Spiderman." A swooshing sound played from a pair of loudspeakers. "When will Kandy be back?"

Ferdinand and Pemberly sat at the workbench wearing headphones. Ferdinand replied, "She's off with Carr and Qigiq gathering materials for tonight."

"That sounds like an ocean wave breaking to me."

"Unfortunately, very little signal penetrated the steel. And why a single rush of sound that doesn't repeat?" Ferdinand studied a squiggling blue line on a white graph. "And these clicks and pops. And later, over here, a rush of air so quiet it might simply be ambient noise from wind."

"I should have listened from all four sides."

"Next time."

"Are you going to lock me in that truck again?"

Ferdinand laughed. "My dear girl, no one will lock you in a truck. But your monitoring efforts have been helpful."

"How about the rusty container?"

"A barely audible signal ticking like a broken clock."

"Bird?" Jill said.

"You are thinking out of the box. Yes, the sound does resemble pecking. Where were these containers?"

"Third row up. And the bottom row."

Ferdinand aligned the graphs. "These were recorded at precisely the same time?"

"Not quite. I placed the low one, then flew the other into position manually. Took me a minute or so. I'm pretty good with video games—kick butt against the alien bugs all the time."

Ferdinand chuckled. "I see. Well, I will align these and attempt to remove common ambient noise."

The rushing sound of a small wave filled the cavernous interior of the aircraft.

Jill sat up. "Wait. That's not a wave. It sounds...like a toilet."

"Perhaps," Ferdinand said, letting the audio play again.

"Breathing?" Pemberly suggested.

"What about the second container? That clicking."

Ferdinand typed at the keyboard.

"Wait," Jill said. "Do that again?"

"Do what?" Ferdinand asked. "I was simply remapping the audio."

"Okay, remap it again."

"But I just..." he sighed. "Very well."

"Not a bird," she said. "Those clicks are from a keyboard."

"We must visit the harbor," Ferdinand said, "and attempt to obtain more definitive data. But this is an excellent start."

Jill rolled onto her back; she wasn't smiling.

Ferdinand kept working.

A matrix of a hundred portraits appeared on the monitor to Ferdinand's left. The computer beeped as it displayed the last one.

The beep motivated Jill off the couch. "What did you find?"

"Win Chong," Ferdinand said. "Or more accurately, Win Chongs, plural." He leaned closer to the monitor. "Ten thousand, five hundred, and thirteen of them."

"You mean ten thousand pictures?"

"I filtered for redundancy, so this data set should contain only unique individuals."

"We'll never be able to look at so many," she said. "Where are they from?"

"Assuming you mean the photos, they are mostly from WeChat, a Chinese social network. Others are from Weibo, a Chinese short message broadcast network, and from scraping websites around the world. Humans are not shy when posting pictures of themselves to attract attention."

He paged through a thousand faces, a hundred at a time.

"Humans have, in fact, created a worldwide surveillance society without the help of a secret government agency with a three-letter name. People do it voluntarily for the tidbits Silicon Valley entrepreneurs offer them. Technologists have known this for years, of course. But if one takes the long view, and tries to warn others of the risks, they are met with blank stares between glances down at a smartphone to post yet another picture that will live in the cloud forever." He reversed the direction of his scan. "But I digress, and risk boring you with needless philosophizing. Using the name Joe Roberts provided, and the geographical area that we know Mylin has visited, we can narrow this group down to..."

Two images displayed side-by-side: female, Asian, 40-ish, dark hair, dark eyes, wide cheekbones.

"You got all those down to two people?" Jill asked, incredulous. "Kandy wasn't kidding about you waving a magic wand."

"Detective Dreeson is too kind. Requiring a residence on Jeju eliminated most candidates. And that may turn out to be a terrible assumption. Perhaps the person we are looking for visits Jeju for brief periods but never resides here. So I have also included any passage through South Korean customs."

"Ferd, you're amazing."

He laughed heartily.

"Sorry," Jill said. "I've heard Detective Dreeson call you that."

"Not to worry, Miss Jill. Kandy has many idiosyncrasies that we overlook because she is extremely capable at her job."

"Thanks," she said. "So you narrowed it down to two

people?"

He gestured to the picture on the left. "One." He moved his hand to the right. "She died ten years ago."

CHAPTER 31

"NO WAY," KANDY SAID, shaking her head. "I should go. This is a job for a woman." She laughed.

"It's three stories up," Carr said.

"You have a bad knee," she countered.

Carr turned to Qigiq, who was reviewing the drone videos of the harbor.

"What do you think?"

"I think it's safer if a drone takes a repelling line to the top container and attaches it to something solid."

"That line needs to be black," Kandy said.

"Agreed. With the right line, any one of us can make a safe ascent." Qigiq paused, staring at a hundred containers—modern societies sure moved a lot of stuff. "I'm worried what we find. Whoever goes will be hanging outside that container without backup."

"Yet another reason to send me," Kandy said. "Highly qualified hand-to-hand."

"Plus, she likes action," Qigiq said. "Think of her job satisfaction."

Carr sighed.

They were using the cockpit of the executive jet while the scientists prepared the lab. Jill had returned to the van prison to ready the drones.

"Where's Roberts?" Carr asked.

"Texted ten minutes ago," Qigiq said. "He went to see a lava tube."

Carr shook his head. "Photographers must think different."

Kandy held up a fist. "Jon Ken Pon anyone?"

"Warning," Qigiq said, "she'll win. I think she's found a way to cheat."

Carr rubbed a hand through his hair. "Okay, Dreeson, it's all yours. But we have to back you up."

"Ferd and Pemberly need backup more than I do."

Carr put his head in his hands and spoke at the floor. "Lot of unknowns, we all need support." He leaned back in his co-pilot's chair. "How about I drive the new Humvee to the gallery and hope the dragon eyes accept it as one of theirs. You take your red sled to the docks, and our moto-buddy floats to wherever he's needed most. It violates all kinds of protocols, but we're short-handed for people with weapons training."

"What about the civilians?" Kandy said.

"Keep them in the truck so they don't get hurt."

"They're doing a good job," Qigiq said. "Joe got the Dragon Lady's name. And Jill came up with those audio recordings."

Carr held up a hand. "I hear you. I'll get them a medal. Or a fat bonus."

"How about a scholarship?" Kandy said. "Jill wants to go to the academy."

He laughed. "She really is as crazy as you are."

"Remains to be seen," Kandy said with a smile. "But she has the basic ingredients. And a heart full of desire."

Carr's expression flattened. "I remember feeling that way once. It's peanuts by FBI standards. I'll see what I can do." He grew quiet for a moment. "Thinking back to my academy days. And *Dragon Lady.* Do either of you remember that plane?"

Kandy and Qigiq looked at each other with blank stares.

"Nope," she said. "What plane?"

"A high-altitude spy plane. Russia shot down one of ours. Captured the pilot. Caused all manner of international troubles."

"The U2?" Qigiq said. "The plane Gary Powers flew. Some new missile shot him down."

"Right," Carr said. "The U2 was nicknamed 'Dragon Lady.'"

Kandy asked, "You think it's not just us? Win actually calls herself the name of a spy plane? And that's why it's always 'dragon eyes?'" Kandy hesitated. "An *American* spy plane? That would mean..."

Carr shrugged. "Seems impossible. But if we can figure out what she's selling, maybe we'd know who she works for." He turned to Qigiq. "What do you want out of this?"

"For it to be over, after we catch whatever we're chasing. And a future for Mylin." He twiddled the wheel in front of him. Nothing happened. "We persuaded Mylin to help us. She was cooperating until they grabbed her out from under my nose. I feel I owe her."

Carr stood. "We'll know where Mylin stands after tonight. Pemberly said she understood his note. She helps us, I get her reduced prison time. If we crack this thing, I'll get her a medal too."

"How about a path to citizenship?" Kandy said.

Carr sucked air through his teeth. "No experience with that. But I'll try."

"Before you go," Qigiq said. "How about an opinion?"

"As many as you like."

"What happened last night?"

Carr sat back down and glanced around until he found his Coke can. He took a long swallow. "You're asking me to deduce why a team hit our aircraft to steal paintings we planned to sell to Win, taking pains not to hurt anybody? And why the stolen goods ended up in an art gallery owned by Uncle Gan?"

"Yep."

Kandy stopped pacing and stretched her back like a bored yoga instructor. "I'll give you two reasons. First, two million dollars. While I'm sure that attack team was paid well, a heist wouldn't cost two million U.S."

"Win negotiated with me," Qigiq said, "but the price didn't seem to worry her. I got the feeling she was going to pass it along to the buyer."

"Or maybe she never planned to pay it. She just wanted you

to get the merchandise to the island. But—," Kandy twisted her back, "she might be like me."

"Now you're beginning to scare me," Carr said.

Kandy grinned. "She likes action. Time is of the utmost importance for reasons unbeknownst to us. Of course, right now, most things are unbeknownst to us."

"So she agrees to my price. I bring the paintings here. She grabs them the moment they arrive."

"Can't get them any faster than that," Kandy said.

"But once she had them in her possession, why put them out in the open where we can see them?" Carr said.

Qigiq released the wheel. "Maybe not us. Maybe Win is proving she has the merchandise to someone else."

"Yeah," Kandy said. "So *they* make their first payment. Part of which she uses to pay you off when you show up to complain about the heist. Most important, it all happens fast. None of this dilly-dallying waiting for banks to move money around."

The cockpit was dark. The sun had set over Hatashan. "And the reason she's in a hurry?"

"She's a woman," Kandy said, and huffed her low laugh.

"Too easy," Carr said. "And besides, she's Asian. Asian women put the word *patience* in the dictionary."

Qigiq turned to Carr. "So she must have a deadline."

Carr nodded. "Impending event. That would explain it."

"Not good," Kandy said. "Because we don't know what or when."

"Or why," Carr added.

The cabin was quiet save for the light hum of an onboard generator. That hum made Qigiq think of how self-contained an airplane was, like his houseboat back in Marin—a place that had started to feel like home in just a few months.

An electronic chirp broke the calm.

Carr read the message and said, "Roberts is outside on the runway. Wants to talk face to face. Says it's important."

CHAPTER 32

I GAZED OUT THROUGH the thick glass of the gallery's front door. A group of young Koreans on the far side of the street sang a song of love. Today, three couples had visited Gallerie Electra seeking an appropriate wedding gift. This beautiful island would be a good choice if one wished to marry. I locked the door with the odd thought that the glass might be bulletproof.

The shadow of the gallery building reached across the two-lane street and bent upward onto a boutique whose front was painted pink by the fading light. I pressed the palm of my free hand against my heart and felt the edge of the professor's note touch the skin beneath my shirt. So many different kinds of people in the world, how was I ever to understand them all? Or learn which ones to trust?

I lowered the polished bamboo blinds to cover the door from top to bottom and withdrew a brass key as long as my finger. Then I circled the gallery, studying each painting and turning off its spotlight.

What was so important about these pictures?

They were pretty, yes. But there was much beautiful art in the world, old and new. Why these? Why now?

I had much to learn about the art business.

I flicked off the last spotlight. Rows of gray beams seeping in from the street striped the dark room and carried me back to my prison cell. I shuddered. I told myself to live the current moment fully, as the Buddha taught. Right now, I was free; I could play the most amazing instrument I had ever touched; I had my own money.

Real freedom contained action.

I smiled while moving receipts from the cash register drawer to the wall safe in the back room. I placed a small lamp on the glass counter, propped my music against the cash register, and filled the gallery with the sound of my Guarneri singing Mr. Long's Beethoven.

His money. Hiding among my shoes. What would I do with my share? I no longer needed a viola. And that was all I had ever wished for.

I turned my attention to the sound resonating in the gallery. It wasn't as large as a concert hall, but it was five times the room where Mr. Long and broken the door. The ceiling was high, so notes soared before coming back to me clothed in richness I barely believed had come from my bow.

Maybe I would buy a house.

The mere thought took my breath away. I had never dreamed of owning anything. Father owned everything. What it would it be like, this world of *owning?*

I lifted the bow from the strings.

My tiny concert hall fell silent.

I had heard growl. The soles of my feet sensed a vibration.

I placed my instrument in its case and hid it in a low drawer under wrapping paper. I removed Madame's high heels and stood barefoot on polished wood. Stripes of light sliced across my toes.

The vibration became stronger.

I flicked off the light on the music stand and waited.

The vibration went away.

I reached inside my blouse for the professor's note, reread it, and put it back. Tonight. He was coming tonight.

I padded silently past the side door to the store room and into the vestibule of the rear entrance. I knelt down and parted the slats with one finger. I blinked and blinked. Everything was pure black, as if I had gone blind. I stared and waited. A black wall close to the other side of the door came into focus.

Motion made me jerk away. There had been no sound. I parted the slats again. A rectangle lit from behind glowed on the glass. Paper. With writing. I squinted.

Mylin, is there an alarm? —Joe

Alarm? I knew of no alarm. Maybe it was automatic. So much of the Internet world—

Joe?

My photographer! He helped me escape from Father! Why was he in Korea?

I turned the lock and opened the inside door. A figure was kneeling on the ground holding a note up to the glass, the face covered by a mask that revealed only eyes. A tiny flashlight in one hand lit the paper. Behind him a black truck on high angry tires pointed away from the gallery.

Joe inched the outer door open and was suddenly so close his scent reached me. I hugged him, wanting to be safe—knowing it wasn't possible in the land of dragons. A corner of the professor's note poked my chest.

I pushed away and whispered, "What are you doing here?"

"Helping you," he said softly through the mask. "Kandy, Qigiq, and the FBI agent you met are here, too."

I grabbed his arm. "I told Qigiq to leave."

Joe eased past me, brushing his chest against mine. He said, "Let me check for an alarm," before disappearing into the striped grayness of the gallery. I pressed my back against the cool wall beside the door to wait.

He returned quickly. "There's an electronic alarm, but it hasn't been armed. Did anyone give you a code?"

I shook my head.

He frowned. "Why wouldn't they have you set the alarm?"

"There is no need," I said. His expression revealed his confusion. "No one on this island would dare touch this property. And if they did, they would be found quickly." I hesitated, but he needed to know. "And severely punished."

He nodded and found my eyes. "We're coming in, OK?"

The professor's note said he was coming back. I had been thinking all day he meant we would again be man and woman, like before...in San Francisco.

"Mylin?"

I focused on Joe's eyes, this man who had tried so hard to save me.

"I...I don't know. I don't know what's happening. I can't tell you if it's safe." Then a thought that was always near intruded. "Dragon's are out at night, too. Especially at night."

"That's why we brought a truck like the ones they used."

"They?"

"The people who stole Qigiq's paintings."

"These are *his* paintings?"

"He rescued them from a house before it burned down." He held my shoulders and looked me in the eye. "Mylin, there isn't much time. We're coming in, OK?"

I nodded gravely, seeing our house burn, feeling his touch. I wished I could kill my brother again. I blurted out, "I'm playing a concert on the top of a mountain."

His eyes held on my face, but he didn't speak.

"Sunday at sunset."

He nodded. "I'll find it." Then he disappeared into the darkness.

Three black-clad bodies with their faces hidden by masks slipped through the door carrying black bags—thieves from a movie. I faced the truck. Who had stolen the paintings? I pushed the door open—stopped myself. Eyes would find me out there. I let the door swing quietly closed and shut the inside one with the slatted blinds. Then I locked us all inside.

I found the Professor with another bearded man in the gallery. They were moving from painting to painting with a black stick that emitted pink light—like a light saber from the movies.

Then, before my eyes, magic happened.

Under the light, the painting transformed from a picture to rows and rows of writing. Writing in Mylinian. My language.

The pink light from the stick turned green; Chinese characters replaced the Mylinian.

I stood dumbstruck as the men worked. This was why these simple paintings were so desired, so important, so dangerous —they held ancient secrets.

Secrets even dragon eyes could not see.

CHAPTER 33

KANDY STOOD NEXT TO THE RED SUV in the shadow of indigenous king cherry trees. The trees weren't in blossom. The ferry dock was empty. She pulled on climbing gloves and adjusted the harness strapped tight to her body, touched each item on her belt and visualized using it. She took one last 360 degree look around, then pulled a skullcap down over her face—her entire being now covered in black. She adjusted the mini-goggles strapped to her forehead.

Her other choice was a bright blue jumpsuit and hardhat. But she was too tall, too white, and too female to convince an observer she was just an innocuous dock worker doing overtime on a South Korean island.

Stealth won that argument. A risky option.

Being dressed like a ninja wasn't explainable if confronted. But she preferred being a dark shadow observers could convince themselves they hadn't seen.

Reaching the containers was the problem at hand. If she swam, the first twenty yards out of the water would expose her. If she ran in, the floodlights would cast a mime's shadow against the whiteness of the building. Not good options.

She chose simplicity itself—crawl.

She stepped back into the SUV, started it, and drove directly toward the storage building, swung in beside a silver Hyundai sedan, and shut off the engine. She waited. Listened. Scanned for eyes paying attention to her, wondering where the driver of the Hyundai was working.

Three minutes past one A.M.

She remained corpse-still in the darkness for seven minutes. No activity. No third shift. Not even a watchman on the near side of the stack of containers. She reached up to verify the switch position to keep the interior light off, then exited the vehicle thinking *move like a snake.*

Speed attracts the human eye.

Three slow-motion steps placed her spine against the building and her face in darkness. Two more and the rungs of a rusty fire escape ladder bolted to concrete block carried her upward. She dropped to her knees and worked her way forward behind the low wall at the edge of the flat roof. At the far end of the building she took three quick steps and leapt toward a newly painted container. Soft soles touched the steel top, followed by a fluid body roll.

Almost silent.

She shimmied over the end of the box, hung from her fingertips, dropped to concrete.

Forty yards of open pier separated her from the five-story wall of stacked containers she needed to reach. A monstrous crane stood stock-still in between.

Life's little trade-offs: motion versus stealth, exposure time versus speed.

She dropped flat onto concrete and inched forward on her belly until she reached the rear of the crane, breathing slowly, imagining a snail. She did another slow motion 360 survey. She knew that Jill had a drone in the sky, but Kandy couldn't see or hear it. That made her wonder if the dragon had drone eyes active tonight. Only thing to do about that was stay in darkness and hope it didn't have infrared sensors.

Hugging the crane, she worked her way around to a tire so large she could crawl into the hub. High in the crane's arms, a pair of floodlights glowed, splashing white everywhere. This time she didn't crawl; she sprinted through the light and disappeared between two containers. With her body sideways, she crabbed between the steel sides to the other end. The ship moored at the pier was barely fifty yards away.

She stabilized her breathing. This was a lot of trouble to look inside a tin box.

She removed binoculars from her belt and scanned the ship. Containers covered half the deck. Lights everywhere. No guards in sight.

1:17 AM.

She turned the glasses up the side of the container stack. Her target was twenty-five feet away. Two more containers sat on top of it. She focused on the upper lip of the top one. A blur arrived. An arm from the drone swung out and hooked a carabiner to a locking rod on the topmost container, then released a coil of black rope. The rope floated directly toward her, straightened, wavered, and ended ten inches from the ground.

"Thanks, Jill," Kandy whispered.

She put the binoculars away, took three deep breaths, stepped out from between the containers, and clipped onto the rope. Her boot tread gripped steel and her gloves worked hand over hand as she speed-walked up the side. In seconds, she reached locked barn doors, located the container's ID code, and verified the digits that Ferdinand had been able to decipher: four-zero-seven-five.

She activated the harness lock to free her hands. Then she flipped open a holster to access Carr's magic tube, pulled the goggles down over her eyes, crouched to bring her close to the container's door, and touched a green button.

Blue light shot from the narrow end of the black tube and touched the locking rod. A narrow slice of the rod turned red, then white. She released the button. Repositioned. Repeated. A ten-inch chunk of rod tilted. Carr claimed it wouldn't be too hot to catch because the laser cut so fast.

She tested his theory.

It was plenty hot, but she managed to place it on the lip of the door she didn't plan to open.

She slid the tube back into its holster and mentally rehearsed her next series of moves as a time-lapse movie—so they would flow like a martial artist's offense.

Only then did she...

Ease the top bar down with right hand, rotate handle with left, reach for pistol with right, swing door open with right toe—hope it doesn't draw attention.

It groaned like a lonely whale.

Her left hand pushed the strobe flashlight into the narrow opening to disorient anyone looking toward the door from the inside. A chemical stench wafted past her. She studied the interior the moment the flashing light stabilized: mostly empty, no lighting, a lump in the far corner. Possible body.

Not moving.

She swung inward.

Releasing the rope from the harness, she moved toward a bald Caucasian female, fingers splayed out on the floor, fingernails damaged. No clothing.

Kandy ducked back to the door, took three quick breaths of fresh air and raced to the woman.

Pulse 50. Respiration 10. She messaged Jill to prepare medical supplies. No cell coverage. She moved closer to the door until the message sent.

A yellow flash filled the box as the gong of a church bell rattled her ears.

Bullet striking steel.

She peeled off her outermost shirt, working it from beneath the harness, draped it over the body, then scrambled on her belly across the rusted steel floor. She crouched behind the closed door on her left. If she were the shooter, she would watch for motion. She waved the flashlight past the opening.

The second shot ignited sparks along the edge above her. She needed that door closed before a bullet got inside and ricocheted around like a BB in a pachinko machine.

She unzipped her nylon belt, dropped the gear to the floor, and attached one end to the center of the closed door she was pressing against with her left shoulder. Unlocked it. Took two deep breaths of fresh air. Pushed the left side door open. Jumped across and pulled the right door closed. The ten-inch rod she had left lying on the lip clanged on the concrete below.

She yanked the belt.

The left door was three-quarters closed when the bullet hit the outside. Her phone vibrated against her leg. The door slammed shut. They were safe. Trapped, but safe.

The message read: *Coming in for you.*

How would Qigiq come in with an active shooter? She'd need to be ready.

Kandy cradled the unconscious figure in her arms: light, maybe a hundred pounds. She wrapped the belt around the woman's body and slipped her arm through for security. The container rang again. The shooter was toying with her; there was no way in.

And no way out. Qigiq had better have something good up his Alaskan sleeve.

She glanced at the phone—no message. No service.

Kandy carried the woman to the doors. With the toe of her boot she inched the right door open two inches and found the rope with her eyes.

No shots. One bar of cell service.

New message: *Diversion in progress.*

The insect whine of a small-bore motorcycle grew louder.

Two deep breaths and she pushed the left door open. Drones were strafing the cargo ship with something that burned like napalm. Half of the ship's containers were mushrooming black smoke into the night sky. She reached for the rope with the woman lying in the crook of her arms, positioned her gloved hands, and stepped into space.

Their bodies swung away from the container, spun, and came back fast. Kandy planted both feet against the closed steel door. With her belt redeployed to support the woman, she had no harness, so she descended in a muscle-driven wrist-over-wrist motion that jostled the woman with each move, her head swaying in the light from the fires like the face of a sacrificial victim. The moment Kandy's feet touched the concrete dock, Qigiq appeared. Wearing black, straddling his motorbike.

"I'll take her."

Kandy draped the body over his arms and released the belt. "You want a ride?"

She shook her head. "Separate targets are better." She turned her eyes toward the ship. "Did you see the shooter?"

"Guard amidship. He's busy with Jill's fire now."

Kandy flashed him a tiny salute. "Later."

The bike revved behind her as she ducked between containers.

CHAPTER 34

KANDY HELD THE TARP while Qigiq carried the body into the cargo-plane laboratory. He lowered her to the couch at the back and checked vital signs. "Fifty-three." He lifted one eyelid, then the other, while waving a small flashlight. "Dilation response delayed, but present."

Kandy stretched a silver space blanket over the woman and retrieved her shirt.

Qigiq sat on the couch and massaged the woman's feet through the blanket. "Cold way to ride a motorcycle even for someone young and strong. She's maybe thirty, but hasn't eaten in awhile."

"How cold?"

"Bike claims fifty-five Fahrenheit. Plus bare skin in the wind. Hard to know how her body will react."

"Where did Jill get napalm?"

"Field operations manual. The drones clip onto payloads like a home delivery system." He glanced at his orange-strapped wristwatch, a souvenir of motorcycle racing he wore for inspiration. Tonight, he felt like he was in the back of the pack, needing some luck. "I wonder how Ferdinand is doing at the gallery?"

Kandy placed a palm on the woman's forehead. "They're running late, maybe found something interesting. Did you ever wonder why the Dragon Lady let you watch her inspect that painting?"

"Calculated risk. She knew I wouldn't let her take the painting out of my sight, that would require too much trust. So she had to guess if I was astute enough to understand, and duplicate, the scans Long did."

Kandy sat cross-legged on the floor beside the couch. "You're saying that Win assumes we're stupid?" She laughed.

"Or thinks we would walk away from the deal if she insisted on being alone with our property."

Kandy popped gum into her mouth. "Or she already had plans to steal the other paintings so you wouldn't have time to analyze them, even if you did figure out how to do it."

Qigiq grinned. "I like that one. Honor among thieves. Show respect. Until she takes what she wants."

"Governments call that diplomacy."

The woman's arm shifted. Qigiq stopped the massage. "Guesses?"

Kandy chewed for a quarter minute. "I'd say stow away if she weren't Caucasian. Not many white people try to smuggle themselves into South Korea far as I know. Maybe Carr's super software can tell us who she is."

"Container could have been going anywhere: Russia, Europe, South America."

Kandy stood in a single smooth motion. "Political prisoner trying to escape North Korea or China ends up trapped on a dock?" She shook her head. "Anyone trying a move like that would have a sleeping bag, warm clothing, plenty of food and water."

"Only if she had time and access. She could have been running from sex traffickers."

Kandy paced the length of the couch while staring out the side window of the aircraft. "OK, say I buy that she leaves everything behind, even her clothing because it can somehow identify her. Still. I didn't see food or water containers, but I did see, and smell, a self-contained toilet."

"She got lucky?"

"Grabbed a shipping container that happened to have an operating toilet? Uh-uh. Would never happen. Remember, the only reason we peeked inside is because Joe figured out that container wasn't being moved around like the rest of them."

"Maybe she paid a human smuggler who stripped her of her belongings, raped her, and stuck her in the container to be delivered at the other end."

Kandy stopped moving. "You're onto something. When Ferd gets back, let's get a blood test."

"A blood—" He thought about how pets were transported in the holds of airplanes. "You're thinking drugged and tossed inside, awaiting pickup."

"That's exactly what I'm thinking. Which means—" She chewed harder. "You and I have interfered with someone's plans."

Qigiq pushed himself up from the couch. "We have company. There's a black vehicle on the runway."

Kandy drew her firearm and moved sideways out of sight. Qigiq positioned himself between the woman and the tarp-covered doorway.

Qigiq's phone received a message from Carr: *All is well.* After the chaos at the docks, he had trouble believing it. Maybe Kandy's paranoia was rubbing off on him.

Ferdinand pushed aside the canvas and stepped into the plane. "Hello, my friends. Mylin sends greetings. She apologizes that the present circumstances prevent her from joining us."

Pemberly entered looking like an exhausted professor during exam week. "We have found much of interest. Confusing, but intriguing."

Carr brought up the rear, closed the tarp, and removed his mask. "Jill and Joe are heading back to the Shilla to rest." He looked like a good night's sleep should be at the top of his bucket list.

Kandy stepped out. "Any trouble?"

Carr shook his head. "Mylin played her viola to cover the noise these two guys made moving pictures around. I sat in the truck trying to locate dragon eyes without success. Joe watched the front of the building. How about you two?"

"We had to start a fire," Kandy said. "And found someone we weren't expecting."

Carr frowned as he turned to her. "Someone?"

"Movie trailer version. Comatose body in container. Shots fired at daring female detective. Ship napalmed by drones. Riveting motorcycle escape."

Carr exhaled like he was extinguishing candles on a birthday cake. "Low profile, huh?"

"The needs of the moment."

"Where is this someone?"

"Here," Ferdinand said. "I have some limited experience, but we need medical assistance."

Carr headed for the rear of the plane.

Qigiq said, "No identification."

Carr stooped beside the couch to one knee. He placed the back of his powerful hand gently against the woman's cheek.

"Everyone, allow me to introduce Shirley Sun, missing FBI agent."

CHAPTER 35

"*THEY DID* WHAT *LAST NIGHT?*" Gan demanded, more loudly than intended.

"I know only what our eyes report," Win said. "A faceless ninja scaled the containers after midnight."

Gan reached for the case he kept in his cherry wood desk. Cherry brought blossoms to mind. Of their brief visit with beauty. Of the samurais who honored the tiny flowers as a reminder to seize the moment, human life, too, is short.

"Why?" he asked, opening the case to retrieve a French-made cigarette: a luxury he allowed himself when circumstances generated excessive tension.

"Why is unclear," she said. "As is who."

He took his time igniting the tip with a gold lighter that glowed orange but had no flame. "Someone capable of scaling flat steel in darkness unassisted. Could one of ours do it?"

"You suspect a traitor among us?"

He exhaled and shook his head, holding the cigarette to one side. "I am simply trying to understand the necessary skill required. But if you think we have reason to suspect..." His voice trailed off like the smoke from his fingers.

"This FBI man has a great deal of money." She paused. "Including some of ours. Bribes are possible. Our dragons are well-paid, but human."

"Your thoughts?"

"One of Carr's people." She shifted in the guest chair. "There was also a fire."

Gan leaned forward and struck ashes into a black stone tray.

Win continued, "A ring of fire erupted on the upper deck of *Golden Lotus*. While the night security guards were engaged controlling it, whoever had entered the container disappeared." She shifted again. "However, before the fire, our dragons fired at the ninja."

Gan held his gaze on the smoke spiraling upward from his hand. "You are about to tell me that we do not have a dead ninja."

"We were slow, far away. The steel, too strong." She stood and paced in small steps left and right across the front of his desk. "The fire distracted him."

Gan flicked ashes. "You mean the fire filled him with fear and he ran to save himself, forgetting his duties."

"Yes."

"Anything else?"

She stopped at a bookcase to his left and touched the binding of a book.

"Sun Tzu is especially interesting," Gan said. "He speaks directly of the use of fire to hobble one's enemies."

She turned around and half-sat on the shelf. "Whether he ran in fear, or attempted to protect the ship is unimportant. The fact remains that in the flames and smoke and confusion —"

"The ninja is gone forever."

"Worse." She lowered her eyes to the floor, then lifted them to stare across the room, avoiding his gaze. "Our cargo is gone with him."

Gan's hand hovered over the ashtray. He waited until she looked his way.

"How is this possible from three stories in the air? And behind locks that even our customers cannot open until we let them?" He flicked. "Yet a single agile enemy removes our precious property."

Win's eyes slipped away to the shaded window behind him. "A closure rod was cut. Yet there are no marks of a saw blade."

"Through inches of steel?"

She remained silent.

Gan ground out the cigarette and waited for the smoke to dissipate. What had happened was done. The past is gone forever. Trying to bring it back pollutes the future. He must move his mind toward a solution.

"How is Mylin?"

"She had a visitor at the gallery last night. Our friends to the north used the same model vehicle that we used for..." she turned to face the book she had selected, "our drive through the jungle."

"What would they want with Mylin?"

She walked her fingers from one spine to the next along the shelf. "We must ask her, but this much we have learned repeatedly: everyone wants Mylin. Perhaps there was an official with a special request. Perhaps a scouting visit and we will soon receive the special request." She moved up a row, touching faded books filled with the wisdom of the ancients. "I sent eyes this morning. Everything remains in the gallery precisely as we instructed Mylin yesterday." She located a book, tilted it from the shelf. It fell open easily to a page that had been read often.

Gan waited, knowing that Win consulted learned texts to quiet her mind. When she hadn't spoken, and he could wait no longer, he said, "Do you think these events so dire?"

She gazed at the pages. "I am uncertain. Deeper secrets elude us." She closed the book and pushed it back into place on the shelf, then turned around to face Gan.

She said, "The hour grows short."

CHAPTER 36

QIGIQ SAT NEAR SHIRLEY listening to the evenness of her breathing and watching saline drip into her forearm. Her vital signs were improving. He wished her a quick recovery and would be pleased when she regained consciousness.

And talked.

Across the cargo hold, the scientists manipulated data while mumbling to each other. Layers of symbols floated across computer screens like hieroglyphics on the wall of a pyramid. Ferdinand had color-coded each layer according to language. Most were Mylinian, others Chinese. A few were English. With computer assistance, the scientists were attempting to translate each layer, but the results thus far were unintelligible. Ferdinand hypothesized that a more complex underlying structure existed that they had not yet identified. The two men were in the process of feeding all known information to a data-mining program and artificial intelligence engine that had been released by Google.

Carr stood behind, watching them work. His face was set mid-frown, like he was trying to wish a solution into existence. He said, "Google is a surveillance platform. The whole world will know what we're up to."

Ferdinand sat up straighter, his eyes locked on the graphics before him. "As a general principle, I agree. Google corporation tracks and remembers everything it can, even occasionally the actions of children using a Chromebook in a classroom. However, in this case, we have control. Google deemed it in their interest to open-source a machine intelligence library they named TensorFlow. It is the basis of Deep Dream visual processing. Perhaps you've seen the hallucinogenic imagery that it produces. I find the results impressive, if inconsistent. I downloaded TensorFlow months ago and have constructed a modified version I call Deep Thought—a frivolous moniker I borrowed from a novel." Ferdinand stretched both arms against interlaced fingers, knuckles crackling like popcorn. "Deep Thought is running on computers inside this aircraft. They are not attached to the Internet."

"So what happens in Jeju stays in Jeju?" Carr asked.

"Should we be fortunate enough to find a solution, it will be ours alone."

Carr patted Ferdinand's shoulder from behind. "In that case, I hope you find something quickly. We surely need the help."

"Deep Thought and I are both working as fast as our processing power allows."

"What about this?" Kandy asked from where she sat on the floor, her legs extended in front of her, one lifted six inches into the air. Strewn around her was an empty mesh backpack and stacks of U.S. currency in denominations up to the hundred.

"How much?" Carr asked.

"Just shy of half a million, not counting the part I slipped into my retirement account." She huffed her alto laugh.

"Joe's friend is freer with money than Madame Win," Qigiq said.

Carr said, "This Natasha woman wants something and isn't shy about paying for it."

"She didn't even tell Joe what it was for."

"In a roundabout way she did," Carr said. "Whatever Win has for sale, Natasha and her friends want to buy."

"That's a lot of leeway," Kandy said, lowering her right leg and raising her left.

Qigiq asked, "Do you think Natasha knows?"

Kandy glanced his way. "You think she's bidding blind?"'

"She gives Win massages," Carr said. "Who knows what they chat about. From what she told Joe, she's an operative for a country that isn't poor. Maybe she gets wind of something interesting coming through, arranges to bid on it. Dragon Lady shuts her out. Cuts a better deal. Maybe the dragon doesn't trust Natasha. Being locked out piques the interest of Natasha's management." A throat noise caused him to turn toward Shirley. "Then along comes Joe. Hmm. An American on the island talking to the Dragon Lady? Her management decides to bait Joe."

"So the money is a bribe," Kandy said.

Carr shook his head. "The money is to get our attention, which it has. Natasha wants us to renege on our deal with Win. Someone, somewhere, thinks what she's selling is worth a lot more than half a million dollars."

Kandy stopped chewing. "Think they got wind of our two-point-six million dollar offer?"

"Do you ever run out of gum?" Carr asked.

She shook her head. "As important as bullets. Keeps me calm."

Carr laughed.

"So who talks to Natasha?" Qigiq asked. "And what am I going to tell her?" He laughed, aware he was the logical choice, because he was the real seller. "We can't keep Joe in the loop, it's too dangerous."

"Agreed," Carr said.

"Why?" Kandy asked.

Qigiq knew Kandy's shorthand. He responded, "Natasha is a potential source. We're short on understanding. Isn't a conversation a good next step?"

Kandy snapped her gum. "Maybe you should get a massage. But I'm having a hard time trusting a gorgeous woman named Natasha who tosses money around."

"Me too," Carr said. "And what conversation do we have that won't interfere with our, uh...deal with Win?"

"I'm not feeling as committed since she stole my paintings," Qigiq said. "And why haven't I heard from her regarding the selling process?"

Kandy said, "Better go see your biker friend. Maybe you have a message."

"Would Win use a foot soldier like Lee to explain a high-profile issue?" Qigiq paused, then asked, "Do you think Win has figured out who was at the gallery last night?"

"If she knows about it," Carr said. "You weren't involved. Mylin will keep our secret."

Kandy said, "Assuming her spies saw our truck, she'll be trying to figure out why nothing is missing."

"And she'll be looking for that truck." Carr glanced at his watch. "Should be on the ferry by now."

Qigiq listened to Shirley's shallow breathing, tossing an idea around in his head. If the artwork had been stolen, or he wanted to claim that as a cover to sell it to someone else, how would he tell Win?

He said, "What if I contact Win? Explain why I haven't delivered the merchandise. She doesn't know we know she's the thief."

"How about we demand she give them back or pay?" Kandy said. "Put some pressure on. Try to force a mistake?"

"Good thoughts," Carr said.

"Remarkable," Ferdinand said from his desk. "Absolutely remarkable."

"Thanks, Ferd," Kandy said.

Ferdinand swiveled toward her. "Were you speaking to me? I'm sorry, I was lost in Deep Thought's discovery. What it has found is astonishing."

"You mean Google helped us?" she said.

"It removed the gauze from our eyes, since it wasn't biased by the medium. We see a flat, two-dimensional artwork. Then we detect hidden writings revealed by specific wavelengths of light. Of course, we naturally think *pages* of information. The creator even encoded each layer so it would masquerade as a message, teasing us that we could understand them independently. However, in reality, only the first layer stands alone, the visible one that originally attracted Petr's artistic eye on the floor of my condo."

"And the other layers?" Carr asked.

"Not layers," Pemberly chimed in. "Data samples. When decoded and interpolated, they produce this remarkable object."

All eyes moved to a huge cube on the screen filled with a billion dots of light, as if a giant cleaver had chopped a chunk out of the Milky Way Galaxy.

"Are you about to tell me what this means?" Carr asked. "Or confuse me more?"

"First, confusion," Ferdinand said. "We assemble data from the layers for each painting into a cube. We decode each layer. Most use ancient Chinese texts as keys: the data in the painting acts as an index into a specific text, where the correct character is found. These are breakable with modern computer tools, and since the dawn of mathematics-based encryption, rarely used."

"Why?" Kandy asked.

"Perhaps because many modern methods have been compromised by government regulations for backdoors. It is difficult to know which ones might be safe. And from whom. This ancient approach contains a custom language, hidden layers, and even if one gets that far, still no information. Unless."

Shirley's condition remained unchanged so Qigiq moved closer to the displays.

"OK, Ferd. I'll bite," Kandy said. "Unless..."

"We do this."

The cube rotated in slow motion to an oblique angle. A translucent red plane sliced down through it, then shifted slowly through the cube. As the red plane moved, pages of text appeared on the screen beside the graphics.

"I can't read that either," Carr said.

"It's not intended to be read by you," Ferdinand said.

Kandy stuffed cash back into the mesh backpack. "More

mumbo jumbo for you to crack?"

"Not this time," Pemberly said.

Kandy stopped packing.

Carr leaned forward. "The rich guy in the penthouse with the five computers. The first condom murder. What was his specialty?"

"Laundering money?" Kandy said.

"Communications. He bought up communication companies. Especially brand new startups with specialized technology."

Qigiq remembered. "That CEO who was with Yubi when she died. What did he do?"

"You guys are thinking Ferd's treasure chest is related to the condom murders?" Kandy said.

Qigiq was thinking *I should have known all along.* He said, "Before he died, Wu was using female musicians to blackmail American men for confidential information, then turning around and paying them handsomely for it. We never figured out what Wu was buying."

"This?" Carr asked.

"Ferdinand is going to tell us. As soon as he waves his magic wand." Kandy laughed.

"Yes...and no. It is difficult to ascertain how much of this information Wu understood. I can confirm, however, that thousands of symbols have been painstakingly encoded onto each painting, deeply hidden behind layers of confusion that require algorithmic reconstruction. But the resulting text isn't for humans. It's code for a computer."

Carr said, "What does it do?"

"Only moments ago we realized the hidden information is a computer program. I will begin analyzing its function immediately. However..."

"Days? Weeks?" Carr asked.

"Too early to guess."

Kandy said, "Weeks is forever in Dragon Girl's world."

"With no guarantee of success, I might add," Ferdinand said.

"This may be only a fragment of a larger system."

Kandy zipped the mesh pack closed. "Well, we know what's on Natasha's shopping list."

Ferdinand stroked a hand down his beard. "There is one more thing. The languages used here are common in the world of computer science."

"Geek heaven," Kandy said.

"All the fault of a woman." The onboard generator hummed. "A portion of this code is written in a variant of a popular language known by the letter C. This variant, called C-plus-plus, was first introduced in the early 1980s"

"Riveting story," Kandy said. "Is there a punch line?"

Ferdinand nodded. "Indeed there is. You must certainly know of Ada Lovelace." He looked around at confused faces. "She lived in the nineteenth century and helped Charles Babbage program his Analytical Engine."

"I missed a plot point," Kandy said.

"Ada was a mathematician and is credited with being the world's first programmer."

Carr said, "I'm betting this is going to be relevant."

Qigiq wasn't so sure. They might be chasing a red herring that Wu was simply trying to pawn off on unsuspecting governments at the highest bid.

"That is for you detectives to decide. Fast forward to the Reagan era of the 1980s. A new computer language is designed for embedded systems to meet what was called the *Steelman language requirements.* It was named Ada."

"This matters why?" Carr asked.

"Much of what I see before me is Ada. Perhaps seventy-five or eighty percent."

Qigiq glanced back at Shirley, but saw no change. "Does that help us?"

"I think it may be pertinent that development of this language was funded by the United States Department of Defense. It has since been used in avionics, air traffic control, railways, military applications, and space exploration."

The generator hummed.

Carr spoke first. "What's it doing here?"

CHAPTER 37

JILL LEANED ONTO THE NARROW desk, eyes locked on monitor six directly in front of her face. Her long sigh resembled escaping steam.

Joe said, "You did a great job with that fire."

"No thanks to you off playing with your Russian doll. It was super tense, I..." She didn't continue.

"The gunfire?"

"Yeah. A guy on deck shot at Kandy. Me in this tin can miles away. I...I thought I'd see her killed." Two long breaths. "Freaked me out."

"She's a smart detective."

"Sure. But she was pinned down in a container. Her only way out was the rope I dropped for her."

"Good job on that too."

Jill's gaze didn't change. The surveillance drone was high and moving like it was late for an appointment. She exhaled slowly through her mouth.

"Thanks. Sitting alone in this truck. When that first bullet hit the container..." She shook her head. "Orange sparks welding bright. Like watching a scary silent movie. I froze."

He waited. She stared at number six—had been for close to an hour. "Was that the screen you saw it on?"

She pointed two-thirds of the way up. "Right there. I knew it was a gunshot. I don't know how—the drone didn't have ears. I guess I figured someone would try to stop her."

"You said you froze."

Jill spoke with her chin resting in both hands. "Sure did.

Stone cold. Could have been a statue."

"But?"

"The second shot made me jump like a some jerk had grabbed my ass on the street. I scrambled through the weapons list, searching for something that didn't require precision. I'm a lousy drone pilot."

"You underrate yourself. You found napalm?"

"Incendiary grenades. The drone can carry a dozen."

"Why did you send two drones? Redundancy?"

"Ha! I wish I was that together under pressure. I was shaking so bad, I pressed the wrong button on the remote."

"You were successful. That matters." He paused. "Sorry I wasn't here to help. I saw Natasha, then did guard duty at the gallery."

Jill sat up straight and took a slow breath. "That's okay, you were working too. I'm just unimpressed with my composure under fire." She leaned toward the monitor. "Where is this thing going?"

"It's taking direction from a satellite. But I have no idea how autonomous mode actually works."

"Tell me about Natasha."

"Tall, athletic, blonde. Gives great massages."

"Ha! What you said sounds crazy. She really thinks you're a spy?"

"Or I'm her last resort." He laughed. "There must be a lot of pressure for her to throw six-figure money around."

"You ever think about how dangerous this is. Those bullets…"

"About every ten seconds. When this is over, I'm only shooting a camera."

"Kandy and Qigiq face this stuff every day," Jill said.

"Special people doing a special job. After you graduate, you will too."

Jill rolled her lips inward. "I hope I can handle it." She dropped her chin into her hands and watched images fly by as though she were a girl on a bullet train.

"Give yourself time."

"Mylin is trapped in this world."

"That's why we're here," he said.

"That's why you and I are here. Carr is using her."

"Without Carr, she'd still be sitting in a prison cell."

Jill stood, eyes on the monitor. "Not a great option."

"Not to be a downer, but she wasn't in a good place before prison, either."

"Trafficked by your own family? Yeah, that's super bad." A car whooshed by on the road outside. "Life is a lot about luck, isn't it?"

"The era you're born into. Who your parents are. The government you live under. The talents you have." He paused. "A whole lot of stuff just gets handed to you."

"Sucks."

"It cuts both ways. Look at you. Kandy says you have a brilliant career ahead of you."

Jill finally smiled. "Guess that makes me lucky, doesn't it?"

"Everyone has luck. Some just get a bigger dose of bad."

Joe involuntarily considered his own luck the day he photographed Mylin smoking beside a colossal pillar in Ann Arbor, Michigan. Back then, he thought he'd never see her again.

"Hey," Jill said.

He turned. "Hey what?"

"The drone."

Joe dragged the folding chair over next to her.

She said, "It's gone to Jeju International Airport."

"Oh man, stay out of their airspace. If we cause an international incident, Carr will get fired for letting us touch this van."

Jill switched to manual control and flew the drone straight up and across a parking lot filled with small sedans, then lowered it vertically onto the roof of the five-story spear-shaped control tower.

Joe said, "Are you trying to see the inside of a Korean jail?"

"Think about it," Jill said. "Air traffic controllers can't see up through the roof. And no plane is going to fly anywhere near that tower. It's a perfect stakeout location."

"That's pretzel logic, but I don't have a better idea. What do you see?"

"Airplanes at gates. One about to touch down that looks like every jet I've ever seen."

"Airline?"

Jill zoomed the drone's camera. "If I remember my languages class, that's Hanja on the side."

Joe looked over her shoulder. "You said that drone is at Jeju International, right?"

"Uh-huh."

"Who runs Air Koryo?"

"Never heard of it."

He leaned in. "What model plane is that?"

"A white one with one engine on each wing." She laughed.

"Let's ask the computer."

She typed. A top and side image of the plane popped onto an adjoining screen alongside a seating diagram. Specifications appeared below the images.

Jill read aloud, "Russian made Tupoler TU-24."

"A North Korean airline?"

"That'd be a good guess."

"Why did your drone go to this airport?"

"It's chasing the flight that is landing now."

"Why would a drone care about a specific flight?" he asked.

"Because its secret software knows something that we don't. Which isn't hard, because we don't know much."

"Ask it," he suggested.

"You mean like, 'Hey Siri, why did you fly there?'"

"Yeah, if it has a reason, it might tell us."

"What if the information is classified? We don't have security clearance. Or what if it's one of those AI things that can't explain why it decides what it does? Or maybe it goes to airports when it's bored to visit other flying machines."

Joe laughed, then grew quiet. "Let's assume a couple of things. I know assuming is risky, but that plane is probably from North Korea. Or maybe it's a North Korean airlines, but the flight is coming from further west, say Moscow."

"Natasha has you thinking like a Cold War spy movie. But, okay, so what?"

Joe stood. "So, our drone has access to whatever its super cameras see, and whatever drone flight control computers get to know about. Maybe something as simple as a newspaper article we can't read because it's in Korean. Or a blog post from a South Korean journalist."

"Do newspapers still exist?"

"Sure, how else would you wrap fish? But if the drone picked that flight out of all possible options on the island..."

"You think it's interested in a passenger on that flight. And you want to know who and why?"

"You're a mind reader," Joe said.

"So we need the passenger manifest."

Joe sat back down. "Easier said than done, huh?"

"Carr's FBI buds probably monitor flight manifests from all over the world. But if we ask, it'll broadcast what we're doing. How about we go inside the terminal and watch faces come off the plane?"

"Someone will see our drone," Joe said.

"Then *you* go inside and stand around with your snoopy camera."

He sat, stretched out his legs, and blew a stream of air at the roof. "Two problems. First, I don't have a ticket. How do I get past security? Second, that plane will be unloading in five minutes. I'd need a rocket belt to get there that fast."

On the screen, the Koryo plane taxied toward an empty gate.

"OK, we can't watch the gate from inside," she said. "What's next?"

"Baggage claim. But if this person is important, he or she won't pick up bags, other people will do it for them. Or maybe it's a short visit and there isn't any baggage."

She said, "You're cheering me up."

"Let's watch the exits."

Jill glanced over her shoulder at him. "It's an international airport. Thousands of people leave every minute."

"Carr's magic computer will find something."

"OK, Mr. Optimistic." She turned back to the screen. "Let's say I'm crazy enough to think this haystack has a needle. We couldn't get closer to a controlled airspace if we walked onto the runway."

Joe smiled. "Afraid we'll get caught?"

"I'm scared we'll screw up Carr's mission." She paused. "Or put Mylin in danger."

"You're right, Jill. I'm used to working alone with nothing hanging in the balance except a couple of snapshots. Sorry."

"So what do we do with a black drone zooming around an airport in broad daylight?"

Joe stood. "I'll drive us over."

She studied him. "Think we have time?"

"No, but I don't have a better idea." He cupped his hand behind one ear and leaned toward her.

She laughed. "No, I don't either. I'll find a perch and watch baggage claim."

* * *

Jill hovered the drone within the branches of a copse of palm trees opposite the main entrance. With a slight rotation, she could monitor both baggage claim and departures. She said, "I have seventeen minutes of flying time left."

Joe called over his shoulder, "Five more minutes. Sorry to be slow. Don't want to attract a traffic cop."

"Don't rush. If there was anyone important on that Koryo flight, they're long gone by now. Who hangs around an airport?"

"People who have to make a connection, in which case our luck just ran out."

Jill panned the drone's camera across the sea of faces departing baggage claim. She wanted to find something, anything, any little hint of...she didn't really know what. "The computer can watch better than I can. Why am I even here?"

"So you can be frustrated with the lack of progress. Computers aren't good at emotion."

"You should do stand-up. How do you handle a shoot when the waiting starts driving you mad?"

He called back, "Move to another shoot."

"I can't..."

Wait. Yes, she could.

Jill switched the drone to manual and took it above the tallest palm, being careful to remain over the roadway and away from drone-roasting jet exhaust. She hoped it would be a speck in the sky to the naked eye, and pass for one of the hundreds of species of exotic birds on the island.

The monitor showed the entire airport from above. She deduced that any pick-up vehicle leaving the airport would first have to arrive. She guided the drone along the inbound two-lane road where traffic entered before being funneled to arrivals, departures, and parking lots. But her drone was too high for facial recognition software to function: a gaping hole in her tactics. She called toward the cab, "We need another drone."

"Go for it, we're close. It'll get there before us."

Jill triggered the launch control. Her peripheral vision caught a structure too long to be a car. She zoomed the drone's camera to the limit and brought it to a lower elevation.

"Hey, Joe. Park quick. I've got something here."

The van slowed and made a sharp right. A few seconds later it rolled to a stop. Joe crawled into the back. "There are two delivery trucks about our size in front of us in this alley. But we shouldn't stay long."

"Look."

The drone was hovering above a parking lot. Jill descended. The cars grew larger.

"Is this live?"

She nodded. "What do you think?"

"I think three black sedans means an official escort. Where are they?"

"Don't laugh. In a cell phone lot a half-mile outside the airport." Two figures in dark clothing stood beside each vehicle. "Look at that second car."

"Maybe he's birdwatching."

"At an airport? I think he's searching for me. Drones. Maybe even checking for a possible sniper nest if his boss is a political figure."

"You're good at paranoid," Joe said. "We could drive over. A van will fit in at an airport."

"I'd love to be closer. But what I really want to know is: Who are they picking up?"

The man with binoculars extended an arm. He wasn't pointing directly her way, but Jill made the drone climb anyway. Just in case the guy wasn't birdwatching.

"We need a plan," Joe said. "You're the tactical genius."

"But you're the master of sneaky. If you wanted to avoid detection while photographing the person who's going to get into that car, how would you do it?"

"If this were the States, I'd hang out at the curb in arrivals and hope that's where those cars are going."

"But not here?"

He shook his head. "I'd stick out. They'll tag me as American and create a commotion trying to sell me souvenirs and services. Hard to stay incognito."

Jill remained quiet for a few seconds. Then said softly, "Do you think I could do it?"

"You're the right size. Dyed hair. Sunglasses. Teen-girl baseball cap. Yeah, you can do it. Do you have gloves?"

* * *

Jill leaned over a low drinking fountain and pressed the button with a finger of her red leather glove. As she drank, she practiced aiming the camera hiding in her left palm as it fed video via her Blackphone to the van's computer for real-time analysis.

She was the drone.

"Good," Joe said through the buds in her ears. Buds like every other teenager was using to listen to the ubiquitous K-pop on the island. "Nineteen minutes since the plane reached the gate. Let's see if our passenger is waiting for luggage."

She tapped her left earbud four times with a fingernail so Joe would hear clicks of acknowledgement, straightened, and walked away from the fountain.

A baggage carousel beeped, spun a blue siren light, and started moving. Saturday—hundreds of well-dressed visitors arriving on the island. Posters all around promising that this was the most desirable place in the world for young Korean couples to tie the knot. The sea of foreign voices merging with indecipherable Hangul made her feel isolated and visible, as if she were a pariah cut off from society.

But no one paid her the slightest attention.

She strolled toward the moving belt, rotating her arm to help the hidden camera find faces. No one appeared obviously important. No one displayed the telltale alertness of a body-guard.

A young skinny girl dragged a pink suitcase from the belt with two hands. Standing on its two-wheeled bottom, it reached to her shoulders. Jill instinctively took a step forward to assist, but stopped herself before attracting attention by touching a stranger's luggage.

Joe said in her ear, "Motorcade on the move."

An Asian man wearing white sneakers and a yellow golf shirt reached a hand out to help the girl. Jill gazed past them at an eight foot high poster on the wall of a smiling bride. She considered her next move.

Joe said, "The computer thinks the guy in yellow is a VIP. I'm rolling your way. Patching computer audio through so you'll hear what I hear."

The voice in her ear changed to the monotone male of a smartphone. "Asian male. Age forty-three. Moving left to right across visual field. Name: Yom Ki. Occupation: Director of the Office of Cultural Development. Residence: Pyongyang, Democratic People's Republic of Korea."

The guy with the little girl.

Jill swung right, keeping the pair in her camera frame by watching the tiny picture projected inside of Joe's magic glasses. The glasses were too large for her face, although he insisted they enhanced her Korean-schoolgirl persona. She walked quickly to keep pace with the man towing the pink suitcase so fast that the little girl had to skip along to keep up. They made a colorful pair. She wondered if the kid—

A hand grabbed her left biceps and spun her around. She faced a guy about her height wearing a blue uniform and a cap. She couldn't decide: security guard, cop, baggage handler. He held out his free hand palm up and spoke rapidly in Korean. He saw her face. His lips stopped mid-word.

She recognized an opportunity.

She opened her mouth to speak.

The idea that English was a poor choice tickled her brain, since it was a kind of international second language for tourist destinations. She had studied a bit of Spanish in high school. A story about a mother taking her child to his first day of kindergarten that she had been forced to memorize popped into her head and began coming out her mouth. Fear tingled up the skin over her shoulder blades as she rattled off Spanish words she barely understood. In a foreign country. Without ID. No ticket, no luggage. And no explanation for why she was at the airport. Holding a hidden camera broadcasting to an un- marked van owned by the FBI.

She spoke louder.

She gestured toward the luggage turnstile and shrugged. Tap tap tapped her wrist to show she was late. Held up both hands and wiggled an imaginary steering wheel to indicate her ride was waiting—striving to be a crazy neurotic creature that he wouldn't want to deal with.

He lowered his palm, but didn't release her arm. Instead, he dragged her toward the exit—in the direction of the VIP and the girl.

Jill held out her arm and leaned in to take a selfie with the guard. He hesitated, realized what she was doing, and smiled. He let her push through the glass doors first, rather than dragging her outside. As sunlight smacked her eyeballs, the yellow golf shirt disappeared into the back seat of the middle sedan in a three-car motorcade.

The guard holding her arm kept talking; she understood nothing.

Her peripheral vision found Joe's van in a row of taxies half its size. Her heart wanted to race to the safety of its boring interior. Then she saw Joe running straight toward them. When he was within earshot, she asked him in Spanish for directions to the train station.

He answered, "Bienvenido Jeju, Señorita Valdez."

Joe took her arm gently and stared at the guard. In English he said, "Thank you so much for escorting my boss to the exit. She gets overly excited when flying. You know how artists have such fragile temperaments."

Joe released her, lowered both of his arms, and bowed to the cop guy.

The cop released his grip and returned Joe's bow. Joe extended his hand American style. He was smooth, but Jill was certain money changed hands.

The cop turned toward the motorcade and said something that sounded unfriendly. Then he touched his cap in a mini-salute to Joe and headed back inside.

"Thanks," she said. "I'm glad you speak Spanish."

"I know about ten words, and one of them is the name of an oil tanker that ran aground in Alaska. Let's get out of here." They reached the van just as the taxi behind it was pulling around. The driver screamed out his open passenger window at Joe.

Inside the van's cab, Joe said, "Good job finding out who. Now we have to figure out what, when, and why."

CHAPTER 38

UNCLE GAN WAS INSISTING that the concert begin precisely at sunset. It was now ten minutes past six, and still no accompanist. We had rehearsed twice. Saturday evening had many false starts. That was the first time we played together, and the only time I had ever been accompanied by the staccato pluck of a harpsichord. The piano was more common, especially in America where everything was bold and loud. Then this morning we had played through the entire concert with only a few small problems.

But it wasn't the music making me nervous.

My heart was pounding because of this place.

I stood in wild grass of a lush deep green that lined a valley inside a crater named Baengnokdam. This crater sat at the top of the Hallasan volcano—in the middle of Jeju Island. I imagined the tallest volcano in all of South Korea below my feet. Within the valley, a blue lake shimmered in the softening light.

But that was only the beginning.

Uncle had promised to build a stage. What he delivered was a masterpiece of modern art. A square stage covered in white silk floated not far from the shore. At its center sat a gleaming red harpsichord made from exotic woods. Its polished surface reflected the ripples on the lake's surface. Beside it, my music stand shot skyward like a spear, made of the same shiny red wood. Behind the harpsichord rose a half-shell covered with thousands of tiny lights able to reproduce the colors of the rainbow.

A young boy had shown me an inflatable raft hidden under a tarp. He assured me it was spotless and would not stain our gowns, for both were nearly white and covered with sequins that I now understood were intended to reflect the rainbow lights. I had never in my life imagined floating across water to take the stage.

The strange newness of the idea excited me.

I touched the necklace at my throat, a heart within a heart. Jilly had given me a necklace before my last concert, but it had been taken from me along with uncle Gan's gun.

The growing audience was seated in three rows of folding chairs on sandy soil, each row lower than the one behind it. The front row almost touched the water and had only four chairs. Uncle Gan and Win occupied the middle two. The others were empty. In total there was seating for thirty people, the smallest concert I had played in years.

But what people!

Floor-length gowns of black, red, and blue matched the South Korean flag hanging on the left side of the floating stage and the North Korean flag on the right. Both flags were based on red, white, and blue, just like the flag of the United States. But the South's flag also included four black trigrams surrounding a Taegeuk symbol that I knew expressed the hope of balance of yin and yang. The men wore tuxedos, or military uniforms in dark greens or deep blues. The women's high-heeled shoes penetrated soft earth and slipped on black stones. Men assisted, holding elbows, occasionally a waist. Everyone wore smiles.

Would there be a speech? And why display the flags of the divided country? Perhaps harmony was the goal, and this concert was a tiny part of something much larger.

A group walked over the rise to the east behind the mostly occupied chairs. I sighed with relief to see my new musician friend among them. When Tim-Su Ki saw me, she waved shyly, flanked by serious-looking men in crisp dark jackets who spoke to no one. Her gown glittered pink in the setting sun as the orange ball neared the western lip of the crater. Perhaps once it dipped below the edge, casting long shadows across our stage, Uncle Gan would let the concert begin.

The group reached the front row. Uncle Gan bowed to two men. Those men separated to sit on either end of the front row with Uncle and Win between them. I had never seen them before. Why would Tim-Su be accompanied by such men?

I smiled as she walked toward me across grass, sand, and small rough black stones that had been formed from the mouth of this powerful volcano thousands of years ago—long before the viola had even been invented. I bowed to greet her, happy to see her again.

She had been a teenager for a month, and this was her first trip outside of North Korea. Her father only allowed it because he himself would be in attendance to watch over her. Of course, one of those two men in the front row must be her father, I should have guessed. Yesterday, I had started to tell her of a concert hall I played in the United States filled with a thousand people. But I stopped because she had begun to cry, believing she would never be allowed to even see the United States, let alone perform there.

After we bowed, she glanced over her shoulder at the front row. The two important-looking men were talking to Uncle Gan, who was gesturing toward the stage. Tim-Su stepped forward, hugged me, and said in English. "Mylin, I am so afraid."

I put an arm around her. I knew the taste of fear. "Our rehearsal went well. We'll do fine."

"I...I...don't know if I can play."

"Of course you can. You have a wonderful instrument and great talent. We have prepared well. And we have the loveliest stage on the island."

She held me close and shuffled her feet until she was facing the stage. "I can't," she whispered.

I squeezed her tightly and felt her body trembling.

"I...I can't swim."

"We have a rubber boat. I'll hold your hand. Once we begin,

the music will carry us and you will forget where we are."

She released me slowly. Tear tracks marked her cheeks. I tried not to remember a girl crying such tears the first time she was sold to a man.

"Tim-Su. If you can play Beethoven, you can ride in a boat. Can you play Beethoven?"

She nodded slightly. Then a faint smile broke the perfect gloss someone had painted on her lips. "His earliest works were for the harpsichord," she said proudly.

"Let's dedicate our concert to Ludwig. And the instrument you play so beautifully."

This time a broad smile accompanied her nodding head, and I realized she had pink sparkles in her black hair that matched her dress.

A Korean boy, not much taller than Tim-Su, cleared his throat to draw our attention. His black suit was cleaned and pressed, but perhaps a size too large for him. He wore black sneakers.

He bowed and spoke in Korean. We bowed in return.

Tim-Su whispered to me, "He is our boatman."

She seemed to grow stronger when he took her hand and led her to a gray raft with polished wooden seats surrounded by fat tubes filled with air. The gentleness with which he helped her into the craft made me think of children playing at court-ing. He placed her in the back facing forward, where he could see her as he rowed.

My turn came.

I could swim well, but I worried for my instrument. It was in my hands, tuned and ready to play. But looking into the now glassy waters of the crater lake made me see it slip from my fingers and disappear into the black depths forever. I stepped carefully over the side and sat in the bow facing the back so I could watch Tim-Su and encourage her.

We slid from the shore and floated on the placid waters. Instead of the fear I had expected, Tim-Su stared at the rower with a fiery excitement that was still present when she seated herself at the harpsichord and sounded a concert A for me to check my tuning. The sky had become sheets of orange, red, and purple. The audience sat in the darkening shadow from the lip of the crater. The stage floated in darkness as it rocked slightly from the weight of our bodies moving to take our positions.

The boy's boat swooshed onto shore. The unlit lights behind us hovered like a giant gray clam. I waited for someone to introduce us or possibly say what this event was celebrating.

Then I realized I was the soloist and on stage. Perhaps they were waiting for me to begin our first piece: a lovely viola melody by Bach that Tim-Su had played for me at rehearsal. It was so beautiful that I read through it with her and we decided right then to open our concert with it. To my utter amazement, Uncle Gan had left the entire concert program up to me. Except for Mr. Long's Beethoven. That was to be our finale.

I tucked the viola under my chin and positioned the fingers of my left hand.

I inhaled and lifted my bow.

I caught Tim-Su's eye so we could begin precisely together, then moved my shoulders and bow into the opening phrase. As the notes rose from my remarkable Italian instrument, the half-shell behind us brightened in astonishing whiteness, as if the music had brought it to life. Tim-Su's fingers synchronized perfectly with my bow, as if we were breathing the same breath. If the bright lights or the surrounding liquid death were bothering her, it wasn't revealed in her playing.

Our sounds floated away from us, across the water, up the hills of the crater valley, into that glorious streaked sky—and beyond.

CHAPTER 39

JILL SAID, "I'M SICK of this stupid truck. I want to be at the concert."

"Look at this panoramic view spread before us on pristine glass paid for by the F B of I. We have our best lens up there, and our bird is wearing binaural microphones that mimic the reception of ears on the human head."

"I want to hug her good luck like I did before the last..." she fell silent.

Joe's shoulders stiffened. He didn't speak—unable to not think about the Reno concert. Only weeks ago he had been sitting behind a sound mixer in the middle of a street filled with thousands of fans. Fifty feet from the stage. Glorious music. The new orchestra doing so well. Then in a heartbeat, helpless to do one single thing for the young women as flames consumed the entire stage.

Jill broke the silence. "Mylin can't see us. She doesn't know that we're supporting her."

"And ready to help," Joe added.

"Yeah. She thinks she's alone in this mess."

"She knows we're watching. That's why she told me about the concert that night at the gallery."

"Knowing isn't the same as seeing," Jill said. "Or touching."

"It's not safe to be there." He paused. "For us...or her."

Jill sighed and leaned her orange hair against the side of the van opposite the cinematic display. "I know, but I want to be there, not watching from a drone hiding in a pile of volcanic rocks."

Joe agreed with her. He'd much prefer hiding where he could feel the temperature of the air, smell grasses on the wind, hear the soft rustle of movement around him. The microphones were good, excellent even. But he wanted to be in that crater taking pictures. "Yeah, not the same," he said softly, staring at the stage as Mylin lifted her bow.

The half-shell behind her and a tiny girl at a red keyboard instrument burst into brilliant whiteness.

"Wow," Jill said. "Look at that!"

The shell changed color. The delicate sound of the harpsichord filled the van.

Their drone was hiding in the crater forty-five degrees to the left of, and behind, the audience. He zoomed and recorded high-resolution face shots of each performer, remembering a moonlit shot of Mylin smoking beside a pillar: the first picture he had ever taken of her. Then he zoomed out to include in the entire stage.

"Not as good as being there," he said. "I need to move the camera."

"It'll be seen. Better settle for what you can get with the swivel, like you did when everyone came in."

He adjusted the camera to a wider angle. His eyes stopped. "Who are those people in front?"

"Left to right we have: Unnamed diplomat from South Korea. Dragon Lady. Uncle Gan. Guy from the airport that our computer claims is a cultural attaché from North Korea named Ki."

"And everyone else?"

"People who have the money to dress like that."

"Guesses?"

"Bodyguards. Businessmen who would rather be elsewhere. Wives who dragged hubby to the event because it's important to be seen when climbing the social ladder."

"North and South doing *anything* together seems like major news." He listened to the rich tone of Mylin's viola and the precision of the young girl's flying fingers. "Who's the harpsichord player?"

"The culture officer's daughter according to Carr's cyber-stalking computer."

Joe leaned back on the one good chair and switched the camera to panorama. "Is this some kind of debut performance to introduce her to the West?"

"Maybe," Jill said. "But the way she plays, she might have debuted at four or five years old."

Joe stood to stretch his legs, then leaned forward to study the screen closely: sand, black rocks, incredibly bright green grass, channels of water erosion, hills flowing upward in all directions from the lake to the lip of the crater. "Where are the professionals?"

"Doing a good job hiding," Jill said. "Detectives are sneaky."

"The FBI is probably sneakier."

"If they need us, we'll get a call. So far, it's just a bunch of people at a swanky concert."

Joe pointed to the last row of polished wood folding chairs. "Him."

"Gan's golf buddy that chased Mylin to the temple. Looks like she scored a ticket for him."

"We only have a profile view. What if we put another drone out there?"

"In open space? That'd be crazy. Look at his eyes glued to her. Mylin has a groupie."

Joe dropped into the chair.

With her head still against the side of the van, Jill said, "The pros have the concert covered. The computers are recording it for posterity. The beards are cracking magic computer code. So what do we do?"

"Stay out of trouble so no one has to save us."

"Ha!" she said.

"We wait. Watch the drone footage. Maybe provide surveillance assistance."

She sighed. "I don't have the genetic makeup for stakeouts."

"No doubt. You're way too patient." He laughed hard.

She tossed a crumpled wrapper from an energy bar. It clipped him on the shoulder. A Blackphone chirped its bird-call imitation. They looked at each other, then rotated to the screens showing the in-progress concert.

A second chirp.

"It's you," Jill said.

Joe slipped the slender phone from his pants pocket. "It says, Nashi."

"You gave your Russian girlfriend the number to the Secure Circle?" Jill asked in a hushed voice, as if whispering were more secure.

"No. No, I didn't."

The phone chirped again.

"And I for sure did not secretly add her phone to the circle and put her name in my contacts list. But it's on the screen."

A fourth chirp echoed in the van.

"Answer it," Jill said.

"Carr said not to talk to anyone outside the circle."

"He said not to *call* anyone. You've been compromised. Let's find out who is trying to reach you. And freaking *why!*"

Joe touched "Accept" and put the device to his ear, thinking carefully about how much to reveal in his words. He finally just said, "Hello."

"Are you good with computers?"

The accent was unmistakable. "Nashi?"

"Of course. Didn't your phone identify me?"

It had, but he didn't know how. "You gave me something. Where were we when you handed it to me?"

"Inside a lava tube. Now, are you good with computers?"

"Not particularly. I'm a photographer."

"You keep telling me that. How secure is this connection?"

"As secure as your end."

She laughed softly. "Good point. I wish I knew for sure. OK, my photographer friend, read between the lines. I have found a thing. It is related to the person who is involved in the business transaction we discussed."

Joe pulled the phone away from his ear, flicked to speaker, and began recording the call.

Jill's eyes widened as she mouthed, "Natasha?"

He nodded and said, "You expressed an interest in that transaction."

"My interest is … peaking. This thing that I have found requires *immediate* attention."

Joe said, "I'm in the middle of another project."

"Drop it," Natasha said. "Get over here. Bring your best digital wizard. You'll want to know about this as much as I do."

Jill opened a text window on a computer screen and typed: **Demanding bitch!**

Joe smiled as he struggled to understand Natasha's hints. "Surely you have people to deal with the sort of *thing* you've found."

"I do. But not nearby." She paused. "And I'm not doing a deal with them."

Jill typed: **Are we doing a deal with her?**

Joe shrugged. "I have to call my boss. If I can get time off, where would you like to meet for…" he glanced at the time on his phone, "dinner?"

Silence.

Jill caught Joe's eye, shrugged.

As he was about to repeat the request for a location his phone vibrated. Before he could read the incoming message, the call terminated.

"That woman is in a hurry," Jill said.

He opened the message app. A picture showed dozens of shipping containers and a ship he had seen before. "She's at the docks."

"Big place to find one blonde-haired Russian babe."

Joe zoomed with his fingers, roamed left, right, up, down. "Nothing but containers. Not one person on the dock when this picture was taken."

The phone vibrated in his hand again. "GPS coordinates."

"Shoot," Jill said.

Joe recited while she typed using one monitor, the other seven showing Mylin. "We don't have a drone in that harbor," Jill said.

"We could use satellite images. Buildings don't move."

"But we need precision. Let me find our drone footage."

In less than a minute the screen filled with images of cranes, a wall of containers, and the ship docked beyond it. "Can't be coincidence." She pointed with her left hand. "Look at the location for her coordinates."

"Inside a container?"

"Not *a* container. *The* container."

Joe leaned closer. "You sure?"

"You're the Tetris player who found two that hadn't moved. With all the excitement of finding Shirley and bullets and fires, we haven't dared to go back to examine that second container."

"The odds are paper thin."

Jill shook her head. "Not at all. Both of these containers have something to do with our mission. *We* found them. Looks like your sexy friend did too."

"You haven't even seen her."

"All female Russian spies are sexy. Haven't you ever seen a James Bond movie?" She laughed. "Now what?"

"Natasha wants a computer expert. That's not me."

"Or me. How about the scientists?"

"Above my pay grade. I'll call Carr."

The agent answered before the second ring. Joe explained Natasha and her request.

"How did she get inside the Circle?"

"No idea," Joe said, feeling a need to defend himself. "I didn't tell her anything."

"Was the phone ever out of your sight?"

"No. I keep it in my pants pocket one hundred percent of the—" Reality flooded over him. "Uh, she gave me a massage in a candlelit room." He hesitated. "My pants were on a chair in the corner."

"Sounds nice," Carr said. "And your fingers were handy to provide the needed print for unlocking your phone. She stole your number and entered hers so the phone would take her call. That means the Russians already have this Blackphone version too."

"Sorry," Joe said, not very loudly.

"Don't worry about it. Maybe this is our break."

Joe heard papers being shuffled. He put his phone on speaker.

"Here's the plan," Carr said. "Drive to the docks. Keep the van far enough away that your Russian friend can't see it arrive. If she has eyes in the sky, we'll have to live with it. Park. Wait for me. I'm bringing Ferdinand—the man says he's never met a computer he didn't like. Pemberly will stay here to work on decoding these crazy dots. Keep Jill on top of that concert, we need to know if anything besides music goes on up there." More shuffling papers.

Joe waited. Jill examined a hundred different views of the harbor.

"Leave now," Carr said. "Do not approach the container until we speak again."

Joe slipped the phone into his pocket thinking about Natasha's massage. "We're going for a drive."

"We?"

"You heard Carr say he wants you to stay on top of Mylin's concert."

"That I can do," Jill said, smiling. She turned up the volume on the audio feed; Mylin's viola filled the van. Joe crawled to the cab and pointed it toward Natasha's container, wondering with every rotation of the tires what *thing* she had found.

* * *

Joe reached the city lights of Soegwipo in fourteen minutes. He searched for a busy street, thinking the activity would help hide them. He pulled to the curb. In less than a minute, a drab green Jeep with a cloudy plastic rear window backed in and parked directly in front of him. He had room to leave if he worked at it but felt trapped anyway.

No one got out of the Jeep.

His phone chirped.

"I'm in the Jeep," Carr said. "Has Natasha contacted you again?"

"No, but she sent GPS coordinates of her location. We might be wrong, but our computer says she's inside the second container we identified earlier."

Silence for ten seconds. Then, "Has Natasha ever seen your van?"

Joe thought back. They had connected in the spa each time. "No, I don't think so."

"You're taking a risk here," Carr said. "You don't have to do this. Trouble is, she knows you and expects you. If I send someone else..."

Joe said, "I'm comfortable sneaking around."

"Good. Have Jill position a drone. I want a look inside of that container the moment Natasha opens the door. If I don't like what I see, we pull you out."

Carr had Joe drive to the docks and park in the shadow of a white storage building. Jill gave two thumbs up. With a glance around the area, Joe slid from the driver's seat to the pavement.

Orange light streaked the sky. The smell of salt air and fish mixed with industrial grease and diesel fuel. Joe imagined Mylin performing in a crater on the top of a volcano; Natasha hiding in a metal box; his life drifting far from making art. He inhaled deeply and started walking.

He didn't try to be sneaky—just headed straight for the rusty container. He held the Blackphone in his pocket with trembling fingers. It could summon Carr and firepower—at least until he stepped inside the box.

He reached the rusted door and pressed an ear to it.

No voices. No whirring machines. A fragment of melody. The lever arm that sealed the door with rods had been rotated to the vertical; the door was unlatched, ready to open. His arms were covered with goosebumps. He told himself it was the cool sea breeze, swallowed, took one last full breath, and knocked.

Quick footsteps approached, followed by silence.

He suddenly realized she might be as afraid as he was. She was just a masseuse.

He said, "Is the spa open today?"

Metallic sounds preceded the wide swing of the door to his left. He leaned right to clear the entrance for the camera on Jill's drone. Bright light silhouetted Natasha's body in the opening. Joe stretched to look over her shoulder. The container was much like the inside of Carr's van, only with more lights.

Natasha stepped onto the pavement and hugged him with her left arm while holding the metal door open with the right. He felt her head swivel as she whispered in his ear.

"Are you alone?"

"For the moment. Is this your new apartment?"

She smiled broadly. "I'm only visiting. Come quickly. We are going to need help."

They stepped inside together; she pulled the door closed. The room had only one good chair—just like his van. It felt isolated, austere. A place where a reclusive author could write spy novels.

She opened a cabinet and handed him a folding chair with padding on the seat. Her crystal blue eyes were ringed with gray shadows that didn't come from makeup.

Joe said, "You're working too hard."

"Occupational hazard of the masseuse." She sat in the good chair and touched a smooth pad on the desk in front of her.

Dark gray water rushing by on the computer screens above the desk made him feel like the container was moving. He unfolded the chair and sat beside her. Only then did he realize the room was filled with music so clear that the musician could have been standing beside him.

Natasha continued to work until one screen filled with rows of characters he could read, though not understand.

"There," she said.

"Where?"

"Right in the center. That's as near as I can get."

"You're deeper into this than me. What's going on in here? I thought these tin cans were used to haul smartphones and Barbie dolls to the United States."

"Correct. However, tailing your buyer eventually led me to this very special one."

"My buyer?" Joe said.

Natasha shot him a tired smile, but said nothing.

"What?" Joe asked.

She turned her entire chair to face him. "Joe, you are excellent at playing the tourist who just happened to stumble into international espionage. You're maybe the best I've ever seen. Each time you do it, I almost believe you." Her blue eyes flicked from his face to his body, to his sneakers, and back to his face. "But wouldn't things go faster if you stopped playing quite so dumb?"

"I'll try. But dumb artist comes natural to me."

She nodded and pulled a band out of her hair; blondness flowed to her shoulders. "I understand. Some weeks I become a masseuse because nothing else is happening." She leaned forward, shook her head, then sat up fast and brushed her hair back with one hand. "But not this week."

"Busy?"

"As you well know, my American friend."

Joe waved a hand at the console.

She sighed, and spoke before he could ask his question again.

"OK, I will spell it out for the uninformed photographer. At this point, it is best to put specifics on the table. This," she swept her arm across the computers and screens, "is a PM-34 mobile control center. Usually it is carried on the back of a truck. But it has been designed to be sufficiently compact to fit into a standard twenty-foot shipping container." She pointed at the screens. "As you can see, a drone is currently flying over open water."

He wondered what drone she was referring to, but said, "Where is it headed?"

"South is as much as I've been able to discern. I need a security specialist to hack into this thing."

"I have a man waiting. But I don't know how much help he'll be on Russian-made machinery."

She looked into him with blue eyes that made him dizzy, then shook her head slowly. "You just don't give up, do you?"

"Should I?"

"Maybe not. The dumb act got you this far. But some of us have to think for a living, so I will explain. I tracked a Chinese man to this container on several occasions. He became a person of interest to me when I saw him with a young Asian girl who is associated with our mutual friend; the one who is buying from you an item that I wish to buy."

"That's why you called?"

She stared at him for a moment. "Yes. I broke inside tonight to see what he is hiding. And I find…are you listening closely, my foolish photographer? I find an American drone console showing a live drone going somewhere fast. Naturally, I conclude that perhaps this system is what you have for sale. But then I realize, of course not, anyone can buy this hardware from a variety of arms vendors on the white or black market. So I ask myself: what is important? The drone? Could you be selling a state-of-the-art UAV, possibly one my colleagues do not yet know about?"

She brushed her blonde hair back again with one hand and continued, "I find this idea of a drone for sale enticing. But we waste time. Machines are available, or can be stolen. Then I think of what is not available."

Joe searched his head for the answer she had come up with and realized he was way out of his league. He said, "A missing piece?"

She scowled and grinned at the same time. "*The* missing piece."

"And now you need a computer specialist?"

"Exactly."

"But why isn't..."

"Because it is all proprietary, naturally. We couldn't have all the countries of the world using the same software and interfering with each other. That would be more of a mess than the Internet."

The images of rushing water were abruptly replaced by blurs of green and brown and gray: hillside, roadway, the flash of a building. They both turned back to the displays.

Natasha said, "That drone could be anywhere in the world. I can't even tell what country it's in."

Joe stood and stepped back to take in the panorama of the monitor array. A vague uneasiness filled him as he watched land rip past beneath the drone's camera. His photographer's eye had seen this place before. Recently. He whispered, "Oh... please...no."

Natasha turned to him.

He headed for the door while pulling his Natasha-hacked Blackphone out. Still inside he stopped and looked back. "I'll get my guy here ASAP." He pointed to the screens, reality becoming clearer with every heartbeat. "That's the east face of Hallasan."

CHAPTER 40

QIGIQ HAD CHOSEN THE WESTERN lip of the crater so the sun would be in the eyes of anyone looking up toward the ridge, searching for uninvited guests. But now the sun was gone. The ridge lay in dark shadows. The valley before him glowed with light from the half-shell behind Mylin and her accompanist. Rich sound rolled up from the stage without electronic amplification, just the natural acoustics of a volcano. He looked for Kandy in the jagged black rock on the opposite side of the crater, but she was too well hidden.

They hadn't been invited.

Rather, Mylin told Joe; Carr chose stake out. So many persons of interest in one place at one time was too good to pass up. Thus far, Qigiq had enjoyed an hour of excellent music and taken photos of attendees who happened to look his way, something Joe Roberts could have done better. He held the Blackphone up at full zoom to shoot Mylin in front of the moving rainbow of lights. As he was about to release the shutter, a thrum mixed with the music. He took the picture of Mylin and one of the audience. The phone vibrated in his hands.

Where is it? Kandy texted.

What's that noise? Jill's microphone must have picked it up. She sent more texts.

Carr's computer says it's a drone.

I'm not flying it.

Qigiq didn't often use messaging, but it sure had advantages when silence was required and cellular coverage existed to satisfy tourists. He wrote:

Propellers?

Qigiq turned slowly in a full circle, scanning the sky, first with his eyes, then with the zoom. Bright stars filled black openness. He had seen such skies often in Alaska, but rarely since relocating to San Francisco. His last night of starlight had been in the desert at Black Rock, the night a motorcycle killed Mylin's father.

He sent: **nothing visible from here.**

And received: *nothing here.*

And then from Jill: *nothing from my drone.*

Could the audience hear the thrumming sound over the music? Qigiq scanned the crowd. A man sitting at the far end of the last row stood slowly. He took a step sideways out of the row, then walked backwards up the hill holding a cell phone in front of him.

Qigiq thought briefly about the way recording an event interfered with experiencing it. People seemed obsessed with capturing the past, instead of living the present.

The man continued toe-heel backwards up the hill. The rainbow lights of the shell became the deep aqua of the ocean in sunlight. Mylin played with greater intensity. The still water around the floating stage rippled as she moved with the music. The ripples scattered the stage lights into a second star field surrounding the young musicians, raising them aloft into a sea of stars.

A dark spot interrupted the aqua.

There.

I see it.

...arrived on his phone.

A black line interrupted his view of Mylin, above the water, halfway between the stage and the audience. He thought of a spider-cam recording the event for video release, but didn't see cables. There was only the helicopter-like thumping of propellers whirling in the dark. The black line rotated left and right, balancing? Searching? If Mylin noticed it, her playing gave no indication.

Why use a camera rig that blocked the audience's view of the performance? The thought about capturing the past rose up again.

He texted to Jill: **Can you identify?**

If it were a common machine, Carr's system would know about it.

Not yet.

The machine was painted a flat dark gray that barely reflected the light reaching it from the stage. Its silhouette had appeared suddenly, which made him think it must have come in low across the lake behind the stage, then up and over the half-shell.

It's called a Crow. Israeli design. CIA uses them for recon.

The man walking backwards neared the lip of the crater. He would be recording a fantastic panorama of the lake and stage from way up there.

Ours? Kandy's question.

Tubes are mini-Predator rockets.

They're capable of

Qigiq stopped reading and elbow-crawled to his bike. A CIA drone carrying rockets in the presence of diplomats from North and South Korea couldn't mean anything good. He threw a leg over the bike, but instead of starting it, he pulled the clutch in. The steep descent into the crater accelerated him toward the lake. Quietly.

Tires crushed slick grass. Shock absorbers swooshed. He stood on the pegs and coasted across rough surfaces he had to feel more than see. The weirdness of the moment distracted him: a lowly Fairbanks detective, loaned to San Francisco homicide, drawn into a classified FBI investigation, on foreign soil. That detective was now approaching what could very well be a CIA drone on an independent mission. He had no jurisdiction. So what was he doing here?

Would Carr know about that drone? Unlikely.

Would Carr choose to intervene? Unclear.

He would prefer asking. But...he was halfway to the lake when the drone rotated in place like a concept car at a motor show. The tips of two rockets came into view.

A rocky section jolted the bike's suspension, slowing his descent. If those rockets fired, engine noise would be meaningless. He released the clutch. The 500cc thumper came to life and he opened the throttle. Faces turned his way.

A glance confirmed the drone was still rotating.

Gunfire.

He hoped that meant Kandy agreed with his own assessment: *stop the drone—protect the people.*

The dull black machine wavered in the sky, as if unsure of what to do next. Then stabilized and continued turning.

Qigiq reached the edge of the lake thirty yards to the left of the audience, skidded to a stop, leaned the bike on its stand, and wished for a more powerful weapon. He scanned. On the opposite side of the crowd Kandy was running fleet-footed over bowling-ball sized chunks of lava. She wasn't in his line of fire. Mylin wasn't. The audience wasn't. He knelt, stretched both arms across the seat for stability and fired three rounds. The piercing sounds echoed up the valley. The drone wavered.

Mylin didn't miss a note.

He jumped over the bike and ran along the perimeter of the lake. Four men in suits ran toward him.

More shots. Kandy again.

The body guards split up. Two headed for Kandy and two for him.

Qigiq waved his pistol and pointed. Soon six people were firing at the drone. It danced left and right and dipped as if it knew how to dodge bullets. Without warning, the rear lifted, the tail pointed up at the stars...and emitted fire. Two missiles launched straight into the lake a dozen yards from the stage as the drone flipped upside down and crashed on the water's surface.

Everyone ceased fire.

The audience sat perfectly still, wax figures in a museum,

all eyes front. A dazzling harpsichord run filled the air. Mylin's viola danced beneath it. Qigiq sighed with relief that the girls were safe.

A column of foam erupted from the lake as if the volcano had come alive. Light from the stage painted the rising water the color of fire.

The column collapsed in slow motion, forming a mound of water that lifted the stage like a helpless raft in a raging river. The stage broke from moorings never designed for such forces, glided down the face like a crazed surfer, and crashed into the trough. Over half of the stage submerged.

Harpsichord and musicians skidded down the slick surface into the lake. The stage bobbed upwards and flipped upside down. The wave kept moving across the lake. Qigiq knew it would reach up the opposite shore—then roar back.

The stage lay turtled, its two fat gray pontoons pointing up at the sky. The half-shell of LEDs glowed underwater, casting a halo around the inverted square as if it were about to lift off. The stage rocked and splashed. Qigiq dropped flat to the ground to place his eyes at water level as the attendees stood and fought to move away from the lake.

No bobbing heads or waving hands in the halo.

From his left a boy in a raft rowed frantically toward the upended stage. Qigiq worried the kid would be swamped by the returning wave.

He jammed the pistol into his pocket, peeled off his jacket, and ran into the water estimating where the girls might be relative to the stage.

He dove.

He had swum in the icy bays of Alaska; this water was warm.

He opened his eyes, expecting the darkness of a mountain lake. Instead, brilliant LEDs showed him the way like a lighthouse beacon. Red lights became white, filling the underwater world with gray objects and shadows. He surfaced near the edge of the stage, grabbed a pontoon, and refilled his lungs. No sign of either musician.

He dove again.

The clamshell lights had become brilliant white spots he could barely look at. A shadow slithered between him and the glare. He followed it. The rowing boy had jumped in. As the bubbles cleared, the boy swam deeper. The lights moved—not the entire shell, just a section.

He aimed for it.

A figure in the underwater murk writhed midst thousands of LEDs, tearing and twisting them from mountings, entangled like a tuna in a fishing net. He wouldn't have known it was human, except for the viola.

He approached cautiously and attempted to free the wires wrapped around her ankles.

She kicked furiously.

He moved to her side. Her hand shot out and raked fingernails down his arm, pulling him toward her and the rat's nest of wire. She trapped his arm against her body.

He grabbed her purple floating hair with his free hand, pulled her head back, pressed his mouth to hers and exhaled slowly. He let go, but she held tight to his arm with the strength of three men. He bent her wrist backward to weaken the grip, yanked his arm free, then pushed away. His left hand dropped to his boot. Going up for air and returning would take too long...

The lights turned sunset pink. She stopped moving. A chance.

He reached the knife between her knees and sliced through wires, moving quickly toward her feet.

Her legs kicked wildly, but they were free.

He reached for her head.

Her shoulders had become hopelessly entangled. Lights painted blotches of red on her forehead.

She went limp.

He yanked the viola away and let it float upward. His lungs burned. He wrapped one arm around her ankles and swam away from the shell. The wires grew taut. He cut fiercely, wrapped an arm around her slender chest—and swam upwards.

Air rushing into his chest released tension in his entire body. He saw stars as a wave lifted their bodies skyward; he swiveled his head and located the crowd on shore.

He pulled her toward the beach.

The rise of the next wave pushed Mylin's body into him. A group of men standing in chest-deep water caught his arms as the wave dropped away. Hands lifted Mylin from his grasp. A woman called out in Chinese—the same words over and over.

Qigiq crawled up the rocky shore on his knuckles, the knife still grasped in his left fist. Thankful he carried it. Thankful he hadn't dropped it. Thankful its blade defeated the wires.

Mylin lay on her back in the grass, a man in uniform giving her mouth-to-mouth resuscitation. Further along the beach the harpsichordist sat in a chair. A young boy in a dripping wet shirt stood behind her draping a jacket over her shoulders.

Four men lifted Mylin and carried her up the side of the volcano. Gan followed. A woman chased after Gan. Qigiq didn't get a good look at her face, but he would bet Kandy dinner she was the Dragon Lady.

Qigiq's body shivered down to his toes, perhaps from exertion, perhaps from Mylin's brush with death, perhaps from awareness of what an armed drone controlled by a faraway foe could do.

But he blamed the wet clothing and night air.

His eyes located Kandy leaping from jagged rock to rock near the lip of the crater. She disappeared midst the black volcanic rubble. An instant later, she was back up and moving fast.

CHAPTER 41

CARR'S EYES HELD ON EACH FACE for a few beats, then moved on. When he had circumnavigated the lab bench the group was using as a conference table, he stood and spoke. "We find ourselves in a precarious situation. Drones guard our perimeter. If the van's computer detects motion, it will us." He began pacing around the table. "What actually happened in that crater is a complete mystery, so we are on high alert. I realize that it's midnight and everyone's had a rough day, but we have new information to sort out." He checked his watch, considered something, then added, "We need to be off this island within the next twenty-four hours."

No comments.

Qigiq was looking forward to returning to San Francisco and sleeping in his houseboat. But they had too many loose ends and still no booty.

Carr said, "First issue. Where the hell is Dreeson?"

Qigiq said, "I pulled Mylin from the lake. From the beach, I saw Kandy running the rim." He gestured to his left. "Way up behind the audience seating. I'm sure it was her, no one else runs over rocks like that." He hesitated. "She fell, but got up fast."

"OK. Last seen at the end of the concert."

Jill said, "I received a text message from her at eight thirty-one. 'In pursuit.'" She looked down at the table. "I don't know why she sent it to me."

"Figured you as the most reliable channel," Carr said. "Or she wanted a drone. But Dreeson doesn't beat around the bush.

If she wanted a drone, that message would have read, 'send drone.'"

"I have some photos," Qigiq said. "A guy was backing away from the concert just before the missile carrier showed up. Same direction Kandy went."

"Could we see them now?" Ferdinand asked.

Qigiq handed his Blackphone to Joe in the seat beside him. Joe took a quick look at the picture, then passed the phone diagonally across to Ferdinand, who said, "This man's face is obscured by the phone he is holding. This will be difficult."

"Deliberate?" Carr asked.

"Hard to know," Qigiq said, "but the timing is suspicious. He gets up in the middle of the finale and walks away just before a missile strike."

"He could have just been recording the climax," Carr said.

"Perhaps Kandy recognized him," Ferdinand suggested.

"Why not use a drone?" Joe asked.

They contemplated.

Jill broke the silence. "He has something Kandy wants."

"Possible," Carr agreed.

"Or she wants him," Ferdinand suggested.

"Qigiq," Carr said, "you've worked with her the longest. Why haven't we heard from her?"

"Only one possible reason. Wherever she is, she can't get a message out. And I mean *cannot*. She's been captured. Her equipment failed." He paused, considering the worst-case scenario. "Highly unlikely that Kandy is dead, more probable she doesn't have cell coverage and can't contact us without giving up the chase." He thought back for relevant data. "By the time the concert scene stabilized and I combed the area, her vehicle was gone. That doesn't mean she has it, but she is partial to driving machinery."

"OK," Carr said. "Let's make operating assumptions. Dreeson is alive and in possession of a capable SUV that can take her anywhere on this island. For unknown reasons, she is unable to reach the Sealed Circle. What do we do?"

Ferdinand said, "Monitor all available channels. Send a drone to search for the red SUV. And try to utilize the dragon-eye network by offering a cash reward."

"Done," Carr said. "Jill, you're on the drone as soon as this meeting adjourns. Qigiq, contact your biker buddy."

They nodded.

"Drooooo...nnn...e."

All eyes turned toward the rear of the aircraft. Carr took long strides to reach Shirley's side and knelt. His six-foot-plus linebacker build dwarfed the emaciated agent, but he touched her hand with the gentleness of a child as he leaned over to whisper in her ear.

They waited.

Carr's forehead was deeply creased when he returned to his place at the head of the table.

"She's repeating that one word. I think she uncovered a smuggling operation."

"To Jeju?" Ferdinand asked.

"Unsure. We'll track the container when she recovers enough to tell us more."

Joe asked, "The drone that attacked Mylin. Would it fit inside of a container?"

"Most are designed to disassemble and fit into a twenty-foot box. The bigger ones need a forty."

"What I saw would have fit in a twenty," Qigiq said. "Minus the propellers."

"Why is the size important?" Carr asked.

"Bear with me for one second," Joe said. "Where did that drone come from? Could it have flown in from the peninsula?"

With a hand gesture, Carr turned the question to Ferdinand.

"The South Korean peninsula is less than a hundred miles away across the East China Sea. A missile-carrying drone could cross it easily."

"Thanks," Joe said. "This might be totally unrelated. Jill and I were bored watching nothing happen at Mylin's residence. So I did an analysis of the movement of containers.

That's how we identified the two that had been on the dock so long."

Carr nodded. "Right."

"We saw something that made no sense at the time." He looked around the table. "Sorry if this is stupid. But I tracked one container from the ship, to the dock, to a truck."

"Quite common," Ferdinand said.

Joe nodded. "Except this flatbed truck then drove directly onto a ferry that was going north to the peninsula."

Ferdinand said, "Fascinating."

"I'm missing something," Carr said.

"Ship the drone north, then have it fly back south. Anyone tracking that container will discover a data trail ends on the island."

Carr hesitated. "You think the attack drone was in that container?"

"Pure speculation," Ferdinand said, "but a fascinating possibility." He thought for a moment. "Especially if we combine it with the control station revealed to us by our friend Natasha."

"Friend?" Carr said. "But a good point. What is that doing here?"

"My skills were unable to crack the system to take control," Ferdinand said. "However, the video feed was clearly from a drone."

"Someone programmed the controller?"

"Correct. With a precise objective. Its artificial intelligence engine would, of course, have some latitude in achieving it. Much as a mapping program can provide alternate routes to the same destination."

"But we don't know who?" Carr said.

"We know Natasha found that container by following a person of interest. A person she refuses to identify unless we sell her the items Win has agreed to purchase. Items that we no longer possess. Though at this juncture, that is a trivial detail."

"Not much to go on," Carr said. "And we don't know if this

person is still on the island."

Ferdinand nodded. "True. But the UAV flight control system is a model not only popular with, but perhaps designed for, our own Central Intelligence Agency. We know the CIA has been fighting the War on Terror for many years via drone strikes around the world against...specialized targets."

Carr watched Ferdinand, nodding slowly. "You think we've stumbled into a CIA operation?"

"Possibly. Or someone else wants us—well not us, no one cares what we think—wants the world to believe that the CIA is flying autonomous drones in Asia."

"That sounds bad, but I don't know why," Joe said.

"A couple of reasons," Carr said. "It's one thing for the CIA to use a human operator to fly a drone on a mission. It's worse to do that secretly over an ally's territory. But it's a whole other issue to launch an armed computer after a target and let *it* decide what to do."

"Lots could go wrong," Joe said.

"And does," Carr agreed. "Look at last night."

"Speaking of which," Ferdinand said. "There is another strange coincidence, if you believe in such things."

"Since arriving on Jeju, I have a hard time believing *anything* is a coincidence," Carr said. "Someone is responsible. We just have to find them."

"The music," Ferdinand said.

Joe added, "When I walked into that container, it was filled with the stuff Mylin plays."

Ferdinand nodded. "A specific viola sonata by Beethoven."

"Why would music matter?" Carr asked.

"I located the file that Joe heard," Ferdinand said. "Apparently it was deemed of insufficient importance to encrypt. The content isn't special: a compressed audio format standard on most smartphones."

"A recording," Carr said flatly.

Ferdinand nodded. "According to the metadata in the file, a two-day-old recording. That same metadata includes a GPS location of where it was made." He pushed his chair back and walked to his research console. A picture popped up on the center monitor.

Jill jumped up. "That's Mylin's house."

"Was it her playing?" Qigiq asked.

"Most likely," Ferdinand said.

Carr rubbed his forehead and sat down. "Can we conclude that the person Natasha tailed had contact with Mylin?"

No one commented.

"Qigiq," Ferdinand said, "when did the drone attack?"

"During the finale."

Music began to play. "This piece?"

Qigiq nodded.

"You're about to tell me," Carr said, "that someone recorded Mylin's playing, then used it as an audio trigger for a drone?"

"That is my current hypothesis," Ferdinand said. "Quite a unique mechanism. And unlikely to fail. Have you ever used a smartphone to identify a song? Music has unique fingerprints, almost like DNA."

"But why?" Jill almost shouted. "Why would anyone want to kill Mylin?"

"You are making an assumption," Ferdinand said gently.

Jill frowned and sat down, but didn't speak. Qigiq did.

"*Someone* at that concert was the target. Mylin's music was used to confirm both time and location to an autonomous machine. That would explain why the drone first faced the stage, then rotated 180 degrees. Wouldn't take very good facial recognition to find one target out of thirty or forty people."

Joe said, "But we don't know who the target was."

"We can make a good guess," Carr said. "North Korea has been making headlines since their first H-bomb test. Most of the world is annoyed with them." He ran a hand through his short hair. "What an international mess that would be. A drone kills a representative of North Korea while he's visiting on a cultural exchange mission of peace. The CIA gets blamed.

The U.S. takes heat for using an autonomous smart weapon, possibly in violation of non-proliferation treaties."

"And his daughter," Qigiq said.

"The fallout would be unprecedented," Carr added.

"We stopped it," Jill chimed in.

"You did," Qigiq said. "Dive bombing that drone with yours was a great idea."

Jill looked down at the table, her cheeks flushed.

Carr said, "We stopped something. I'm waiting for a call from POTUS asking me what the hell I think I'm doing out here."

"You think the U.S. arranged this?" Jill asked.

Carr shrugged. "I'd feel better if I knew it *wasn't* us. Who the hell else can fly our drones?"

The room grew quiet. Qigiq missed Kandy's cracking gum.

"Oh my," Ferdinand muttered. He dropped into the chair in front of his monitors and typed. One of the screens filled with Ada text.

Carr straightened like he had heard a shot in the dark. "No possible way. No one has access to that."

"What?" Jill said.

Qigiq ran through a mental list. He said, "Mylin's father was paying military suppliers."

"Who?" Jill asked.

"Win has access to this," Carr said. A statement, not a question.

"And is selling it," Qigiq added. "To someone who isn't Natasha."

"Perhaps already sold it," Carr said. "Unless this whole thing was a verification process."

"Is this what we've been chasing?" Qigiq asked.

"Adds up for me," Carr said and whistled a dive-bomb sound. "No wonder she was offering millions. You did her a huge favor saving those paintings from the fire."

Qigiq felt like Benedict Arnold. "Sorry. I had no idea."

"No, no," Carr said. "This is great. Look what we've uncovered. We need to know this."

"Know what?" Jill asked.

Qigiq said, "Mylin's father and his orchestra were acquiring, exporting, and selling classified U.S. military information. By very creative and unusual means."

"Like what?" she said.

"Like hookers seducing, blackmailing, then paying guys to reveal the computer code to our entire drone program." Carr turned to Ferdinand. "Am I right?"

Ferdinand stared at the Ada code as it scrolled slowly up the screen. "I cannot be certain without more analysis."

"But if you had to bet right now?" Carr insisted.

Ferdinand didn't hesitate. "Win and at least one other party have this computer code."

"Oh my gosh," Jill said, her voice tight. "Where's Kandy?"

The space fell quiet. Qigiq was confident Kandy was tailing the man with the camera.

An audio squawk caused Jill to jerk upright. "That's a drone alarm." She pulled out her Blackphone. "It's at the docks watching the Natasha container. Has a code red." She jumped up. "I'll grab what it has from the van and be back posthaste."

CHAPTER 42

I WAS PLAYING THE THEME in Mr. Long's Beethoven piece.

The recapitulation.

Before my eyes. An apparition. A black thing blocking the starry sky—insect.

I played.

It examined me. Turned away.

I played.

Pops. Like the sound when I shot my brother. The thing dancing.

I played.

A cannon roared—the 1812 Overture by Tchaikovsky used a cannon.

Water poured upward into the sky.

The earth tilted under my high heels.

I tried to play but fell...and fell...I clutched my beautiful instrument to my breasts.

Falling. Lights. Falling. Cold darkness.

Water. I must swim. Which way?

The sky fell onto me.

Bright clouds enveloped me. Clutched me.

I struggled against their whiteness.

Kicked...twisted...my viola was torn away.

The dragon gods kissed my lips. Filled me with air.

I tried to swim, to rise, to kick...kick...kick...

* * *

The gods filled me over and over. Their breath was fire inside with each rise of my chest.

"Over here. You. Four of us. Lift."

Bouncing on the back of a running dragon. Fiery flashes bright against my closed eyes.

Chinese. "Please. Please. I am her mother."

The dragon ran faster.

A dragon claw covered my mouth. Shouted, "Breathe, Mylin. Breathe."

The claw held tight. Soft joy deep, deep inside replaced the breath of fire.

* * *

My eyelids glowed red, but I could not lift them. My chest rose and fell. My left arm screamed like a sharp knife was separating the flesh. A viola played the ending of Mr. Long's sonata over and over again. *No. My ears were fooling me.* My mind was playing the sonata like a skipping record from the days of my father, who had music on black disks the size of a sunhat.

A fan humming—almost on pitch with my mind's viola.

Swooshing.

Automobile traffic. The endless presence of human pollution. I longed to move my arm away from the pain. But it ignored my requests.

"He must have planned it."

A male voice. Not close. Not far away. Floating to my ears through cotton mountains.

"He insisted there be a demonstration."

A woman, the intonation, who...

"...of technical capability, yes. As proof. Not a murderous attack on innocents. And on home soil. This madness will draw great powers down upon us."

Uncle Gan's voice. Angry. What had I done wrong? I had tried so hard to play well.

"No one was hurt," the woman said.

"Fool's luck the Americans were there."

She laughed. "Such irony the gods deliver to us."

"Our business will vanish if we cannot be trusted. This may

well destroy us."

Her laughter continued. "No one *trusts* us. They desire our wares."

"You are careless," Uncle Gan said. "He could have been killed. And his daughter with him." He paused for several seconds. The fan stopped humming. "And both of us."

"He wouldn't dare hurt us."

"No? Mylin lies unconscious. Her brain may be damaged from lack of oxygen."

"The doctors—"

"Yes," he cut her off. "They are always confident until it is too late. Then they deliver the bad news before going golfing."

"Mylin is breathing on her own."

"More luck. He planned destruction. We were unaware. The dragon eyes failed us. And the yellow coward ran."

"Have faith," she said. "Mylin will be fine."

"Faith? You sound like a foolish American. She is—"

"Special. I know. We must care for her."

"And teach her." He paused. "There is no one else."

"We—"

"Were almost killed. Let us go pay a visit to Mister—"

I was so thirsty. I tried to say "water." A groan escaped my throat.

Footfalls. The woman said, "Call the doctors."

A warm hand wrapped around my left fingers—the ones that could dance over steel strings with the speed of a viper.

"Mylin. Mylin," she whispered. "There has been a terrible... accident."

I moaned, "w a...t e r."

CHAPTER 43

THE GUY IN THE LAST ROW had risen to leave just when the missiles showed up. Hand-holding a camera. Anticipating? Wanting a visual record of the explosion? Proof?

Sure seemed that way to her.

Kandy drove with her right hand, pushing the SUV hard to keep the black Kia sport sedan in sight as they descended the curvy mountain road. She massaged the swelling in her left kneecap with her free hand; lava was sure hard. She wouldn't be running fast anytime soon.

The man with the camera had jumped behind the wheel, but the exhaust pipe said the sedan had already been idling. Left it running? Remote start? Other occupants? The windows on the sedan were too dark to provide an answer.

She followed the Kia to the ferry dock in the same harbor as the stacks of containers that had become the focus of their mission. The chubby guy she had seen hop in up on the volcano got out the driver's side and headed for the footbridge that arched over the water. Maybe the same chubby guy she had seen on the drone recordings chasing Mylin to a Buddhist temple. She wasn't close enough to be sure, but would be happy to bet. The footbridge let tourists view the docks from high in the sky. Therefore, her prey now had a panoramic view of the entire area.

She pulled into line four cars behind the sedan and shut off the engine, sat perfectly still, and listened.

The diesel engines of the ferry boat were idling. No cranes moved. Three guards walked the deck of the ship whose containers were blackened from the fire. Her target walked up the footbridge and lifted his collar to the ocean breeze. Or maybe to hide his face. It was a good place for a meeting. If so, she wanted to get close enough to take pictures. ID the attendees.

She checked her weapon and stepped out of the truck into the glow of the dock's blue-white vapor lights. The bridge itself held no place to hide. The docks were well lit. That left the row of cars waiting for the ferry.

She popped a stick of Juicy Fruit and ignored the throbbing from her knee. She pulled her Blackphone out to check the distance to the bridge. The screen was black. Entirely black—not a single pixel glowed anywhere behind shattered glass.

She glanced at her target making his way up the sloping walk and rebooted her phone.

Nothing.

The phone had taken a fatal hit while protecting her hip. Fair trade, but now she had a new problem. She couldn't let Qigiq know her location. Therefore, no backup.

She dialed down her internal risk-taking meter; she had to play it safer, for the sake of the mission. She weighed her limited options:

Abandon the tail. Drive back to the airport for help.

Remain here. Hope Jill spots her red SUV from a drone.

Move forward at an unknown risk level with no backup.

She popped another stick of gum and surveyed the bridge.

Her man had stopped at the apex, his neck craned upward over the docks, facing the stars. She tried to follow his line of sight, but ended up at the Seven Sisters, which reminded her of the starred Subaru logo, which made her think of a turbocharged WRX she once liked.

A fireball erupted from the end of a container in the bottom row of a wall of containers. The trees surrounding the harbor flickered. The black water glowed orange.

She clasped her palms over her ears. The blast wave swept through the line of vehicles with the energy of a hurricane. She dropped behind the SUV and watched the bridge. Like dozens of others up there, her man was standing at the rail watching the fireball lift into the sky and turn to gray smoke.

Metal clanged as a container door slammed onto concrete to her left. The hurricane wind weakened. The breeze cleared the smoke. She located the container with no doors, now a black shell spewing flames. The second container from the end—the one she never reached because she found Shirley.

Her man was walking toward his car.

She crawled in through the passenger door of the SUV.

He reached the black Kia...and kept coming. She remained low across the front seat, knee complaining, pistol ready.

His shadow passed over her driver's window.

She counted ten chews, then eased up to check the rearview mirror. He wasn't walking on the left of the row of cars. She twisted around. Nor on the right.

She silently swore at herself for taking her eyes off of him, even for a count of ten. She hooked two fingers into the door release, intending to cover the area on foot, when a white, snub-nosed truck pulled out of the ferry line a dozen cars behind her. A pizza with Frisbee-sized pepperonis was painted on the side. Her target being inside seemed unlikely, but it was the only vehicle moving.

Reflections of fire in the windshield prevented her from seeing the driver's face.

She rolled dice in her head.

He could have stepped into any car while she was down on the seat. But why had a pizza van suddenly decided it didn't want to wait for the ferry?

Coincidence?

Like the coincidence of a drone attacking Mylin's concert just as this man was leaving. Or that a specific shipping container exploded moments after the same man arrived on the bridge.

Circumstantial evidence. Not much use in a court of law.

But plenty fishy.

Kandy started her truck and waited for the van to complete

its U-turn. Then she pulled out of line, swinging the tight right turn that off-road vehicles are famous for, placing the row of waiting cars between them. She inched along the line, searching for her man and keeping one eye on the pizza van. She'd prefer her Volvo coupe that hid so well in traffic it was almost invisible, but focused on her good fortune that he was now in an ungainly vehicle that would be difficult to hide. Yet...he didn't really seem to be hiding.

He was confident. Maybe overconfident that the chaos at the crater was occupying everyone, giving him ample cover. Cover to do what?

Destroy evidence and escape.

What other loose ends needed to be eliminated? Fires from the past came to mind: art gallery in Sausalito, house for musicians with bodies entombed in the basement wall, flaming instruments on stage. What was left?

Shirley Sun. Mylin.

The pizza van headed north. Guessing with her gut—she turned south. Carr was guarding Shirley, and Mylin was in a hospital surrounded by people. That left the gallery in Jeju City unattended. Qigiq had pulled paintings from a burning house on a hunch. Ferdinand had examined them and unwound layers of secrecy to reveal computer code.

The paintings, too, were a loose end.

Kandy needed a road across the island that the pizza driver wouldn't use. Fortunately, three Humvees had shown her the way. She pressed the accelerator. And smiled.

* * *

Front or back? Kandy couldn't watch both at the same time. The street was well lit, and therefore risky, even for a confident criminal. Back. She parked her truck thirty yards down the alley facing away from the rear entrance of Gallerie Electra. The name gave her flashbacks of dragging Ferdinand out of its sister gallery in Sausalito as it burned around them. How long ago?

Only a couple of months.

Ten minutes of staring at the dark back door of the gallery left her wondering if her intuition had failed. Maybe the guy wasn't coming to destroy the magic paintings after all. She dug around in the glove box and found the receipt for the SUV rental, turned it over, and wrote the number of Qigiq's Blackphone from memory. She began to write a note telling him she was watching the gallery, thinking she could hand it to a bystander to make the call for her. Then remembered Carr explaining the Secure Circle. She stopped writing. She couldn't inform anyone of where she was without driving back to Carr's jet.

And losing the target.

She checked her new Kimber carry piece, then pulled a 17-round Glock from the glove box; she always stored a second piece in the car. Even a rental. Especially a rental.

Nothing moved in her mirrors.

He was driving a slow pizza van, but even so, how could she have beaten him by so many minutes?

He made another stop.

Where? And why?

That drone at the concert had been bold. It *wanted* to be seen. A fast strike from a distance would have had a higher chance of success than hovering while people shot at it. So this guy wanted credit for something. Yet he had been at the docks when the drone control center vaporized. Proving it had ever existed would be all but impossible. Seemed inconsistent.

If she had guessed wrong, he might be gone forever, or—

A vehicle arrived at the end of the alley, barely three car lengths away. As it turned in, its headlights went out. For the second time in an hour, she tossed her body down across the console, twisting her knee into sudden agony. The vehicle passed by her passenger window. Slowly, she reached her right arm straight up to tilt the inside rearview mirror. Adjust, adjust...

Pizza van.

She crawled between the seats all the way through the big Chevy SUV until she sat low and comfortably while gazing out the rear window. It was dusty from her trip, so she couldn't see out well, but he couldn't see in either.

The snub-nosed van backed up to the gallery's back door.

Score one for intuition.

The passenger door remained closed. The rear door didn't open. No light came on inside the cab. Her mind raced through options:

Stop him before he destroys the gallery.

Wait until he acts.

Call the locals from a phone booth to report a break-in.

Move in for a closer look.

A figure filled the shadows between the rear of the van and the gallery. A bright light flared at the doorknob and sputtered out. The figure pushed the door inward with one arm.

No key.

Kandy stepped out of her SUV and moved to the nearest trash bin. Then she gumshoed forward to a small white pickup that was half rust. On to another trash container and into a doorway. She was close enough to read the address of the pizza shop on Parangdo Drive. She didn't usually worry about the future, but this gig was way different than an SFPD homicide case. So she tried to predict the fallout Carr would have to deal with if she, a city cop and part-time FBI agent, took down a foreigner in a foreign country. Then she performed the same mental calculus for doing nothing while chubby commits arson with the paintings inside.

No lights came on in the gallery.

She would cast the deciding vote based on how he came out that back door.

She let the semi-automatic hang at her side. Using it would create even more problems for Carr. She half-snickered that this decision should fall to her—the member of the team who opted for action over deliberation.

Yet here she was, deliberating like Ferdinand over a computer problem.

The door opened.

A figure emerged with paintings under his left arm, his body silhouetted against the light-colored backs of the artwork. The belly convinced her she had found the Buddha man. A man now removing paintings from the gallery. Stealing? Possibly. Or maybe he had paid Dragon Lady and was collecting his property and taking it off the island—eliminating evidence in the process.

Kandy rocked her left foot to ease the pressure on her knee. The motion didn't help much, but it did remind her not try to run and not jump anything higher than a conclusion.

Buddha man opened the back of the truck, slid two paintings in horizontally like giant pizza boxes, then turned and stared down the alley directly toward her. She held her breath and remained stone still with the gun at her side, not wanting the slightest reflection.

He went back inside.

Buddha man would unload the gallery, maybe torch it as he left, leaving her with the same problem she had at the ferry: tailing with a red Lego block of an SUV in a sea of small cars. She glanced back at her monster. A feeling in her gut fought to become an idea. Her eyes ran along vehicles parked in the alley. Modern cars had computer chips for keys, but she remembered seeing...

Her gaze landed on the white pickup whose rusty rocker panels and rotted bumpers suggested it had been on the island for decades. The letters TO OT showed across the tailgate.

It might be old enough.

Kandy moved quietly in the shadows. She eased open a driver's door that no one had bothered to lock, pulled it carefully closed, then lay on her back with her head under the steering column—the Glock between her knees where she could reach it without looking. She sorted colored wires that appeared shades of gray in the darkness and stripped them with her teeth. When she finished, she exited in silence, dropped to the pavement and slithered underneath the pickup to the tailgate. The man was loading a painting nearly as wide as the pizza van itself.

She wanted new gum. Decided against risking wrapper noise. Wondered how Qigiq was ever going to be paid for his paintings—almost laughed aloud at herself.

The man closed up the rear of the snub-nose van and turned to the door of the gallery. He stared inside as if debating, then pulled the door closed with one hand. She saw clearly for the first time that he was wearing white gloves. He was also still wearing a tuxedo, its bow tie in perfect position. He disappeared to the far side of the truck.

She crawled between the little Toyota pickup and a cement block wall with *HAPPY BAKERY* sprayed across it in red paint. The pizza van rolled forward without headlights and retraced its path. Gravel crunched as it passed the opposite side of the white pickup, not ten feet from where she stood. When it reached the end, its brake lights splashed red over the entire alley. She froze in place, feeling exposed by the light. When the red disappeared, she started breathing and worked her way around the tailgate to slip behind the wheel. She pressed the clutch, eliciting a spike of pain behind her kneecap, touched two wires together, and gave it gas.

An ancient four-cylinder engine stumbled to life.

With effort she eased the clutch out and rolled to the end of the alley. The pizza man was stopped at a traffic light fifty yards to her left. She waited for the light to go green and the van to begin moving, before turning onto the two lane road. When he was well ahead, she switched on her headlights and blended into the sparse flow of Korean vehicles. She cracked her gum to take her mind off the stupidity of slipping on a loose rock and banging her knee. Not to mention crushing her smartphone.

The pizza van moved with traffic, seemingly not in a hurry to be anywhere. Or else carefully timing arrival at a rendezvous point. Which made her think of time. The plastic lens over the pickup's clock was cracked and the second hand wasn't moving. Phone was dead. She glanced at the wide athletic band on her wrist; the watch that was normally attached had been torn off. She thought back to the start of the concert and ran through her actions.

Best guess? Almost ten p.m.

* * *

The pizza van pulled into a parking lot surrounded by office buildings ten stories high. She continued past the lot's entrance, holding her speed, hoping the next light would turn red so she could stop and watch him.

It didn't cooperate.

She turned right at the light and glanced in the mirror. The van was sitting in an angled space with its brake lights illuminated. Kandy slowed. No parking on either side of the street. The silver car behind her honked. She drifted toward the curb and waved him around. He shouted in Korean as he pulled past, but stopped when he saw her face. Whether not shouting was a courtesy to tourists or he was shocked to see a white woman behind the wheel, she would never know.

She climbed the curb with the right front wheel and stopped the truck halfway on the sidewalk. Yanking wires under the dash apart stopped the engine. She flicked on the left turn signal, hid the Glock under the back seat, stepped out, and joined pedestrians walking toward the corner she had just turned. One man took the trouble to explain with hand gestures that her truck would be towed.

She bowed, smiled, and thanked him while hiding as best she could near the back of the group of eight. They stopped at the corner to wait for the light. Standing there, she recalled that Qigiq had learned the pizza driver's name. The man with the magic colored lights that revealed secrets.

Mr. Long was standing directly across the street from her, his face in shadows cast by overhead streetlights.

Had he seen her at the concert? She had shown herself only

after the drone arrived, and he was already leaving. Not worth the risk. She turned right and crossed the street, kept walking for ten yards, moved close to a building and knelt to retie a shoelace she didn't have. Behind her the group went toward Long. He weaved through the other pedestrians mid-street, then continued toward her illegally parked truck. Concentrating on messages from her knee, she began to jog: to the next corner, right, corner, right. As she neared the third corner she eased over to hug the building and peek back at her truck.

Long wasn't on the street.

Maybe thirty seconds for her trek around the block. He couldn't have walked far, and he didn't look like he could run fast.

Starting from her truck, she scanned the signs over entranceways: Yi Financial, Crescent, Bank of Jeju, all closed, signs dark. Her eyes continued left, crossed the street. Retail boutique selling slinky dresses, pharmacy, Jeju Health Clinic, signs lit, all open.

Bingo.

The explosion had dumped the musicians into the lake. Mylin had been injured and needed a medical facility. Somehow, Long knew which one.

Kandy moved fast, on the lookout for any sign of Long watching his back. A middle-aged Korean woman with a black stripe on her cap shuffled papers on her desk even though computer screens sat to her left and right. She looked up as Kandy entered, smiled, and said:

"Welcome to the Jeju Health Clinic," with a British accent. "How may I help you?"

CHAPTER 44

THE WOMAN'S EYES DROPPED to the rip in Kandy's pants that exposed her swollen left knee.

"Let's get you over to emergency and let Dr. Phi take a look."

Resting hadn't even crossed Kandy's mind. "I'm okay, thanks. A heavyset man just came in here."

The woman met Kandy's eyes, but she said nothing.

Kandy flipped her San Francisco detective badge onto the desk, knowing she had no jurisdiction whatsoever. "I'm a detective. There was an accident up on the—"

"Oh yes. A girl almost drowned. He asked to see her." She smiled. "She regained consciousness and played for us to test her arm. She is very talented."

"Can you get me to her room without anyone seeing me?" She met the woman's eyes. "The young lady is in danger."

"Well, I...uh...yes, perhaps." The woman stared at Kandy for a long moment, nodded, stood quickly, and hustled around the counter. "Please follow me." Her soft-soled shoes made no sound on the tiles as she led Kandy to an elevator with scratched gray doors. It smelled of laundry soap. The woman held a button to keep the doors open.

"When you reach the third floor, turn right and stay close to the near wall. The second door along that wall will be room three-oh-eight." The woman paused, then looked down at Kandy's knee. "Should I call the police?"

Kandy considered the paintings in the van. And the complications.

"Would you recognize the guy?"

The woman nodded without hesitation.

"If he comes down alone, call the police. Tell them he's parked in the lot a block east of here, and that he's driving a pizza van filled with stolen artwork."

The woman's forehead creased, her face serious. "Pizza van. Stolen artwork. East of the clinic."

"Only if he's alone."

She nodded.

"Thank you," Kandy said. The woman wasn't wearing a name tag. Kandy held out her hand. "Kandy Dreeson."

"Su Min."

They shook hands. Then bowed.

Su Min released the button, leaving Kandy alone in the car. She pulled her weapon from behind her back and held it in her right hand as the elevator made a slo-mo ascent. Leaning her shoulder against the wall, she attempted to flex her left knee. It blocked at thirty degrees. The elevator shuddered, inched upward, creaked, groaned, stopped.

Kandy stepped into the antiseptic hallway of a hospital ward. No people, no carts, 311 above the door across the hall. Four doors to her right, two on each side, then a ninety-degree turn at the end of the hallway, which meant she couldn't tell if anyone was approaching. To her left, a waist-high window revealed the street below. She placed her face near the glass and could just make out the left front fender of her borrowed pickup. Its turn signal was still flashing.

She pressed her shoulder blades against the near wall and moved toward the open door to 310. One second to debate and another to step past 310 briskly enough that anyone inside would think *scurrying doctor,* not *skulking detective.* She stopped short of the entrance to 308. Male voice.

"All has gone well. The morning papers will describe the 'accident.' But America will know."

A woman said, "You requested a demonstration, not a disaster."

Silence. Light laughter. "And what a demonstration it was."

Kandy couldn't see into the room. She mentally tagged the laughing voice as Long.

"If he had been killed—" A different male voice.

"A lowly cultural attaché?" Long said. "The news media would bluster for a few weeks, no one would care enough to take action, and my colleagues would have successfully instilled precisely the fear they desire."

"What about the girls?" the woman said.

Dragon Lady. Kandy would bet on it.

"Americans call it 'collateral damage.' But the little ladies weren't even scratched."

A thud like a phone book being dropped. She gritted her teeth, wishing she had the blasted Blackphone to record this.

"There's your money," Long said. "You delivered what you promised." Silence. "Count it if you wish. Our organization also keeps its promises."

The sound of paper being shuffled.

"That's not necessary," the second male said.

Kandy figured, if Dragon Lady, then Uncle Gan.

"Let her," Long said. "She will be happier. Now, Mylin, come with me."

A long pause full of emptiness.

"Me?" Mylin said in a breathless whisper.

"Do you not remember? I told you I would be back, even if things went wrong."

"I thought...you meant you would return to visit your tiger girl." A hesitation. "Someday."

Long laughed. "I plan to visit my tiger often. You are coming to the mainland to become my wife."

"No!"

Gan's voice.

Kandy adjusted her trigger finger.

"No?" Long said. "Who are you to refuse now? We struck a deal. You delivered for my organization. And I paid what you asked."

"Mylin was to be only…a temporary gift."

"You misunderstood our terms. I accept your gift. Now she is mine."

"No, she's not," Gan said. "My daughter is too valuable to waste on your kind."

Kandy felt her eyebrows knit together: *My* daughter?

Long laughed louder. "You risk my wrath for a whore? Are you unaware of the extent of our power?"

Feet shuffling against hard flooring preceded a sound she couldn't mistake—the muffled spit of a silenced handgun.

Without thought of the international complications she was about to unleash, but with the crystal-clear objective of protecting Mylin, she spun on her right foot and pressed the door to room 308 inward with her left forearm.

A one second sweep told her:

Long. Standing. Six feet away, back to her.

Mylin sitting on bed. Holding viola. Stacks of money, open briefcase.

Win pressed against the window, the night's blackness surrounding her.

Gan kneeling at Win's feet, bent forward.

Long heard, because his head was turning to look over his left shoulder, revealing the weapon extended in his right hand.

Her knee was too weak to support a kick, so Kandy struck with her left elbow just below Long's ear as her right hand drove his gun upward. As Long collapsed, she caught his biceps with her left hand and snapped his wrist backwards. The silenced weapon dropped away.

Long's fall stopped on his knees. "You shall die for this," he spat out." "Hunted like a—"

Kandy punched him on the left side of his face.

He bent forward and drooled blood.

She pressed him flat to the floor, yanked both wrists behind his back, and slipped a zip-tie cuff from her back pocket around them.

Gan groaned.

Kandy pressed her pistol to the back of Long's head until he knew it was there. She said, "Stop talking."

"Thank you, Detective," Madame Win said.

Kandy looked up at a 38 caliber revolver pointing at her head.

"Please relinquish your weapon."

"What are you doing?" Mylin said with surprising strength. "She saved Uncle Gan."

"For that we are grateful, but we must leave without your friend. I am afraid there will soon be great political turmoil."

"She helped us," Mylin said. "He was trying to take me away."

"As intended. But your silly father interfered."

Staring at Win, Mylin blinked hard, as if to make the scene disappear.

"With your brothers gone, I hoped you would take over for me. But you must marry Mr. Long to maintain our...business opportunities."

"My father died in the desert."

Kandy carefully measured the distance to Win's 38 with her eyes. She noted the four feet between Win and the window behind her. Pain from pressure on her kneecap fought for her attention.

"Your sentimental fool of a father lies before me with a bullet in his belly. I fell in love like a naive schoolgirl and ran away with him the day you were born. Your uncle, who fancied himself the great Mr. Wu, died in the desert—another fool chasing after you."

"My mother is dead."

"Wu also believed I died bringing you into the world." Win released one hand from the weapon and pointed at Mylin. "The scar on your temple you hide with that silly tattoo was put there by Doctor Fan's forceps. It convinced the idiot Wu I had a difficult, fatal delivery."

Mylin stammered, "You lied about your own death?"

"I lie about most things, but each to a purpose. I even stole my sister's identity after the cancer took her." She put her hand back on the gun. "But we speak too much of the past. Tell your friend to release Mr. Long. We must move quickly."

Mylin turned toward Kandy. Kandy saw a young woman going into shock.

Mylin said, "Thank you for trying to help me. I have known few friends in my—"

"Enough!" Win shouted. "The weapon, detective. Slowly. I assure you I require only one bullet to end your capitalistic existence."

"You'll never leave this island," Kandy said, confident Qigiq would hunt this woman to the ends of the earth.

"American hubris. We will see who becomes the hunter."

"Put down your gun, Dragon Lady."

Eyes swung toward Mylin, still seated on the bed, her viola lying beside its case.

Win laughed. "Dear, dear girl, you would never shoot me. I've managed your career from afar for years. And wherever did you get that little pistol?"

Gan lay still on his side. Soundless.

"Uncle gave it to me the day he gave me this beautiful viola. He said I should protect myself."

"You could never pull that trigger," Win said. "You are weak. An instrument to be used by others."

"You don't know?" Kandy said, still not having moved a centimeter.

"My dragons see everything," Win scoffed.

"Then they saw Mylin fire a Smith and Wesson, just like the one she's holding now, when she ended Shen's life."

Win squinted. Her eyes flashed toward Mylin and back to Kandy.

"You are lying."

"Shen abused me. This I could accept. But he murdered my musician friends." Mylin trembled. "That was too much."

"You killed him? My last male heir. Over a bunch of silly

girls?"

Mylin said, "I wish I could kill him again."

Win's gun swept toward Mylin.

Kandy lifted her pistol.

A white-handled knife struck Win's chest to the right of her heart. Her face jerked toward it in surprise as her arms dropped away. Her gun hit the floor. Kandy pressed hard against the back of Long's neck, her weapon on Win. Mylin remained corpse still, her revolver trained on Win's face.

Footfalls sounded behind Kandy.

"Mylin," Qigiq said softly, "she's not worth wasting your life in a Korean prison." He lifted his hand and placed two fingers on her outstretched forearms. "Let Agent Carr deal with them." He pressed until her gun pointed down at the mattress. "It doesn't matter who they are. They're going away. You have new friends now."

The roar of an un-silenced 38 revolver ricocheted through the room. Tears flowed down Mylin's cheeks. Qigiq gently unwrapped her fingers from the gun and took it away. Then he reached into the case and placed the viola bow in her hand.

The door to the room slammed closed.

Carr stood with his back against it, his hulk nearly obliterating the door.

CHAPTER 45

I SAT IN THE FRONT ROW of a luxurious jet made for businessmen. It wasn't large, but dark wood and soft leather
made the interior as welcoming as an intimate concert hall.
My Guarneri viola sat strapped on the seat beside me, having
floated to safety in the crater lake, protected now by the pack
with the precious padding. Mr. Long's briefcase, containing
his money packed beside mine, rested on the floor beneath my
seat. The packet I had spilled out in the closet remained hidden within it. No one had even mentioned the colored gems.
I dreamed of jewelry containing them in the future I harbored
secretly within me. I reached to my throat and touched the
heart within a heart.

The handsome Mr. Carr, standing now at the front of the
cabin, said that the paintings had been delivered. Long had
decoded their mysterious messages and used the information;
therefore, he should pay for them. Long had paid by tossing
the money onto my hospital bed.

But the Dragon Lady. The woman claiming to be my
mother...

And Uncle Gan...

*Could he really be my father? Of course he could. I knew nothing
of the lies that had sent me on my journey to America.*

...were now in Carr's custody. Since he was taking them
away, he suggested that after the case against me regarding my
brother's death was "handled," I should occupy the house on
Shorean Road. The house where Mr. Long used my body, recorded my performance for his mission, and gave me my own

money for the first time in my life.

The bedroom door would need a new lock.

Agent Carr said I might live in the house for years, so should also have the assets. He said Win and Gan wouldn't need them where they were going. Thus, the stuffed briefcase beneath my wonderful leather seat.

Kandy Dreeson sat across the aisle from me, her left leg stretched straight out in a strap-on cast the health center had provided. She was alternately packing ice around her knee and dismantling her gun onto a tray table, even though she hadn't fired it.

Qigiq sat beside her by the window. I had caused much trouble for my two friends; yet, they didn't appear angry. They had even thanked me for helping them.

"What brought you to the hospital?" Kandy asked.

After a moment, Qigiq said, "Slow thinking. I should have gone straight to Mylin to protect her, but assumed doctors would be watching her closely. Jill's drone found your SUV behind the art gallery, so I headed over. That's when Carr had the idea of listening to the local police dispatch radio. Ferdinand rigged a computer translator and Carr picked up an address near the gallery and the phrase 'stolen Toyota pickup.' Too much coincidence, so Jill flew expanding circles around the gallery until finding a pickup parked on the sidewalk."

"How long were you in the hallway?"

"First words I heard were 'sentimental fool.'"

"Good timing," Kandy said. "When Win's eyes shifted, she gave me an opening. Not sure I had time for an accurate shot. And I was her next target."

"Bothered me when she stopped talking, so I peeked around the door frame. Three people holding guns in a Mexican standoff. I figured Win for the bad guy." He smiled.

"Nice throw," Kandy said, abandoning her ice packing and returning to wiping down gun parts.

"Thanks. Easier to estimate distance inside a room."

Kandy leaned forward. "Hey Carr, what happens next? Or is

this mission classified and I don't have a need to know?" She laughed.

He shrugged his muscular shoulders as Kandy's words *what now* hung in my thoughts.

Carr said, "First step is easy. We fly to a U.S. air base in South Korea to get advanced medical attention for Shirley, Kandy, and our three guests."

I listened to his words, but thought of myself. Was it possible they would send me back to my chopsticks and sunbeam? My brother Shen deserved to die for killing my friends. The dragon gods had simply chosen me as executioner. Now I had helped recover secrets people were willing to kill for—shouldn't I go free?

"After everyone is healthy," Carr continued, "we'll send them on vacation to a nice resort in Cuba."

I longed to find Jiao and Dia, the other members of my quartet, and again play the elegant, transcendent sounds of master composers from all places and times. My eyes grew damp remembering my foolish sister Pé, our fourth member, and her desire to run away to a new life with a rich American man. Father, well *her* father, had ended her life for that simple wish.

Carr added, "And if Cuba doesn't have room, Uncle Sam operates resorts all over the world. One way or another, I will avenge Graham's murder."

Three people sat handcuffed in the back of the plane: a woman using my deceased aunt's name and swearing she is my mother—begging me to help free her; a man claiming to be my father who gave me two guns and a priceless viola, who fell in love with his brother's wife; and a rotund man with much money and ruthless friends who demanded I marry him—although he had never actually asked me.

But what did all that matter now?

"How long?" Qigiq asked.

Carr compressed his lips, making me think of a famous bust of Beethoven.

"Given the military nature of what was stolen, kidnapping, murder of American citizens, the orchestra—if we can connect them to Shen's actions—something measured in lifetimes. Of course, a great deal depends on how much they share about their, shall we say, sales channels. I suspect we might discover mutual objectives. If they reveal something important..." he shrugged.

No matter who these people turned out to be, I never wanted to see them again. Ever.

"What about Long?" Kandy asked.

"Above my pay grade," Carr said. "As soon as we get back, he's the CIA's problem."

I twisted around. Mr. Long sat in the last row alone, his head leaned back against the seat, bruised mouth open, snoring. He seemed an odd choice for a spy—but he did have passion.

"You going to need us anymore?" Kandy asked.

"I sure hope not," Carr said. "I'm optimistic these three will reveal the dragon eyes inside the department. Then we can get back to business as usual."

"Need help with your report?" Qigiq asked. "Kandy writes them for fun on weekends." Kandy elbowed him in the arm. He laughed.

Carr shook his head slowly. "I'm not going to write much down. Have you seen this?" He handed Qigiq a thin newspaper. "Came out early this morning."

Qigiq read the paper, but I knew what was in the article. Win and Gan had whispered about it in the hospital, thinking I was still asleep. At the time, I had thought I was dreaming. "Tell them it was a pyrotechnics accident," Win had said. "An explosion sank the stage. The girls were saved by brave members of the audience."

"But the audience saw the drone," Gan had countered.

"An airborne camera to record the auspicious proceedings. Have our friend from the North, the Director of the Office of Cultural Development, endorse our version. He was an eye witness. No one will dare contradict him."

"But why would he lie?" Gan had protested.

"To protect himself. If the world finds out he was attacked while in South Korea, he will never be allowed to leave the country again. Nor will his talented daughter."

Gan had been silent for so long I was almost asleep when he said, "But how will Long's objectives be met if the world doesn't know what he accomplished with American technology?"

"Foolish, foolish, Gan. It is better the *world* doesn't know, so long as North Korea knows what the United States tried to do with that drone. Our Northern friend will inform the few people who matter. Someone may even dive into the crater lake to retrieve the drone, if we don't get there first. Never forget that the dragon is the middleman. We find, we sell. The wars are not ours."

Gan had agreed. I wondered what would happen, what unstoppable forces would be set in motion, when the truth behind the pyrotechnics *accident* leaked beyond North Korea. To the United States. Maybe to Mr. Long's bosses in China. I thought about my money.

Qigiq finished the article. "An accident?"

"This way, no one loses face," Carr said.

My thoughts floated back to my quartet: the Geisha Quartet. We must choose a new name. Something symbolic. Maybe the Ouroboros Quartet. I touched the scar on my temple courtesy of Doctor Fan and imagined the dragon devouring its tail tattoo I had gotten to hide it. And to remind me that I had killed my mother. For years that black thought had pressed downward on a child's frail shoulders.

And I hadn't.

So. Many. Lies.

The door to the aircraft stood open. The engines were still silent. I reached left and unbuckled the belt holding my viola. I slid the briefcase below my seat forward across plush carpet. Agent Carr had warned me that even though it was mine, I should be careful how I used it—dangerous people watched the way others spent money and could come to take it away.

I thought he was talking about thieves, but he had meant governments. I grabbed the handle and stood.

Carr said, "We'll be taxiing shortly."

I smiled, picked up my money-encased viola in my other hand, walked to the muscular agent, and wrapped both arms around him. "Thank you for coming to the prison to free me," I whispered in his ear. "Did you get what you wanted?"

He was quiet for a moment, returning the hug. "Yes."

I kissed his cheek and released his body. "Then I wish to remain here to start my new life."

He stared down into me with a mixed expression I had never seen on anyone's face: compassion, pain, wonder, even a touch of joy. I held his eyes with mine and tried to smile. Finally he said:

"I planned to wait until we were back in the U.S." He gestured with his head. "Step into my office."

I ducked to enter the place meant for pilots. Carr followed and pulled the door closed behind him. The cool isolation of my old prison cell wavered through my limbs. I didn't turn to look at him. Instead, I sat in the wide chair on the left, placed my luggage on the floor, and imagined flying through the clouds as the pilot of this amazing machine.

Agent Carr placed a box on my lap. His hands were large, but the motion was gentle. For a brief moment I wondered how they would feel on my body. I studied the box. At first, I thought it was a shoebox from my room, but it was taped shut down the middle. There were no markings.

"Another gun?" I asked.

He sat down in the co-pilot's chair, looked into me again, and shook his head.

I peeled back the tape and flipped the top off. The pouch jammed inside was made of fine silver cloth. I lifted it out and a delicate chain dropped across my knee.

"A purse?"

"Woven titanium. Prevents the contents from being read electronically."

I snapped it open. A small book rested in a pocket. I removed the book. The seal of the United States of America adorned the front. I opened it. Many pages were covered with colorful stamps. It belonged to someone named Fong.

"You are giving me a fake passport?"

A smile appeared slowly on his face. "No. It is very real. Nothing shouts fake like an empty passport, though. That's why the stamps."

"Who is she?"

He pointed at my small breasts.

"I am to become..." I checked the little book, "Lin Fong." I stared at a picture that seemed oddly familiar. "She looks scared."

"It's been altered a bit digitally."

"I don't even know who my parents are. Or if I'm really Chinese."

"No one cares. What matters is that you can come and go as a U.S. citizen to most countries in the world. Play your music wherever you like."

"Who was this girl?"

"There is no girl. Joe Roberts told me you named yourself after Maya Lin, the renowned architect. He thought you'd like Lin in your name. We took that picture during the prison interview. Spy camera hidden in a pen."

The silver purse wasn't empty. I slipped my passport to a new life back inside and removed a black rectangle.

"Top secret smartphone," Carr said. "Like most things in life, that passport has a price. As of this moment, you are an FBI informant in our witness protection program. You're also on probation for the next three years. Call me once a month using that phone. It contains the number. Don't use it for anything else. Only call where not even your best friends can overhear you. *No one* is to know you are part of this program. That's for your protection. Many people are upset about these paintings. More are going to be.

"Going forward, keep your eyes and ears open. I'll have

questions for you once Win and Gan start talking, to verify that what they tell me isn't all lies. If I have anything for you to do, I'll call that phone. Only answer if you're alone. Do not show that phone to anyone. Not Joe. Not Jill. No one. Only two people know you are in this program, and they're both in this cockpit.

"In the side pocket, you'll find a credit card in the name of Lin Fong. Use that for your purchases. Our computers will track the location and keep me informed of your where-abouts. If credit card charges stop coming in, I'll come find you. Don't worry about the bills, your Uncle Sam will pay them."

I stared into the little purse and imagined a secret passage-way to a whole new life, like in a childhood fairytale. I said, "I have something for you," and dug into my pocket to remove the two capsules that hadn't left me since my grandmother delivered them at the prison. I held my hand out, palm up.

Agent Carr's eyes moved from my face to my palm to my face to my palm—and held there.

"A gift from my uncle," I said.

He reached out, lifted one, held it up, and rolled it between his fingers. "I'll have them tested."

I gestured with my head toward the rear of the plane.

"I don't want them to be able to use these."

He said only, "Understood."

"What about Mr. Long's...um, briefcase?" I asked.

"Hide it. As far as I'm concerned, you inherited money from your mother." He paused. "If she turns out to be your mother. But you shouldn't need it. Just use that card."

He stood and picked up the other capsule from my palm.

I said, "Please come back to visit me."

He smiled slightly, nodded slightly, and returned to the main cabin, leaving me alone in the captain's chair. I put the magic phone into the silver purse. I placed the purse inside the briefcase. I stared out at the clouds, wondering how high dragons could fly. Time passed. Eventually, I realized that I didn't have to make a choice; it had been made for me.

I exited the cockpit and went to my detective friends. I placed my cases on the floor. "Thank you both so much." I kissed Kandy on her left cheek, and Qigiq on his right. Tears of separation, fear, and joy formed in my eyes. I said, "May I borrow your knife?"

Qigiq looked deep into me, then reached into his boot and held out a beautiful handle of white ivory—a bird in flight etched along its length. I wrapped my bow hand around it, lifted the purple and black hair that had covered my tattoo for years, and sliced it away. I walked down the rows of seats and dropped the hair on the lap of the bearded scientist who knew more than anyone I had ever met. I smiled at his surprise, then continued along the narrow aisle until reaching the woman calling herself Win. I pointed the knife at her. Fear formed in her black eyes. Footfalls approached from behind. I lifted her hair, dyed jet black to make her appear younger and more vicious, and sliced away ten centimeters. Then I turned to the man I knew as Uncle Gan sitting beside her, lifted the hair on the top of his head, and cut.

When I turned around, Qigiq was standing behind me. Smiling.

I placed the hair in separate piles on the lap of the scientist.

The bearded man said, "The hair shaft does not contain the nucleated DNA required for a paternity analysis. A saliva sample would be much more accurate."

I picked up my hair from his lap, turned my eyes at the dragon woman, and spit into my palm.

He handed me a clear bag. I slid the wet clump of hair inside. How was it possible that this man always seemed prepared with precisely what was needed? Perhaps he did it the way I prepared for a concert: endless repetition of the key ingredients.

I bowed and held the knife across my palms to return it to Qigiq.

I retrieved my cases.

I marched to the open door in the purple high heels that Win thought frivolous. I turned around to face the luxurious cabin. A cabin designed for rich men to jet around the earth making deals to exploit the people of yet another country. I avoided eye contact with my friends.

Afraid of what I would feel.

Afraid I would stop.

I looked away from my (maybe) parents: Win of the stolen name; the sentimental Gan who sent pills and semen to me in prison to control my life. My eyes touched on a sleeping Shirley Sun. Another woman. A woman who made her own choice to become an FBI agent and serve her country. I stared at Mr. Long, who had awakened from his nap. I wanted to spit in his face for using my body; I wanted to thank him for the money; I wanted to kill him for sending missiles to my concert; I wanted to vomit on him for thinking that I would be his bride and service his bloated body every day for the rest of my life. Hateful words filled my heart and fought to rise up my throat. Words I realized I had longed to say to many men. Maybe every man who had ever used me. But the words that finally came out I didn't expect:

"Enjoy your vacation in America, Mr. Long."

I spun, stepped through the open doorway, and wobbled down the folding stairs.

A voice trailed me. "After all this action, I could use a vacation. I think I'll stay on the island and take pictures for a month."

I clanged down the metal stairs afraid to look back; afraid to keep going; afraid my life would spin away from the slight grasp I had on it. When my shoes touched the tarmac I ran toward a long black van parked nearby, thinking I could hide behind it...and cry.

Footfalls followed me down the stairs. I must not let them catch me and take me back. But I couldn't run fast in the purple shoes. A hand closed around my biceps. I fought to shake it off.

"Mylin, it's Joe. Can I hang out with you for a few weeks?"

I turned and let him see my tears. This young man who had kidnapped me on a motorcycle, trying to help me escape the Mr. Wu who had been my father all my life.

Perhaps Joe had finally succeeded.

I nodded slowly, seeing him clearly with both eyes now that my hair was cut away.

An arm reached around my shoulders.

"Me too," Jill whispered into my ear. "The academy will still be there later. Agent Carr is trying to get a scholarship for me."

We three stood in a silent clump as the stairs folded up into the sleek plane and the twin engines began to make sighing noises. My heart filled with warmth for my friends, and anger at the prisoners on that plane, and relief that I wouldn't be alone on the island, and joy at the beautiful instrument in my hand with its hidden gun to protect me. My thoughts tumbled forward: I could fly Grandma to the island from San Francisco. Fulfill her dream of visiting mainland China before dying. Bring joy to the woman who had mothered and comforted me as a child.

The fat tires under the jet began to turn.

I tucked the briefcase holding my fortune under my left arm. We three waved at the departing roar. Tears dripped on my purple-clad toes.

A cell phone chirped beneath the roar of jets.

Joe lowered his eyes. "It's Natasha, inviting me for a massage."

I said, "I'm happy your friend didn't die in the explosion Kandy saw."

Joe nodded solemnly. "Thanks."

Jill added, "Or maybe she did. And someone stole her metadata."

I thought about Lin Fong's passport. And her bottomless credit card. My awareness flowed outward like water from my body after swimming. It landed on the veiled words of the handsome FBI agent. And on my new job for the United States of America—that would keep me out of its jails. This man who had freed me from prison would want to know. My eyes drifted to Jilly's eyes, once purple, now green. And over to the stress lines in Joe's forehead. I thought about a beautiful Russian girl who had become a spy. Had it been her choice, or had others chosen for her? Even though she was tall and beautiful, was her heart so different from mine?

I wavered, fearful of entering this new life.

I looked at my friends, far from their own homes. I thought of detectives Qigiq and Kandy—all of the people who cared about me.

I took a deep breath as if beginning a challenging concerto, and said:

"Let's go help her."

———

If you enjoyed *Lock Up,* please help other thriller fans discover Joe Klingler by writing a review at your favorite retailer. Your efforts are greatly appreciated in this age of eBooks. Thank you.

For the latest news, please sign-up
for The Klingler_Report at
www.joeklingler.com.

ACKNOWLEDGEMENT

Thank you for supporting my writing. It is you, the reader, who closes the circle of the scribbler with a story to tell. Thanks also to the many readers who have taken the time to post reviews of my books at their favorite retailer. Reviews are an integral part of the Information Age, and each one helps new readers find works that are right for them. Thanks to Jessica Klimesh for her careful edits, insightful suggestions, and keeping me honest on word choices. I greatly enjoyed our first project together. Once again my longtime editor, Robyn Russell, traveled along with every paragraph from beginning to end, providing her unique sensitivity into what Norman Mailer referred to as The Spooky Art. As always, a warm thank you to R: my first reader and tireless supporter extraordinaire.

ABOUT THE AUTHOR

Joe Klingler

Born and educated in the Midwest, Joe Klingler moved to California with the Silicon Valley gold rush, and worked in its hi-tech morass of innovation and disruption for years. He is the author of diverse award-winning suspense novels, including: the Daemon Thriller: RATS, four books featuring detective Qigiq and his partner Kandy Dreeson: Mash Up, Tune Up, Burn Up, Lock Up, and the Tommy Cuda Mystery: Missing Mona. He writes from his home in California, plays blues guitar, and continues his quest for the perfect motorcycle.

Made in the USA
Monee, IL
16 March 2021